A Time to Embrace

Jennifer Miller

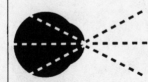

This Large Print Book carries the
Seal of Approval of N.A.V.H.

— *Women of Faith Fiction* —

A Time to Embrace

A Story of Hope, Healing, and Abundant Life

Karen Kingsbury

Walker Large Print • Waterville, Maine

Published in 2003 by arrangement with Thomas Nelson, Inc.

Set in 16 pt. Plantin by Elena Picard.

Printed in the United States on permanent paper.

Library of Congress Control Number: 2002115067
ISBN 1-4104-0079-4 (lg. print : sc : alk. paper)

DEDICATED TO . . .

My husband, in honor of his fourteen years as a varsity basketball coach. You have suffered much this past season, but always you held your head high and believed. "God has a plan," you would say, leaving me and everyone else awe-struck at your faithfulness. Without a doubt you are the most honest, most loyal man I've ever known. How blessed I am to be your wife . . . truly. Your character stands as a shining beacon for all who have had the privilege of even the briefest contact with you. Yes, my love, God has a plan. And one day in the not so distant future, the name Coach will ring once more, and you'll wear the whistle again.

I have two prayers for you. First, that we savor every minute of this season of rest. For the basketball program's loss is most certainly our gain. And second, that the loving legacy of your coaching days will change forever the lives of those boys who called you Coach.

Kelsey, my precious little teenager, whose heart is so close to my own. I watch you on the soccer field, giving everything you've got, and I am grateful for the young woman you're becoming. Nothing pushes you around, sweetheart. Not boys or friends or the trends of the day. Instead you stand at the front of the pack, a one-in-a-million sweetheart with a future so bright it shines. Wasn't it just yesterday when you were teetering across our kitchen floor, trying to give your pacifier to the cat so he wouldn't be lonely? I can hear the ticking of time, my daughter. The clock moves faster every year . . . but believe me, I'm savoring every minute. I am blessed beyond words for the joy of being your mother.

Tyler, my strong and determined oldest son. Since the day you could walk, you wanted to entertain us. Singing, dancing, doing silly tricks. Whatever it took to make us laugh. And now here you are, tall and handsome, writing books, and learning to sing and play the piano, putting together dramas in a way that glorifies our Lord. All that and you're only ten years old! I've always believed God has a special plan for your life, Tyler, and I believe it more all the time. Keep listening for His lead, son. That way the dance will always be just what He wants it to be.

Sean, my tender boy. I knew when we brought you home from Haiti that you

6

loved God. But it wasn't until I saw your eyes fill with tears during worship time that I realized how very much you loved Him. "What's wrong, Sean?" I would whisper to you. But you would only shake your head, "Nothing, Mom. I just love Jesus so much." I pray you always hold that special love in your heart, and that you allow God to guide you to all the glorious plans He has for you.

Joshua, my can-do child. From the moment I met you I knew you were special, set apart from the other kids at the orphanage. Now that you've been home a year I can see that all the more clearly. God has placed within you a root of determination stronger than any I've seen. Whether you're drawing or writing, coloring or singing, playing basketball or soccer, you steel your mind to be the best, and then you do just that. I couldn't be prouder of the strides you've made, son. Always remember where your talent comes from, Joshua . . . and use it to glorify Him.

EJ, our chosen son. Yours was the first face we saw on the Internet photo-listing that day when we first considered adopting from Haiti. Since then I've been convinced of one thing: God brought you into our lives. Sometimes I think maybe you'll be a doctor or a lawyer, or maybe the president of a company. Because the things God has done in the one year since you've been home are so amazing, nothing would surprise me. Keep your eyes on Jesus, son. Your hope will always only be found there.

Austin (MJ), my miracle boy, my precious heart. Is it possible you are already five? A big strapping boy who no longer sees the need for a nap, and who has just one more year home with me before starting school? I love being your mommy, Austin. I love when you bring me dandelions in the middle of the day or wrap your chubby arms around my neck and smother my face in kisses. I love playing give-and-go with you every morning. And wearing my Burger King crown so I can be the Kings and you can be the Bulls in our living room one-on-one battles. What joy you bring me, my littlest son. You call yourself MJ because you wanna be like Michael Jordan, and truly, I don't doubt that you will be one day. But when I see you, I'll always remember how close we came to losing you. And how grateful I am that God gave you back to us.

And to God Almighty, the Author of life, who has, for now, blessed me with these.

One

The kid made Coach John Reynolds nervous.

He was tall and gangly, and he'd been doodling on his notebook since sixth period health class began. Now the hour was almost up, and John could see what the boy was drawing.

A skull and crossbones.

The design was similar to the one stenciled on the kid's black T-shirt. Similar, also, to the patch sewn on his baggy dark jeans. His hair was dyed jet black and he wore spiked black leather collars around his neck and wrists.

There was no question Nathan Pike was fascinated with darkness. He was a gothic, one of a handful of kids at Marion High School who followed a cultic adherence to the things of doom.

That wasn't what bothered John.

What bothered him was a little something the boy had scribbled *beneath* the dark symbolism. One of the words looked like it read *death*. John couldn't quite make it out from the front of the classroom, so he paced.

Like he did every Friday night along the stadium sidelines as the school's varsity football coach, John wandered up and down the rows of students checking their work, handing out bits of instruction or critique where it was needed.

As he made his way toward Nathan's desk, he glanced at the boy's notebook again. The words scribbled there made John's blood run cold. Was Nathan serious? These days John could do nothing but assume the student meant what he'd written. John squinted, just to make sure he'd read the words correctly.

He had.

Beneath the skull and crossbones, Nathan had written this sentiment: *Death to jocks*.

John was still staring when Nathan looked up and their eyes met. The boy's were icy and dead, unblinking. Intended to intimidate. Nathan was probably used to people taking one glance and looking away, but John had spent his career around kids like Nathan. Instead of turning, he hesitated, using his eyes to tell Nathan what he could not possibly say at that moment. That the boy was lost, that he was a follower, that the things he'd drawn and the words he'd written were not appropriate and would not be tolerated.

But most important, John hoped his eyes conveyed that he was there for Nathan Pike. The same way he had been there for others like him, the way he would always be there for his students.

Nathan looked away first, shifting his eyes back to his notebook.

John tried to still his racing heart. Doing his best to look unaffected, he returned to the front of the classroom. His students had another ten minutes of seatwork before he would resume his lecture.

He sat down at his desk, picked up a pen, and grabbed the closest notepad.

Death to jocks?

Obviously he would have to report what he'd seen to the administration, but as a teacher, what was he supposed to do with that? What if Nathan was serious?

Ever since the shooting tragedies at a handful of schools around the country, most districts had instituted a "red-flag" plan of some sort. Marion High School was no exception. The plan had every

11

teacher and employee keeping an eye on the classrooms in their care. If any student or situation seemed troublesome or unusual, the teacher or employee was supposed to make a report immediately. Meetings were held once a month to discuss which students might be slipping through the cracks. The telltale signs were obvious: a student bullied by others, despondent, dejected, outcast, angry, or fascinated with death. And particularly students who made threats of violence.

Nathan Pike qualified in every category.

But then, so did 5 percent of the school's enrollment. Without a specific bit of evidence, there wasn't much a teacher or administrator could do. The handbook on troubled kids advised teachers to ease the teasing or involve students in school life.

"Talk to them, find out more about them, ask about their hobbies and pastimes," the principal had told John and the other faculty when they discussed the handbook. "Perhaps even recommend them for counseling."

That was all fine and good. The problem was, boys like Nathan Pike didn't always advertise their plans. Nathan was a senior. John remembered when Nathan first came to Marion High. His freshman and sophomore years Nathan had worn conservative clothes and kept to himself.

The change in his image didn't happen until last year.

The same year the Marion High Eagles won their second state football championship.

John cast a quick glance at Nathan. The boy was doodling again. *He doesn't know I saw the notebook.* Otherwise wouldn't he have sat back in his chair, covered the skull and crossbones, and hidden the horrible words? This wasn't the first time John had suspected Nathan might be a problem. Given the boy's changed image, John had kept a close eye on him since the school year began. He strolled by Nathan's desk at least once each day and made a point of calling on him, talking to him, or locking eyes with him throughout the hour. John suspected a deep anger burned in the boy's heart, but today was the first time there'd ever been proof.

John remained still but allowed his gaze to rove around the room. What was different about today? Why would Nathan choose now to write something so hateful?

Then it hit him.

Jake Daniels wasn't in class.

Suddenly the entire scenario made

sense. When Jake was there — no matter where he sat — he found a way to turn his classmates against Nathan.

Freak . . . queer . . . death doctor . . . nerd . . . loser.

All names whispered and loosely tossed in Nathan's direction. When the whispers carried to the front of the classroom, John would raise his eyebrows toward Jake and a handful of other football players in the class.

"That's enough." The warning was usually all John had to say. And for a little while, the teasing would stop. But always the careless taunting and cruel words hit their mark. John was sure of it.

Not that Nathan ever let Jake and the others see his pain. The boy ignored all jocks, treated them as though they didn't exist. Which was probably the best way to get back at the student athletes who picked on him. Nothing bothered John's current football players more than being looked over.

That was especially true for Jake Daniels.

No matter that this year's team hadn't *earned* the accolades that came their way. The fact that the team's record was worse than any season in recent history mattered

14

little to Jake and his teammates. They believed they were special and they intended to make everyone at school treat them accordingly.

John thought about this year's team. It was strange, really. They were talented, maybe more so than any other group of kids to come through Marion High. Talk around school was that they had even more going for them than last year's team when John's own son Kade led the Eagles to a state championship. But they were arrogant and cocky, with no care for protocol or character. In all his years of coaching, John had never had a more difficult group.

No wonder they weren't winning. Their talent was useless in light of their attitudes.

And many of the boys' parents were worse. Especially since Marion had lost two of its first four games.

Parents constantly complained about playing time, practice routines, and, of course, the losses. They were often rude and condescending, threatening to get John fired if his record didn't improve.

"What happened to Marion High's undefeated record?" they would ask him. "A good coach would've kept the streak going."

15

"Maybe Coach Reynolds doesn't know what he's doing," they would say. "Anyone could coach the talent at Marion High and come up with an undefeated season. But losses?"

They wondered out loud what type of colossal failure John Reynolds was to take a team of Eagles football players onto the field and actually lose. It was unthinkable to the Marion High parents. Unconscionable. How dare Coach Reynolds drop two games so early in the season!

And sometimes the wins were worse.

"That was a cream puff opponent last week, Reynolds," the parents would say. If they had a two-touchdown win, the parents would harp that it should have been four at least. And then John's favorite line of all: "Why, if *my* son had gotten more playing time . . ."

Parents gossiped behind his back and undermined the authority he had on the field. Never mind the fact that the Eagles were coming off a championship season. Never mind that John was one of the winningest coaches in the state. Never mind that more than half of last year's championship squad had graduated, placing John in what was obviously a rebuilding year.

The thing that mattered was whether the sons of John's detractors were being used at what they believed were the proper positions and for enough minutes each game. Whether their numbers were being called at the appropriate times for the big plays, and how strong their individual statistics appeared in the paper.

It was just a rotten break that the biggest controversy on the team had, in a round-about way, made Nathan's life miserable. Two quarterbacks had come into summer practices, each ready for the starting position: Casey Parker and Jake Daniels.

Casey was the shoo-in, the senior, the one who had ridden the bench behind Kade up until last year. All his high-school football career had come down to this, his final season with the Eagles. He reported in August expecting to own the starting position.

What the boy hadn't expected was that Jake Daniels would show up with the same mind-set.

Jake was a junior, a usually good kid from a family who once lived down the street from John and his wife, Abby. But two years ago, the Danielses split up. Jake's mother took Jake and moved into an apartment. His father took a job in New Jersey hosting a sports radio program. The divorce was nasty.

Jake was one of the casualties.

John shuddered. How close had he and Abby come to doing the same thing? Those days were behind them, thank God. But they were still very real for Jake Daniels.

At first Jake had turned to John, a father figure who wasn't half a country away. John would never forget something Jake asked him.

"You think my dad still loves me?"

The kid was well over six feet tall, nearly a man. But in that instant he was seven years old again, desperate for some proof that the father he'd counted on all his life, the man who had moved away and left him, still cared.

John did everything he could to assure Jake, but as time passed, the boy grew quiet and sullen. He spent more hours alone in the weightroom and out on the field, honing his throwing skills.

When summer practices came around, there was no question who would be the starting quarterback. Jake won the contest easily. The moment that happened, Casey Parker's father, Chuck, called a meeting with John.

"Listen, Coach —" the veins on his temple popped out as he spoke — "I heard my son lost the starting position."

John had to stifle a sigh. "That's true."

The man spouted several expletives and demanded an explanation. John's answer was simple. Casey was a good quarterback with a bad attitude. Jake was younger, but more talented and coachable, and therefore the better choice.

"My son cannot be second string." Casey's father was loud, his face flushed. "We've been planning for this all his life! He's a senior and he will not be sitting the bench. If he has a bad attitude, that's only because of his intensity. Live with it."

Fortunately, John had brought one of his assistants to the meeting. The way accusations and hearsay were flying about, he'd figured he couldn't be too careful. So he and his assistant had sat there, waiting for Parker to continue.

"What I'm saying is —" Chuck Parker leaned forward, his eyes intent — "I've got three coaches breathing down my neck. We're thinking of transferring. Going where my kid'll get a fair shake."

John resisted the urge to roll his eyes. "Your son has an attitude problem, Chuck. A big one. If other high-school coaches in the area are recruiting him, it's because they haven't worked with him." John leveled his gaze at the man. "What exactly are your concerns?"

"I'll *tell* you my concern, Coach." Chuck pointed a rigid finger at John. "You're not loyal to your players. That's what. Loyalty is everything in sports."

This from a man whose son wanted to toss his letterman's jacket and transfer schools. As it turned out, Casey Parker stayed. He took snaps at running back and tight end and spelled Jake at quarterback. But the criticism from Casey's father had continued each week, embarrassing Casey and causing the boy to work harder to get along with Jake, his on-field rival. Jake seemed grateful to be accepted by a senior like Casey, and the two of them began spending most of their free time together. It didn't take long to see the changes in Jake. Gone was the shy, earnest kid who popped into John's classroom twice a week just to connect. Gone was the boy who had once been kind to Nathan Pike. Now Jake was no different from the majority of players who strutted across Marion High's campus.

And in that way, the quarterback controversy had only made Nathan's life more miserable. Whereas once Nathan was respected by at least one of the football players, now he didn't have a single ally on the team.

John had overheard two teachers talking recently.

"How many Marion football players does it take to screw in a light bulb?"

"I give up."

"One — he holds it while the world revolves around him."

There were nights when John wondered why he was wasting his time. Especially when his athletes' elitist attitudes divided the school campus and alienated students like Nathan Pike. Students who sometimes snapped and made an entire school pay for their low place in the social pecking order.

So what if John's athletes could throw a ball or run the length of a field? If they left the football program at Marion High without a breath of compassion or character, what was the point?

John drew a salary of $3,100 a season for coaching football. One year he'd figured it came out to less than two bucks an hour. Obviously he didn't do the job for the money.

He glanced at the clock. Three minutes of seatwork left.

Images from a dozen different seasons flashed in his mind. Why was he in it, then? It wasn't for his ego. He'd had more strokes in his days as a quarterback for University of Michigan than most men received in a lifetime. No, he didn't coach for pride's sake.

It was, very simply, because there were two things he seemed born to do: play football . . . and teach teens.

Coaching was the purest way he'd known to bring those two together. Season after season after season, it had worked. Until now. Now it didn't feel pure at all. It felt ridiculous. Like the whole sports world had gone haywire.

John drew a deep breath and stood, working the tendons in his bum knee — the one with the old football injury. He walked to the chalkboard where, for the next ten minutes, he diagramed a series of nutritional food values and meticulously explained them. Then he assigned homework.

But the whole time there was only one thing on his mind: Nathan Pike.

How had a clean-cut student like Nathan once was become so angry and hateful? Was it all because of Jake Daniels? Were Jake's and the other players' egos so inflated that they couldn't coexist with anyone different from them? And what about the words Nathan had scribbled on his notebook? *Death to jocks.* Did he mean it?

If so, what could be done?

Schools like Marion High grew from the safe soil of Middle America. Most did not have metal detectors or mesh backpacks or video cameras that might catch a disturbed student before he took action. Yes, they had the red-flag program. Nathan had already been red-flagged. Everyone who knew him was watching.

But what if that wasn't enough?

John's stomach tightened, and he swallowed hard. He had no answers. Only that today, in addition to grading papers, inputting student test results in the computer, holding afternoon practice, and meeting with a handful of irritated parents along the sidelines, he would also have to talk to the principal about Nathan Pike's scribbled declaration.

It was eight o'clock by the time he climbed into his car and opened an envelope he'd found in his school mailbox just before practice.

"To whom it may concern," the letter began. "We are calling for the resignation of Coach Reynolds . . ."

John sucked in a sharp breath. *What in the world?* His gut ached as he kept reading.

"Coach Reynolds is not the moral example we need for our young men. He is aware that several of his players are drinking and taking part in illegal road races. Coach Reynolds knows about this but does nothing. Therefore we are demanding he resign or be let go. If nothing is done about this, we will inform the media of our request."

John remembered to exhale. The letter wasn't signed, but it was copied to his athletic director, his principal, and three school district officials.

Who could have written such a thing? And what were they referring to? John gripped the steering wheel with both hands and sat back hard. Then he remembered. There had been rumors in August when practice first started up . . . rumors that a few players had drunk and raced their cars. But that's all they'd been: rumors. John couldn't do anything about them . . .

He leaned his head against the car window. He'd been furious when he'd heard the report. He'd asked the players straight out, but each of them had denied any wrongdoing. Beyond that there wasn't a thing John could do. Protocol was that rumors not be given credence unless there was proof of a rule violation.

Not a moral example for the players?

John's hands began to tremble and he stared over his right shoulder at the doors of the school. Surely his athletic director wouldn't acknowledge a cowardly, unsigned letter like this one. But then . . .

The athletic director was new. An angry man with a chip on his shoulder and what seemed like a vendetta against Christians. He'd been hired a year ago to replace Ray Lemming, a formidable man whose heart and soul had been given over to coaches and athletes.

Ray was so involved in school athletics he was a fixture at the school, but last year, at the ripe age of sixty-three, he retired to spend more time with his family. The way most coaches saw it, much of the true heart of Marion sports retired right alongside him. That was especially true after the school hired Herman Lutz as athletic director.

John drew a weary breath. He'd done everything possible to support the man, but he'd already fired the boys' swim coach after a parent complaint. What if he took this absurd letter seriously? The other coaches saw Lutz as a person drowning in the complexities of the job.

"It just takes one parent," one of the coaches had said at a meeting that summer. "One parent threatens to go to Lutz's boss, and he'll give them what they want."

Even if it meant firing a coach.

John let his head fall slowly against the steering wheel. Nathan Pike . . . the death threat against jocks . . . the change in Jake Daniels . . . the attitude of his players . . . the complaining parents . . . the inexplicable losses this season . . .

And now this.

John felt eighty years old. How had Abby's father survived a lifetime of coaching? The question shifted his thoughts and he let everything about the day fade for a moment. Thirteen hours ago he'd arrived at school, and only now could he do what he wanted more than anything else. The thing he looked forward to more with each passing day.

He would drive home, open the door of the house he'd almost lost, and take the woman he loved more than life itself into his arms. The woman whose blue eyes danced more these days, and whose every warm embrace erased a bit more of their painful past. The woman who cheered him on each morning, and filled his heart when he couldn't take another minute of coaching and teaching.

The woman he had almost walked away from.

His precious Abby.

Two

———◆———

Abby was writing the opening paragraph for her latest magazine article when it happened.

There, between the third and fourth sentences, her fingers suddenly froze at the keyboard and the questions began to come. Was it true? Were they really back together? Had they actually dodged the bullet of divorce without even their kids knowing how close they'd come?

Slowly, Abby's eyes moved up away from the computer screen toward a shelf on her desk, to a recent photograph of her and John. Their newly married daughter, Nicole, had snapped the picture at a family softball game that past Labor Day weekend. There they were, Abby and John, side by side on the bleachers behind home plate, arms around each other. Looking like they'd never been anything but happily in love.

"You guys are so cute," Nicole had said at the time. "More in love every year."

Abby stared at the photo, her daughter's voice ringing like wind chimes in the corners of her mind. There was no obvious sign, really, no way of seeing how close they'd come to losing it. How very nearly they had thrown away twenty-two years of marriage.

But when Abby looked at the picture, she knew.

It was there in the eyes, too deep for anyone but she and John to notice. A glistening of survivor love, a love tested and tried and so much stronger because of it all. A love that had placed its toes over the edge of a cold, dark abyss, steeled itself against the pain, and jumped. A love that had only at the last moment been caught by the nape of the neck and snatched back to safe pasture.

Nicole had no idea, of course. None of their kids did, really. Not Kade — now eighteen and in his first year at college. And certainly not their youngest, Sean. At eleven he had no idea how close she and John had come to walking away from each other.

She glanced at the calendar. Last year at this time they were making plans to divorce. Then Nicole and Matt announced their engagement, which delayed their timetable. But Abby and John planned to tell the kids after Nicole and Matt got home from their honeymoon.

Abby shuddered. If she and John had divorced, the kids might never have recovered. Especially Nicole, who was so idealistic and trusting in love.

Baby, if you only knew . . .

And yet here they were . . . she and John, exactly the way Nicole believed them to be.

Abby often had to pinch herself to believe it was true, that she and John weren't filing for divorce and looking for a way to tell the kids. They weren't fighting or ignoring each other or on the verge of having affairs.

They had survived. Not only that, but they were actually happy. Happier than they'd been since they'd said their vows. The things that tore so many couples apart had — through God's grace — made them stronger. One day, when the time was right, they would tell the kids what had almost happened. Maybe it would make them stronger, too.

Abby turned her attention back to the computer screen.

The article was one that grew from the roots of her heart: "Youth Coaches in America — a Dying Breed." She had a new editor at the national magazine that bought most of her work. A woman with a keen sense for the pulse and conscience of American families. In September she and Abby had discussed possible articles. An exposé on coaching had actually been the editor's idea.

"The whole country's sports crazy," the woman said. "But everywhere I turn it seems another quality coach is calling it quits. Maybe it's time we took a look at why."

Abby almost laughed out loud. If anyone could write honestly about the pain and passion of coaching youth sports, she could. She was a coach's daughter, after all. Her father and John's had been teammates at the University of Michigan, the school where John played before getting his degree and doing the only thing that seemed natural — coaching football.

Her entire life had taken place around the seasons of the game.

But after sharing the past two decades with John Reynolds, Abby could do more than write a magazine article about coaching. She could write a book. And she'd include it all: parents complaining about playing time, players ignoring character and responsibility, unrealistic expectations, second-guessing, and catcalling from the stands.

Fabricated accusations spouted in behind-the-scenes gossip circles designed to pressure a coach to step down. Never mind the team barbecues in the backyard or the way John used his own money to buy the guys breakfast a dozen times after a Saturday practice.

It always came down to the bottom line: win more games or else.

Was it any wonder coaches were quitting?

Abby's heart softened. There were still players who made the game a joy, still parents who thanked John after a hard-fought contest or dropped him a card in the mail expressing their gratitude. Otherwise there wouldn't be a man like John left in the coaching ranks. A handful of players at Marion High still tried hard in the classroom and on the field, still showed respect and earned it by their hard work and diligence. Players who appreciated the barbecues at the Reynoldses' house and the time and love John put into every season, every player. Young men who would go on to get college degrees and good jobs, and who years after graduating would still call the Reynoldses' house and ask, "Is Coach there?"

Those players used to be the norm. Why was it that now — for coaches across America — they were the exception?

"Yes," Abby had told her editor. "I'd love to write the story."

She'd spent the past few weeks interviewing coaches of longtime, successful programs. Coaches who had stepped down in recent years because of the same troubles that plagued John, the same reasons he came home tired and dejected more often.

The front door opened, and Abby heard her husband sigh as he closed the door. His footsteps sounded across the tiled entryway. Not the firm, crisp steps of spring or summer, but the sad, shuffling steps of a football season gone awry.

"I'm in here." She pushed back from her computer and waited.

John slumped into the room and leaned against the doorframe. His eyes found hers, and he held a folded piece of paper out to her.

She stood and took it from him. "Long day?"

"Read it."

Abby sat back down, opened the note, and began to read. Her heart sank. They wanted John's resignation. Were they crazy? Wasn't it enough that they harassed him daily? What did the parents want? She folded the note and tossed it on her desk. Then she went to John and slipped her arms around his waist. "I'm sorry."

He pulled her close, hugging her the way he'd done back when they were first married. Abby relished the sensation. John's strong arms, the smell of his cologne, the way they drew strength from each other . . .

This was the man she'd fallen in love with, the one she'd almost let get away.

John straightened and studied her. "It's nothing to worry about." He leaned close and kissed her.

A ripple of doubt sliced through the waters of Abby's soul. "It says a copy was sent to Herman Lutz. Athletic directors fire coaches when parents complain."

"Not this time." John shrugged. "Lutz knows me better than that."

"Ray Lemming knew you best of all." Abby kept her tone gentle. "I get a bad feeling about Herman Lutz."

"Lutz'll support me." He uttered a heavy chuckle. "Everyone knows I'd never let my players drink or have . . . what was it?"

"Street races."

"Right. Street races. I mean, come on." He angled his head. "One or two parents will always complain. Even when we win every game."

Abby didn't want to push the issue. "God's in control."

John blinked. "What's that supposed to mean?"

"It means God'll back you. No matter who else does or doesn't."

"You sound worried."

"Not worried. Just concerned about the letter."

John leaned against the wall, took off his baseball cap, and tossed it on the couch. "Where's Sean?"

"In his room." Their youngest son was in sixth grade. In the past few weeks, girls had begun to call. "His social life's left him a little behind at school. He'll be doing good to finish by ten."

"No wonder it's so quiet." He released the hold he had on Abby's waist and brought his fingertips up along her face, tracing the outline of her cheekbones. "It isn't supposed to be like this."

The feel of his hands against her face sent a shiver down her back. "Coaching?"

He nodded. "We won state last year." His tone was tired, his eyes darker than she'd seen them in a while. "What do they want from me?"

"I'm not sure." Abby studied him for a moment, then lowered her chin. "I know what you need, though."

John's expression softened. "What?"

"Dancing lessons." Abby could almost feel the sparkle in her eyes.

"Dancing lessons? So we can fox-trot over Jefferson next Friday night?"

"No, silly." She gave him a light push. "Stop thinking football." Her fingers linked with his and she waltzed him one step away from the wall and back. "I'm talking about *us*."

A quiet moan rumbled up from John's chest. "Come on, Abby. Not dance lessons. I'm tone-deaf, remember? And not a stitch of rhythm."

She led him into the room a few more steps, her body close to his. "You dance with me on the pier." Her tone was pleading, and she did an intentional pout. She sounded like Nicole when she wanted her own way.

"Oh, Abby . . . no." His shoulders slumped forward a bit, but there was a light in his eyes that hadn't been there before. "Dancing on the pier is different. Crickets and creaking boards . . . the wind on the lake. I can dance to *that* kind of music." He arched his arm and twirled her beneath it. "Please, Abby. Don't make me take dance lessons."

She'd already won. Still, she grinned at him and held up a single finger. "Wait." In a flash she darted to her desk and snatched the piece of newspaper she'd clipped earlier that day. "Look. They're at the high school." She held up the article.

With a slight roll of his eyes he squinted at the headline. "Ballroom Dancing for *Mature* Couples?" He planted his hands on his hips and raised his eyebrows at her. "Great. Not only will I be sashaying for the first time in my life, I'll be doing it in the company of people twice my age." His head fell back a notch. "Abby . . . please."

She pointed to the smaller print. "Forty and older, John. That's what the article says."

"We're not that old." He was playing with her now, teasing her the way he'd done back when she was a high-school senior, surprised beyond words that this college-age star quarterback who'd been a family friend forever, wanted to date her. Her, of all people.

A giggle slipped from her lips and she drew close to him once more. "Yes, we are that old."

"No." His mouth hung open for a moment and he pointed first to her, then to himself. "How old are we?"

"I'm forty-one and you're forty-five."

"Forty-five?" He mouthed the words, his expression a twist of mock horror.

"Yes, forty-five."

"Really?" He took the news clipping from her and studied it again.

"Really."

"Well, then . . ." The article drifted to the floor. This time he took her hand in his and waltzed her toward the doorway. "I guess it's time for dancing lessons."

John led them from the center of her office into the entryway. "Mature, huh?"

"Yep." She loved moments like this, when it felt like she and John shared one heartbeat. They waltzed down the hall toward the kitchen.

"*You* don't think I'm mature, though, do you?" As he said the words, his feet became tangled with hers, and he fell backward, pulling Abby down with him. They smacked the wall as they landed, one on top of the other.

The shock lasted only a few seconds.

When it was clear they were both okay, a ripple of laughter burst from both of them. "No, John . . ." Deep waves of giggles sent Abby rolling onto the floor beside him. "No worries. I don't think you're mature."

"That's good." He was laughing harder than her, even. So hard there were tears in his eyes. "I wouldn't want that."

"But you *do* need dance lessons."

"Apparently." His laughter grew. "It reminds me . . . of the time you . . ." He tried to catch his breath. "The time you fell down the stairs at Sea World."

"That's right." Her ribs hurt from laughing so hard. "I had to get that seat."

"I'll never forget the sea lions." John imitated how the animals had swung their heads in Abby's direction that day.

"Don't . . ." Abby sucked in a breath. "You're killing me."

"People sticking out arms and legs trying to stop you." John sat up and rested his elbows on his knees.

She exhaled, finally catching her breath. "We're . . . quite a pair."

John struggled to his feet and leaned against the wall. "It worked." He stuck his hand out and helped Abby to her feet.

"What?" Abby's heart felt lighter than a summer breeze. How good it was to laugh like this, rolling around on the floor, being silly with John.

"I know you don't think I'm mature now." They linked arms and entered the kitchen.

"Definitely not."

"Starving, maybe." He rubbed his backside. "But never mature."

Three

Dinner was in full swing. It was Wednesday, and every seat at the table was taken. John and Abby and Sean filled out one side, while Nicole and Matt and Matt's parents, Jo and Denny Conley, took up the other.

Abby loved nights like this, when the gang gathered at the Reynoldses' house, laughing and sharing updates about their lives. Across from her, Abby admired the glow on Nicole's face. *Thank You, God, for bringing Matt into her life. Don't ever let them go through what John and I did . . .*

The group was giggling about something Denny had said, something about a fishing hook getting caught in the pastor's hairpiece the previous weekend.

"Thing is —" Jo set her fork down, her face red from laughing — "none of us knew about the hair thingy. I mean Pastor stands up there every Sunday as honest as a trout in summertime." She gestured around the table. "You know what I mean . . . the man's not one of those big-hair types you see on TV. He's the real deal. Gen-u-ine."

Abby didn't know the man, but she felt for him all the same. "He must've been mortified."

Denny shrugged, but before he could respond, Jo leaned forward and held up her finger. "Know what he told me. He says, 'Jo, don't you go tellin' no one at church about this. The good Lord took my hair, but that don't mean I can't wear a hat.' " Jo slapped the table and the water in her glass jostled over the rim. "A hat! Isn't that the funniest thing y'all ever heard?"

Abby studied the red-headed woman, tiny and full of fire, a woman Abby never would have chosen for her daughter's mother-in-law. But Jo had grown on Abby and Nicole, and now they found her charming. A bit talkative, and maybe a little too interested in fishing, but wonderfully real and full of love. Their family get-togethers weren't the same without her.

Nicole wiped her mouth and looked at John. "Heard anything from Kade?"

"Nothing new." John shrugged. "School's going well, football, too."

"He's a redshirt this year, isn't he?"

Denny anchored his elbows on the table.

"He is. It'll give him an extra year of eligibility."

"The whole redshirt thing doesn't sit well with me." Jo made a face. "Like a bad bucket o' bait."

Abby smiled. "It's a coach's call. There's a lot of talent ahead of Kade on the depth chart. He's okay with redshirting."

"I don't care." Jo's tone grew loud, more passionate. "Young Kade's good enough to start, after all, and I'd tell 'em so myself if I had the coach's number." She cocked her head in John's direction. "You don't have it, do you?"

Everyone laughed except Jo, who glanced about the table as though they'd all taken leave of their senses. "I'm serious as a thunderstorm on Lake Michigan. The boy's good."

"It's okay, Jo." John grinned at the woman, and Abby savored the effect. Lately, John's smile did wonderful things to Abby's heart. His voice was kind as he helped Jo understand. "Kade *agreed* to redshirt. He has a lot to learn before he takes the field."

"Yes —" Nicole looked at Abby — "and he's coming home soon, right?"

Abby admired the way her daughter handled herself around Jo. In the few months since marrying Matt, Nicole had become expert at dealing with her mother-in-law, knowing when to steer the conversation and how to distract Jo when she became too excited.

"That's right." Abby nodded. "Iowa plays at Indiana, October 20. It's only a four-hour drive from here. The school has that Monday off, so Kade'll come home with us, stay Sunday, and fly back to school Monday."

"Yep." Sean looked up from his dinner. "Ten days and counting."

"Well, don't you know I want in on that surer than a flea on a billy goat. Me and Denny, here, why we'll be tagging along right behind you down the turnp—" Jo gasped. "Wait." She jabbed her elbow into Denny's ribs, and the man jumped. "That's the weekend we have the mission thing, isn't it?"

Denny thought for a moment. "I think it is."

Matt looked up, his fork hanging in the air. "Mission thing?" He loved Abby's cooking and usually spent dinner letting the others talk while he worked on cleaning his plate. Abby had made stuffed pork chops and glazed potatoes, and Matt was already on his third serving. His eyes twinkled as he met his mother's gaze. "What mission thing?"

"Aw, shucks." Jo exchanged a look with Denny, and then exhaled hard. "We weren't going to tell you young folks yet. Wanted it to be a surprise."

Nicole leaned forward so she could see her in-laws more clearly. "You're taking a mission trip?"

"Actually —" Denny reached for Jo's hand — "it's a little more involved than that."

Abby could feel the anticipation building around the table. After all, Matt's parents had divorced when Matt was a small child. They'd lived separate lives until Matt and Nicole's engagement. Then — in a series of events that was nothing short of miraculous — first Denny, then Jo became believers. Two months ago they remarried and got involved at church. Now they spent Saturdays fishing with their pastor.

"Mom —" Matt set his fork down and leaned on the table — "what're you guys talking about?"

"Dag-nabbit." Jo shot an apologetic look at Denny. "I must have the biggest mouth this side of a steelhead." Then she turned and faced her son. "The truth is, your dad and I are thinking about spending a year in Mexico. Working at an orphanage down there and . . ."

For maybe the first time since Abby had known Jo, the woman was silent. The news was so amazing, so unlike anything Jo had ever done, even she could think of nothing to add.

Nicole squealed. "That's *amazing!*" She bounced up from her chair and positioned herself behind Jo and Denny, placing an arm around each of them. "You'll love every minute of it."

Jo shrugged, her cheeks suddenly red. "Well, it's not like we can do much for 'em, you know. But we're willin'. Pastor says that's what matters."

Denny cleared his throat. "We'll help build a second room for babies and do general maintenance. Sort of act as care-takers for the place."

"Dad, that's great." Matt reached out and shook his father's hand. "I guess I can't believe it. I never thought my parents would spend a year in mission work."

John flashed Abby a quick look. "We serve a God of miracles — that's for sure."

Abby let her eyes fall to her plate. She understood the secret meaning in John's words, and at times like this, she wanted desperately to tell the kids about their own miracle. How they'd almost divorced and then somehow, found the way to the old pier in their backyard. How, there and then, in the hours after Nicole's wedding, God had opened their ears to hear the music once more — the music of their lives — and they'd remembered again how to dance.

The miracle was this: they'd stayed together and made something beautiful of their marriage. It wouldn't have happened without God's divine hand, and as such, it was a miracle worth sharing.

But they couldn't. Abby and John had never told any of them about what had almost happened. The kids would have been too shaken, especially Nicole. No, the kids had no idea. She doubted they ever would.

Abby looked up and let the thought go. Congratulations continued around the table, and Jo and Denny answered a host of questions. If all went well, they would leave for Mexico in July and return a year later.

"They asked us if we could teach the children anything while we were there." Jo winked at Denny. "I told 'em I'd have those kids baitin' a hook in no time."

Matt gave his mother a warm smile, his

tone light and teasing. "If I know you, you'll probably bring back a couple of little fishermen."

"Right." The tips of Jo's smile faded and her laugh sounded suddenly forced.

The change wasn't enough for everyone at the table to notice, but Abby caught it. Something about Matt's mention of the orphans had caused Jo's heart to stumble. Abby would have to look for opportunities in the coming months when she and Jo could talk. She was almost sure the woman harbored deep feelings on the topic, feelings she maybe hadn't shared with Matt or Nicole.

"Wait a minute —" Denny nodded his head in Matt's direction — "your mother and I aren't looking to be parents again."

"What he means is, I wanna be a grandma. Sooner the better."

"A grandma?" Nicole's mouth hung open in pretend shock. "Sorry, Jo. We're years away from granting that wish."

"I'd say." Matt slipped an arm around Nicole's shoulders. "I think the game plan is four years, isn't it?"

"Exactly."

Abby had to bite her lip to keep from laughing out loud. "If only it worked that way."

"Yeah." John narrowed his eyes. "We got married July 14, 1979. And what was our plan on children?"

"Five years, I believe."

"And when was Nicole born?"

"April 16, 1980." Abby gave Nicole a quick smile. "But that's okay, honey. You can pretend you have a plan. Less stress that way."

On the other side of the table, Jo was still working out the math. Her fingers moved one across the others, then came to an abrupt stop. She gasped and stared at Abby. "You mean Nicole was born nine months and two days after the weddin'?" The light in her eyes was full strength once more. She leaned across Matt's plate and patted Nicole on the hand. "No wonder you're so sweet, darlin'. I always thought it was your upbringing." She sent a quick look John's way. "And it's that, too, of course." She looked back at Nicole. "But I had no idea you were a honeymoon baby. Honeymoon babies are better than a week on the lake. All gushy and drippy and believin' in happily ever after."

Jo sucked in a quick breath and shifted her eyes to Matt. "You better take good care o' her, son. She ain't no ordinary girl. She's a honeymoon baby." She lowered her voice, and the others had to strain to hear it. "Good for you, son. You got yourself a catch better'n anything a rod and reel will ever land you. Besides, honeymoon babies beget honeymoon babies. That's what I always heard, anyway."

"Excuse me." Nicole held up her hand, her smile sincere. "*This* honeymoon baby will not be begetting anytime short of four years." She leaned against Matt and gazed at his eyes. "My brilliant husband has a law career to launch first."

It was only then that Abby noticed John's eyes. They'd grown distant in the past few minutes, like he'd already left them and headed up for bed, leaving his body behind as a means of being polite.

Abby looked harder. No, it wasn't distance. It was depth . . . depth and pain. Then it hit her. He was thinking about football again. The topic hadn't come up all night, and Abby was glad. They'd both spent most of their recent days battling the questions all people in coaching have to ask themselves if they stay in long enough: What's it all for? Why are we involved with this? Isn't there more to life?

The dinner wound down, and Nicole and Matt left with Denny and Jo behind them. Sean turned in with promises to finish his math homework. Abby followed John up to their bedroom.

"What's on your mind?"

Only then, when they were finally alone, did his feelings find words. They were words she hadn't ever expected John Reynolds to say. He simply rubbed the back of his head and studied her. Then in a voice filled with conviction and fatigue, he said it.

"I'm quitting football, Abby. This is my last year."

The statement knocked around in her mind and rattled its way down to her gut. She had always known the day would come. But she had never expected it to come now. Not on the tails of a championship season. Oh, sure this season was harder than others. But John had dealt with complaining parents before, handled bad attitudes and unexplainable losses. Those things happened to every coach. But the idea that he might hang up his whistle now, with so many years of teaching left, was more surprising than anything John could have said.

Almost as surprising as the feelings rising within her.

All her life, in the cellar of her heart, Abby had dreaded the day when football would no longer be part of her routine. But here, now . . . with her eyes locked on John's, she felt no dread whatsoever.

She felt relief.

Four

Even parked, the car looked fast.

Jake Daniels and a handful of his teammates were leaving practice Saturday morning when they spotted it. A red Acura Integra NSX. Maybe a '91 or '92.

Unable to keep from gawking, the group stopped. Casey Parker was the first to recover. It was the nicest car Jake had ever seen.

"Tight, man." Casey slung his gym bag over his shoulder. "I'll bet that baby can run."

The car was so shiny Jake almost had to squint. It had two doors, a spoiler in the front, and a riser across the back. The body hugged the ground, snug against a hot set of Momo wheels.

Suddenly the black-tinted passenger window lowered, and a man waved in their direction. Jake narrowed his eyes even more. *What the . . . ?*

"Hey, Daniels, isn't that your dad?" Casey punched Jake in the arm. "Where's the blonde?"

Jake gulped. It was his dad, all right. He'd showed up at last night's football game — the first he'd attended since moving to New Jersey. Beside him had been some blonde girl in a spandex shirt, leather pants, and spiked heels. She couldn't have been more than twenty-five. Big-time bimbo, working a wad of gum and batting her eyelashes.

The other guys razzed Jake about her all morning at Saturday's practice.

"She available, man . . . or does your dad have first dibs?"

"Your dad into sharing, Daniels? That's the hottest stepmom I've *ever* seen."

"She's not his stepmom . . . she's his girlfriend. He and his dad take turns."

The comments had gotten old after the first hour, but the guys kept at it. Still, whoever the blonde was, she wasn't in the Integra. Jake nodded to his teammates, shouldered his bag, and headed for the car. Normally his mother met him after practice in their old van, faithful and sure, always on time.

But not today.

"Hey . . ." His father waited until Jake

54

was closer before he said anything. "Climb in."

Jake did as he was told. The car must be a rental. Apparently his dad was making big bucks at the radio station. Back when he worked for the Marion paper, before the divorce, his father never would have rented an Acura NSX. But then, he wouldn't have had an airhead for a girlfriend either. A lot had changed.

"Well . . . what do you think?" His father's smile was practically bursting through his skin.

"Where is she?"

His expression went blank. "Who?"

"The girl. Bambi. Bimby . . . whatever her name was."

"Bonnie." A shadow fell across his eyes, and he looked older than Mom. They were the same age, but there were more lines on Dad's forehead now. He worked them with his thumb and forefinger and cleared his throat. "She's getting a massage."

"Oh." Jake wasn't sure what to say. "Thanks for picking me up." He patted the dashboard. "Nice rental."

His dad leaned forward, sunglasses in one hand, his arm resting on the steering wheel. He looked like one of those guys in a *Sports Illustrated* ad. "What if I told you it wasn't a rental?"

It took a moment for Jake to remember to breathe. "Not a rental?"

The grin was back on his father's face. "Remember last summer, that conversation we had about cars?"

"Cars?"

"That's right." An unfamiliar chuckle slipped from his dad's mouth. Something about it made Jake feel like he didn't know the man. Almost like he was trying too hard to be cool.

"Uh . . ." Jake tried not to be bugged. Where were these questions going, anyway? "You asked me which cars were hot right now, right? That conversation?"

"Exactly. You told me the hottest car would be a used Acura NSX . . . maybe a '91. Remember?"

"Okay . . ." Jake's heart rate doubled. It wasn't possible, was it? After all, he would be seventeen next week. But would his dad really come all the way from New Jersey to bring him a —

He swallowed hard. "Dad . . . whose car is it?"

Moving his arm off the wheel with more flare than usual, his father turned off the engine, pulled out the key, and handed it to Jake. "It's yours, son. Happy birthday."

Jake's mouth hung open a moment. "No way."

"Yes, way." His dad grinned again and slipped on the sunglasses. "I'm busy next weekend so I brought it down now. That way you'll have it for your big day."

A million thoughts crowded Jake's ability to think. Was his father serious? A car like this had to cost forty grand! And what about Jeni and Kindra and Julieanne? For that matter what about Kelsey? The superbabes would all be after him once they got a look at this thing. Man, she could probably do zero to sixty in five flat. Probably reach one-thirty, one-forty in a street race.

Jake gulped. What would Mom think? She didn't want him owning *any* car yet — let alone the hottest street racer this side of the Illinois state line.

His father was staring at him, the grin still in place. "Well . . ."

"Dad, it's awesome. I'm in shock."

"Yeah, well . . . it's the least I can do." He removed the sunglasses again, his eyes serious. "I've missed a lot, being gone, son. Maybe this'll make it up to you. At least a little."

"A little? How 'bout a lot." Jake's fingers and toes tingled; the flesh on his arms and legs all but buzzed with excitement. He wanted to stand on the roof and shout it to the world. *I own an Acura NSX!* His dad might have changed, but the man did love him, after all. He must. And Jake loved him, too. Especially now.

His father was watching him again, waiting. But what could Jake say? How did a kid thank his dad for something like this? He lifted his shoulders a few times. "I don't know what to say, Dad. Thanks. It's perfect. I . . . I can't believe it's mine."

His dad laughed again, the kind of polished laugh he probably did often on his radio program. "I think you're in my seat, son." His father released the hood latch and climbed out. Jake did the same. They met near the front of the car, and Jake couldn't resist. He slipped his fingers beneath the hood and popped it open. Jake pulled in a sharp breath. No way! He cast a quick glance over his shoulder. Did his dad know this wasn't a stock engine? *Act normal,* he told himself. *Don't give it away.*

The engine block was raised, with a reshaped combustion chamber and a custom intake manifold. Forget fast. This car was going to fly.

"Good stuff, huh?" His dad patted his shoulder and left his hand there. The feel of it made Jake miss the old days. Back when there wasn't this . . . this awkwardness between them.

"Yeah . . . nice."

His dad did a little cough. "It's a fast car, son."

Jake twisted around and met his father's eyes. He probably had plans to take the engine back to stock first thing next week. "Yes, sir."

"Let's keep that little detail from your mother, okay?"

"Really?" Jake's mouth was dry. What would the guys say about this? They'd want to hang with him every weekend, for sure. He'd be the most sought-after kid at Marion High. Mom would be furious if she knew how fast it was . . . or how much it cost. But Dad was right. No point bothering her with the details. "I won't say a word."

Dad raised a finger and pointed it close to Jake's face. "But no tickets, now, you hear?"

"Not a one." Jake nodded, serious and certain. This was a car he could have fun with, but he'd be careful. No risk taking. No street racing. Well . . . maybe a little street racing, but nothing dangerous. A few of the guys on the team had started racing lately. But even if he did, it wouldn't be much. Once a month, maybe. Besides, he had a reputation for being one of the safest drivers at school. "You can trust me, Dad."

"Good." His father dropped the sunglasses back in place and glanced at his watch. "Better get you home. Your mom'll wonder what took us so long."

Besides, Bunny — or whatever her name is — is waiting. Jake let the thought go. He moved to pass his father en route to the driver's seat. It was a moment when, in years past, Jake would have hugged his dad hard, or crooked his elbow around his neck and given him a few light, playful punches in the gut.

But not now.

Since his parents' divorce, everything had changed. First his father's address and job title, then his clothes and the ways he spent his Saturday nights. Girls like what's-her-name were a dime a dozen for his dad. And why not? His dad was a looker. Handsome, strong, former jock, smooth voice . . .

Girls liked men like his dad.

What Jake didn't get, though, was what his dad saw in the girls. Especially with someone as wonderful as Mom living at home alone.

With each passing second, the moment grew more awkward, and finally Jake thrust his hand forward. His dad did the same, and the two shook hard. "Thanks again, Dad. It's awesome."

Jake made his way around the car, climbed in, and started the engine. As he drove back home, careful to keep to the speed limit, the car felt like one of those racehorses chomping at the bit in the moments before the big event. Something told him his Integra wouldn't hit stride until it was cruising well over a hundred.

Of course, he didn't share that thought with his dad. In fact, he doubted he'd share it with the guys. This car would blow away anything they drove, so what was the point? Racing would only get him in trouble. It was enough merely owning a car like this. He smiled. His father had nothing to worry about. He would be the most careful Integra NSX driver ever.

The moment his mother walked out of the house, her feelings were obvious. First shock, then awe, then a fierce and pointed anger aimed directly at his father. She barely shot a look at Jake as the two of them climbed out and anchored themselves on either side of the car.

"What's this?" She gestured at the car

the same way she gestured at his math papers when he fell short of a C.

"This?" Dad looked from the car back to Mom. "A birthday present for Jake. I'm out of town next week, so I brought it a few days early."

"You mean the cruise you and *Bonnie* are taking?" His mother's smile made Jake's skin crawl . . . it was practically evil. "Your girlfriend talked, Tim. Word gets around."

Jake winced at the pain that cut him deep in his gut. *It's because of Mom's tone,* he insisted to himself. Not because his father would rather take a cruise with some blonde than be there for his own son's birthday. He lifted his eyes in his father's direction.

Dad's mouth hung open, and he seemed to search for something to say. "How'd you . . ." He crossed his arms. "Look, what I do on my own time is my business, okay?"

"So that's what this is."

"What?"

"The fancy sports car." Jake's mother laughed once, but there was nothing funny in her voice. The pain in Jake's gut worsened, and he thought he might be sick. He hated when she acted like this. His mother waved at the car and continued. "I get it,

Tim. It's some kind of atonement for everything you're not doing for Jake this year. A makeup for all the hours you're spending with the girlfriend."

"You have no right saying that in front of —"

"In front of who? Jake? Like you care." She huffed. "No boy Jake's age should be driving a car like that."

Wait a minute . . . Jake wanted to interject but one look at his mom's rage-filled face and he decided against it.

"You're crazy, Tara. The car's perfect."

"What do you take me for, a fool? That's an *Integra.*" Her voice grew louder. Jake clutched his stomach. His parents were acting like kids fighting over some stupid toy. Only *he* was the toy — and it wasn't so much that they wanted him, really, but that they each wanted to win.

"So what?"

"It's too fast, that's what." She paced a few steps back toward the apartment and then spun around. "If you want him to have transportation, Tim, buy him a Bronco or a truck." Her eyes narrowed. "But an Integra?"

Jake had heard enough. He swung his bag over his shoulder and slipped past his parents without either of them seeming to notice. This was why they'd divorced. The fighting and yelling. The name-calling. Jake hated it, especially today. Hated the way it shot darts at his good feelings.

He flopped on his bed and buried his face in the pillow. Why couldn't they love each other like they used to? And why'd they have to fight all the time? Didn't they know how much it hurt him? Other kids had divorced parents, but at least they tried to get along. Not his parents, though. Every time they were together it was like they hated each other.

Jake rolled over and stared at the ceiling. Why was he letting their problems ruin the day? Nothing would change the thrill of what had just happened. The car was his, and it was a dream. Tons better than the heap of rust that dork Nathan Pike drove.

His parents' fights were their problem. No matter how determined they were to ruin the weekend, Monday would be the greatest day of Jake's life for one simple reason.

He was the proud owner of a shiny red Integra NSX, a car faster than just about anything in Illinois.

Five

―――――◆―――――

Maturity had nothing to do with it.

Thirty minutes into the dance lessons at the Marion High gymnasium, John felt like a freshman struggling through gym class, bumbling about on two left feet and not sure of his next step.

The instructor was a white-haired woman in her late fifties named Paula. She wore a microphone headpiece and was dressed in thick tights and a leotard. Her tone was condescending, with a forced cheerfulness that made John feel anything but mature. On top of that, she clapped her hands often. "Okay, class." She let her eyes drift down the line of fifteen couples.

Two, maybe three cups of coffee too many. John grimaced.

Paula clapped her hands again. "Line up." Her eyebrows seemed permanently raised. "Let's try that again."

Abby was holding her own, except when

he stepped on her foot. Trouble was, he'd been doing that often enough to make it part of the dance routine. He gave Abby a quick grin. "Here we go again. Hope your feet can take it."

"Stop it, John." She giggled. "The teacher will hear you."

"Perky Paula, you mean." The music had started, and already they were struggling to keep up with the other couples. John kept his voice to a whisper. "She's too busy counting out the beat."

John twirled Abby, and she nodded once in his direction. "Very nice."

"Sure, next thing you know I'll be up there with Paula." John danced a bit straighter and tried the next series of steps without looking. As he did, he came down on Abby's foot, sending her shoe skittering across the gym floor.

Paula shot them a stern look — the type usually reserved for students who shot spit wads. She clucked her tongue. "Please . . . hurry back in line."

Abby's lips were tight, the last line of defense before she burst into laughter. She ran after her shoe with tiptoe steps, ducking down as though that might help make the two of them less of a distraction. When the shoe was back on her foot, she returned to

John's side, and they did their best to blend back into line with the others.

It was no wonder John couldn't concentrate on the dance steps. Abby looked simply radiant. She could easily have been a decade younger, and the sparkle in her eyes made him feel as giddy as it had back when they first started dating. Why hadn't he seen her beauty last year or the year before? Or the year before that? How could he possibly have allowed himself to be distracted by another woman?

What could have made him think anyone might fill that place in his heart the way his precious Abby did?

"What are you thinking?" She whispered the words, and they found their way straight to his heart.

It no longer mattered that their dance steps weren't perfectly in time with the other couples around them. "That you're beautiful. That you've always been the most beautiful woman in the world."

A blush fell across Abby's cheeks. "I love you, John Reynolds."

His feet stopped, and Abby danced her way up against him. As she did, he leaned down and kissed her. "Thank you, Abby . . . for loving me."

The couple back one spot in the line

bumped into them and then danced their way around.

"Keep moving, people." Paula clapped her hands, her eyes fixed on John and Abby. "This is dance class . . . not the prom."

They fell back into line with the others once more. But no reprimand from the instructor could stop Abby and him from locking eyes, from allowing the rest of the world to fade as they danced in a way they'd always meant to. But for the grace of God, where would they be right now? For that matter, where would God be in the mix of things? And who would John be sharing his bed with?

A shudder gripped his gut.

God . . . thank You that I didn't fall the way I could have. Let me always love Abby like I do right now. Don't ever let us wander from each other again. Or from You . . . please.

A chord of three strands is not quickly broken, my son.

The silent whisper in his soul, the reminder of a Scripture he and Abby had used at their wedding, was enough to break John's concentration. Almost in perfect time to the music, he stepped on Abby's foot again.

This time she let out a quick squeak and jumped. Behind them in line, two other women did the same sort of jump, apparently thinking it was part of the dance. When Abby realized what was happening, she lost it.

Her laughter was silent, but relentless. And John was helpless to do anything but join her. Several times Paula shot them a look of pure frustration, shaking her head as if to say Abby and John would never be mature dancers. Not in a hundred years.

By the time the lesson was over, Abby was limping.

They were halfway to the car when John hunched down in front of her. "Your chariot, my dear."

Her laugh sounded like the wind chimes on their backyard deck in spring. John savored the sound, reveling in her nearness. She played out a gentle beat on his back. "You don't have to do that, John. I can walk."

"No, come on. I damaged your toes. I can give you a ride." He reached back for her legs, and as he did, she hopped onto his back. At first he walked, but the harder she laughed the faster he went until he was galloping. He went past the car and did a small circle around the parking lot. Everything about the moment felt free and un-defined and alive. As though time had stopped for them to celebrate the joy of being together. He let out a shout that echoed against the wall of the school. "Yeeee-haw!"

"I wonder —" Abby's words were broken up by the bumpiness of the ride — "what old Paula would think of *this* dance move?"

Finally he ran back to their car and set Abby down near the passenger door. The parking lot was empty, all the mature dancers having gone home to chamomile tea and early sleep. Abby leaned against the car door, breathless from the ride and the laughter. "What a night."

John grew quiet and he moved up against her, leaning close so their bodies were molded in all the right places. Passion colored the moment, and he studied her in silence. The only sounds were the occa-sional drone of a car on the distant road and the intoxicating whisper of Abby's heartbeat against his. He traced her chin, the delicate line of her jaw. "I feel like a teenager in love."

"Well . . ." She tilted her head back, her throat slim and curved in the moonlight. There was a raspy sound of desire in her voice, the way John had heard it often these past months. "Maybe that's because we're in a high-school parking lot."

"No." He angled his head so he wouldn't block any of the light. He wanted to see her face . . . all of it . . . wanted to memorize everything about her. "That's not why."

"It isn't?"

"Nope." He ran his fingers lightly down the length of her arms. "It's you, Abby. You make me feel this way."

They were quiet a minute, their bodies moving subtly until they were even closer than before. John nuzzled her face, breathing in the scent of her perfume as he dusted his lips along the side of her neck.

When he looked up, he saw her eyes were watery. Fear stabbed at him — he'd sworn to never make her cry again. "What're you thinking, baby?"

A single tear made its way down her cheek. "It's a miracle, John. What I feel . . . what we feel for each other. Six months ago . . ."

She didn't finish the sentence, and John was glad. He held his finger to her lips. "Have I told you lately how beautiful you are?"

"Yes." She lowered her chin and gave a few slow blinks. It was a look of both shyness and flirtation, a look that had driven him mad since he was a college boy.

"When did I tell you?"

"During the dance lesson, remember?" The corners of Abby's mouth lifted and her eyes twinkled.

"That was a long time ago." He placed a soft kiss, one at a time, on each of her eyes. "I mean lately. Have I told you *lately* how beautiful you are?"

Another tear fell, and she uttered a sound that was more laugh than cry. "I guess not."

"Well . . . you're more beautiful than a sunrise, Abby Reynolds. More beautiful than spring. In case I don't tell you often enough, I want you to know. I couldn't think about anything else in that dance lesson." He gave her a lopsided grin. "Not when all I wanted to do was . . ."

He was suddenly out of words. In their place, he moved toward her in a dance step he was far more familiar with. Then he kissed her as he'd been longing to do for an hour.

When they came up for air, both their heartbeats had quickened. "Hey . . ." He kissed her twice more and then held her gaze. "Wanna come back to my place?"

"Not for dancing, I hope." One of her

eyebrows lifted just a bit, the way it always did when she teased him. "My feet are sore enough."

"No —" he framed her face with his fingertips, letting a slow smile ease across his mouth — "not ballroom dancing, anyway."

"Hmmm." She gently brushed her lips against his, then put her hands on his shoulders and pushed him back a few inches. "Lead the way, Mr. Reynolds. Lead the way."

They crept into the house like a couple of delinquents breaking curfew. Not that it mattered. Sean was spending the night at a friend's, so they had the house to themselves.

Abby felt better than she'd felt in years as she followed John into the living room. "Okay, so where's the ballroom for this dance?"

"I'll show you, Mrs. Reynolds." He took her hand and led her up the stairs toward their room. "Follow me."

The hour that came next was more wonderful than Abby dared dream. She had heard from other women that after rocky times in their marriages, physical intimacy was never quite the same. Especially if another woman had been in the picture.

But from the moment she and John stood on their backyard pier in the hours after Nicole's wedding and recognized the impossibility of walking away from each other, Abby had fallen in love with her husband all over again. It really was a miracle. Their relationship now was like an intense, passionate release of all the feelings they'd buried for those three awful years.

Now they spent their intimate moments making it up to each other. Celebrating the joy of having rediscovered something that was almost lost for good. Never mind that conventional wisdom would have them struggling in this part of their relationship, taking a year or more to build back what those bad years had cost them.

Abby trusted John completely. And he trusted her.

Before they fell asleep, John rolled on his side and studied her. "Have I told you lately . . ."

The moonlight played across his face, and she smiled. "Yes . . . you've told me."

"You know what I liked best about tonight?"

She inched onto her side so they were facing each other. "The dance?"

He chuckled soft and low. "Always that.

But you know what else?"

"What?"

"It made me forget about coaching. Even just for a night."

A pain sliced through her heart. "It's that bad?"

"Worse." His smile faded. In its place was a look that was more sad than frustrated. "Know what I read in the paper yesterday?"

"What?"

"Some high-school basketball player's parents are suing his coach for seven million dollars."

"Seven million?" Abby propped her elbow up on the pillow. "For *what?*"

"For costing the kid his chance at an NBA career."

"What?" The story didn't make sense. "How is that the coach's fault?"

"Because —" John drew a slow breath — "the coach put the kid on JV instead of varsity."

Abby gasped. "You're kidding, right?"

"No." John's chuckle was so sad it almost broke Abby's heart. "I'm serious. That's what it's come to, Abby. Sometimes I don't think I'll survive the season."

"I'm sorry." She moved her elbow and let the side of her face rest on the pillow. "I wish there was something I could do."

"I keep thinking about that note. How one of my player's parents wants me fired badly enough to go to the district level to see it happen." He rolled onto his back again. "Me? Letting players drink and race their cars? Don't they know me at all? Don't they appreciate what I've done for that school since I've been there?"

The pain in Abby's heart spread to her soul. How could they possibly attack this man's character? If she could, she would walk into the school, take over the public address system, and tell the entire school population that Coach Reynolds did not and never would have done anything unethical where his players were concerned. She would demand they recognize his efforts and treat him with the respect and gratitude he deserved.

But she couldn't do that.

She couldn't even write a letter on his behalf, though she wanted to. Badly. "There's only one thing I can do, John. But it's the most important thing of all."

"Pray?" He turned his head so he could see her again.

"Exactly." She ran her fingertips lightly through his hair. "Pray that God shows you how much the kids still love you, the kids who wouldn't play ball for any other coach."

"Okay." He smiled, and for the first time since he'd brought up the topic, his features relaxed. "You pray. It's only because of your prayers that I've coached there this long."

"You know what I think?" She laid her head on John's shoulder and snuggled close to him.

"My season's falling apart?"

"No." She rested her hand above his heart. "I think something very big's about to happen."

"Like we win three games straight?"

"No, again." Abby gave a muffled laugh. "Something spiritual. Like God's got something major going on. Maybe that's why the season's starting so rough. We may not see how all the pieces fit right now. But maybe we'll see it soon. You know?"

John was quiet.

"You awake?"

"Yeah. Just thinking." His chest rose as he inhaled. "I'd forgotten about that."

"About God having a plan?"

"Mmmhmm." He hesitated. "It must be that."

"Yep. And whatever it is, it's going to be huge."

"How do you know?"

"It's something I feel."

"Oh. Okay." John's breathing was slower, his words running together the way they did just before he fell asleep. "I'm sorry."

"For what?"

"For stepping on your feet tonight."

"That's okay. We have another lesson next week."

"I love you, Abby. G'night."

"Goodnight . . . I love you, too."

She drifted off to sleep, her head still on John's shoulder, her mind filled with a dozen happy memories from the evening.

And with the increasing sense that somehow, someway, God was up to something very big at Marion High School. Something that involved football and parents and most especially her wonderful husband.

Coach John Reynolds.

Six

Nicole was afraid.

There was no other way to say it. After the whirlwind weekend with Kade home, she wasn't merely tired; she was exhausted. Too exhausted. Now it was Wednesday, and she and Matt had plans to eat dinner out. But as Nicole slipped into a pair of jeans and a sweater, her arms and legs felt like they were made of lead. Every movement was a colossal effort.

It couldn't be the flu. She didn't have a fever or a cough or an upset stomach. She raised the zipper and studied her reflection in their bathroom mirror. Pale . . . ashen, even. True her summer tan had faded, but Nicole couldn't remember her face ever looking this white.

She sighed. Maybe the events of the past few months had finally caught up to her. After the honeymoon they'd come home and immediately helped Matt put together his résumé for a position with the district attorney's office. Now that he was hired, Nicole was knee-deep in studies, trying to balance running their home with the demands of being a college senior.

On top of that, there were constant discussions with Matt about his parents' impending yearlong missionary trip. And then there was her younger brother Kade.

Last week, when he was home, something about him had been different. Older maybe, quieter. He was anxious to get playing time at the University of Iowa and he had a lot on his mind. On Sunday night he stopped by Matt and Nicole's apartment. They talked until 3 a.m. about whether he'd made a mistake taking the scholarship at Iowa when he'd rather be playing closer to home at Illinois.

"It's too far away," Kade said an hour into the conversation. Matt had gone to bed back at the beginning, leaving Nicole and Kade in the living room. Kade had tossed his hands in the air. "I feel like I'm on another planet." He sat on the floor, his back against the wall.

"It's only a day's drive from here." Nicole didn't want him pulling out of Iowa just because he was homesick. "It's always hard the first semester."

"Yeah, but Dad's been my coach forever, Nic." His knees were up, legs wide apart the way he always sat when they'd had these conversations over the years. "I'd at least like to see him in the stands, you know?" He rested his forearms on his knees. "This was the first weekend he and Mom have been to a game."

Nicole could see his point. "Why didn't you consider Illinois before? They sent you a letter didn't they?"

"Yeah." Kade frowned. "A bunch of letters. I thought being away from home would be fun."

"Maybe it will be. You've only been there two months."

"I know . . . but now I want to be here. Does that make sense?"

The discussion went in circles that way until the only thing Nicole could tell him was what he wanted to hear. "Transfer, then." She muttered a tired laugh. "We'd love to have you closer, bud. Then we could have these talks every weekend."

Kade grinned. "Just like the old days."

"Right. Just like the old days."

Memories of the discussion faded and Nicole checked the mirror once more. The morning after their late talk, she'd had class at eight o'clock. Every hour of the day and night had been booked since then. No wonder she was tired. Her body was merely trying to catch up.

Unless . . .

Nicole swallowed hard and turned from the mirror. She put a quick spritz of perfume on her neck. *Don't think about it . . . it's impossible.* But her mind refused to change the topic. Especially in light of the one memory that wouldn't go away.

It had happened three weeks after their honeymoon. They'd agreed to wait three or four years before having children, so birth control was a must. By waiting, Nicole could finish school and find a teaching job. She would teach two years and then take a decade off to have babies. When the kids were in school, she'd resume teaching. That way she could be with them after school and miss almost none of their at-home family time.

That was the ten-year plan, anyway. And they'd intended to follow it to the letter. All of which meant being very careful. Not only because of the ten-year plan, but because of something else. Something she hadn't wanted to share with anyone. Something she couldn't voice even to herself.

They'd talked about birth control pills,

but Nicole was concerned about the side effects. In the end they decided to use condoms instead.

"You probably learned about condoms in school," the doctor told Nicole when she was in for a checkup just before her wedding day.

"We did. They're one of the safest ways to prevent pregnancy, right?"

The doctor chuckled. "Not hardly." He gave her a crooked grin. "Every month someone whose husband used a condom comes into my office pregnant."

Nicole had been surprised, but also fairly certain the doctor was exaggerating. Obviously condoms worked or they wouldn't sell them.

Still, there was that one time . . .

Late that night, just weeks after their honeymoon, in the moments after being physically intimate, Matt had come out of the bathroom with a strange look on his face.

"What's wrong?" Nicole had sat up in bed, holding the sheet to herself.

"I think it broke." Matt ran his fingers through his hair and shook his head. "I thought that only happened in the movies."

A wave of alarm came over Nicole and

then passed. There was no way it broke. "Maybe it just looked that way."

Matt climbed back into bed. "Let's hope so."

Now, ten weeks later, the conversation came back to Nicole every few hours. Not just because she was more tired than usual, but because she hadn't had a period since before her wedding.

She'd heard her mother talk about being pregnant before, how she'd known from the moment of conception — known without a doubt — that a new life had begun to grow within her.

Nicole had searched for such signs, but there'd been nothing. Her period had always been irregular. Sometimes she'd missed three months in a row before it showed up again. So there wasn't any real reason to think she might be pregnant.

Was there . . . ?

The bedroom door opened and Nicole jumped. Matt stuck his head inside. "Ready?"

"Sure." She forced a smile. "I'll be right down."

She was quiet through dinner, and finally when Matt was finished eating, he pushed his plate away and looked at her. "Okay, Nic. What's wrong?"

"Nothing." Her answer was too quick. She stared at her food. More than half her cheeseburger was still untouched. Her eyes lifted and found his again. "I'm fine."

"You're not fine. You've been sleeping late and going to bed early. You yawn all the time and hardly have any appetite." Matt's voice was gentle, but concerned. "I'm worried about you."

Her gaze fell again. She pushed a fork through the small dish of beans beside the burger. The food looked old and uninteresting. A sigh slipped from her lips. It was time. If they were going to build a marriage of closeness and trust, she couldn't keep her fears from him another minute.

"Okay." Drawing a quick breath, she looked at him once more. "I think I might be pregnant."

She had expected him to look shocked, even upset by her statement. After all, a baby now would mean their plan was out the window.

Instead, Matt's face lit up like a Christmas tree. "Nicole? Are you serious?"

"Matt —" she lowered her head so people at the other tables wouldn't hear her — "it's too soon. You *can't* be excited about this."

His face went blank for a moment, then

he let loose a single, quiet laugh. "Yes, I can. Babies are a miracle, honey. Whenever they come."

Her heart dropped to her socks. His enthusiasm made the entire possibility seem more real. What if she really was pregnant? How could she be a mother when she hadn't finished college? And what about her worst fears, the ones she couldn't admit even to herself? Question after question assaulted her until she felt Matt's hands on hers.

"Sweetheart, I don't get it. You're upset because you think you might be pregnant?"

"Yes!" Nicole felt the sting of tears in her eyes. "We wanted to wait four years, remember?"

"Sure." He sat back a bit and blinked. "But if you're pregnant now, there's no point being upset. God will work out the details." He took her fingers in his. "Besides, maybe you're not. We've been careful."

"Yeah, but what about that one night? When you thought it broke?"

A knowing look filled Matt's eyes. "You think that's when it . . ."

"Maybe. The doctor told me it happens all the time." She dropped her head back for a moment and then found his eyes again. As she did, two tears slid down her cheeks. "I didn't believe him."

"Okay." Matt took her hand. "But, honey, you've always said you can't wait to be a mother. So why . . . are you crying? I mean, our plan can be adjusted, can't it?"

"I guess."

"Then . . . why the tears, honey? I don't get it."

Nicole wanted to climb across the table and hug him. He was such a good guy, so full of love for her and the future family they would one day raise. She steadied herself and decided to tell him her fears. The ones that had kept her up at night even when she desperately needed to sleep. "I guess I'm afraid."

Empathy filled in the lines on Matt's worried face. "Of what?"

Nicole sat back and took a sip of water. "Remember last year? When we were planning the wedding?"

"Of course." Matt studied her, his body halfway across the table as he leaned toward her.

"Something was wrong with my parents' marriage." Nicole gave Matt's fingers a gentle squeeze. "I think I told you I was worried about them."

"Right. You prayed for them, and as we checked into the hotel the night of our wedding, you felt the Lord had answered your prayers. That everything was going to be okay."

Nicole nodded. "I've thought about it a lot since then and I've decided maybe . . . just maybe their marriage isn't all it seems to be. You know?"

"Okay." Matt looked as lost as a child alone at the zoo. "So . . ."

"So I think I've figured it out."

"Figured it out?"

"Yes." Nicole stared at him. "The reason why my parents aren't really happy like I thought they were."

Matt blinked again. "Just a month or so ago you told them they looked like newly-weds."

"That was before I put the pieces together. It was something your mother said at dinner one night." Nicole released his fingers and sat back. If only he could understand. "Now I think I know the problem."

"Which is . . ."

"I was a honeymoon baby, remember?" Couldn't Matt see it? She worked to make her tone patient. "They had kids too early."

"Sorry, Nic." This time Matt sat back and crossed his arms. "I don't get it."

"How can you not get it?" Nicole held her hands out palms up. "My parents never got those crucial years, the years when the two of them could have bonded and built their love."

Matt looked at her for a moment. Then he stood and eased himself around the table and slid onto the bench seat beside her. He placed his arm over her shoulders and pulled her up against him. "I have the surest sense that you're wrong, Nicole. Your parents love each other very much. Having children early in their marriage hasn't hurt that. Not then or now."

Her husband's nearness, the warm shelter of his arm around her, made everything somehow better. Her defenses fell like autumn leaves. Maybe Matt was right, but this was something Nicole had thought about ever since they'd been back from the honeymoon. "You don't think it hurt them?"

"No." He kissed the side of her face and smoothed her hair back behind her ears. "But if it worries you, why don't you ask your mother? She'll tell you the truth."

Ask her mother? Why hadn't Nicole thought of that? Rather than imagining the reasons her parents had struggled last year, it couldn't hurt to come out and ask. She shifted her position so she could see Matt more clearly. "Okay. I'll do that."

"Now, how 'bout we pay this bill and do some shopping before we go home. I think there's a little something we have to get before another day goes by."

Nicole's heart was lighter than it had been in weeks. With God on her side and a husband like Matt, everything was going to be okay. "What's that?"

He grinned. "A pregnancy test."

Seven

The information was all there, on the Internet.

Whatever research Abby had done for her article could easily be supplemented with information from the Web. She signed on and waited for the connection. She'd been so busy catching up from the weekend with Kade that she hadn't had time to work on her coaching article until late that evening. Last night she might have had a few hours, but John needed the computer. He had to look up some new Internet site that gave coach's tips and defensive tricks. John had heard about it from one of the other coaches.

Abby hadn't minded. She had plenty of time to pull the article together.

The screen danced to life and a digital voice announced, "You've got mail."

For the briefest instant she remembered how badly she'd looked forward to those words a year ago. Back when she and John were speeding in opposite directions, headed straight for divorce. She'd been E-mailing an editor almost daily, a man who wanted to spend time with her.

If she hadn't found John's journal after Nicole's wedding, hadn't read it and learned the real way he felt about their marriage and the mistakes he'd made, she might never have forgiven him. In fact right now she might be in the midst of a full-blown relationship with the editor.

The thought turned Abby's stomach. She let it pass as quickly as it had come. These days her E-mail was almost all business related. She was working with several new magazines and keeping her relationships with editors at a strictly functional level. Occasionally there'd be an E-mail from a friend or a forward from one of the women at church.

But that was about it.

And even though John was spending more time on the computer, he never got E-mail. He merely surfed the Web for football strategies and plays he hadn't thought of before. Once in a while he'd check out a site with ranch property for sale and report to Abby that they should buy a hundred-acre piece in northern Montana. But he was only kidding, only looking for a way to ease the tension brought on by the football season.

Abby clicked the mailbox and immediately a list of mail appeared. There was more than usual, and it took a moment for her to scan the list. Something from a new magazine, three from her current editors, then . . .

Her heart stopped.

The next E-mail on the list had a subject line that read, *"More excitement than you can imagine!"* It was from someone named Candy at a Web site called *Sexyfun*.

Abby's heart thudded hard and resumed beating, twice as fast as before. Her eyes did a quick check down the rest of the list and there were five more E-mails like it. All from girls at Web sites with similar names as the first.

Her mind screamed it wasn't so. It couldn't be. Everywhere she turned someone was talking about Internet pornography. She and John had talked about the phenomenon, but neither of them had really understood the fascination. There was no way John had been accessing pornographic sites, was there? He'd been on the Internet, yes. But only to look at coaching sites, right?

There was one way to find out.

Abby maneuvered her mouse through a series of clicks until a list of Web sites appeared on her screen. The last fifty sites that had been accessed by their computer. The most recent were three that were clearly football related. But beyond that the list was horrendous.

Names of Web sites Abby could barely read let alone utter out loud. She closed her eyes. *God, no . . . don't let this be happening. Please*. After all she and John had been through, as much as he seemed to be in love with her . . . he couldn't be turning to pornography. It was impossible.

Yet, what other explanation was there? They were the only two people who used the Internet on this computer, other than Sean. And he only used it for homework. Abby thought back. It had been at least a month since Sean had been anywhere near the computer.

So that meant . . .

"No, God! I can't take it." She covered her face with her hands. Dealing with her husband's fascination with another woman had been one thing. But this?

You pulled us through that time, God . . . so why this? Why now?

She waited, but there were no reassuring

utterances in her soul, no verses that came to mind. Only an awful empty pit in her stomach, a pit that grew larger with each passing moment.

She opened her eyes and looked at the list. Maybe they weren't porn sites. Maybe they were coaching sites with stupid names. Yes, that had to be it. A thin veil of perspiration broke out across Abby's nose and forehead. She felt faint, desperate, terrified. Her heart couldn't take the shock, couldn't believe the list of Web site names staring back at her.

There was only one way to find out.

She picked the first one, something about naked girls, and clicked the link. *Let it be coaching information . . . defensive plays . . . anything but —*

A picture began to take shape and Abby gasped. Immediately she found the *X* in the upper right corner and closed the window. It wasn't coaching plays; it was exactly what one would expect to see on a Web site with that name.

Pornography.

Somehow in the midst of his distress and discouragement, John had used his late-night hours on the Internet to click his way into a seedy underworld of sin. Anger bubbled up from Abby's gut and filled her with a burning rage. *How dare he* . . .

She shut down the computer and spun her computer chair toward the dark window. The moon was only a sliver that night, but Abby stared outside anyway. What was he thinking? They'd been doing so well, enjoying each other both as friends and lovers. How could he —

Then another thought hit her.

Maybe that's why he had enjoyed their physical love so much lately . . . maybe he wasn't thinking about Abby at all, but these . . . these . . .

Nausea welled within her and she wondered if she would be sick to her stomach. How dare he sleep upstairs like nothing was wrong, when all the while he was keeping this terrible secret from her? And how could her body, her love ever compare with the images on his computer screen?

The array of emotions assaulting her was almost too much to bear. Sorrow . . . fury . . . regret. She'd trusted him, after all. Believed him that he wanted to be like the eagle — strong by her side until death parted them. Why in the world, then, would he begin experimenting with pornographic Web sites? Especially when he knew from friends of theirs how addictive and destructive they could be?

For more than an hour Abby sat there, her stomach in knots, until finally she went upstairs and studied her husband. Last year she'd had no trouble knowing John was interested in another woman. His distance, the hours he was gone from home, the strange phone calls. The signs had all been there. But this . . . this pornographic thing? He'd been masterful at hiding this. Abby blinked in the dark, sickened by the innocence on his face.

She lay down on the far edge of their bed, turned her back to him, and fell asleep. But not before two simple thoughts filled her mind . . .

How could they possibly stay together now?

And most of all, why hadn't she been enough for him?

The game that Friday was away, and John's Eagles won with a last-minute field goal. Rumors were spreading about the players who drank and took part in the street races. It was so bad John could almost hear the parents whispering about him.

"Coach Reynolds isn't the man we thought he was . . ."

"We need a man with better moral character than that . . ."

Of course the real reasons were as obvious as his record. The Eagles had only won three games. A dismal feat considering the hopes everyone had once held for this team. Winning had a way of shutting up the critics. Lose and a coach immediately became fair game.

The stands were rife with parents who would have run on fourth down or passed the ball on first. People whose sons didn't play much were the worst. Most of them figured the team would win if only their boys were in the mix. Those whose sons did play had another answer: poor coaching.

Either way the bad start this season fell on John's head.

As John boarded the team bus back to Marion that night, he felt only a small amount of relief from the victory. Jake Daniels's head hadn't been in the game no matter what John tried to do to inspire him. John had seen Jake's new Integra NSX. The entire school was talking about it.

Rumor had it Jake was looking to race it as soon as football season was finished.

John stared out the dirty window of the bus and gritted his teeth. What was Jake's father thinking, getting the boy a car like that? How was a teenager supposed to focus on his studies and his role as quarterback with a racecar sitting in the parking lot?

Not only that, but Jake and Casey and a handful of players had stepped up their teasing against Nathan Pike and his gothic friends. John had told the administration about Nathan's awful, scribbled words — *death to jocks*. Apparently the principal had pulled Nathan into the office and questioned him. Nathan acted calm and casual.

"It's a song, man." He shook his head at the principal. "You people are so out of touch."

The principal could do nothing but believe Nathan and issue him a warning. Song or not, he wasn't to be writing death threats on his notebook. Nathan agreed, and the incident passed. At least as far as the administration was concerned.

The reality was something else altogether. Nathan and his dark friends had gotten more hateful, more distant. At the same time, the cruel, arrogant remarks from Jake and Casey and the others had only come with more frequency. At times there was so much tension between the two groups, John felt certain the situation was about to erupt.

Several times he'd pulled Jake and Casey aside and said something, but always their answer was the same: "We're just playin' around, Coach."

Their parents didn't seem to care whether their sons were bullying kids like Nathan Pike. They were too worried about the Eagles win-loss record, too concerned with whispering and rumoring and getting John fired, filling the stands with enough negative energy to kill the rest of the season.

No wonder Abby hadn't wanted to go tonight.

Until this one, she hadn't missed a game since the season began. John had been in a hurry when he breezed home, grabbed his coaching bag, and headed back out for the game.

"You're going, right?" He went to plant a quick kiss on her lips, but at the last second she turned and it landed on her cheek instead. The gesture had seemed odd, but John hadn't had time to dwell on it. He had a bus to catch.

"Not tonight." She'd seemed distracted. In fact, she'd seemed that way since Thursday morning. Not angry, exactly. Just . . . distant.

The bus ride seemed longer than usual,

and John settled back in his seat. What was eating her anyway? He thought for a moment, then it hit him. It must have been her magazine article. Sometimes she got quiet right before deadline on a big piece. The best solution, he'd found, was to let her be. Give her as much time and space as possible to get her work done, then she'd be fine.

Still, he'd missed her tonight. It was always better coaching from the sidelines knowing Abby was there somewhere behind him in the stands. Everyone else might complain about him, but Abby would have cheered. Especially tonight, since they pulled out a win.

John stretched. Enough of the negative thoughts. Jake Daniels . . . Nathan Pike . . . the complaining parents. All of it was only part of a passing season. He would pray for the kids and look for opportunities to reach them. But everything about Marion High was something he was learning to leave behind when he finished up for the day.

Life was too short to bring his troubles home. Especially when things with Abby were so unbelievably wonderful.

It was nearly eleven when he walked in the house. The lights were out. Abby must have finished writing and gone to bed. John shut the door behind him and took three steps. Then he heard her voice.

"John . . . I'm in here."

He squinted into the dark and flipped on the light in the entryway. "Abby? What are you doing?"

"Praying." She paused. "Come here, will you? We need to talk."

He wasn't sure if he should feel honored or concerned. She'd obviously waited up for him to come home, intent on talking to him. But there was nothing light about her tone. He set down his bag and took the chair opposite her. "What's up?"

"This." Moving like an old woman, Abby reached down and picked up a piece of paper from the floor. "I found it a few days ago, but it took me a while to know how to bring it up."

Bring it up? What was she talking about? He took the paper, and in the half-light from the foyer, he stared at its contents. In no time he could see what it was, and it turned his stomach.

"Where'd this come from?" He brought the page closer to his face so he could read it clearly.

It was a list of pornographic-type sites. One after another after another. Probably twenty of them in all. John glanced up the page and saw their E-mail address listed at the top. Suddenly he understood. Abby was here, waiting in the dark, because she'd found this list on their computer Internet log and wanted an explanation.

The whole time he'd been looking at the list, Abby had said nothing. Now John lifted his eyes to her, his heart racing. "You got this off *our* computer?"

"Yes." Her arms were folded tight against her waist. "You're the only other person who uses the computer besides me, John." Her voice broke. "Obviously we need to talk."

He wanted to scream at her. Did she honestly think he was visiting porn sites in his spare time? That with everything going on at school and with the team, he could possibly be crazy enough to get involved with Internet smut? When he was married to the only woman he'd ever loved?

The idea was outrageous.

"You think *I* looked up these sites?" He planted his fingertips on his chest.

"What am I supposed to think?"

John wadded the paper up and threw it against the wall. Then he stood and paced a few steps in either direction. "Abby, are you out of your *mind?* I've never looked at a pornographic Web site in my life." His tone was sharper than his words. "How could you think such a thing?"

"Don't lie to me, John." Clearly she was as angry as he, but she stayed in her chair. "You've been on the Internet more often than usual and always at night. Why?"

He stared at her, stunned. "You really doubt me, don't you? After all we've been through, you still don't trust me."

"I *did* trust you." She lowered her voice, but her intensity remained. "But I trusted you three years ago, too. Back when you and Charlene were spending every morning together."

He felt the blood drain from his face. "That's not fair, Abby, and you know it." John bent at the waist, firing his words at her. "We were *both* wrong back then, but those days are behind us. Remember?"

"I thought so, too." The fight left her voice. "Until I found that list."

She might as well have slapped his face. Wounded and furious and not sure what to say, John fell back into the chair and buried his head in his hands. "You don't know me any better than the parents of my players."

Abby was silent, and for a moment neither of them said anything.

There had to be an explanation for the sites. Abby obviously hadn't looked them up, but neither had he. And how dare she accuse him even after he'd denied having anything to do with them.

God, give me the words here . . . how can Abby doubt me on this?

Love is not easily angered . . .

The holy response flashed across the scoreboard of his mind and took the edge off his temper. His shoulders slumped, and he shook his head. Of course Abby didn't believe him. After the times he'd spent with Charlene . . . the lies he'd told Abby when their marriage was unraveling . . .

For the first time since their reconciliation, John realized something he hadn't before.

It would take years before either of them would feel completely secure again. No matter how good things were between them. Sin always had consequences. Abby's doubts about him now were one of those.

She broke the silence first. "Aren't you going to say anything? I've been carrying this around for two days wondering why I'm not enough for you." She was crying now. Not angry sobs or out-of-control weeping, but small, soundless cries that strangled his heart.

John dropped to the ground and crawled on his knees until he was up against her legs. "Abby . . ." His words were calm, quieter than before. He lifted her chin so she'd have to look at him. "I promise you with everything I have, I didn't do this. I've never looked at a porn site. Not ever."

She sniffed and wiped the back of her hand across her cheeks. Nothing came from her mouth, but John could see it in her eyes. Doubt . . . fear . . . concern. Thoughts that somehow it was happening again, that their marriage was falling apart.

God . . . please give me wisdom. There has to be an answer.

Two seconds passed, then a third, and suddenly he knew the answer. The realization brought him as much pain as it did relief. The explanation was bound to satisfy Abby, but it left them with a problem neither of them had anticipated.

"Did you forget?" Their eyes were still locked. "Kade was here last weekend. He stayed with us through Monday afternoon."

It took a moment for the information to register.

As it did, John could see his wife's expression shift. Like melting wax, her face softened and her anger fell away. In its place was a sadness and guilt so raw it was painful to look at. Nearly a minute passed before Abby opened her mouth. "Kade?"

"He was here. I'm not sure if he was on the computer, but he must've been. Because —" he met her eyes squarely — "the only thing I looked at were coaching sites. I . . . found three of them."

Abby stared into the night, her eyes distant. After a long while, she lifted her gaze back to John's. "Sunday night he was with Nicole. But Saturday . . . Saturday he was here. He didn't get to sleep until after one o'clock because I got up and . . ."

John caught her hands in his. "And what?"

"I came down for a drink of water." Tears flooded her eyes. "He was on the computer. I . . . I didn't realize it until I was halfway up the stairs and heard the clicking sounds. I completely forgot about that."

There was nothing for John to say. Abby's doubts cut to his core, but he couldn't deny they were deserved. Thankfully, Internet pornography was not something he'd ever even considered. Still, he could hardly be upset with Abby for thinking it possible.

"John . . ." She took his face in her

hands and searched his eyes. "I'm so sorry. How could I have thought — ?"

"Shh, Abby. Don't." He lay his head against hers and stroked her hair. "It's my fault. If I hadn't let you down in the past, you never would've wondered."

"But I'm such a jerk." Her tears became sobs, and she clung to John as though her next breath depended on his being there. "Why didn't I *ask* you first? Instead of accusing you?"

"It's okay." Peace flooded his heart. This was his Abby, fighting for their marriage, determined to let go of the past. What he'd seen when he came home was merely a momentary lapse in trust, the kind of thing that was bound to happen in light of the trials they'd weathered. "Of course you're going to have doubts, honey. It's over with. Let it go."

Abby struggled to sit up, her eyes bloodshot, her breaths quick and jerky. "I never want to doubt you again, John Reynolds." She sniffed and shook her head. Her voice was little more than a whisper. "It's not okay. What we have is too precious to waste it doubting each other."

She was right. There was no way they could build on the love and joy of the past few months without trust. Suddenly he wondered if this was the first time. "Have you had doubts before this? About me, I mean?"

"No, I —" She started to shake her head but she stopped herself. "Well . . . sometimes." She took a quick breath. For a long time she said nothing. "I guess I wonder if someday another Charlene will move into the picture, or if I'll be enough for you. Pretty enough . . . smart enough. Young enough."

If he hadn't already been on his knees, her admission would have sent him there. "You were *always* enough. It wasn't you; it was life. Time. Busyness. We let too much come between us."

"I know." Her voice was calmer, more controlled. "But the Charlenes of this world will always be there."

"Never again, Abby. Remember the eagle?"

Abby tilted her head. "Kade's English paper. He wrote how the eagle mates for life . . . clings to its mate, even falling with her to his death rather than letting go."

"Right." John worked his fingers up her arms to the sides of her face. "I'm clinging like I never did before." He leaned forward and kissed her forehead. "Nothing could make me let go of you. Nothing."

She slid to the edge of the chair and hugged him. "I believe you. I've believed you since Nicole's wedding. The doubts are just . . . I don't know, stupid I guess."

He searched his heart and knew there was something else. If he was going to be completely honest, he had to tell her his thoughts as well. "You're not the only one."

She pulled back enough to see his eyes. "Not the only one?"

"With stupid doubts."

A softness settled over her eyes. "Really?"

"Really." John let his gaze drop for a moment before looking up again. Things had been going so well between him and Abby, he hadn't wanted to admit his fleeting thoughts. Not even to himself. "I wonder sometimes what would've happened if I hadn't come back the night of Nicole's wedding. I mean, there I was, packed to leave for good. Only God could have made me stop the car and come back." He bit his lip. "But what if I hadn't come? Would you be dating that editor or having some sort of Internet relationship with him?"

"I never should have let you go." She slipped her fingers through his hair, her eyes shining. "Then you wouldn't have to wonder."

"I don't worry about you now. Just the past and where we might be if I hadn't come back."

Abby rested her head against his once more, and they held each other. A long while later, Abby fell back into the chair again. "We still have a problem, though, don't we?"

John could read her soul as easily now as he had back when she was a teenager. "Kade?"

"Kade." Her eyes narrowed, less in anger than confusion. "Why would he do that, John? That's not how we raised him. That garbage will strangle the life out of him."

"I'll talk to him."

"On the phone? What if he denies it?"

She was right. This called for more than a phone call. "They have a bye coming up the second week in November. Let's fly him home. I'll talk to him then."

"What if he's addicted? It happens all the time." Abby hesitated. "I wish we didn't have to wait."

"We don't have to." John took her hands in his again. This time he folded them within his. "We can do something right now."

Then with hearts and hands linked in a way that filled John's being, they bowed their heads and prayed for their older son. That he would be honest about the Internet sites he'd looked into. That he would be willing to discuss the issue with John.

And that together they could eliminate the problem. Before it was too late.

Eight

Perky Paula was going to kick them out for sure.

Abby could tell the moment she saw Jo and Denny at the gymnasium door. It was the first Saturday in November, and Abby had invited Nicole's in-laws — as if John dancing on her feet wasn't enough humor for the hour. They'd agreed to meet at the entrance.

Abby wore a dress, and John, nice pants and a khaki button-down. Church clothes. It was *ballroom* dancing, after all. In Abby's mind that connoted elegance and taste. Even with her husband stepping on her toes.

Jo and Denny, on the other hand, looked ready for a country hoedown.

Abby would have felt sorry for them, except neither of Matt's parents seemed to care how they were dressed. *Maybe they've never seen ballroom dancing.* For that matter it was quite possible they'd never seen a ballroom.

Denny wore pointed cowboy boots and a tall black hat. Jo was squeezed into a pink-and-black miniskirt with a matching pink-fringed shirt and pink boots.

As they approached, John bent down and whispered in Abby's ear, "Didn't you tell them what to wear?"

Abby waved at Jo as she whispered back, "I thought they'd know."

Both couples signed in and took their places.

Jo fell in place next to Abby. "You sure the teacher won't mind us buttin' in and all?"

"Positive." John and Denny led the way. "The class is an ongoing thing."

John shot a quick look at Denny. "Aren't you glad?"

Denny gave a lopsided grin and twirled his finger in the air. "Barrel of fun, I'm sure."

"Oh, stop." Jo whacked her husband in the arm. "You love dancin' with me and you know it."

Paula had been flitting about, connecting with various couples. Now she approached Abby and John with a hurried smile. "Welcome back, I see you've

brought your —" Instantly the smile became a frown as Paula scrutinized Jo and
Denny. "My goodness —" the muttered
comment was just loud enough for them to
hear — "completely inappropriate." She
shook her head and turned to the front of
the gym.

Abby could feel Jo's ire from five feet
away. *Here we go.* Abby took John's hand
and waited.

Jo spun around, her eyebrows furrowed.
"That woman has a lot of nerve! What's
her problem?"

"Nothing." John patted Jo on the back.
"She takes her dancing very seriously."

Abby could almost see the hairs rise on
Jo's neck as she planted her hands on her
hips. "I take my fishin' seriously, but you
won't see me sticking fishhooks in the first-
timers over it."

The couples lined up while Paula
worked the tape player. Abby and John positioned themselves next to Jo and Denny.
Jo hissed in Abby's direction.

"Besides, *look* at her! Dressed in tights
and a lee-tard at her age!"

Denny gave her a discreet nudge.
"Jo . . ."

"What? She looks ridiculous."

Jo shot a laserlike glare at Paula's back.

"She better not look at me like that again or I'll . . . well . . ." Jo caught Denny's look and relaxed some. "Never mind. Sorry." She shot Abby and John a weak smile. "I get a little carried away."

"Right." Denny used his eyes to apologize for his wife. "And water gets a little wet."

Abby grinned and squeezed John's hand once more. "Don't worry about it, Jo." She gave the woman a tender smile and tried to imagine what Nicole would do in this situation. Abby drew a deep breath. "Hey, how's the mission thing going? You guys still thinking about a year in Mexico?"

"Absolutely." The scowl fell from Jo's face. "Can't wait. Those little babies need people to love 'em, and me and Denny are just the folks." She winked at her husband. "Besides, the fishin' down there'll be heavenly. Just like if I died and the Lord met me at the pearly gates with a brand new rod and reel."

One of the couples was talking to Paula so they still had a moment before class began. John poked his elbow at Denny. "Watch her feet. I had to carry Abby out after our first lesson."

"No!" Jo gave John a slap on the arm. "The graceful star quarterback from Michigan University? I don't believe it."

"It's true." Abby winced and laughed at the same time. "My toes are still bruised."

"Hey, you seen the kids lately?" Jo gave her shoulders an exaggerated shrug and reached her hands over her head in a full-body stretch. The kind usually reserved for aerobic classes. Two of the couples near the front of the line noticed her and began whispering.

"Uh . . ." Abby tried to remember Jo's question. "Yes. Nicole stopped by yesterday."

"Well . . . what'd you think?"

Denny exchanged a bewildered look with John, as if to say he had no idea what his wife was talking about. Again.

"Think?"

Jo huffed lightly. "About Nicole. Isn't she glowing?"

Abby thought for a moment. "I guess I haven't noticed."

"Okay, class." Paula clapped her hands. "Everyone in position, please. Let's do a quick run-through of the steps we learned last week. Ready? And one and two and . . ." The music started.

Abby and John lurched into action, getting halfway across the gym floor before John waltzed across her foot. "Ouch!"

Abby tripped a bit and then fell back into step. This time they circled the room without incident. "Not bad." She smiled at him. "You're maturing quite nicely."

John nodded at something behind her. "That's more than I can say for Jo and Denny."

Abby glanced over her shoulder and nearly tripped.

Jo and Denny were completely ignoring Paula's lead. Instead they had linked arms and were doing a side-by-side, high-stepping country line dance, oblivious to the waltzing couples around them.

Abby spun back around to face John, eyes wide. "Paula's going to kick them out!"

"I don't think so." John's eyes sparkled. "She's been watching them the whole time. She's too shocked to say anything."

As it turned out, Paula didn't say a word until midway through the lesson. That's when Jo let loose a loud "Yeeee-*haaaw!*" in the middle of a subdued classical piece.

With that, Paula adjusted her headset and clapped her hands again. "There will be no shouting out from the students. Just follow the couple in front of you or I'll have to ask you to leave."

Jo gave Paula an angry look, opened her

mouth, and did it again. "Yeeee-ha —"

Denny placed his hand firmly over Jo's mouth before she could complete the sound.

Abby peered over John's shoulder for a better view. "Wow." She worked hard to keep her laughter quiet. "The woman's unbelievable."

"You invited her." John did a playful roll of his eyes. "I could have predicted this."

"Come on . . . she's just more intense than most people."

"The way a tornado is more intense than a gust of wind."

Jo and Denny were two-stepping now, and Denny whispered to her midstep. Something close to remorse filled Jo's eyes, and after that she seemed more sedate. Abby was awed. Clearly Denny's influence over Jo was considerable.

For the rest of the hour, every time Abby looked at them, they were lost in their own world of two-stepping and line dancing. Not once during the session did either of them even attempt a ballroom step.

When the lesson was over, the couples stood outside the gym catching their breath. "I think that teacher had something against me."

"No . . . Do you think so?" Denny

looped his arm around Jo's neck and pulled her close. He flashed a grin at Abby and John.

"And why was she teachin' us that old-folk style dance? Someone oughta take her to a country dance hall and show her how to lighten up a little before she gets too caught up in herself and —"

Denny placed his hand over Jo's mouth once again. "What she means is, thanks for asking us to come. We had a great time."

Abby stifled a giggle. As she did, she remembered something. "Hey, what was that you were saying about Nicole earlier?"

Jo started to talk but Denny's fingers muffled the sound. He chuckled and let his hand fall. She raised her eyebrows at him. "Thank you." Then she turned to Abby. "Just that she's glowing brighter than a rainbow trout if you haven't noticed."

Glowing? What was that supposed to mean? "That newlywed look?"

John and Denny exchanged another curious look.

"No . . ." Jo leaned in as if she had top-secret information. "That *glowing* look."

"Meaning . . ." Abby was desperate for Jo to explain herself. She couldn't be suggesting . . .

"Okay." Jo straightened up again.

120

"Nicole's a honeymoon baby, right?"

John shifted his weight and glanced at his watch. Abby's signal that the conversation could wait.

"Right, so?" Abby willed the woman to make herself clear.

"So —" Jo grinned — "honeymoon babies beget honeymoon babies. That's the way it works."

"Jo, come on." John chuckled. "You don't think Nicole's pregnant?"

"Now, now." Jo held up her hand and lifted her chin. "You didn't hear that from me."

A pit formed in Abby's stomach. Certainly if Nicole *was* pregnant, she wouldn't have told Jo and Denny first. Would she? But then, maybe Nicole hadn't said a word. Maybe — "Did Matt tell you?"

"Nope. Nothing like that. The kids haven't said a word." Jo tapped a finger against her temple. "It's just a hunch. That and the way Nicole's been glowing."

John gave a gentle tug on Abby's arm. She responded with a few subtle steps backward. "Well, we need to run. I wouldn't think too much about Nicole being pregnant. The kids are planning to wait awhile."

"I think we all know how plans like that

work out, don't we?" Jo looked at Denny. But this time there was nothing funny about her tone. In fact, if Abby wasn't in such a hurry she would've taken more time with Jo. Because the look she and Denny shared was almost sad.

The couples bid each other good-bye, but later that night Abby couldn't shake what Jo had said. She and John helped Sean with a Native American flathouse he had to complete by Monday. When they were done, she motioned for John to follow her out back.

Without saying a word, they strolled hand-in-hand to the pier. When one of them had something on their heart, knowing what to do was as instinctive as drawing breath.

When they reached the end of the pier, they sat on a small bench John had placed there a month ago. Abby waited a minute before saying anything, gazing instead at the ribbon of light across the water. She loved this lake, loved the fact that they'd lived there since the children were young. Way back since their tiny baby daughter Haley Ann died suddenly in her sleep.

There was never a time when they sat here together that Abby didn't remember their second daughter, the one whose ashes they'd sprinkled across this very water. Over the years they'd come to this spot to share the highs and lows of life. When Abby's mother was killed by the Barneveld tornado . . . when John's father died of a heart attack . . . when John led the Eagles to their first state title — and when the parent complaints got to him.

They would sit until words came. Then, when they were done talking, John would take her by the hand and sway with her, back and forth. Not the kind of dancing that required lessons. Rather the kind that required listening. Leaves rustling in the trees beyond the pier, crickets and creaking boards. The whisper of the wind. The faint refrains of distant memories.

"Can you hear it?" he would ask.

"Mmmm." She would rest her head against his chest. "The music of our lives."

"Dance with me, Abby . . . don't ever stop."

Abby drew in a long, slow mouthful of the cool night air. It tasted of the coming winter, cool and damp. It wouldn't be long before they'd have to bundle up on evenings like these. And Abby had a feeling there would be several of them, between John's coaching troubles and their concerns about Kade.

She turned to John and reached for his hand. He was looking at her, watching her. Abby held his gaze for a moment. "I wonder if he'll admit it."

"Probably." John stared out at the water. "He doesn't usually keep secrets from me."

"Yeah, but . . ."

"I think he'll tell me."

"I'm nervous about it."

Their fingers were still linked, and John soothed his thumb over the top of her hand. "I'm not. He's a good kid, Abby. Whatever he's doing on the Internet . . . I doubt he's addicted to it."

"I know. But what if he gets angry that we know?" She tried to will away the knots in her stomach. "Things like this could cause a rift between him and us. A rift that could take him away from God, even."

"Abby . . ." John faced her again and gave her the same look he gave the children whenever a bad thunderstorm came up. Calm and confident, gently understanding. "We've prayed for that boy since he was born. God's not going to let him go that easily."

She nodded and something in her stomach relaxed. "You're right."

"What else?"

"You know me too well."

"Yep." He flashed her the grin she loved best. "So what else?"

"Remember that kid you told me about? Nathan Pike?" Her thoughts were all over the board tonight, but John wouldn't mind. He was used to conversation like this. Random neural firings, he called them.

"How could I forget him? He's in my class every day."

"I don't like it." Abby's heart rate quickened. "He worries me, John. What if he does something crazy?"

"He won't. Kids like that aren't the ones who buy a gun and go ballistic." John released her hand and laced his fingers behind his head. "Nathan wants attention, that's all. The gothic look, the casual threats — those are his way of getting someone to finally notice him."

"I don't like it."

They were quiet again, and overhead an eagle swooped low over the water, snagged a fish, and soared over a thicket of trees. John watched it disappear. "He must be taking food back to the nest."

"Probably." Abby leaned her head back. The moon was full tonight, dimming the brightness of the stars. Abby felt herself relax. John was right. Everything was going to be okay with Kade . . . and with Nathan Pike. Even with the football team. God would work it out somehow.

"You don't think Nicole's pregnant, do you?"

John stood and stretched, twisting first to the right, then to the left. When he was finished, he exhaled hard and held a hand out to Abby. "No, I don't think Nicole's pregnant. They want to wait awhile before having kids, remember?"

"I know." Abby clutched tightly to his fingers as he pulled her to her feet. "But what if Jo's right? Now that I think about it, she has had a kind of glow about her."

"Believe me, Abby —" John eased her into his arms — "if our daughter was pregnant, she'd tell Matt first, and you second. She's just happy, that's all. Who wouldn't be glowing?"

"You're right." Abby hesitated. "But if she was . . . wouldn't that be something? You and me, *grandparents?*"

John chuckled. "I guess I'd *have* to be mature then."

Abby studied John's features, the subtle lines across his forehead, the hint of gray at his sideburns. "It's weird to think we're getting old."

"Weird?" John drew her closer. "I don't

126

know; I think it's nice."

"Yes." Abby pictured them together this way, dancing on the pier, laughing and loving and finding strength from each other. "It'll be fun to grow old with you, John Reynolds."

"One day we'll put our rocking chairs out here."

"So when we're too tired to dance, we can rock?"

"Right." The corners of his lips raised, and Abby felt tingles along her spine. "Remember our first date?"

"You came with your family for a Michigan football game." He raised his eyebrows. "Finally."

"I was seventeen, John." She lowered her chin, remembering the shy girl she'd been. Their families had known each other forever, but John was older than her. Abby hadn't thought she stood a chance until that pivotal football game. "How could I believe that John Reynolds, star quarterback for the Wolverines, wanted to date me?"

"I'd been planning it for two years." He traced her jaw line, his eyes locked on hers. "I was just waiting for you to grow up."

"Now the tables have turned."

"Is that so?"

"Mmhhmm. Now I'm waiting for you to grow up." Abby sent a playful kick at John's foot. "At least on the dance floor."

"I can dance when it matters." He glanced up and out at the lake, taking in the beauty of this favorite spot. Then, ever so slowly, he began to sway. His gaze fell to hers, as it had so often over the years. "Dance with me, Abby."

His tender words melted her heart. "Always, John." She moved with him. "Forever and always."

She nestled her head against his shoulder, drawing strength from each beat of his heart. They moved together to the far-off cry of a hawk and the lapping of lake water against their private shore. Abby closed her eyes. What would life be like without her husband? A life where they couldn't come to this place, this pier they both loved, the spot where their daughter's ashes lay and where they'd shared so much of each other? A life where they wouldn't have nights like this one?

It was impossible to imagine.

Yet there was no denying they were getting older. And one day — when their years of being grandparents and great-grandparents were finished — the music would stop. The dance would be over. It was inevitable.

Abby pressed her cheek against John's chest once more, savoring his closeness. *Thank You, God . . . thank You for saving us from ourselves.*

Later that night, before she fell asleep, Abby uttered another prayer. One she'd said more often in the past few months.

God, I've never been more in love with John. Please . . . let us have a thousand more nights like this one. Please.

Nine

———◆———

The confrontation was set for Saturday afternoon.

Kade didn't know it, of course, but John had long since had the day planned out. The Eagles had won their football game the night before, so it was a light practice that Saturday morning. Kade had come along, enjoying the chance to catch up with dozens of his former teammates.

"Hey, Dad, I think I'll go throw a few balls for the freshmen." Kade motioned to the adjacent field, where the younger Eagles were practicing.

John watched from his place near the varsity squad. The moment Kade appeared in their midst, the freshmen gathered around him, shaking his hand, looking awe-struck at his presence. Big college quarterback Kade Reynolds back from school. It was enough to make their week.

John's gaze shifted to his older players.

"Okay. Line up; let's do it again. This time I want you linemen shoulder to shoulder. You're a wall, not a picket fence. Let's remember that!"

When the drill was underway, John glanced once more to the other field. Kade was throwing passes for the young receivers, airing them out in a way that made even John's mouth hang open. The boy had potential, for sure. John couldn't be prouder of him.

Later that day, though, Kade wouldn't be Mr. Big-time Athlete. He would simply be John Reynolds's boy. And the father-son conversation wouldn't be about Kade's talents.

Give me the words, God . . . how I handle this could affect his life forever.

Two hours later they were at home and finished with lunch. Sean needed new soccer cleats, and Abby had arranged to take him to the store. That way John and Kade could be alone.

When they were by themselves, Kade headed for the television. "Ahhh . . . Saturday football. Time to check out the competition."

Before he could grab the remote control, John cleared his throat. "Let's take the boat out instead. You and me."

Kade hesitated for a moment and then shrugged. "Sure. Why not? I can catch the highlights on *SportsCenter*."

The day was unseasonably warm, as though fall was doing its absolute best to steal a few hours from the impending winter. A light cloud layer kept the sun's glare down, but there was no rain in the forecast. It was the perfect afternoon for a few hours on the lake.

They made idle chitchat at first, joking about the time when Sean was four years old. Abby had been at the supermarket, and John was in charge of the children. He, Nicole, and Kade were playing Frisbee on the grassy hill behind their house, when Sean snuck off, donned a life jacket, climbed into their family rowboat, and loosed the moorings. By the time John realized Sean was missing, the child had drifted a hundred yards out onto the lake. He was standing up in the boat screaming at them for help.

"I was scared to death." John worked the boat's oars as he laughed at the memory.

"You thought Sean would drown?"

"Are you kidding?" John huffed. "He had a life jacket. Besides, he knew how to swim." He winked at Kade. "I was scared of your mother. She would've killed me if she'd gotten home and found Sean out in the middle of the water by himself!"

The lake was a private one, frequented mainly by the homeowners whose houses sat along the three-mile shoreline. Today, the water had only a few other boats on the far side. John rowed out a bit further and then pulled in the paddles.

Kade leaned back and positioned his face toward the thinly veiled sun. "I forget how good it feels. Quiet. Peaceful." He sent John a quick grin. "Good idea, Dad."

"I can think out here." John hesitated. "Or have a real conversation."

It took a moment, but Kade sat forward again and met John's gaze. "Something you wanna talk about, Dad?"

"Actually, there is."

"Okay, shoot."

John searched his son's features for a sign . . . some flicker of apprehension or guilt. But Kade's expression was the picture of trusting innocence. John's heart tightened. Was Kade so far into this thing that he didn't feel even a hint of guilt?

Here I go, Lord . . . give me the words. John rested his elbows on his knees and looked deep into Kade's eyes. "After your visit last time, your mother and I found some questionable Web site addresses on her Internet history page."

Kade's face was blank. "Questionable?"

"Well, worse than questionable, really." John resisted the urge to squirm. "What I'm saying is, we found a list of pornography sites, Kade."

"Pornography?" His eyebrows lowered into a baffled *V.* "Are you . . . accusing me of checking out porn sites?"

Doubts assaulted John. "Look, son. Your mother thought *I'd* looked them up. And I know it wasn't me. Obviously it wasn't your mother. Sean hadn't been on the computer for a month, and even then he has his own screen name that wouldn't allow those types of sites." John motioned to himself. "What am I supposed to think?"

For a beat or two, Kade's mouth hung open. John could see the battle in the boy's eyes. He wanted to deny it, wanted to yell at John to stay out of his business and quit nosing around. But with each passing second, the anger fell from his face. In its place was a hodge-podge of emotions, led by a strong and undeniable shadow of guilt. It was easy to recognize because John had looked that way, himself, not long ago.

When Kade said nothing, John dropped

his voice back to normal. "I'm right, aren't I?"

A tired sigh slipped from Kade's throat. His gaze fell to his feet.

"We need to talk about it, son. When did you start doing this?"

The boy's shoulders slumped and he brought his head up. "I'm not the only one." He crossed his arms. "All the guys are into it."

There was a hardness in Kade's features, a defiance almost. It was something John had never seen on any of his children, and it frightened him. "That might be true, but it's wrong, Kade. You know that better than anyone on your team."

Kade tossed his hands in the air. "It's like a virtual girlfriend, Dad. Don't you get it?" His tone was strained, and he glanced around as though he was searching for a way to make John understand. "No strings, no ties, no sex." His cheeks looked hot. "Well . . . not really, anyway."

"It's still immoral, son. And for a lot of people it becomes an obsession."

"Okay, then you tell me what I'm supposed to do? I'm a Christian, so I'm not allowed to have sex until I'm married — however many years away *that* is. I'm a football player, so I don't have time for a girlfriend. And I don't have any money, even if I did have time." He huffed. "Don't you get it? The Internet solves all those problems with a few clicks. It's there whenever I feel like it. Besides, it's better than getting some girl pregnant."

John wanted to scream. "There's nothing better about it." Did Kade really think pornography was no big deal? Had the college culture so quickly undermined everything they'd taught him? "In God's eyes pornography is every bit as wrong as illicit sex, Kade. It's the same thing."

"It's *not* the same." Kade was angry. "There's no people involved, Dad. Just pictures."

"Yeah." John leaned back, his heart thudding hard within him. "Pictures of people."

Kade was quiet. The twists in his expression eased some. "They're getting paid for what they do. It's their choice."

"Listen to yourself, son. You think those women *like* making money that way? Some of them are slaves to the business, handcuffed, threatened, forced at gunpoint to do horrific things. Others are runaways, teenagers barely old enough to drive, desperate for a way to live on the streets. Some are drug users, needing that next hit so badly they'd do anything for it." John paused, his tone softer than before. Sadder. "Is that the kind of industry you want to support?"

"The guys talk about it like it's okay, like there's nothing wrong with it." Kade wrung his hands and stared at the floor of the boat again. "Most of the time . . . it seemed like they were right."

"Of course it seemed that way." John studied his son, willing him to understand. "That's what the devil wants you to think. Oh, it's just a bunch of pictures, no big deal. But pictures like that lead somewhere, Kade. Have you thought about that?"

He looked up. "What do you mean?"

"Still pictures lead to videos . . . and pretty soon, even that's not enough." Kade flinched, and John's heart fell to his knees. "You're into videos, too?"

Kade looked from one side of the lake to the other, and then at John. "Just a few times. After practice the guys sometimes get together at one of the dorms. They have a bunch of movies, and well . . ."

The boat might as well have disappeared. John felt like a drowning man, buried in a kind of water he could not escape. "It's not long before videos aren't

137

enough, either. Then it becomes prostitution."

"No!" Kade's answer was quick. "I've never done that."

"The guys?"

Kade hesitated. "A few of them . . . once or twice. Before the season started." Sweat beaded up across Kade's forehead. "But not me, Dad. I swear!"

The problem was worse than John had dared imagine. *Come on, God . . . give me something profound here.* "Pornography is a lie, son."

"A lie?" Despite Kade's humbled tone, his expression told John he still didn't see the severity of the problem.

"Yes, a lie. It makes women look like nothing more than sexual objects with no purpose except to please men." John cocked his head. "That's a lie, isn't it?"

"Yeah, I guess."

"You guess?" John worked the muscles in his jaw. "Think about your sister . . . or the girls you've dated. How would you feel if you ran through a series of computer clicks and found *their* naked pictures on the Internet?"

"Dad!" Kade narrowed his eyes. "How can you say something like that?"

"Well . . . the girls you're looking at belong to someone, too. They're someone's sister, someone's daughter. Someone's mother, in many cases. Someone's future wife. Why is it okay to treat them that way?" John grabbed a quick breath. "That's the first lie: that a woman is merely a body."

Kade looked up. Was he listening more closely, or was John merely imagining it?

"The second lie is this: true sexual satisfaction can come from sinful behavior." John stared at the sky for a moment. The clouds were clearing, and suddenly he knew exactly what to say. He met Kade's eyes once more. "It might feel good to your body, but not to your soul. And it can never come without intimacy."

"You mean like actually having sex?"

"No. Intimacy and sex are totally different things, son. Intimacy . . . is the bond that God brings about between two married people. It comes from years of commitment, of sharing and talking and working through problems. Years of getting to know that person better than anyone else in life. A physical relationship with someone like that — that's intimacy. And anything less is a lie."

Kade leveled his gaze at John. "You mean like you and Ms. Denton?"

It took several seconds for John to breathe again. Was it possible . . . ? Did Kade know John had nearly gotten involved with Charlene Denton? She'd taught at the school with John. For years, though they were both married, Charlene would flirt mercilessly with him. After she divorced her husband, Charlene found her way to John's classroom often.

In the year before she moved away, Kade had walked into his father's classroom and found him with her more than once, but always John had talked his way out of the situation. One time Kade had found them holding hands . . . John had lied and said he was praying with the woman. As wrong as that had been at the time, John always thought Kade had believed him.

At least until now.

"What about me and Ms. Denton?" John was desperate, buying time. The look on Kade's face told John his son had doubted his father's wrong relationship from the start.

"Come on, Dad. She was with you all the time. The guys on the team even talked about it. Ms. Denton would come out to practice and stand next to you, she hung out in your classroom . . . I'm not stupid."

John felt like a dying man. "How come

you never said anything before this?"

"You told me she was just a friend. That she needed your prayers." Kade shrugged. "I guess I wanted to believe it."

A breeze drifted over the lake and washed away any pretense John had left. "Everything about my friendship with Ms. Denton was wrong. It was a lie, just like pornography's a lie."

"So you slept with her?" Kade looked like he was about to cry.

"No." John considered telling Kade about the two times when he and Charlene kissed. But there was no point. That was behind him now. "I did things I'm not proud of, son. But I never crossed that line."

"So, it's true." Kade shook his head. His shoulders slumped forward, and John couldn't tell whether the shadows on his face were disgust or despair. "The guys used to razz me all the time and I'd tell 'em to get lost. My parents were different. They loved each other. And now . . . all the time . . . what a joke."

"Wait a minute, Kade. That's not fair."

"Yes, it is. Porn stuff isn't the only lie. You and Mom are, too. It's all a lie. So, what's the point of —"

"Stop!" John leaned forward until his

knees were touching Kade's. "What your mother and I share is not a lie. We struggled, yes. And we came back together stronger than before." He looked straight into Kade's eyes, trying to see into his soul. "You know why we drifted apart?"

Kade said nothing, his lips tight and pinched.

"Because we forgot about being intimate. We stopped talking and sharing our hearts with each other. We let life and busy schedules rule our relationship, and because of that we almost walked away from a love that, other than God's, is greater than any I know." He uttered a single laugh. "No, son, what your mom and I share is as honest as anything I'll ever have. Charlene Denton — now that was a lie. And every day I thank God for letting me recognize the fact before it was too late. For helping your mom and me remember the importance of intimacy."

Kade straightened some, his eyebrows still knit together with doubt. "So . . . you're fine? You and Mom?"

"We're much better than fine. I think we love each other more now than ever before." John took hold of Kade's shoulder with a light grip. "But we're worried about you."

"I'm okay."

"No, you're not. If you believe the lie now, if you convince yourself that satisfaction can be found in visual unrealities, how will you ever share intimacy with a real woman?"

"That's different."

"You'll meet someone one day, and she'll want to know about you. Everything about you. If she finds out you've had a fascination with porn sites, my guess is she'll drop you like a bad pass. What girl wants to measure up to those kinds of images? Besides she wouldn't respect you, not if you see women as nothing more than objects, sex slaves."

Kade's expression changed. This time John was sure about it. The boy was finally listening.

"Relationships take work, son. Hours and days and years of getting close to that person. That's real love, real intimacy. If you train your mind to believe that the work isn't important, you'll not only be going against every plan God has for your life . . . you'll lose out on a chance to experience the greatest gift He's given us. The gift of true love."

"So you really think it's a sin?"

"Yes." John kept his tone calm, reasonable. "Absolutely."

Kade looked away. "We talked about that, a few of the guys and me. They told me it wasn't a problem because the girls agreed to have the pictures taken, and we weren't really doing anything wrong." Kade's face clouded. "But inside . . . I guess I always knew it couldn't be right."

"And the other thing is the temptation to get involved with it again anytime you feel frustrated with the real thing."

Kade sighed.

"The question is this —" John leaned back against the edge of the boat — "how hard will it be to stop?"

Kade squinted at a line of trees in the distance. "Hard."

The word hit John like a rock. "Have . . . have you tried to quit before?"

"Once." Kade looked eight years old again. "But my computer's right there in the dorm, and . . . I don't know . . . you get used to it."

For the first time, John caught a glimpse of why Internet pornography was so addictive. Computers were everywhere, access to the Web as easy as finding a telephone. If a person got on those sites once and experienced pleasure, the body would cry out for more.

"There are filters you can buy. That might help."

"Yeah. One of the guys did that. He had to get counseling, too. Maybe he and I could help each other."

"We can get you help, son. Whatever it takes. You have to believe me that this is bad stuff. If you let it continue, it'll destroy you."

Kade nodded slowly. "I guess I never thought of it that way. You know, like where it could lead."

"That time . . . when you tried to quit . . ." John let his hand fall back to his knees. "Did you ask God for help?"

"Not really. I didn't think it'd be that hard to stop."

"It's something you need to walk away from, son, and never look back. Not ever."

"I know." Kade fidgeted, his eyes glued to his hands. "I bought a book about stopping. Before I came here. It's in my bag."

"A book?" Relief flooded John's soul. "Then how come you fought me, Kade? You acted like porn sites were a good thing."

"I guess I felt cornered. Everywhere I turn someone's telling me it's bad." He looked up, and his eyes were wet. "What if . . . what if I can't stop?"

John slid his way closer to Kade and

hugged him. "You'll stop, buddy. God'll give you the strength." He thought of Charlene again. "He can give you the strength to walk away from anything bad, no matter how trapped you feel."

Kade sniffled and gripped John's neck with the crook of his elbow. There were tears in his voice. "Pray for me, Dad. Will ya, please?"

It took a moment for the lump in John's throat to subside.

When it did, he let his forehead fall against Kade's, and there in the rowboat, in the middle of the lake, he prayed for his son with an intensity he'd never known before. He asked that Kade would have the strength to walk away from the seedy, sinful world of pornography. That he would find the right friendships and counseling and support to help his eyes be opened to the horror of that world. That God would erase the images captured by Kade's mind, and replace them with a true understanding of a woman's beauty. And that Kade would grasp the reality of real intimacy in the example John and Abby provided. That as the two of them had learned from their mistakes, so would Kade.

And in the end, that he'd be a stronger, more godly man because of it.

Ten

The anonymous letters were coming more frequently now.

Not only did they accuse John of being a poor ethical example for the young men of Marion High, but they blatantly marked him as "a coach whose time has passed." The administration, which at first had assured John that they were completely behind him, now was waffling.

"People are worried about the program," Herman Lutz told him that week. "As the school's athletic director, that concerns me. I think you can understand my position."

Though a year ago it would have been unfathomable to think so, John now carried around the sinking feeling that before he could quit the job, he was going to be fired. That Lutz was going to let the parents bully him into a decision that would be easiest for him. John tried not to think about it. If he lasted long enough, he would resign after the season's final whistle.

Thing was, the team's performance had turned around.

John packed his duffle bag and headed for the team bus. They'd won their last four games and a win tonight over the hapless Bulldogs up in North County would send the Eagles to districts.

All of which meant the season wasn't nearly over.

But that afternoon, football and fanatical parents didn't even make the list of John's greatest concerns. He was about to do something he hadn't done since he'd started coaching. The boys' athletics office was open and John stepped inside. He only had a few minutes before the bus left.

The phone rang three times before she picked up. "Hello?"

"Abby, it's me."

"John?" She hesitated. "Aren't you supposed to be on the bus?"

"Yeah. Hey, real quick. Don't go to the game tonight."

There was another pause and John prayed she'd understand. He didn't have enough time to go into lengthy details. She finally recovered. "Why not?"

"A threat came into the office today. Something about the game." John steadied himself against the office desk. "The police think it's a hoax, but you never know . . . I don't want you there. Just in case."

"Was it Nathan Pike?"

"They're not sure. It might be." He glanced at his watch. "Look, I gotta run. Just know that I love you. And please . . . don't come to the game."

"But John —"

"Don't come, Abby. I gotta go."

"Okay." There was concern in Abby's voice. "I won't. I love you, too."

"See you in a few hours."

"Wait . . ." She hesitated. "Be careful, John."

"I will."

He hung up and jogged to the bus. He was the last one on. The ride to North County took fifteen minutes, and though the team was in high spirits, John stared out the window at the countryside wondering how it had come to this. He hadn't told Abby all the details. They would have terrified her.

Apparently the phone call came into the office about one o'clock that afternoon. A raspy voice told the school secretary that a suicide bomber would be in

149

attendance at that night's game.

"It's gonna be big, lady." The caller had chuckled. "Ya hear me."

The secretary motioned for the principal to pick up the line, but he was busy talking with a parent at the front counter. "Who . . . who is this?"

"Right!" The caller laughed again. "You'll know soon enough. Just tell Coach it's too late to help me now. Tonight's the big night."

"If this is a prank, you better say so." The secretary scrambled for a piece of paper and a pen. "It's a felony to make these kinds of threats."

"This is no threat, lady. People are going to die tonight. You heard it here first."

Then he hung up.

Pale and shaken, the secretary pulled the principal into a private office and told him what happened. Police were on campus asking questions within fifteen minutes. Had anyone made death threats at the school before? How were such incidents handled? Did anyone have knowledge of a student with access to explosives? Where was that night's game being held? And how many entrances to the place were there? Did anyone have something against the football team?

Time and again the answers pointed to Nathan Pike, but there wasn't a thing the police could do. They couldn't even talk to the boy about the phone call.

Nathan Pike was out sick that day.

Determined to question him, police had gone to Nathan's house. Apparently his mother had answered the door, a bewildered look on her face. Her son was at school as far as she knew. She hadn't seen him since that morning.

All of it turned John's stomach. Okay, so police would be at the game, posted at every entrance and scattered throughout the crowd. What good would that do? Suicide bombers didn't advertise. They merely walked into a crowded setting and blew themselves and everyone around them to the moon. By the time the police spotted Nathan Pike, he'd be just another body in a line of corpses.

It was no comfort that John and the team were a safe distance from the stands out on the field. Hundreds of teens would be at the game that night. Thousands, even. If a bomb went off amid that crowd —

John couldn't bring himself to think about it. Of course the person could wait until after the game when the stands emptied onto the field. Then there'd be nothing the police could do to stop a kid from —

"Coach?"

His fears dissipated as he turned around. It was Jake Daniels.

The boy had been one of the bright spots in the past few weeks. He'd let up quite a bit on Nathan. Three times he'd even stopped in to talk to John about the pressures of high school and his concerns for his mother. Apparently she was furious with his father. The two fought whenever they were forced to talk, and Jake felt caught in the middle. Jake always seemed more relaxed after a half hour of sharing life with John.

This was why John still coached, to help young men like Jake. And since they'd started talking again, Jake seemed happier, more at ease. Less likely to join in with Casey Parker and the others who thought they ran the school.

John had even wondered if that's why they were doing better on the field. There was no question Jake's numbers had led them to their recent victories. Now, though, Jake looked troubled.

John managed a smile. "Hey, Jake."

"Uh —" the boy glanced around as though he wanted to make sure no one saw the two of them talking — "can I sit here for a minute?"

"Sure." John slid over. "What's on your mind?"

"There's a rumor going around that . . . well, that Nathan Pike's going to shoot people at the game tonight."

John held his breath. If the media ever had to compete with teenagers for getting a news flash to the public, the teenagers would win every time. He exhaled hard. "A threat came into the office. Yes. Police have checked it out. They're not worried about it."

"Serious? There was really a threat?" Jake's eyes grew wide. "Coach, what if the police are wrong? Nathan Pike's a freak; don't they know that?"

"The police are aware of Nathan." John worked to appear calm, but inside he was as anxious as Jake. What business did they have showing up at a game where there were threats of murder and mayhem? What football game could ever be that important?

"So no one's doing anything about it?"

"The police'll be at the game."

"Yeah, but that won't stop him. I mean, what if he doesn't care about dying?"

"The police are pretty sure it's not a serious threat, Jake. If it was, they'd call off the game."

"I doubt it." Jake held his helmet in his lap and now he hugged it to his middle. "All everyone cares about is winning this game. You know, so we can go to districts."

Jake was closer to the truth than he knew. "You have a point."

"Coach —" Jake lifted his eyes to John's, but only briefly — "I know who's writing the letters."

"Letters?"

"Yeah, the ones that talk about getting you fired."

John's heart sank. It was enough that *he* knew about the angry swarm of parental protests against him without his players knowing. Especially kids like Jake, who had always looked up to John. He wanted to know what the boy knew, but he wouldn't ask. He patted Jake on the knee. "A coach will always have his critics."

"Casey Parker was talking in the locker room the other day. He said his dad had it out for you, bad. They've had meetings."

"His dad and him?"

"His dad and some other parents. At first the other people didn't want to come but . . . well, after we lost. More people came. They've talked to Mr. Lutz."

"That's their right, I guess." John worked his mouth into a smile. "All I can do is my best."

"You're not leaving, though, are you?" Jake's eyes were wide, and John wished he could say something to encourage the boy. "I mean, you won't quit on us, will you? I still have one more year."

"I'd love to be here next year, Jake."

"So you will, right?"

"We'll see." John didn't want to share too much information, but he didn't want to lie either. The odds of him coaching another season at Marion High were growing slimmer all the time.

"You mean you might quit?"

John sighed. "I might not have to quit if Mr. Lutz fires me first."

"He won't fire you! Look at everything you've done for football at Marion High."

"People don't see it that way. They see their sons not getting playing time, the team not winning enough games. If you get the wrong parent upset with you, well . . . sometimes there's nothing anyone can do."

John refrained from saying anything more about Herman Lutz. It wasn't his place to undermine the man's authority in front of a student. But ultimately John's professional fate lay in Lutz's hands, and he was notorious for letting parents have their way. If Casey Parker's father wanted him out, Lutz would likely oblige.

If John didn't quit first.

"If it matters any, Coach, I'll win the game big for you tonight."

John smiled. If only it were that simple. "Thanks, Jake. That means a lot."

Jake fiddled with the chin strap on his helmet. "What can I do about Nathan Pike and the whole threat thing?"

"Pray about it."

Jake's eyes grew wide and his mouth hung open for a moment. "Me?"

"Not just you — the whole team." John lowered his brow but kept his eyes on Jake's. "You guys haven't exactly been kind to Nathan this year. The threat isn't a surprise, really."

Jake swallowed hard and stared at the seat in front of him. "So you want me to pray with the guys about it?"

"You asked."

For a moment, Jake was quiet. "Coach, I think he's jealous of my car."

"The Integra?"

"Yeah. A few days after I got it, I saw Nathan's mom drop him off at school. She has this, like, beat-up old station wagon with a dent on the side. Right then he looked at my car and then at me. Usually he looks at me like he hates me, but that time it was more like he wanted to *be* me. Like he would've given anything to trade places with me."

"Is that why you've let up on him these past few weeks?"

Jake nodded. "It wasn't right. I was such a jerk before."

"You were."

"But now . . . what if it's too late? What if he really does do something?"

John searched the boy's eyes. "I told you what I'd do."

"Okay, Coach." Jake tightened his grip on the helmet. "We'll pray. I'll make it happen."

Nothing in the world could have kept Abby from the game that night.

Yes, John would be upset with her. She'd have to deal with that later. But if someone was going to harm students or players or even her husband, Abby wanted to be there. What if there was something she could do, a student she could help, or a life she could save? What if it was the last time she saw her husband alive?

These thoughts went through her head in an instant, the moment John told her what had happened at school that day. He was late for the bus, so she couldn't argue with him. But there was no way she was staying home.

She filed into the stands and took her place at the far end, near parents from the other school. Bomb threat or not, she didn't enjoy sitting with the parents of John's players. Not this year, at least. Rarely ever, in fact. It simply didn't work to be involved that way.

After John took the job at Marion High, Abby had reveled in her role as the head coach's wife. She had the idyllic sense that she would sit with the parents, chat with them, befriend them. And at first, she did just that. Those were the years when she invited parents over for Thanksgiving dinner and Saturday night socials.

"Be careful, Abby," John would warn her. "You think they're your friends now, but wait and see. Sometimes people have an agenda."

Abby had hated his insinuation that the wonderful people she sat with at games were merely being kind to get their sons in good with Coach Reynolds. She disagreed with him time and again, insisting that people weren't that shallow; football wasn't that important.

But in the end John had been completely right.

One couple — people who were Christians and had shared many meals with the Reynolds — was the first in the office complaining about John's coaching when their son didn't get enough playing time. Other parents turned out to be phony as well, talking about Abby behind her back and then presenting big smiles and happy hellos when she came around.

They weren't all that way, of course, but she'd learned her lesson about players' parents, and she no longer took chances. For years now she sat by herself or with one of the other coachs' wives.

Tonight, though, she had no intention of sitting with anyone. She would camp out in the far side of the stands and watch. Not the game, but the stands, searching the students for any sign of unusual behavior, any sign of Nathan Pike. She had seen Nathan enough times on campus to recognize him. Of course, Nathan and his cronies were easy to spot, dressed as they were in black clothes and spiked collars. Tonight Abby wanted to be the first to notice them, the first to recognize any indication that one of them might be about to blow the stadium to pieces.

The minutes ticked off the clock and halftime came, all without incident. Police were stationed throughout the stadium, some — Abby guessed — in plain clothes. But so far the most remarkable thing that had happened all game was Jake Daniels's five touchdown passes. Abby was fairly certain that was a league record. Kade had been one of the best quarterbacks to come out of that area, and he'd never come close to throwing five TDs in one half.

The second half was uneventful as well. Jake was pulled in the third quarter and replaced by Casey Parker, who had two passes intercepted. Despite that, the Eagles went on to win by thirty points. As the final buzzer sounded, the crowd spilled onto the field, embracing the Eagles as though it hadn't been a season wrought with controversy and parental complaints.

What did it matter now? The Eagles were going to districts.

Abby stood and made her way down to the field. *Where is he, Lord? Where's Nathan Pike? If he's here, please, Father, show me.* She scanned the crowd . . . and then hesitated. Had something moved along the far fence of the stadium? Cornfields surrounded the huge structure on three sides. A parking lot was on the fourth side.

Abby stared, eyes narrowed . . . Yes. There amid the tall corn . . . Abby could swear she saw movement.

Taking the stairs in an almost trancelike manner, Abby walked along the bleachers, drawing closer to the place where John and his players were receiving congratulations from hundreds of students and the entire marching band. The whole time she kept her eyes locked on the place in the cornfield.

Suddenly a figure emerged — a figure dressed in black.

Before Abby could do anything — before she could get close enough to be heard by John and the others, to run or duck or grab a police officer — the figure slipped through a hole in the fence and jogged through the crowd toward her husband.

"John, look out!" Abby shouted the words, and around her, a handful of parents stopped their conversations and stared at her.

Abby ignored them and set out in a full run, bounding down the stairs as fast as she could. *Please, God . . . save them from this. Please, God. In Jesus' name, I beg you . . .*

She was on the field now, but the figure's face was closing in quickly on John,

161

placing himself in the center of the crowd of students and players. Even from fifty yards away, Abby could see the boy's face.

It was Nathan Pike.

He was dressed in his usual black, but this time he had on a new garment. A bulky jacket.

"John . . . run!" Abby screamed the warning and drew the stares of dozens of students. "All of you, run! Quick!"

Some of the students did as she said, but most of them only stood planted in place, motionless, staring at Abby as though she'd lost her mind.

She was ten yards away from John when Nathan walked up to him and put his hand on John's shoulder. At the same time, four officers darted through the crowd and gang-tackled Nathan to the ground.

"John!" Abby was faint by the time she reached her husband's side. Her stomach was in knots and she couldn't breathe. "Come on." She grabbed his arm. "Let's get out of here."

"What in the world . . . ?" John's face was white, his eyes wide.

The circle of students had grown and tightened around the place where the police had Nathan pinned to the ground. The boy appeared to be cooperating. A slew of officers came from every direction and in a matter of minutes directed the students away from the action and out into the parking lot. John directed his assistants to accompany the team bus back to school.

"He's clean," an officer announced. "No bombs."

Every muscle in Abby's body felt weak with relief. She gripped the sleeves of John's jacket and buried her face in his chest. "I thought he was going to kill you, John. I . . . I was so scared."

She whispered the words, so the other coaches couldn't hear. The entire staff was privy to the bomb threat, so none of them was surprised at what was happening.

"It's okay, Abby. It's all over." John ran his hand over her back and took her fingers in his. Then they walked to the place where Nathan still lay on the ground in handcuffs.

The police nodded their okay, and John walked up to the boy's side. "Did you do it, Nathan? Did you make the call?"

Nathan shook his head, his eyes wide and frightened. "They keep asking me that." He gulped, his words sticking in his throat. "I don't know what they're talking about."

Abby clung to John's arm, her body

shaking from the adrenaline rush. The kid was lying. He had to be.

John tried again. "You weren't in class today."

Nathan blinked. "I . . . I went to the library. I had an English paper due and I needed some place quiet. I swear, Mr. Reynolds. I don't know what they're talking about."

An officer stood near Nathan's head. "Why'd you sneak in through the hole in the fence?"

"I was coming back from . . . from the library and thought I'd swing by. I saw the score and wanted to . . . to congratulate Mr. Reynolds. It was a big game."

The story had more holes than a sieve, but that wasn't Abby's problem. All that mattered was that John was okay. John and the students and players. She closed her eyes and rested her head against John. *God, thank You . . . thank You so much.*

The police pulled Nathan to his feet and led him to a waiting police car. Before they left, an officer approached John. "You think he could be telling the truth?"

"It's hard to tell with Nathan." John thought for a moment. "I'll say one thing though. In all the time I've known that boy, I've never seen him afraid until today.

If I didn't know his past, I'd swear he was being straight with you."

The officer jotted something on his notepad. "Thanks. We'll take that into consideration."

Before long, John and Abby were the only people left in the stadium. He folded his arms around her and held her close. "You're shaking."

"I thought . . . I thought he was going to blow you up right there. Before I could do anything to help you."

"I told you not to come." Despite the reprimand, his voice was gentle, and Abby was glad. He wasn't mad at her.

"Right. Like I could sit home while someone might be out here trying to hurt you." She pulled back and looked him straight in the eye. "I had to come, John. Nothing could have kept me away."

"Why doesn't that surprise me?"

She grinned. "Guess what?"

"What?"

"You won!"

"We did."

"Congratulations."

"Thanks." The scoreboard was still lit, as were the stadium lights. Grounds-keepers would clean up for another few hours before shutting the place down.

"Now we get to go to districts."

"You don't sound thrilled." She worked her hands up the side of his face.

"I'm not. The parents hate me, remember?"

"Not if you're winning." Abby ran her finger lightly over his brow.

"These parents are different. Jake Daniels told me who's writing the letters. It's Casey Parker's father."

"No surprise there."

"Hey." He brought his face close to hers and kissed her. "Thanks for being here tonight. Even though I asked you not to. It means a lot to me."

"You're welcome." She kissed him back, breathing in the scent of him, trying not to imagine how different the night might have played out if . . .

She couldn't finish the thought.

"You look tired."

"I am. I've never been so scared in my life."

"Ahhh, Abby." He brushed his face against hers, clinging to her the way she clung to him. "Sweet, Abby. I'm sorry. I hate thinking of you afraid like that. Why don't you go home and get some rest?"

"What about you?"

"I'm a little wired for that." He pulled

his gym bag over his shoulder and led her toward the parking lot. "I think I'll go back to school and correct papers. I'm about two weeks behind. Can you give me a ride?"

She grinned. "I'd love to."

"My car's at the school."

They talked about the game on the ride home, and when Abby pulled up in front of the school, she turned to John and yawned. "Will you be late?"

"Maybe. Could take me until one or two if I have enough energy."

"Don't forget about our dancing lesson tomorrow." She gave him a quick peck on the cheek as he climbed out.

"I won't be that late, don't worry."

"Yeah, but I want you to have enough energy. Paula's pretty demanding, you know."

John laughed. "See ya later, Abby. Love you."

"Love you, too."

Abby drove away knowing it was never more true.

Eleven

The party was packed with teenagers and Jake Daniels was on top of the world. All except one thing.

He couldn't stop thinking about Nathan Pike and Casey Parker.

Nathan, because Jake had watched the whole arrest thing go down. In fact, he had the best view of anyone, since he'd been standing a few feet from Coach Reynolds when it happened. At first he'd been terrified, certain Nathan was going to whip out a gun and they'd all be dead.

But then he saw Nathan's eyes.

Jake and Nathan had never been good friends, but back a few years ago they'd been acquaintances. They'd known each other enough that they'd say hi and help each other with an occasional homework assignment. As Jake had risen in athleticism and popularity, Nathan had spiraled in the opposite direction.

Jake had been honest when he told Coach Reynolds Nathan was a freak. That's what the guy had become. But that night on the field when he saw Nathan's eyes, he knew deep in his gut that Nathan had nothing to do with the threat that day. He was scared as a guy could get.

And that bothered Jake for two reasons. First, because it wasn't right that Nathan was arrested over something he may not have done. And second, because if Nathan didn't do it, who did? Whoever it was, he was very likely still walking around, making plans.

Then there was Casey Parker.

Jake had entered the locker room before the game that night and told everyone first off that the rumors were true. Someone had called the school and threatened to kill people at the game that night.

When the commotion settled down, Jake told the guys there was only one thing they could do about the threats. They could pray. Two and three at a time, the guys had dropped their gear and made their way over to Jake. In less than a minute, the whole team was gathered in a huddle — everyone except Casey Parker.

"This is a public school," Casey snapped at them. "It's against the law to pray."

In the past three weeks — since Jake had been meeting with Coach Reynolds again and being kinder to kids like Nathan Pike — the friendship with Casey had cooled. In the locker room earlier, Jake would have refuted Casey, but one of the other players did it first. "A kid can pray anywhere he wants."

Several others reiterated this truth with grunts and "Yeah, that's right" and other such things.

Casey sat off to the side while the rest of them prayed for God's protection over not just the game but every person in attendance. When the prayer was over, the team formed a tight circle and did their usual chanting and cheering to get fired up for the game.

Casey didn't join in any of it.

He sat by himself all night. Coach didn't call his number until Jake had six touchdowns. It was no surprise to the other Eagles when Casey took the field and promptly threw four incompletes and two interceptions. After that the coaches went to a running game to kill the clock.

On the bus ride back to school, Casey didn't say a word to the rest of them. When talk about the party came up, he split without a good-bye or anything. Jake tried to forget about it. After all, this was *his* night. His team had survived some sort of weird death threat *and* won the game. Big time. They were even going to districts.

It was time to celebrate. Big time.

He looked around. The party was at some girl's place, a freshman cheerleader, Jake thought. The girl had a huge house, lots of food, and parents who didn't mind them gathering there. Most of the team had showed up, but not Casey. A group of guys Jake didn't know that well walked up to him.

"Nice game, Jake . . . way to throw it."

"Yeah, was that like a record or something? Six touchdowns?"

Jake had been asked a hundred times so far, but he was polite as he answered. "A school record. Tied with a league record."

"That's so cool. Way to go."

The guys left, and Jake leaned against the kitchen counter. Some of the kids had beer in their cars outside. They drifted in and out, downing a few beers and then returning to the house. The girl's parents didn't mind the kids drinking as long as it wasn't on their property.

That was fine for them, but not Jake. Not tonight. He'd promised his dad that he wouldn't drink and drive, and since getting the new car, he'd kept his word. He grabbed a plastic cup and filled it with ice water. Besides, he wanted to savor the night, not lose it in a haze of drinking. He'd done that too many times over the summer. He was smarter now.

The party had been going on for two hours already, and it was after midnight. Jake wanted to be fresh for practice in the morning. A few more minutes and he'd call it a night.

At that moment, the front door opened and Jake stared. Casey Parker walked in, his arm around Darla Brubaker — the girl Jake was planning to ask to prom. Jake set his cup down and gritted his teeth. Whatever sort of stunt Casey was trying to pull, it wasn't going to work. Casey searched the room until his eyes landed on Jake. Then he turned to Darla and kissed her on the cheek.

Jake looked away. What was Casey's problem, anyway? He was acting like a total loser. If Darla wanted to hang out with a jerk like that, let her. Still, he couldn't help but look back at the couple, still standing near the front door.

Casey whispered something in Darla's ear, and the girl giggled and took a seat in the corner of the room. When she was gone, Casey sauntered into the kitchen. Something about his expression looked almost hateful.

"Jake." He nodded once and leaned against the opposite counter. "Nice game tonight."

"Thanks." Jake grabbed his cup again and took another swig of water. "Hey, what's eatin' you, man? You weren't yourself out there."

"Let's just say the praying thing freaked me out, okay?"

Jake uttered a single laugh. "It worked, didn't it? No one shot us while we played the game."

Casey slammed his fist onto the counter. "Enough about prayer, okay? If you weren't a junior, I'd take you out for pulling a stunt like that before the game."

"Stunt?" Jake frowned. He didn't like Casey's insinuation.

"I saw you . . . talking to Coach the whole ride up to North County." Casey crossed his arms. "The thing I don't get is this: You're already his favorite little go-to guy. Did you really have to let him talk you into praying? I mean, haven't you sucked up enough these past few weeks? Dropping into Coach's room and acting all buddy-buddy."

Jake set his cup down and took three steps closer to Casey. "What's that supposed to mean?"

"Oh, come on. You're part of Coach's C-squad. Guys like me don't have a chance."

"C-squad?" Jake's mind reeled. What was Casey talking about? What the heck was a C-squad?

"You know, Jake. The *Christian* squad. Coach always gives the best spots to the Christian kids. Everyone knows that."

Jake felt his face go hot, then ice cold. "You're crazy, Parker. That's a lie and anyone on the team'll tell you so."

Casey grabbed a handful of Jake's T-shirt and jerked him close so their faces were only inches apart. "I'm the best quarterback on the team." He hissed the words, giving Jake another jerk for emphasis. "So tell me why I'm sitting the bench and you're getting all the p.t."

"Playing time is *earned*." Jake placed his hands squarely on Casey Parker's shoulders and shoved him. "Anyone who's played for Coach Reynolds knows that."

"That right?" Casey shoved Jake, this time into the kitchen counter.

Before Jake could retaliate, a group of girls rushed into the kitchen squealing at them.

"Break it up, guys."

"Yeah, come on . . . let it go."

Jake straightened his shirt and glared at Casey. When the girls left, Casey shot an angry look at Jake, his expression pinched. "It's time we got to the bottom of this thing."

"Let's take it outside."

"Fine. But not on the grass."

"Where then?"

"The streets." He sneered at Jake. "You think you're the only one with speed?" Casey spat at him. "Well, you're wrong."

"You're talking about a race?" Jake's spine tingled. No one was listening to their conversation. It wouldn't be a big deal. Just a simple race between the two of them. Then Casey would know once and for all not to mess with Jake Daniels. "Any time, Parker. Your car'll look parked next to mine."

"Only one way to find out."

"Where do you want to do it?"

Casey narrowed his eyes, his voice strained with anger. "Haynes Street . . . the milelong stretch in front of the high school."

"Done."

"Meet me at Haynes and Jefferson in thirty minutes." Casey turned and headed back to Darla.

Jake had just one more thing to say, and he said it loud enough for Darla to hear. "Don't forget to bring the winner's trophy."

Late-night hours after a game were John's favorite times to catch up on his classroom work. He taught six health classes each day, and it was easy to fall behind. Especially during the season. Good thing he had more energy than usual tonight.

Generally, he'd get into his office, go through a day's worth of papers, and start feeling tired. Then he'd head home and crawl into bed with Abby sometime around eleven o'clock. But tonight he had enough stamina to work until morning. Not that he would. He'd promised Abby he wouldn't stay out too late. Besides, she was right. He needed his energy for their Saturday night dance lessons.

John scanned a series of papers and entered the tests in his grade book.

He'd never been one of those coaches who watched game films on Friday nights. As much energy as it took to coach a football game, he needed to fill his mind with something completely different. Grading was just the thing. So far that night he'd breezed through three days' worth of papers.

All the while he couldn't stop thinking about Nathan Pike.

Something deep in his gut told him Nathan hadn't come to the stadium for any reason other than the one he'd given — to congratulate John on coaching the team to a victory. He paused and thought about the scenario that had unfolded after the game. No doubt there were troubling pieces to the way it played out. Why hadn't Nathan entered the stadium through the main gates like everyone else? And why would he spend the entire day at the library only to drive ten miles out of the way to a football game? John couldn't remember seeing him at any other game so far that season.

Still, John was an expert at looking into kids' eyes and finding the truth. And something about Nathan's story rang truer than anything the kid had ever said before.

John corrected another batch of papers and then stretched. The framed picture near the edge of his desk caught his attention. He and Abby, at Nicole's wedding. Abby had thought it a strange choice. After all, there was nearly two feet of space between them, and even a stranger could see the tension on their faces. It was hardly a happy picture.

But it was honest.

They had made their decision to divorce, and that night, when the kids had gone on their honeymoon, John had planned to take his things and move in with a fellow teacher — a guy who had divorced his wife a year earlier. In fact, when the picture was snapped, John's car was already packed with his belongings.

The deal was all but done.

Kade and Sean had been spending the week with friends, and Abby had plans to fly to New York and meet with her editor. Their entire lives were falling apart, and the children had known nothing about any of it.

That night, after the wedding, John was only halfway down the road when he stopped and parked the car. He didn't know how to turn it around, didn't know how to erase the mistakes they'd made . . . but he knew he couldn't drive another inch away from the only woman he'd ever loved. The woman God intended for him to love forever. At that point, the divorce plans were all very neat and tidy, the arrangements they'd made about how to tell the kids and how they'd split time . . . everything was set. Everything but one troubling detail.

He still loved Abby. Loved her with

all his heart and soul.

So he climbed out of the car and walked back home. He found her outside, where he had known he'd find her. On the pier, in their private spot. And in the hour that followed the walls they'd built around their hearts came crashing down until all that remained were two people who had created a life and a family and a love that could not be thrown away.

John sighed.

How he loved Abby . . . more so now than ever before.

He could hear her voice the last time she'd visited his classroom. "Take the picture down, John." She'd stared at it, her face filled with disgust. "It's awful. I look like an old, bitter woman."

"No. It makes me remember."

"Remember what?"

"How close we came to losing it all."

Besides, that wasn't the only picture on his desk. There was the other one right beside it. A smaller photo of John and Abby laughing at some family function a few months ago. Abby was right. She looked a decade younger in the later photo. It was amazing what happiness could do for a person's face.

He looked up at the clock on his classroom wall. Twelve-thirty. Abby would be asleep by now. The thought made him suddenly tired. He shot a look at the papers on his desk. The pile was half finished, but the rest could wait. If he had to, he could stay late Monday night, too.

The restlessness he'd felt earlier had worn off. If he went home now, he wouldn't lie awake wondering about this play or that one. He'd cuddle up to Abby, breathe in the fragrance of her sleeping beside him, and drift off to sleep in a matter of minutes.

That settled it.

He gathered his papers, stacked them neatly, and slipped them in the appropriate folders. Then he grabbed his keys, closed up his classroom, and headed for the parking lot.

As he pulled out of the school entrance, he worked the muscles in his legs. He was more tired than he'd thought. The streets were long since deserted, and because John and Abby only lived a few minutes from the school, he could almost count on being home in bed with Abby in five minutes flat.

He looked both ways, began to buckle his seat belt, and swung his car right onto Haynes Street.

A sound came up behind him, almost like an approaching freight train. All within an instant's time, John reminded himself that there were no train tracks in that part of Marion. He glanced in his rearview mirror just as a series of lights blinded him from behind.

What in the world? He was going to be hit. *Dear God . . . help me!*

There was no time to react . . . no time to think about whether he should hit the brake or the gas. The roaring noise behind him became deafening and then there was a terrible jolt. Screeching tires and breaking glass filled John's senses — along with something else.

A blinding pain burned through John's back, an indescribable hurt like nothing he'd ever felt in his life.

His vision blurred, leaving him gasping for air in complete darkness. He found his voice and screamed the only thing that filled his mind, the only thing he could put into words.

"Aaaabby!"

His voice echoed for what felt like forever. It was impossible to draw another breath.

Then there was nothing but silence.

Twelve

———◆———

The air bag inflated immediately.

One minute Jake was barreling down Haynes Street, stunned at the speed Casey Parker had gotten out of his Honda. The next, there was the most horrific crash Jake had ever imagined possible.

His car was still now, but the bag smothered his face. He punched at it, gasping for air. What had happened? Had he blown a tire or lost control? Jake tried to shake off the dizzy feeling. No, that wasn't it. He'd been racing . . . racing Casey Parker.

Jake had the lead, but just barely. He'd stepped on the gas and watched the speedometer climb toward the one hundred mark. It was faster than he'd ever intended to drive, but the race would be over in half a mile. Then he'd seen movement, a truck or a car turning onto the road just ahead of him.

Was that what had happened? Had he hit

someone? His mouth was dry; he couldn't catch his breath. *Oh, God . . . not that.* Jake kicked at the air bag, fighting free from it enough to open his door. He set his feet on the pavement, his chest heaving. Why couldn't he grab a mouthful of air?

Stand up, you idiot! But his body wouldn't cooperate. His muscles were like limp noodles, unable to move. A few seconds passed until, slowly, his lungs began to fill. Then it hit him. He'd had the wind knocked out of him.

Breathe . . . come on, breathe.

Finally he felt the oxygen make its way through his system. As it did, his legs jerked into action. He stood and looked around. Casey Parker was gone. "God, no . . ."

His heart thumped wildly against the wall of his chest as he turned and looked at the roadway in front of his car. There, about twenty yards ahead, was the crumpled remains of what looked like a pickup truck. It was impossible to tell what color it was. Jake wanted to throw up but instead he began to cry. He had no cell phone, no way to call for help. The entire school was surrounded by open fields, so no residents would have heard the crash.

He stared at the twisted metal and knew

without a doubt that the driver was dead. Passengers, too, if there were any. In driver's ed they'd taught them to wear seat belts because usually, almost always, there was room to live in a smashed-up vehicle.

But not this one. The front end was all that was left. The back was crumpled like tinfoil, and the cab . . . well, the cab seemed to have been swallowed up by the other pieces.

Something inside him told him to run, flee as fast as he could. If he'd just killed someone, he would spend years in prison. He glanced back at his car. The front end was totaled, but there was a chance it might still run.

He shook his head, and the thought vanished.

What was he thinking? However impossible it looked, someone might be alive in the wreckage! He walked closer. Whatever . . . whoever lay inside the totaled pickup, he didn't really want to see it.

His heart raced so fast now, he thought he might pass out. The trembling he'd felt earlier had become full-blown shaking. The sound of his teeth chattering filled the night air as he approached the back of the other vehicle.

Suddenly something caught his eyes.

He looked down at the ground and there, in the ten feet that separated him from the destroyed pickup, was a license plate. Jake inched toward it and his heart stopped.

GO EAGLES

Go Eagles? No, God . . . please . . . it can't be. Only one person had a license plate like that. And he drove a pickup truck.

"Coach!" Jake felt his eyes grow wide, his heart stop as he ran the remaining steps to the side of the wreckage.

From inside there was a moaning sound, but the doors were so mangled, Jake couldn't see anything, let alone find a way in to help him. "Coach, is that you?"

Of course it was. Jake gripped the sides of his face and made jerky turns in a dozen different directions. Why hadn't anyone else come by? Where was Casey Parker? He pulled his hair and shouted again. "Coach! I'll get help. Hang on!"

With every bit of strength Jake had ever mustered, he pulled on what looked like part of the door. *Open, you stupid door . . . open. Come on.*

"Coach, hang in there."

Panic came upon him like a tidal wave. What had he done? He'd taken his car past a hundred miles an hour and hit Coach

185

Reynolds . . . How could that possibly have happened? Coach should have been home hours ago. And now what? Coach was lying inside the twisted metal dying, and there was nothing he could do about it. "Coach . . . can you hear me?"

Nothing.

"God . . ." Jake threw his head back and tossed his arms in the air. He wept, shouting like a crazy person. "Please, God, help me! Don't let Coach die!"

At that moment, Jake heard a car coming up behind him. *Thank You, God . . . whatever happens to me, let Coach live. Please.*

He positioned himself in the middle of the road, waving his arms frantically. Almost immediately he recognized the car. Casey Parker. The Honda came to a screeching halt and Casey jumped out.

"I think it was Coach's truck." Casey looked as bad as Jake felt. Shaking, pale-faced, deeply in shock. "I . . . had to come back." He held up a cell phone. "I already called 9-1-1."

"He's . . . he's . . ." Jake was jerking violently, too frightened to speak.

Casey ran up to the wreckage. "Help me, Jake. We have to get him out."

The two boys worked with frantic determination, trying to find a way inside the pickup truck. But there was none. They didn't give up, not even when they heard sirens — not until the emergency vehicles pulled up and EMTs ordered them away from the vehicle.

"That's . . . that's my coach in there!" Jake couldn't think straight, couldn't make his mouth work. "*Help* him!"

Casey took over. "Our coach is trapped inside. We're sure it's him."

One of the paramedics hesitated. "Coach John Reynolds?"

"Yeah." Casey nodded, licking his lips. He looked like he might faint at any moment, but at least he could talk. Jake thrust his hands in his pocket and stared at the ground. He wanted to crawl into a manhole and never come out, or fall asleep and have his mother beside him, waking him, promising him it was all just a bad dream.

Instead, a police car pulled up.

Jake and Casey stood ten feet from the wreckage, alternately watching the rescue effort and staring at the asphalt. Jake hadn't given the police much thought. He was too concerned with whether the paramedics would be able to reach Coach Reynolds and, when they did, whether they could save him or not.

He was so distracted that when the officers positioned themselves in front of him and Casey, Jake stepped to the side for a better view.

"You the driver of the red Integra?" The officer shone a flashlight at his face.

Jake's heart skipped a beat and he squinted. *Oh God . . . help . . .* "Yes . . . yes, sir."

"You injured?"

"No, sir." Jake's throat was so tight he had to force the words out. "I had an air bag."

The other officer shone a flashlight in Casey's face. "You the driver of the Honda?"

Casey's teeth were clattering. "Yeah."

"We had a tip from a driver a mile down the road, said she saw a yellow Honda and a red Integra racing like a couple of speed demons down Haynes Street." The first officer took a step closer to Jake. "That true?"

Jake shot a look at Casey. This was a nightmare. What were they doing here? Why had he ever agreed to race Casey? Wasn't he going to go home? Just a few more minutes and then he'd call it a night, wasn't that what he'd told himself?

"Get your license." The officer pointed to Jake's car. Then he gestured to Casey's Honda. "You, too."

Jake and Casey did as they were told. The first officer handed the laminated cards to the second. "Run a check on them, will ya?" Then he turned back to Jake. "Listen, pal. Make it easier on yourself here. Forensics teams will tell us how fast you were going — down to the mile. You don't cooperate now, and we'll make the process miserable for you *and* your parents."

The sound of a power tool filled the air. *Please, God . . . let them get him out of there.*

Jake tried to swallow, but he couldn't. His tongue was stuck to the roof of his mouth. This time he didn't look at Casey. "Yes, sir . . . we . . . we were racing, sir."

"You aware there's a law against that?"

Jake and Casey nodded in unison. The other officer joined them again. "Clean records for both."

"Not after tonight." He nodded to his partner. "Cuff 'em. Then call their parents."

Jake's blood ran cold — not because he was going to jail but because they were taking him away from Coach. He wanted to scream, shout at everyone to back off and let him stay until he knew everything was okay. His heart felt heavier than cement as the realization set in. Coach might die . . . he might already be dead. And even if he wasn't, nothing would ever be okay again. Jake was the worst, most awful sort of person, and whatever happened to him after this, he deserved every minute of it.

The first officer grabbed Jake's wrists and held them tightly together behind his back. The metal pinched his skin, and Jake was almost glad. In seconds the handcuffs were on, and the officer walked back to his car. The other officer did the same to Casey, and then left, so the two of them were alone on the road, cuffed and staring at Coach Reynolds's destroyed vehicle.

The medics were still working frantically around what was left of Coach's truck, still desperate to get him out. Jake closed his eyes and willed them to hurry up. *God, how could You let this happen? It should be me in there, not Coach. He didn't do anything wrong. Get him out, please . . .*

"I got it!" A paramedic shouted from amid the workers. He tossed a mangled truck door behind him. It landed on the neatly manicured grass that bordered the Marion High parking lot. "I need a backboard, stat. And an airlift. The guy's not going to make it by ground."

They were going to get him out! Jake's knees shook, and again he couldn't catch his breath. A wild splash of hope colored the moment, and Jake fought the urge to shout Coach's name above the chaos.

The paramedic began barking out orders, shouting words Jake had never heard before. The one thing he did pick up was this: Coach Reynolds was still alive! That meant there was a chance . . . a prayer that maybe he might make it! Jake's legs could no longer hold him, and he fell to his knees, his heart thudding hard against the surface of his chest. *Hang in there, Coach . . . come on. God, don't let him die.*

Jake had no idea how long he and Casey stayed there, stone still, watching the rescue. Finally, a helicopter appeared overhead and landed on the empty street. About the same time, one of the paramedics waved his hand at the others. "I'm losing him."

"No!" No one heard Jake above the sound of the chopper. He struggled to his feet, took three steps toward the huddle of medics, and then returned to his place.

Beside him, Casey began to sob.

There was a rush of motion and someone began doing CPR. "Let's get him out of here!"

A team of paramedics lifted a board, and for the first time, Jake could see the man they were working on. There was no question it was Coach Reynolds. He still had on his Marion Eagles jacket.

A wave of sobs strangled Jake's heart. What sort of monster *was* he, to race that way on a city street? And what about Coach, the man who had been more of a father to him than his own dad these past years.

"Please don't let him die!" Once more Jake's agonized cry drowned in the whirring helicopter blades and engine noise.

They loaded Coach Reynolds into the chopper, and it lifted off the ground, disappearing into the sky. Jake watched it go until he could no longer hear the whirring of the engine. When it was gone, an eerie, deathly silence fell over the street. He looked around, suddenly aware of the action taking place near the damaged cars. Other police had arrived and were taking measurements, marking the spot from Jake's car to the wreckage of Coach's truck. As the paramedics left the scene, two tow trucks pulled up. The drivers climbed out and waited by their rigs.

Jake began to shake again, and his arms ached from being cuffed behind his back. "We're going down," Casey whispered beside him. "In flames, Jake. You know that, right? The season's over."

The season? Jake wanted to vomit. What kind of a person was Casey anyway? The *season?* Who cared about the stinkin' season? He turned to Casey, his eyes so swollen from crying he could barely see. "Is that all you can think about?"

Casey wasn't crying anymore, but he shook like someone having a seizure. "Of . . . of course not. I'm worried about Coach. It's just . . . this'll stay with us the . . . the rest of our lives."

Jake's anger blazed, cutting off his tears. "Yeah, and we *deserve* it."

Casey opened his mouth, and at first it looked like he was about to disagree. Then he hung his head and finally, the tears came again for him, as well. "I . . . I know it."

Jake was disgusted with both of them. The officers were right. Coupla rich kids driving cars that were way too fast. He gritted his teeth until his jaw ached. It didn't matter what kind of trouble they faced. The police could toss him in jail and throw out the key for all he cared. In fact, Jake would have gladly given his life for the only thing that still mattered.

That Coach Reynolds survive the night.

Because if Coach didn't live, Jake was pretty sure he wouldn't be able to either.

Thirteen

It was a nightmare.

It had to be. Abby squinted at the clock and saw it was just after two in the morning. There was no way John would have been out this late. Car accidents didn't happen to men like him . . . men who should have been home asleep by now.

Yes, it was just a nightmare. Abby almost had herself convinced, except for one troubling detail: John's place in bed beside her was empty, untouched. She tried to swallow, but her throat was too thick. Why was she trying to scare herself? It wasn't so unusual that John be missing from bed at this hour. Not after a football game. He could be downstairs watching television or eating a bowl of cereal. He did that lots of times.

Still, as convinced as she was, she had to tell the caller something.

"Did you hear me, Mrs. Reynolds? Are you awake?" The voice was calm, gentle. But the urgency was undeniable. "I said we need you down here at the hospital. Your husband's been in an accident."

The man was relentless. "Yes." Abby huffed out her answer. "I'm awake. I'll be there in ten minutes."

She hung up, then called Nicole. If the dream was going to be persistent, she might as well work it out, and that meant playing the role expected of her.

"Your father's been in an accident."

What? Nicole's voice was half shriek, half cry. "Is he hurt?"

Abby forced herself to be calm. If she lost it now, she'd never make it to the hospital. And only by going through the motions would she ever break free from the awful nightmare. "They didn't tell me. Just that we need to come." Her eyes closed, and she knew she was right. It had to be a nightmare. And no wonder, especially after the bomb threat earlier. Her dreams were bound to be bad.

"Mom, are you there?"

"Yes." She forced herself to concentrate. "Is Matt home?"

"Of course."

"Have him drive you. I don't want you

going out at night alone."

"What about you? Maybe we should pick you up."

"Sean's already dressed and waiting for me."

"Is he okay?"

"He'll be fine as soon as this nightmare is over."

The entire ride to the hospital, Abby was shocked at how real everything felt. The cool breeze on her face, the steering wheel in her hands, the road beneath the wheels. Never in her life had a dream felt like this.

But that's what it had to be.

John hadn't been doing anything dangerous tonight. The danger had been back at the football stadium, when he could have been blown to bits. But driving home from school? There couldn't have been a soul on the road.

Abby whipped the car into the hospital parking lot and saw Matt and Nicole just ahead of her. They entered the emergency room together and were immediately led to a small room behind the double doors, out of sight from the rest of the public.

"What's going on?" Nicole started to cry, and Matt put his arm around her. "Why'd they bring us in here?"

Abby clenched her fist as a realization

slammed into her. She had no information whatsoever. Not about the type of accident or whether another car was involved. Not about the extent of John's injuries or how he got to the hospital. She was completely in the dark, and in some ways that brought her comfort. Dreams were like that — strange, missing details, disconnected . . .

Beside her, Sean began to cry, too.

"Shhh." Abby hugged him to her side and stroked his back. "It's okay."

A doctor entered the room and shut the door behind him. The first thing Abby noticed was his face. It was marked with tension and sadness. *No, God . . . don't let this be happening. Not really. Make me wake up. I can't take another minute . . .*

Lean not on your own understanding, daughter . . . I am here with you even now.

The words seemed to come from nowhere and speak straight to her soul. They gave Abby the strength to look up, to meet the doctor's eyes straight on, and ask the hardest question in her life. "How is he?"

"He's alive."

The four of them straightened some at the doctor's words. "Can we see him?" Abby started to stand, but the doctor shook his head.

"We have him on life support in the intensive care unit." The doctor lowered his brow. "It'll be touch and go for the next few days. There's still a significant chance we could lose him."

"No!" Nicole screamed the word and then buried her face in Matt's chest. "No, God . . . not my daddy. No!"

Abby closed her eyes and held more tightly to Sean. She remembered then that she hadn't called Kade. There he was five hundred miles away and he didn't know his father was fighting for his life. It was one more disconnected piece, a part of the nightmare.

But the dream was growing more terrifyingly real by the moment.

Nicole finally quieted down, her face still smothered in Matt's plaid, flannel shirt.

There was sanity in staying calm. Abby looked down and saw that her hands were trembling, but she managed to meet the doctor's gaze. "What . . . what are his injuries?"

"He suffered a severed trachea, Mrs. Reynolds. That type of injury is fatal in most cases. My guess is that the way his body wound up after the accident somehow held the trachea in place long enough to save his life. As soon as they moved him, he stopped breathing. They kept him on life support until he arrived here by helicopter."

"Helicopter?" Abby was seeing spots before her eyes, circling spots that threatened to take up her entire field of vision. She shook her head. No, she couldn't faint. Not now. "What . . . what happened?"

The doctor's eyes fell to his clipboard, and he grimaced. "Apparently he was the victim of a couple street racers — high-school kids."

"Street . . ." Abby's world began to spin around her. "Street racing?"

No doubt about it, it was just a nightmare. Real life didn't have that kind of coincidence. John Reynolds, the coach accused of looking the other way while his players participated in street races . . . hit by teenagers doing that very thing? It was so ridiculous, it couldn't possibly be real.

"The boys were probably going about a hundred miles an hour when your husband pulled out of the school parking lot. He was hit from behind."

"So . . ." Abby pushed her fingers hard against both sides of her head. Again her body wanted to faint, but she wouldn't let it. Not until she heard it all. "So his trachea? That's the problem?"

The doctor's expression grew even

darker than before. "That's the most critical problem at this point."

"There's more?"

Nicole moaned and clung to Matt. Abby glanced at Sean and realized he was sobbing into her sleeve. Poor babies. They shouldn't have to hear this. Still, if it was only a bad dream, it wouldn't hurt anything. Besides, the sooner she worked through it, the quicker she'd wake up.

The doctor checked his notes again. "It looks like he broke his neck, Mrs. Reynolds. We can't really be certain at this point, but we think he's paralyzed. From the waist down, at least."

"Noooo!" Nicole screamed again and this time Matt shot Abby a pleading look.

But there was nothing she could do. The word was still making its way into her conscious. Paralyzed? *Paralyzed!* It was completely impossible. John Reynolds had just coached the Eagles to victory. He had walked her to the car and climbed the school stairs to his office. Later that night they had dance lessons to attend.

Paralyzed?

"I'm sorry." The doctor shook his head. "I know this must be very hard for you. Is there anyone I can call?"

Abby wanted to tell him to call Kade. Instead she stood and gathered Sean to her side. "Where is he? We need to see him."

The doctor studied the group and nodded. He opened the door and motioned to them. "Follow me."

They looked like a trail of walking wounded as they moved along behind the doctor down one hallway and then another. The clicking of the man's heels against the tile floor reminded Abby of some macabre clock, counting down the hours John had left. She wanted to shout at him to walk more quietly, but it wouldn't have made sense. Even in a dream.

Finally the doctor stopped and opened the door. "The group of you can only stay for a few minutes." He looked at Abby. "Mrs. Reynolds, you can stay beside him all night if you wish."

Abby led the way as they crept inside, and only then did her veneer of shock and disbelief give way. As it did, she collapsed in a heap near the foot of his bed, her head spinning.

It was real. *Dear God . . . it's really happening.*

Light narrowed, darkness swept in, overflowing her. "I'm fainti—"

That was the last thing Abby remembered.

When Abby came to, she was sitting in a chair beside John's bed. Nicole, Matt, and Sean were gathered around her. At her feet was a nurse with smelling salts. "I'm sorry, Mrs. Reynolds. You passed out."

Abby looked beyond them to the bed, to her precious John lying there. Tubing ran in and out of his body from his mouth, his neck, his arms and legs. A full brace was fixated to his head and neck, making John looked trapped. Abby wanted to throw it off him, free him and take him away.

But she couldn't.

All she could do for the rest of the night was stay beside John and try not to cry too loudly. Because if he was here, then he wasn't at home. He wasn't watching television or eating cereal or grading papers into the wee hours of the morning. He was strapped to a hospital bed, clinging to life.

And that could only mean one thing.

She wasn't dreaming after all.

Her dear husband, the man who had run like the wind across the football field at the University of Michigan . . . the man who played tennis with her and jogged with her and ran patterns for his players when a diagram wasn't enough . . . the man who danced with her on the pier behind their home a hundred different times . . . might never dance again.

This wasn't the kind of nightmare a person woke up from.

It was the kind that lasted a lifetime.

The hours became little more than a blur.

By Saturday afternoon Kade had joined them at the hospital. He arrived sometime between lunch and dinner, Abby wasn't sure. But they were all there, gathered around John's bed. Praying for him. Jo and Denny had come, and with them a dozen people from church and the high school.

Word was getting out.

Coach Reynolds was in an accident; he might never walk again. Teary-eyed football players kept vigil in the waiting room with the others. Only immediate family was allowed in the room, which meant Abby and the kids and Matt. Abby never left John's side except to use his private rest room. She completely avoided any conversation in the waiting room about who had been arrested and what penalty they might face for hitting John's car. She didn't care about that right now. All that mattered was John's survival.

So far he hadn't regained consciousness,

although doctors thought it could happen anytime.

Abby had long since let go of the idea that what was happening was merely a dream. It was reality. But a reality she prayed would turn out differently than the doctors imagined it would. John would wake up sometime that evening, look around the room, and flash that silly grin of his.

Then he'd wiggle his fingers and toes and ask the first passing nurse to take off the neck brace. His throat would be sore, of course — any time a person had a severed trachea that was bound to happen — but other than that he'd be fine. A few days in the hospital and they could walk away from the scare of the accident and get on with the business of living and loving and taking dance lessons with Perky Paula.

That's how it would happen. Abby was sure of it.

For now, the group of them was quiet. Kade stood anchored against one wall, his gaze locked on his father. Eyes dry, face pale, Kade hadn't moved from his spot for two hours. Beside him on the floor was Sean, his knees pulled up to his chin, his face in his hands. Most of the time, Sean cried quietly to himself. At times when he would stop crying, Abby could see it wasn't because the sadness had passed. It was because he was too scared even for tears.

Matt and Nicole had taken up their position on the opposite wall, Nicole in a chair, and Matt standing beside her. The doctor had encouraged them to talk, explaining that John was more likely to wake up if he heard their voices. Occasionally Abby and the boys would say a few words, but Nicole was the most verbal of them. Every ten minutes or so she would cross the room and stand near the head of John's bed.

"Daddy, it's me." Her tears would come harder then. "Wake up, Daddy. We're all here waiting for you and praying for you. You're going to be okay; I just know it."

After a few sentences, her tears would be too strong to speak through, and she would walk around the bed and hug Abby for a long while. Then she would return to her place next to Matt. Occasionally one or more of them would leave the room for something to eat or drink.

The only good news of the day had come that morning when the doctor upgraded John's condition from critical to serious. "He's had a great night. I'd say his chances of surviving are very strong."

Abby had no idea how long ago that was or whether night had come again or not. She knew only that she didn't dare leave, didn't consider being gone from the room when John first opened his eyes and told them all the truth: that he wasn't that bad off after all.

Finally, as the nurses were pushing dinner carts down the hallway, John let out a quiet moan.

"John!" Abby moved closer to the bed and took hold of his hand, the one without the wires and tubing. "We're all here, honey. Can you hear me?"

The kids gathered closer, waiting for his response. But there was none. Abby studied his face. It was bruised and swollen, but she was almost certain his eyes were twitching beneath the lids. That hadn't happened since Abby arrived at the hospital.

Nicole ran her fingers lightly over John's other hand, careful not to bump the various lines attached to him. "Daddy, it's me . . ." She sucked in two quick breaths and fought to keep her tears at bay. "Are you awake?"

John gave the slightest nod of his head, enough that Sean muttered a soft *"Yes!"* under his breath. It was one thing to have

John injured and facing a life that might never be the same again. But to lose him . . . that was something none of them could bear to think about.

Even the subtlest movement now was like a sign from God that no matter what else might happen, John was going to live.

Another moan escaped his throat and his lips moved. A nurse entered the room and saw what was happening. "Move back. Please. He can't be too stimulated right now, not while he's intubated."

She checked his monitors and brought her head near his face. "John, we need you to stay very still. Can you understand me?"

Again his head moved up and down, no more than half an inch in either direction, but enough to show that he'd heard the nurse. Abby's heart soared. She was right all along. He was going to be fine. They merely had to help him get past his injuries, and then everything would be okay.

The nurse held her hand behind her, indicating that the rest of them needed to keep their distance until she was finished with him. "Are you in pain, John?"

This time he moved his head side to side. Once more the motion was barely detectable, but it was there all the same.

"John, you've been in an accident. Do you know that?"

His head was still. From where Abby stood, she could see him working his eyes again, struggling to make them open. Finally, almost painfully, the lids lifted and he squinted. At almost the same time his arms twitched, and he brought one hand toward his throat.

There! See? Abby wanted to shout. He could move! If he could lift his hands, then he wasn't paralyzed, right? She blinked, and her heart sank. Even if he wasn't paralyzed, he must feel miserable. Tubing stuck down his throat, his head and neck stuck in a brace, unable to speak. John hated having his temperature taken, let alone this. Before he could pull out the lines, the nurse caught his hand and returned it to his side. "I need you to leave your throat alone, John. You've had an injury and we need to keep the tubes in place. Do you understand?"

The nurse's voice was loud and measured, as though he were a dim-witted child. Kade glared at the nurse from his spot against the wall, but Abby was glad for her directness. Otherwise her husband might do something to harm himself, and they couldn't have that.

"Do you understand, John? You mustn't make any sudden movements and don't try to remove your tubing. None of it. Okay?"

John blinked, and his eyes opened a bit wider. For the first time, it looked like he could see. He met the nurse's gaze and gave a more definite nod. Then, without waiting for the nurse to speak again, John turned his head and, using mainly his eyes, found each of them around the room. First Kade, then Sean, Nicole, and Matt. And finally Abby.

She had no idea what the kids read in John's searching eyes, but what she saw said more than any words could. His eyes told her to hang in there, that he was okay, and everything was going to be fine. But there was something else there, too. A love so deep and strong and true it couldn't have been put into words even if John could speak.

The nurse took a step backward. "I'm going to let your family visit with you for a few minutes, John, but after that you have to sleep. You must lie very still. We're working as hard as we can to get you better."

She didn't ask him about his legs, whether he could move them or feel them. Was that because the staff no longer thought he had a problem? Or because there was no point giving him that type of emotional jolt moments after he'd regained consciousness? Abby tried not to think about it.

Instead she made her way closer to the bed, her eyes still locked on his. *Don't lose it, Abby; don't let him see your tears. Not now.* She held her breath and urged the corners of her lips up, where they belonged. "John . . ."

He lifted his fingers off the hospital sheet, and she took them in her own. He couldn't speak, but he squeezed her fingers. Abby refused to notice the way his feet and legs still had not moved.

She let out a small bit of air, caught a quick half breath, and held it again. It was the only way to keep from sobbing. "God is so good to us, John. You're going to be just fine."

His expression changed, and she knew instinctively what was going through his mind. What had happened? Who had hit him? Where was the other driver and was he okay? Abby knew few details herself, so she shook her head. "It doesn't matter what happened. It wasn't your fault, John. The important thing is you're awake and you're here with us now. You're getting the very best possible care, okay?"

The muscles in his face relaxed a bit and he nodded.

At the foot of the bed, Nicole gripped John's toes. But it wasn't until she called his name that he looked at her. "Daddy, Matt and I have something to tell you."

Matt placed his hand on Nicole's shoulder. "Hi." His cheerfulness sounded forced. "It's good to see you awake."

Nicole put her fingers to her throat, and Abby knew it was probably too thick to speak. After several painful seconds, she swallowed and shook her head. "We wanted to tell you tonight, before you and Mom took your dancing —" Her voice broke and for a moment she hung her head.

Matt took over. "We had some news we wanted to share with the family. When we found out about your accident, we were going to wait, but Nicole . . ."

"I want you to know, Daddy. Because you have to do everything you can to get better." She stroked his foot, her eyes never leaving John's. "We're going to have a baby, Daddy. It wasn't something we planned, but it's a miracle all the same." She sniffed twice. "We . . . we wanted you to be the first to know, because we need you, Dad. I

211

need you. Our baby needs you."

Tears filled John's eyes and spilled onto his cheeks. Then he gave a very deliberate nod and the corners of his mouth lifted just enough so they knew what he was feeling. No matter that he was strapped to a hospital bed . . . no matter what lay ahead on his journey to recovery, John was going to be a grandfather. And he was thrilled with the news.

Abby didn't know whether to laugh or cry. Jo had been right, after all. Nicole's glowing look was exactly what her mother-in-law had guessed it to be. She was pregnant! Here, in the midst of Abby's greatest nightmare, was a ray of hope, a reason to celebrate.

The conflicting emotions warred within her. She left John's side and put her arms around Matt and Nicole. "I can't believe it. How long have you known?"

"A few weeks. We wanted to make sure before we told anyone."

Congratulations came from Sean and Kade, though their voices were hardly enthusiastic. Abby let her head rest on Nicole's shoulder. She was too drained to do anything but stand there, motionless. She and John were going to be grandparents. It was something they'd talked about since they got married, only always it had seemed like some far-off stage. An event that happened to other people, old people. When Nicole got married, they knew the possibility was closer than ever, but still . . .

No one had expected Nicole to get pregnant so soon. No one except Jo.

An ocean of sorrow choked Abby as terrible thoughts assaulted her. Would John ever get to run and play with this first grandchild? Would he be able to walk the child around the block or bounce Nicole's baby on his knee?

Please, God . . . let the doctors be wrong about his legs. Please . . .

In this world you will have trouble. But take heart! I have overcome the world.

The verse was one she and John had looked at a month ago, when the troubles at Marion High had intensified. There had been many times in life when the words from the book of John had not comforted her, but caused her fear. "In this world you will have trouble"? What peace could be gained from that?

But over the years she'd come to understand it better.

Troubles were a part of life . . . even events like losing their precious second daughter to sudden infant death syndrome or having her mother killed by the Barneveld tornado. Some troubles were brought on by a person's own actions — like the years she and John lost because of their own selfishness. Other troubles were part of a spiritual attack — like what had happened this year at the high school.

But sometimes you simply stayed late at school correcting papers, pulled out of the parking lot for home, and found your life changed in an instant.

Troubles would come. After more than two decades together, this much Abby and John knew. The point of the verse wasn't to dwell on the certainty of hard times, but rather to be assured of God's victory through it all. If the Lord walked through the door of John's hospital room right now, He would cry with them and feel for them.

But before He left, He would give them a certain, knowing smile, and these parting words: "Cheer up! I have overcome all of it!"

It was true.

The new life growing within her daughter was proof.

Fourteen

———◆———

The jail cell was freezing cold.

Jake huddled in the corner on a cot. He had one roommate, a strung-out kid who he gathered had been picked up for attempted robbery. Jake peered at the guy when he was first brought into the cell, but neither of them had said a word since.

The past twenty-four hours had been like something from a scary movie.

Paramedics had given him and Casey a quick check, and then police had brought the two of them to the station. From there they were sent in different directions. Casey was already eighteen, an adult. Jake, at seventeen, was still a minor. That meant he had to spend the first night in a cell full of teenagers, all with attitudes.

The booking officer told Jake his mother was in the lobby, but he was being charged with a felony. He couldn't have visitors until he was properly booked and placed in his own cell, all of which happened Saturday afternoon.

He still hadn't been able to see his mother.

Everything she had warned him about had happened. He could hear her voice each of the dozens of times he'd gone out with friends since getting the car.

"Stay home, Jake. You'll be too tempted. A car like that could kill someone . . ."

It had been the primary source of his parents' recent arguments. Mom thought the car was only his father's way of making up for lost time, an apology for taking off to another state and living the life of an unfettered single man.

On more than one occasion, his mother had yelled at his father over the phone, trying to convince him that Jake was too young to handle a car like the red Integra. "You're a poor excuse for a father. If you loved him, you'd be here in Illinois. Not gallivanting around with some . . . some floozy on the East Coast."

The last thing Jake had wanted to do was prove his mother right, deepen the rift between his parents. Yeah, well . . . no question he'd done just that.

He rolled onto his side and pulled his legs up. He was lonely and scared and sick to his stomach. What if Coach had died? And if he was still alive, where was he and how was he doing? What were his injuries? Though Jake dreaded facing his mother, at least she would know what was happening with Coach.

For that reason, when the booking officer rattled the bars on his cell, Jake jerked himself upright.

"Jake Daniels." The man used a key to unlock the cell door. Across from Jake, the ratty teenager fixed his gaze on the barren wall once more. The man with the key barked at him. "You have a visitor."

Jake felt like a mess. He'd been stripped of his street clothes and wore a plain blue cotton jumpsuit — the kind you saw on criminals when they testified in court and their pictures ran in the newspaper.

"This way." The man's voice was terse. He led Jake down a hallway of small cells into a half room. There were a dozen chairs facing a solid glass wall, each with dividers that formed a series of small cubicles. At each chair was a telephone. The officer pointed to the last one at the far end of the line. "Down there."

Jake's steps sounded hollow as he made his way to the last chair and sat down. Only then did he see her. His mother sat on the other side of the glass, a telephone in her hand. Her face was swollen, her eyes bloodshot. *Look what I've done to her.* Jake gripped his sides, his heart beating out a strange, fearful rhythm he didn't recognize.

I've ruined her life. I've ruined everyone's life.

His mother motioned to the telephone, and Jake picked up the receiver. Sweat beaded up on his forehead and his palms were wet. His jailhouse breakfast lodged somewhere at the base of his throat. "Hello?"

She started to speak, then she dropped her head in her free hand and cried instead.

"Mom . . . I'm sorry." Jake wanted to put his arms around her and hug her, but the glass was in his way. Could he burst through it? If so, maybe the glass would slit his wrists and he would die the way he deserved to. He stilled his thoughts and cleared his throat. "I . . . I'm so sorry."

Finally she looked up and ran her fingertips beneath her eyes. There were black smudges there, remnants of yesterday's mascara. "What happened, Jake? The police say you were racing."

The running feeling was back. Maybe he could slip out a door somewhere and leave everything about Jake Daniels behind . . .

But the doors on every side were locked, and the mountain of misery standing before him was not going away. Jake massaged his temples. "That's right. We were racing."

His mother's expression changed, and Jake felt his breath catch in his throat. In all his life, he would never forget the shock and sadness, the disappointment that marked his mother's face in that instant. She opened her mouth, but for a long time nothing came out. Then she said just one agonized word. *"Why?"*

Jake hung his head. There was no good answer, none at all. He looked up and saw his mother was waiting. "I . . . uh . . . Casey challenged me." He was suddenly desperate to explain himself. "No one shoulda been on the road at that hour, Mom. When Coach pulled out, there wasn't time to . . ." His voice trailed off.

Through the smudged glass, his mother's eyelids closed in what looked like slow motion. "Oh, Jake . . . it's more than I can stand."

"Is . . . is Dad coming?"

She bit her lip and nodded. "He'll be here tomorrow afternoon."

The question was gnawing a hole

through his gut. All day he'd wanted to ask about Coach, but now that his mother was here, Jake was terrified to do so. Finally he had no choice but to put his thoughts into words. "How's Coach?"

"He . . ." His mother sniffed, her eyes full of new tears. "He made it through the night."

A wild relief exploded in Jake's soul, a relief like nothing he'd ever known. It made him glad he was sitting down, because otherwise his knees would have certainly buckled. Coach was alive! They could lock Jake up forever and he wouldn't mind now. Not as long as Coach Reynolds was okay. He met his mother's eyes again, then frowned.

She looked upset, like there was something she hadn't yet told him.

"Jake, I talked to Mrs. Parker. She knows a family from the Reynoldses' church." His mother hung her head for a moment before looking up. "Coach is in bad shape, son. If he survives . . . he will almost certainly be paralyzed from the waist down."

Paralyzed? Coach? Paralyzed . . . from the waist down? No way . . . not Coach! Jake felt like he'd wallowed into quicksand. Coach couldn't be paralyzed. He was strong as an ox. The guys teased him that he was in better shape than anyone on the team. "Maybe Mrs. Parker's wrong. What's the news saying?"

"It hasn't hit yet. The accident happened too late to make yesterday's paper."

Jake was shaking again. He ran his hand over the top of his head and down the back of his neck. "Mom, you can't leave me in here like this. I gotta know what's happening to him. It's all my fault!"

She squeezed her eyes shut and sat perfectly still. He'd only seen her do that one other time — when his dad left home a few years earlier. Jake wasn't sure, but he thought it probably meant she was having a breakdown. Once more he wanted to punch a hole in the glass, climb through, and give her a hug, but he couldn't even do that. So many lives had fallen apart in one single moment, and it was all because of him.

"Mom, stop. I need you. The guy's watching me and any minute he'll take me back to the cell." Jake's urgent tone caused his mother to open her eyes once more. "I have to know what's going on with Coach."

"The officer told me you'll stay here until Monday, maybe Tuesday. Whenever they can get you before a judge. They're charging you with —" her voice broke, and fresh tears spilled onto her cheeks, "with felony assault and gross vehicular negligence. Also something about street racing and using a car as a deadly weapon. They want to try you as an adult, Jake. That could mean . . ." Her voice faded.

"Staying here a while." Jake gripped the phone. "That's okay, Mom. I deserve it."

"More than a while, Jake. The officer said you'll be lucky if you get out in five years."

His mother didn't understand. She could have told him he was in for thirty years and it wouldn't have mattered. What was he going to do? His football days were over, so were his days behind the wheel. He could hardly go back to Marion High where everyone would know he was the one who'd ruined Coach Reynolds's life. Yet he was only a junior, without a degree or training or any idea of how to support himself. He could hardly move to another town and start over.

No, he was trapped, and for now that suited him fine. This was where he belonged. And even here he could still walk down the hallway or pace across his cell.

If what his mother said was true, that was more than Coach Reynolds could do.

Hanging up the phone and walking away from Jake that afternoon was the hardest thing Tara Daniels had ever endured. But seeing Tim in the lobby of the city jailhouse the next afternoon was pretty close.

He walked in, his tie askew, eyes wide and bewildered, and immediately found her. After hearing the news, he'd taken the first flight he could find. This was the soonest he could get here.

Tara could think of a hundred things she'd wanted to tell him. When the phone call came from the police department telling her they'd arrested Jake for felony vehicular assault and that he'd been racing at the time of the accident, she wished they'd arrest Tim, too. Hadn't she told him? Hadn't she warned them both that a car that fast was dangerous for a teenage boy? Just like she'd told Tim their marriage was worth fighting for, that by leaving for New Jersey he'd only lose everything that mattered most: the love they once shared, the son they'd raised, and the closeness in faith that had once been so important to them.

She'd been right then, and she was right now.

But when Tim approached her, his face

a mask of agony and regret, it didn't matter that she was right or that Tim was wrong. All that mattered was their son had nearly killed someone, possibly paralyzed him. And life would never be the same again.

It was hardly the time to point fingers. In all the world at that moment, only one other person could understand the pain of what Tara Daniels was going through. And that person was the man standing before her. A man she still loved, even if it had been years since she'd liked him.

"Tim . . ." She held out her arms, and he came to her, slowly, like a man stretching out his dying moments. His arms came around her waist, and hers moved around his neck. There — amid meandering petty criminals and empty-eyed drifters, with an assorted number of officers and jail clerks going about their business — Tara and Tim did something they hadn't done in years.

They held tight to each other and cried.

Fifteen

The swelling along John's spine started to recede two days later.

His doctor explained that until the swelling went down, it was impossible to know if John's paralysis was permanent. So far, John was unaware of the possibility. Though he'd had visitors streaming in and out of his room around the clock since Saturday, he was mostly sedated. Too much awake time meant too much movement, and that could interfere with the respirator and trachea tube.

It was early Monday afternoon, and Nicole and Abby were alone in a quiet alcove at the back of the waiting room. John was napping, so they'd planned to catch some sleep themselves. Instead they sat together, exhausted but wide awake, staring out the hospital window at the changing leaves in the trees that lined the parking lot.

They hadn't been there ten minutes when Dr. Robert Furin appeared. Abby and Nicole sat up straighter. Abby's heart soared within her. The doctor's smile could only mean one thing. John had moved his feet!

She felt the corners of her mouth lift some, despite the exhaustion that hung on her like double gravity. "He's got movement in his legs?"

"Uh . . ." The doctor's expression shifted. "No, Mrs. Reynolds. We're still waiting to determine that. Could be sometime in the next hour." He tapped the side of his pen against his pant leg. "I do have good news, though."

Beside her, Abby felt Nicole's body react to the letdown. She must have been thinking the same thing about John's legs. "Okay. We could use some."

"It looks like the trachea wasn't severed like we thought originally. We were able to get a better picture this morning, and it seems to be intact. That happens sometimes when a person receives a severe blow to the throat." The doctor paused. "The good news is we can take him off the respirator. In fact, they're doing that right now. So the next time you see him he should be able to talk." He shook his head. "It's a miracle really. Anyone hit by a car traveling that fast shouldn't be alive."

Abby was glad for the good news. It wasn't what she'd been hoping to hear, but the doctor was right. God had delivered John from what otherwise might have been certain death. They had much to be thankful for.

"When will we know about his legs?"

"We're taking him in for more X rays before the sedatives wear off." The doctor gave a single shake of his head. "I'd say we should know something within the hour."

Within the hour.

News that would alter their lives one way or the other would come like every other piece of information that had shattered their existence these past few days. By a single sentence, delivered as a matter of fact.

"Thank you, doctor." Abby smiled, but the action felt odd. "We'll be here. Please let us know as soon as you have any information."

Nicole was quiet until the doctor left. "Did you bring the article?"

"Yes. I'm not sure when I'll show him, but at some point he'll want to know."

Matt had brought the newspaper yesterday morning and showed them the story. It had a photograph of John's truck, but not a bit of it was recognizable. Abby had covered her mouth with her hands when she saw it.

The doctor was right. Truly, it was a miracle John was alive.

The article said two teenagers had been arrested for street racing, including one who hit John's car as he pulled out of the high-school parking lot. That information hadn't come as a shock to Abby. She'd heard from the beginning that John had been the victim of an illegal street race. It was the names of the teenagers that took her breath away.

Jake Daniels and Casey Parker.

John's quarterbacks. Good kids who had made a series of poor choices and would pay the price for the rest of their lives. According to the article, Casey was being charged with reckless driving, participation in an illegal street race, and being an accomplice to vehicular assault. He had been released on his own recognizance and was expected to plead guilty to several of the charges at a hearing sometime in the next month.

Jake's charges were far more serious.

First, the district attorney's office was determined to try him as an adult. If they succeeded — and chances were strong that they would — Jake would most likely wind up with a jury trial facing a handful of charges, including felony assault with a deadly weapon. The combination of crimes could send Jake to the state penitentiary for as many as ten years.

"This town is tired of illegal street races," the district attorney was quoted as saying. "If the people choose to make an example out of this young man, he could receive the maximum sentence."

Another quote came from Jake's mother, Tara, who apparently was holding vigil for her son at the county jail. "Jake is horrified at what's happened. He's ready to accept any punishment given him." The article went on to say that Mrs. Daniels hoped the district attorney's office would be lenient with her son since he had no prior record.

Abby didn't know what to think about that. If the driver of the speeding car had been a different teenager, one she didn't know, Abby could've ridden the district attorney's bandwagon, hoping for the toughest penalty ever.

But . . . Jake Daniels?

The kid had eaten dinner at their house a dozen times, swam in their lake, and jumped off their pier. How could she hope for a boy like Jake to spend the next decade of his life in prison? Abby couldn't picture him spending ten days there, let alone ten years.

She glanced at Nicole. "Have you thought about Jake's mother? How awful she must feel?"

"She wants leniency for her son." Nicole crossed her arms. "That's the only part that stands out in my mind."

The bitterness in Nicole's voice broke Abby's heart. Nicole was never bitter, never jaded. All her life Nicole had been the first one to pray about a situation, the one who always had a bit of wisdom or Scripture or hope for a person in need.

Bitterness did not become her.

"Jake's a nice boy, Nic."

Her daughter said nothing, and Abby let it go. She couldn't imagine how awful the ordeal had to be from Jake's mother's perspective. How strange it was that just a few weeks ago, Abby and Tara Daniels had been talking about the very car that had nearly killed John.

"What was Tim thinking, giving Jake a car like that?" Tara had said. "Do you know what that thing *cost*? Nearly forty thousand dollars. That's outrageous! He could have bought him four years of college for that. And all it does is tempt a kid like Jake to do something wrong."

Prophetic words, indeed. Jake, who had only recently made the decision to spend less time with the likes of Casey Parker . . . who had stopped teasing the Nathan Pikes at Marion High and started talking more frequently with John about his future. Jake, who might have earned a college scholarship in football . . . . had made a decision that had altered all their lives. Forever.

Rather than be there to love and support Tara in her most dire hour, Abby was living a nightmare of her own, and reading the details of the story from the newspaper, just like everyone else in Marion.

Beneath a smaller headline at the back of the paper was a brief article about the bomb threat at Marion High. It mentioned that a student had been questioned after the football game and released to his parents.

Abby clipped the article about the accident, folded it, and stuck it in her purse. One day soon, John would want to see it. So far, they'd had no discussions about the accident because John couldn't talk. Now that the tubes were coming out of his throat, he would have questions.

Abby prayed he would survive her answers.

Nicole turned to her, her body tense. "Can I talk to you about something? Not about the accident, but something else?"

"Sure." Abby reached over and took Nicole's hand. "What's on your mind?"

There were delicate lines on Nicole's forehead. Abby could feel her daughter's tension as strongly as if it were her own. "It's about the baby."

"Everything's okay, right?"

Nicole nodded. "It's just . . . well, I wanted to tell you I was pregnant a few weeks ago, but I couldn't." She hesitated and her eyes lifted to Abby's. "I wasn't happy about it at first."

Poor Nicole. As if she didn't have enough to worry about with John's condition, she had her own to consider as well. "That's very normal, sweetheart." Abby shifted so she faced Nicole. "Especially when you weren't planning on having babies for another few years."

"Four years."

"Right." Abby waited, giving her daughter time to voice her thoughts.

"I love children; it isn't that." Nicole's face mirrored the struggle going on within her. "It's just . . . I didn't want them to come between me and Matt." She stopped. "The way I came between you and Dad."

Abby sat back a little. What in the world was Nicole talking about? "Honey, you never came between your dad and me."

Nicole blew at a wisp of her bangs and leaned back against the vinyl hospital sofa. "Yes, I did. You might not see it that way, but it's true. That's why . . . why your marriage hasn't always been what it could be."

"Nic, that's not —" Abby couldn't put her thoughts into words. Obviously her daughter was more aware of what had almost happened last year than Abby gave her credit for. But what was Nicole thinking? Their struggles had never had anything to do with the children.

"Mom, I know it sounds crazy, but it's been stuck in my head since Matt and I got married. I've always wanted to believe you and Dad had the best relationship in the world. But last year there were lots of times I knew that wasn't true. Sure, I say you look like newlyweds, but that's only because it's what I *want* to believe." She spread her fingers across her chest. "Deep inside I know you guys aren't always happy. And I think it must be because you never had those years alone together. Without kids."

A small laugh slipped from Abby's throat, and she covered her mouth. Nicole was perceptive, but her reasoning was completely wrong. So wrong it was almost funny.

"Mom —" Nicole lowered her brow — "how can you laugh?"

"Honey, I'm not laughing at you. It's just . . . that wasn't the problem with your dad and me. Not at all."

Nicole was quiet for a moment. "Ever since I found out I was pregnant, I've been scared to death. Deep inside. Because there hasn't been enough time for Matt and me to bond, to build the kind of marriage that will last."

"Oh, Nic." Abby slipped her arms around Nicole's neck and hugged her. "Having children will only strengthen what you and Matt share. It did for your dad and me."

Nicole drew back and her eyes met Abby's. "Then what happened? I know you and Dad have struggled. You try to hide it, but sometimes it's obvious."

"Have you noticed any problems lately? Say, since your wedding?"

"Since my wedding?" Nicole worked free of Abby's embrace and stared out the full-length window. "I guess not." She spun around. "How come?"

Abby stood and joined Nicole near the

window. What exactly should she tell this precious daughter? How much should she say? "Because having you nine months into our marriage was never the cause of our problems."

"What was?"

"In a nutshell, we forgot to dance."

Nicole squinted. "Meaning what?"

A tired laugh slipped from Abby's throat. "Meaning ever since your dad and I moved to the house we live in, we would go out back and dance on the pier. Not real dancing. Just a sort of swaying back and forth, listening to the sounds around us and remembering what was important."

"Really?"

"Mmmhm." Abby felt a lump in her throat. Had they shared their last dance? Was John really lying in a hospital room down the hall paralyzed? She banished the thoughts and found her voice again. "We . . . we would talk about you and your brothers, about the good and bad times with your dad's job as coach, about the victories and tragedies life dealt us over the years."

"Did you talk about Haley Ann?"

"Always." The lightness was gone from Abby's voice. "But about three years ago we stopped meeting out there, stopped taking time to talk about life and our place together in it."

"Was that when Dad started being friends with Ms. Denton?"

Abby nodded. "He wasn't the only one making mistakes, though. I spent more time talking with an editor friend of mine than with your dad. That didn't help. Pretty soon we felt like strangers."

"I didn't know it was that bad."

"It was worse." Abby paused. If she told Nicole the whole story now, she might forever be jaded toward their marriage. But if she didn't, Nicole might not grow.

"You never considered . . ." Nicole's voice faded.

"We did. Last year in fact." Abby stared out the window. A pair of birds were sitting in the tree outside. "Remember the day you and Matt announced your engagement?"

"Yes." Nicole let her head fall back a bit. "We were supposed to have a family meeting, but Matt showed up and we surprised everyone."

"Us, most of all." Abby turned and met Nicole's eyes. "We had picked that day to tell you kids it was over. We were going to get a divorce."

"Mom!" Nicole backed up a step, her eyes wide. "No way!"

"It's true. When you made your announcement, your dad and I met in the kitchen and decided we had to wait. We couldn't go through with it until you were back from your honeymoon."

Nicole grabbed her head and took slow steps back to the sofa. "It all makes sense now."

"What?" Abby turned and leaned against the window.

"Every time I prayed, no matter what I was praying about, you and Dad were on my heart. I told Matt about it. He thought it was probably because you guys were under a lot of stress what with us getting married." Nicole uttered a sad chuckle. "I always thought it was something bigger. But not this big."

"We were at the end of our rope, Nicole. All I can tell you is we felt your prayers."

"So you mean, when Grandpa was dying that day and we were all gathered around his hospital bed . . . you and Daddy were planning to divorce?"

Abby nodded.

"That's unbelievable. I had no idea." A sudden look of alarm filled Nicole's features. "Did Daddy have an affair?"

For months she had worked to keep this information from Nicole and the boys.

Now . . . now she knew that hiding the truth had been wrong. *God . . . You want her to know, don't You?*

The truth will set you free . . .

Abby let the verse roll around in the basement of her heart. Of course! The truth wouldn't only set Abby free . . . it would set Nicole free, as well. After all, Nicole was a married woman. She might have to face something similar herself one day. It was crucial that she see the truth here — that any marriage could be saved so long as both people were willing to hear God's voice above their own.

She drew a calming breath. *God, help me say this so she can understand . . .* "He came close. We both did."

Nicole stood and paced to the window and back. "I don't believe it." She stopped in midstep, her voice angry. "What happened? How come you never made the announcement?"

"The night of your wedding . . . Dad had his things packed. He was going to move in with a friend after you and Matt took off for your honeymoon."

"Ms. *Denton?*" Nicole's cheeks were pale, the dark circles under her eyes more pronounced.

"No, nothing like that. By then Ms.

Denton had moved away. Her friendship with your father was over."

"Then who?"

"A divorced man, a teacher from the school."

"That's terrible." Nicole sank back onto the sofa once more. "So what happened?"

"Sean and Kade went to friends' houses, and after you left, your dad did, too. Or he started to. He got halfway down the road before he turned around and came back. God wouldn't let him leave."

"What about you?" There were doubts in Nicole's tone, but she looked less panicked than before.

"I was angry and upset. Devastated, really. But too stubborn to stop him from leaving. I went upstairs and slipped on one of his sweatshirts. When I did, I found his journal." Abby could still picture the moment as clearly as if it had just happened. "I didn't even know he kept a journal until then."

"What'd it say?"

"It talked about how sorry your father was for letting our marriage grow cold, how wrong he'd been to befriend Ms. Denton. How badly he wished things would work with me, but how certain he was that I'd never be willing to try again."

"Was that when Dad came home?"

"No." Abby's vision grew dim and tears filled her eyes as she remembered. "I finished reading and went out to the pier, past the tables still set up from your wedding, past the empty glasses and crepe paper and streamers, out to the place where your dad and I had always connected." Abby glanced at Nicole. "A few minutes later, your dad came up behind me. He told me something I'll never forget."

"What?" There was the hint of hope in Nicole's eyes, and Abby knew she'd done the right thing. Her daughter needed to hear this story. Especially in light of all the years she and Matt had ahead of them.

Abby closed her eyes for a moment. "He said he needed to tell me about the eagle."

"The eagle?"

"When the eagle mates, he mates for life." Abby gazed into the distance again, seeing John the way he'd looked that night as he walked onto the pier, hands outstretched. "At some point in the eagles' courtship, the female eagle will fly to the highest heights and then free-fall to the ground. The male eagle will then swoop down and lock talons with her. In doing so, he conveys a simple message: he is committed to her."

"I didn't know that." Nicole's features were softer than they'd been all afternoon. "That's beautiful."

"Your father took my hands and told me he didn't ever want to let go again. Never. That if it killed him, he wanted to love me like an eagle loves his mate. Like the Lord wanted him to love me. Holding on until death made him finally let go."

Abby blinked and the memory faded. She looked at Nicole and saw tears in her eyes.

"So . . . that was a turning point for you?"

"Yes, very much so." Abby stroked Nicole's hand. "We're happier than ever, now. It was a miracle really. So, you see, honey. Don't be afraid about the baby. God will use this — and every other season of your life, even the hard ones — to bring you closer to each other, and to Him."

Nicole gave a sudden gasp. "Wait a minute. I just remembered something." She stared at Abby. "That night, when Matt and I were checking into our hotel, I had the strangest sense that God had talked to me."

"About what?"

"About you and Dad. Like He reached down, tapped me on the shoulder, and told me my prayers for you had been heard." Nicole thought for a moment. "I even told Matt about it."

A chill ran down Abby's spine. *It really was You, Lord . . . thank You . . . thank You.* "God's so much bigger than we give Him credit for. We see something like this accident and we think, 'If only God would make it all better.' But nothing gets by God, absolutely nothing. He has it all figured out, and one way or another, everything He does happens for a reason."

Someone was approaching them, and Abby turned. It was Dr. Furin. This time he wasn't smiling. His steps were slow and measured, and he looked at both Abby and Nicole before taking a seat across from them.

"Mrs. Reynolds, I'm afraid I don't have very good news."

Nicole slid closer to Abby and linked hands with her. *Calm, Abby . . . be calm. Remember the words you just spoke . . . God is in control.* She found her voice. "Did you . . . do the tests?"

"Yes." He frowned. "We did several. They all point to the same thing. The accident injured your husband's spinal cord in a very delicate area. The result is something we've been concerned about since the beginning." He paused. "Mrs. Reynolds, your husband is paralyzed from his waist down. I'm sorry."

As bad as the accident had been, as close as they'd come to losing John, Abby never for a minute believed this would be the final diagnosis. Not for John Reynolds. The doctor was saying something about how if the injury had been a centimeter lower, he might have walked away from it . . . but if it'd been a centimeter higher, it could have killed him. And something about rehabilitation and special wheel-chairs.

Nicole was crying softly, nodding as though everything the doctor said made perfect sense.

But Abby barely heard any of it. No longer was she sitting in a stuffy hospital waiting room getting the worst news of her life.

She was fourteen again, stretched out on a blanket near the lakeside bonfire, with a young John beside her, tossing a football in the air, grinning at her, his blue eyes shimmering with the reflection of the moon on the water. *You got a boyfriend, little Miss Abby Chapman?* Then she was seventeen, seeing him for the first time in three years, just before he played in the Michigan football game. *You're beautiful, Abby. Do you know that? Go out with me tonight, after the game . . .* And suddenly he was on the field, reeling back and throwing a football like he was born to do so, running with it, bigger than life, the wind beneath his feet. The image disappeared and she was in a church, John gazing at her with all the love he could muster. *I, John Reynolds, take you, Abby Chapman, to be my lawfully wedded wife.* Then they were dancing, but the image changed and they were in the Marion High gymnasium and Paula was telling them to keep the beat.

"Mrs. Reynolds?"

Abby blinked, and the memories vanished. "Yes?"

"I said you two could go see him now. He knows about the diagnosis. He asked, and, well . . . we thought he should know."

"I don't want to go." Nicole's expression was etched with fear. She shook her head at Abby. "I can't see him. Not yet."

"Now?" Abby looked at Dr. Furin. She felt like she was underwater, like everything around her was happening in slow motion at a level she couldn't quite understand.

"Yes. He asked for you." The doctor stood. "I'm sorry, Mrs. Reynolds."

Abby nodded, but her mind was numb, desperate for the chance to go back in time even a few minutes. Back to the place where there was still a chance John might walk again. They'd lost so many years . . . was this really God's plan? That just when everything was better than ever, John would be paralyzed?

Abby's heart raced. How could she face him? What would she say? John had spent his life using his legs. Even now, in his midforties, he still ran as easily as he breathed. In the classroom he was the most active teacher on campus, spinning off impromptu comedy routines or outjumping the basketball players in his class to see whether they'd have a pop quiz that day.

Once they'd gone to Chicago to see Riverdance. The next day John entered every class by Irish-dancing his way to the front of the room. No wonder the kids loved him. Deep in his heart, he was still one of them. And that was especially true now that he and Abby were happy again. It was as though a decade had slipped off the aging process for both of them.

And now . . . *this?*

What would they do now that John would never walk again? Maybe never make love to her again? Her heart sank like an anchor. She hadn't thought about that before, the idea of never knowing John in that way again. It was unimaginable that their physical love might be a thing of the past. What in the world was she supposed to say about that?

Abby had no answers for herself. She was too terrified to cry, too shocked to feel anything except the certainty of one thing: John needed her. And because of that, she would go to him. Even if she had nothing to offer, no comforting words or bits of hope.

She would hug him and love him and cling to him, talon to talon, even if life would never, ever be the same again.

She entered his room without a sound, but his eyes found hers immediately. She made her way across the room and sat on the edge of the bed.

"John . . ." Only then did the tears come. "I'm so sorry."

There was a fresh bandage on his neck, where they'd pulled the tube. His body looked older somehow, smaller. Like he'd lost three inches off his six-foot-four frame. Then, for the first time since the accident, he looked deep in her eyes and spoke.

His voice was the only thing that hadn't changed.

"Tell me what happened, Abby." The words were painfully slow. His throat must have been raw after having tubes there for the past few days. "Tell me. I have to know."

And for the next half hour, she did.

He said nothing while she shared the article and carefully told him every detail she was aware of. When she was finished, when the facts were laid out for him to accept or rage against, he spoke. What he said told Abby that the John she loved was still in there, that an accident could take his legs, but not his heart and soul. "How . . ." He hesitated, his eyes searching hers. "How in the world is Jake?"

Sixteen

———◦◦◦———

Chuck Parker couldn't sleep.

Sure, his son was facing hundreds of dollars in fines and who knew how many hours of community service for being involved in that stupid accident. And yeah, the boy had blown any chance of an athletic scholarship or even acceptance to one of the better schools.

But that wasn't Chuck's trouble. Coach Reynolds was.

The man was going to live, and Chuck supposed that was good — but there was one detail about the accident that troubled him. What was Coach doing at the school after midnight?

That detail — combined with others that had come out in yesterday's paper — kept him up most of the night. And that never happened to Chuck. Never.

In fact before the accident he'd slept even better, mostly because he was so tired. The smear campaign he'd orchestrated against Coach since the season began was a tough job.

For the past few months Chuck had worked the stands like a car salesman, sidling up to parents and subtly swaying them to his way of thinking: Coach Reynolds needed to go.

"He's a nice guy," Chuck would say to whomever he was seated beside. "Don't get me wrong. But we have the most talented boys in all the state right here at Marion High. Our kids need a visionary, a coach with fire in his blood. Someone who understands today's kids. Besides, Coach Reynolds needs a break. He should concentrate on his younger son, spend more time with his family."

Chuck smiled often in the course of such a statement, and before long — it almost never failed — the parent would be nodding and agreeing and making promises to attend one of Chuck's meetings.

That was where the gloves came off. In those meetings, letters were formulated, plans were made. Coach Reynolds would be fired. He had to be. It was the parents' prerogative. They'd held three such meetings so far, and after each, Chuck Parker made sure the athletic director got a report.

"Herman, the parents want him out. The Eagles need a new direction."

Most of the time Lutz would sit back in his office chair, mouth shut. Then, just to seal his plan, Chuck would remind Lutz of the drinking and street racing the players had done during summer training . . .

"Is that the kind of coach you want at Marion High?" Chuck would raise his voice just enough to make Herman nervous. "Someone who looks the other way while the kids break every rule in the book? We need a coach with courage, a man who'll demand the best from our boys without compromising moral character."

The plan was working, too.

Lutz had assured him the last time that he was taking notes, making arrangements. Finally the man admitted the one thing Parker had longed to hear: "I'm not planning on renewing his contract, if that helps."

Chuck could hardly believe it. Lutz was totally and utterly spineless. But that was the beauty of the situation. Herman Lutz was putty in his hands, and Coach Reynolds was all but fired. A few more games and it would be a done deal.

Of course, Chuck didn't really believe Coach Reynolds knew about the drinking and street racing. Shoot, he wasn't even a bad coach.

But Reynolds had made a fatal mistake: he'd chosen to sit Chuck's son.

Casey was one of the best quarterbacks in the state. Okay, so he had a few Fs on his report card. And yes, he got in trouble sometimes for mouthing off to a teacher. So what? Casey was an intense kid, as driven as they came, one of those superathletes who — and Chuck was convinced of this — would one day lead an NCAA Division I team to a national championship.

Or he *would* have, if Coach Reynolds hadn't been so particular about his players' attitudes. Jake Daniels wasn't a better QB. Just a better kiss-up. And now it was too late for Casey. His entire high school and college football careers had been ruined by Coach Reynolds's ridiculously high standards.

But it wasn't too late for Billy.

Chuck's younger son had an even better arm than Casey. The kid was a freshman this year, tearing up on the ninth-grade team. A full-ride college scholarship was a given for a kid like Billy, and that would only be the beginning. Chuck believed fully that one day Billy would wear a Super

Bowl ring. He could picture him, accepting the award of NFL Most Valuable Player.

Too bad Billy's attitude was worse than Casey's.

Not a problem to Chuck. But to a man like Coach Reynolds? If Chuck didn't do something, Billy would wind up riding the bench just like his older brother. And Chuck simply could not have that.

For that reason, the campaign against Coach Reynolds would've come regardless of the Eagles' wins and losses that year. The fact that they'd lost far more games than they should have only made Chuck's job that much easier. Especially with Herman Lutz in charge. What the man knew about scheduling and practices and sports in general could fit in an ashtray. But one thing Lutz knew: what it took to keep his job. And since the man was already making a poor showing, he absolutely insisted that his coaches win.

All of it — the evenings spent working player parents, the after-hours meetings, the discussions with Herman Lutz — was going exactly as Parker planned, and not once had he had trouble sleeping.

Until the accident.

There had been two articles in the paper since then. The first was factual. It told the story of the street racing and the seriousness of Coach Reynolds's injuries. There had been a chance the man would die. Of course, like everyone else, Chuck Parker prayed Coach would live. And like everyone else, he was relieved when Monday's article said his condition had improved.

But that wasn't all Monday's article had said.

The reporter had gone into the hospital waiting room and interviewed as many kids as he could find. It was *their* story — along with Coach being at school so late that night — that Chuck found most troubling.

According to the article, the kids at Marion High loved Coach Reynolds as much as they loved football. One player said that football and Coach were one and the same, and would forever be for anyone who called himself an Eagle.

Their quotes told the story.

"Some Saturday mornings he shows up with bags of breakfast burgers, enough for the whole team."

"Coach cares about more than football. He's someone you can talk to and he'll always have the right advice. A lot of us think of him like a second dad."

"Every season we go to Coach's house for his famous Backyard Barbecue the night before one of the home games. He treats every one of us like sons. The thing with Coach is he loves us."

The kids' statements felt like they were written in permanent ink across the stone tablet of Chuck Parker's heart. If Coach Reynolds was so wonderful, why hadn't Casey done better?

Coach's answer never changed on the matter: Casey had an attitude problem. Chuck had always dismissed that. His son was just intense and competitive.

But ever since the accident, Chuck wondered if maybe . . . just maybe . . . Coach was right.

After all, what was Casey doing racing in the first place? The way the story went, Casey and Jake exchanged words at a party, and Casey challenged Jake to take it to the streets. The boy had been honest with the police, at least. It was his idea to race, his idea to beat Jake Daniels in at least one thing. And if it meant breaking the law, then so be it.

Talk about a bad attitude! A defiant, privileged attitude that couldn't possibly help Casey succeed in life.

All of which left Chuck wondering if

maybe he'd been wrong about Coach Reynolds. There was only one reason Chuck could think of to be at the high school after midnight on game day. Reynolds must have been catching up on whatever it was teachers do when they're not coaching. Writing assignments . . . planning class time . . . correcting papers. Something like that.

It was something Chuck hadn't ever considered. Coach Reynolds was just a hardworking, honest, devoted guy . . . and Chuck had spent all season trying to undo him. He knew there wasn't one stitch of truth in what he'd wanted people to believe about Reynolds. The truth was there in the article.

No wonder he couldn't sleep.

It was Tuesday morning, and after another sleepless night, Chuck was so tired he felt drugged. He stumbled out of bed, splashed cold water on his face, and found his way down the stairs to the front porch. The newspaper was his window to the world these days. Casey was back at school, but he'd been kicked off the football team and couldn't drive. He was useless at providing Chuck with information about the case.

But the paper would have something.

The story had played on the front page each of the past two days. There was bound to be another update that morning. He picked up the paper, shuffled into the kitchen, and spread it out on the counter.

The headline at the top of the page caught him cold, stopped his heart for more than a beat, and turned his stomach: *Marion High Coach Paralyzed in Street Racing Accident.*

There had to be a mistake. Reynolds was in great physical shape. The guy was tall and built, probably as strong now as he'd been in his college heyday. A man like that couldn't be paralyzed.

Chuck read the article.

Doctors announced Monday that Marion High Coach John Reynolds sustained a permanent spinal injury when his car was hit by a teenage street racer early Saturday morning. The injury has left Reynolds paralyzed from the waist down.

Chuck pushed the newspaper away. His stomach lurched and he bolted for the bathroom. There he fell to his knees and retched. Again and again his insides convulsed until he felt like his gut was turning inside out.

He fell back with a groan. What kind of creep was he, leading a charge against a man like John Reynolds? Coach had only done what was best for the kids at every turn. Even Chuck's own son.

His stomach heaved again.

He leaned his head on his arm, drawing in deep breaths. Coach Reynolds wasn't the problem. Casey was. Casey and Billy . . . and most of all himself. He had used his charm and influence among the parents to convince them of lies, to sway their thinking and basically ruin a man who had given sixteen years of service to the Marion High football team. A man who had built the program with nothing but hard work and determination.

The spasms in his belly finally stopped, and Chuck Parker struggled to his feet. As he stooped to wash his hands and face, he was certain a mountain had sprung up between his shoulder blades.

How much of what had happened to Coach Reynolds was his fault?

If he'd listened to Coach, if he'd done something about his son's attitude a few years ago, maybe Casey wouldn't have challenged Jake to a race. Maybe today they would merely be another high school about to enter the district play-offs, instead of front-page news, with a coach who could no longer walk.

It was all his fault.

Not only that, but he'd been responsible for making Coach Reynolds's last season with the Eagles nothing but a nightmare.

Chuck dried his hands and turned away from the mirror. He couldn't look, couldn't face the man he'd become. But there was one thing he could do, something he should have done at the beginning of the season. And in that instant he made the decision to do it.

He would call in sick and spend the day making sure it happened.

If he hurried, it might not be too late.

Jake Daniels was arraigned before a judge in juvenile court. He still wore the jailhouse blues, and because the hearing required a public appearance, the escorting officer made certain he was cuffed.

The moment Jake stepped into the courtroom he knew something was wrong. His mother and father sat almost together on one of the benches, but as he entered, they barely looked at him. His dad had paid for an attorney, some slick dresser named A. W. Bennington, who had an office downtown and a reputation for getting bad guys off easy. The kind of man Jake wouldn't have associated with — until now.

"The judge will read your charges and ask you how you plead," A.W. had explained when the two of them met on Monday afternoon. "You'll plead not guilty. I'll do the rest."

"Will they keep me here?" Jake didn't know why he asked. He didn't really care. Where would he go if they let him out? Not to the hospital with his other teammates, who'd been holding vigil there. Not to Coach Reynolds's room. Hardly. And not back to school. He'd be a freak, someone the other kids whispered about and mocked and downright hated. Coach Reynolds was easily the favorite teacher on campus. Loyalty for him might have been shaky among the Eagle parents, but it was stronger than cement among the kids on campus.

Besides, Jake belonged in jail.

But A.W. had shaken his head. "You'll be out as soon as the hearing's over."

His mother and father had taken turns visiting him after the attorney left yesterday. They knew he'd be coming home, so why did they both look like they'd been handed a death sentence?

Jake was led into the courtroom and

took a seat at a long table. A.W. was already seated, looking far more dressed up than any of the other adults. No telling what his father had paid the man. Anything to keep Jake from spending a decade in prison.

A.W. frowned at Jake and leaned close. "The coach is paralyzed. Your parents said it was in the paper this morning. Could make things a little tricky."

Jake spun around and found his mother. She was watching him, and as their eyes met, he saw she was crying. Slowly, firmly, she nodded her head and mouthed something Jake couldn't understand. He shifted his glance to his dad, who only bit his lip and looked down.

The muscles in Jake's neck unwound, and his eyes found their way back to the front of the courtroom. He wanted to die, to simply hold his breath and let God take him away from the horror of living.

Coach Reynolds was paralyzed. No, that wasn't it at all. He'd paralyzed Coach. That was the truth of the matter. He'd seen the pickup truck turn in front of him that night, hadn't he? He could have jerked his steering wheel and flipped his car. Sure, he might have died, but Coach would be fine. He'd been a selfish jerk, driving the car smack into the pickup. Now a man's life was ruined. A man Jake looked up to and respected, a man who was a hero to a thousand kids at least.

Coach would never again take a lap with them or run plays with them or lead them in drills. The guys would never see Coach — his equipment bag slung over his shoulder, baseball cap low over his eyes — walking across the field toward practice. Never again.

And it was all Jake's fault. He dropped his head in his hands. What had A.W. said a moment ago? It could make things a little tricky? He gritted his teeth. Was that all that mattered to these people? Didn't they understand what he'd done? What he'd stolen from Coach Reynolds?

"All rise."

The judge was a formidable looking woman with white hair and a pinched face. *Good. Maybe she'll lock me up forever.*

A.W. was on his feet. He motioned for Jake to do the same.

"Jake Daniels, you are being charged with a series of crimes that include the following." She read the list, but there was nothing new. Same things the officer had told him and his mother, the things A.W. had gone over with him yesterday. "At this point we are treating you as a minor. How do you plead to the charges?"

Jake said the first words that came to mind. "Guilty, ma'am."

"Just a minute, Your Honor." A.W. took a giant step in front of Jake and held up his hand. "May I have a word with my client in private?"

The judge's forehead lifted. "Hurry. This is a busy place, counselor. Your client should have been prepped before coming here this morning."

"Yes, Your Honor." A.W. sat and took a firm hold of Jake's blue cotton sleeve, pulling him down as well. He moved his lip almost on top of Jake's ear and hissed at him, "What're you doing?"

Jake wasn't as careful about being quiet. "She asked me how I wanted to plead."

"Keep your voice down." A.W. glared at him. He was so close it looked like he had one giant eyeball. "You're supposed to tell her, 'Not guilty.' Remember? Like we talked about."

"But I *am* guilty. I did it. I hit Coach's car, so why lie about it?"

Jake was pretty sure A.W. was going to have a nervous breakdown. Sweat was beading on his upper lip. "We aren't talking about whether you hit the guy.

We're talking about what sort of crime you should be charged with." A.W.'s hands were shaking. "What we're saying today is that we don't think you're guilty of felony assault with a deadly weapon."

The words swam around in Jake's head in no certain order. It felt like everyone in the room was staring at him, including his parents. Whatever the hearing meant, he had no choice but to cooperate. He sat back in his chair, his arms crossed. "Whatever."

A.W. stared at him a bit longer as though he wasn't quite sure Jake was ready to speak the right answer. Then he gave a slow turn to the judge. "We're ready now, Your Honor."

"Very well." The judge looked bored. "Will the defendant please rise?" She paused for effect. "Again."

Jake stood.

"How do you plead to the charges leveled against you?"

He cast a quick glance at A.W. The man was staring at his notepad, refusing to watch. Jake looked at the judge once more. "Not guilty, Your Honor."

"Very well. You may be seated."

Immediately the other guy, the district attorney, rose and approached the judge.

"The state would like to request that Jake Daniels be tried as an adult, Your Honor. He is seventeen years old, mere months away from the legal age of adulthood." For a brief moment, the state's lawyer hung his head. When he looked at the judge again, he almost looked like he was going to cry. "We learned this morning that the victim in this case was paralyzed in the accident. His condition is permanent, Your Honor. Therefore, because of the severity of the crime, we are convinced Mr. Daniels should be tried as an adult."

Jake wasn't sure what the difference was, exactly, only that A.W. didn't want him tried as an adult. Jake didn't care. The other lawyer was right. He wasn't a little kid. He'd known exactly how dangerous street racing was, but he'd done it anyway.

The judge said something about making a decision in two weeks as to whether Jake would be tried as an adult or not. Then it was A.W.'s turn again. He asked that Jake be released to his parents because he was really, basically, a good kid. No prior record, no alcohol in his system the night of the accident. Just a stupid mistake with tragic consequences.

"I want his license revoked immediately." The judge made a notation on a pad of paper. "Also, I want him enrolled in a continuation school so that he isn't attending classes with the other young man involved in the case. With those stipulations, your motion is granted, counselor. Mr. Daniels may be released to his parents pending the outcome of his trial."

The hearing was over as quickly as it had begun, and a uniformed man approached Jake. "Turn around."

He did as he was told, and the man removed the handcuffs from Jake's wrist.

A.W. smiled at Jake. "You're going home, Jake. You're a free man."

But it was a lie.

Coach Reynolds was paralyzed.

And as long as Jake lived, he would never, ever be free again.

Seventeen

It was like dragging around a hundred pounds of dead weight.

Four weeks had passed since the accident, and doctors had moved John to a room in the rehabilitation unit. They had certain goals, certain benchmarks for him to attain: transferring himself from a bed to a wheelchair, and from a wheelchair to the toilet and back again. They wanted him to dress himself and know how to look for sores on his legs and torso.

Today's lesson was about knowing when an open wound needed medical treatment.

"Sores represent an insidious threat, Mr. Reynolds." The physical therapist was slender, in his late thirties. Clearly he was passionate about his job, intent on bringing independence to those like John, who had recently joined the ranks of paraplegia.

John hoped the man would forgive him

for being less than enthusiastic.

"Mr. Reynolds, are you listening?"

"Hmmm?" John hadn't realized how many people called him *Coach* until he'd been admitted to the hospital. Even after four weeks it didn't sound right . . . *Mr. Reynolds*, not *Coach* Reynolds. It was as though the doctors and nurses and rehab technicians were talking about someone altogether different than the man he'd once been.

But then that was exactly right, wasn't it? He wasn't the man he'd been before the accident. "I'm sorry. Say it again."

"Sores . . . see, they develop on areas where your body gets rubbed on a regular basis. The problem is, with paralysis you can't feel the rubbing. The situation becomes especially dangerous after you've been in a state of paralysis for several months or more. That's when your body begins to show signs of muscle atrophy. Without the muscle barrier, bones have been known to rub clear through the skin. So you can see the problem, Mr. Reynolds."

John wanted to knock the man over with his wheelchair. Better yet he wanted to yell, "Cut!" at the top of his lungs and watch a dozen stagehands rush onto the scene to tell him he could get up now. The filming was over.

Of course, he could actually do neither of those things. If he wanted to get home before Christmas, he could only sit here and listen to some stranger tell him how his legs were going to waste away and that sores were going to appear on his body in the process. John settled against the back of the wheelchair, his eyes on the man's mouth. It was still moving, still explaining the reality of John's situation in meticulously vivid detail.

But John was no longer listening. His body might be a prisoner, but his mind could go wherever it wanted. And right now he wanted to think back over the past month.

From the moment he'd come to that Saturday after the accident, John had known he was in trouble. He had no memory of the accident, nothing at all. One moment he was pulling out of the Marion High parking lot, the next he was waking up in a hospital bed, feeling like he was choking to death. And something else, something even worse.

At first he'd been too distracted to notice.

Abby was there, and Kade and Sean and

Nicole and Matt. He'd known whatever was happening, it had to be serious if everyone was gathered around him. He'd reached for his throat, and then the nurse had stepped in and warned him to stay still. The stiller the better.

Calm me down, God. And in seconds he felt his body relax. The tubes weren't choking him; it only felt that way. The more he relaxed, the easier it was to breathe.

It was only then, when he was able to draw a breath more normally, that John realized it. Something was terribly wrong. His body ached from lying in one place and he wanted to stretch. His brain sent down a series of instantaneous commands. Toes — curl back . . . feet — point forward . . . ankles — roll around . . . legs — shift positions.

But his body wouldn't obey a single one.

Alarm shattered John's peacefulness, but he refused to let it show. His family was watching, looking to him for strength. Besides, at first he hoped maybe he was wrong. Maybe it was part of the medication they'd given him, something to make him tired and lethargic. A painkiller maybe. Perhaps his legs had been hurt in the accident and they were still under some kind of deep anesthesia.

By Sunday he still slept most of the time, but he was aware enough to know that none of those things should have taken away the feeling in his legs. That evening he began experimenting whenever he was awake. During the few minutes when no one was in the room, he'd slip his hand beneath the sheet and feel around. First his stomach, then his hips and thighs.

Above his bellybutton he could feel his hand quite normally. He could sense the coolness of his fingers and feel pain when he pinched himself. But below that, nothing. No sensation whatsoever. It felt like he was touching someone else, as though someone had taken his lower half and replaced it with that of a stranger.

Then he'd glance around the room, and if no one was coming, he would stare at a part of his body and order it to move. His pelvis or his legs. Even his toes.

It was always the same: nothing. No movement.

So when they pulled the tubes from his throat and performed a series of X rays and tests on his back, John knew what they were looking for. He could have saved them the time. Finally John asked what was going on, what had happened to him.

When Dr. Furin entered the room, closed the door, and announced that he had bad news, John beat him to the punch.

"I'm paralyzed, aren't I?"

"Yes." The doctor looked pained. As though he wished he'd become a plumber or a lawyer or an accountant. Anything but a doctor forced to tell a healthy man like John Reynolds that he'd never walk again. "I'm afraid so. We were hoping once the swelling went down that . . ." The doctor struggled to find the right words. "We were hoping the paralysis might be temporary."

The moment John knew the truth, he had only one concern. How would Abby take the news? In those early hours, he'd refused to be devastated. He was up to the challenge, wasn't he? He would take to a wheelchair and do all the things he'd done before. And one day he'd learn to walk again, no matter what the doctors said. Not just walk, but run. Yes, he'd be running again in a few months or a few years. Whatever it took. He'd show the doctors how it could be done.

The only thing that mattered was whether Abby could stand the shock.

As soon as he saw her, he knew he needn't have worried. Her face was a direct reflection of her heart and the love she

271

felt for him. A love that couldn't possibly be affected by something like paralysis. In her eyes was a strength that reflected his own. They would fight this thing, battle it. And one day, together, they would overcome it.

Then, when she'd told him about the accident, that he'd been hit by none other than Jake Daniels, his concerns shifted completely to the boy. Jake would be devastated by the news, distraught beyond his ability to carry on. For the next two weeks John survived by praying for Jake, begging God to bring good out of what had happened, asking Him to give Jake the courage to visit John. That way the boy could see for himself that John wasn't about to check out on life just because of a lack of feeling in his legs.

Hardly.

One of his visitors that first week had been Nathan Pike. The boy looked uncomfortable, dressed in his usual black garb. But something was different . . . It took John a few minutes to figure it out, but then it was clear. The defiance was gone.

"I heard what happened." Nathan scuffed his feet around, his hands stuffed in his pockets. "I had to come. Health class's no fun without you."

John chuckled. "Health's not much fun, anyway."

"Yeah." Nathan shrugged. "You know what I mean."

There was a silence, and Nathan looked uncomfortable.

"You okay, Nathan?"

"Actually . . . about what happened at the game . . . I was gonna call you up the next day, but then . . . well . . ." He stared at his feet. "You know. You got hurt."

"What'd you want to talk about?"

"The threat . . . whatever it was." He lifted his head, his eyes more earnest than John had ever seen them. "Mr. Reynolds, I didn't do it. I swear. I've done a lot of stupid things, but I didn't do that. I was at the library all day. Really."

"Okay." It went against all reason, but John believed him. "Whatever you say."

"You believe me, right?"

John made a fist and brought his knuckles up against Nathan's. "I believe you."

"You know something, Coach?"

"What?"

"You're the only one who does."

There were other visitors after that, dozens of students and players. All of them helped distract John from the gravity of his situation. But when John started rehabilitation, the reality came crashing in on him.

John had told Abby that after a few days of therapy, he was certain he would have movement in his toes again. At least that.

Instead, a therapist spent the better parts of two days teaching him how to slide from the bed to his wheelchair. Movement in his toes or anywhere else beneath his waist was as impossible as willing a body part on another person to move.

"How much rehabilitation before I'll be able to move my feet?" John asked Dr. Furin the question on the evening of the second day of therapy.

The doctor had been on his way out of the room and he stopped, frozen in his tracks. "Mr. Reynolds, paralysis is a permanent condition. Some people have made miraculous strides, depending on their situation. But at this point we don't expect you to have feeling in your legs ever again. No matter how much time we spend on rehab."

It was the first time since his accident that John had felt anger. "Then why bother?"

"Because —" Dr. Furin's voice was kind — "if we don't, you'll never get out of bed."

The answer infuriated John, and he told Abby as much that night. "They could at least give me a reason to hope."

Abby had been strong as steel, rarely crying — at least not in front of him. He knew her well enough to know she was crying somewhere, sometime. But he appreciated the fact that she kept her chin up around him.

She had worked her way onto the hospital bed and soothed her fingers over his weary forehead. "Since when do you find your hope in what doctors tell you, John Reynolds?"

His anger had faded. "I hadn't thought of that."

"Yep." A smile filled her face. "That's why you have me. To remind you of the truth."

"That my hope can only be found in God, is that it?"

"Exactly."

"Okay, then, Abby . . . you gotta do something for me."

"What's that?"

"Pray for a miracle." His eyes were wet, and he blinked twice to see her more clearly. "Don't ever stop praying."

In the days since then, the Marion Eagles finished their football season with a second-round play-off loss. John's assistant coaches had taken over since his accident, and a quarterback from the junior varsity squad was brought up to lead the team. Nearly all the players and coaches had been by, most of them making only a brief appearance to bring John a signed football or a card or a bouquet of balloons.

When the season ended, the visits tapered off and John put his energies entirely into rehabilitation.

Day by day, he learned the things his therapists asked of him. He could balance his torso with the strength of his arms and swing himself into a wheelchair. His efforts at getting on a toilet were trickier, but he could do so unassisted now. In fact, Dr. Furin had assured him that he was maybe one week away from going home.

"Definitely before Christmas." Dr. Furin had grinned at him the other day. "I'll bet that's the best news you've heard in a while."

It should have been, but somehow it wasn't. After a month in the hospital, a month of not coming a single centimeter closer to moving his feet or legs, John's usually fiery determination was cooling fast.

Christmas? From a wheelchair?

The past few days he still prayed for a miracle, but not with any real sense of it actually happening. He was no longer thinking about fighting his diagnosis or beating the odds or somehow gaining the ability to walk again.

Rather, he was thinking of all that he'd lost.

Last night was the first time Abby had noticed it. She gave him the update about Jake. The judge had delayed making a decision about whether to try the boy as an adult, and at the same time, the district attorney was refusing any sort of plea bargain. The hearing on how he would be tried was set to take place in ten days. But either way, it looked like Jake would have to stand trial.

When Abby was finished talking, she planted her hands on her hips. "John Reynolds, you're not even listening."

John blinked. "I'm listening. That's too bad. About Jake, I mean."

"Too bad?" Abby huffed. "When you first got hurt, you couldn't stand the thought of Jake going to jail. Now it's just, 'too bad'?"

"I'm sorry."

"Don't be sorry, John, be *mad*. Be furious. Be upset. But don't lie there with that monotone and say you're sorry. That's not the man I married."

John's voice remained the same. "You're right."

"What's that mean?"

"I'm not the man you married, Abby. I've lost the fight."

"You've *what?*" Abby seethed, pacing from one side of his hospital room to the other. "Don't tell me about losing the fight, John. The fight hasn't even begun! You can't ask me to pray for a miracle if you've already given up. I mean, come on . . ."

The conversation went on that way for an hour until finally Abby broke down and wept. She apologized for expecting so much and assured him he had the right to be discouraged. Before she left, she admitted he wasn't the only one. She was discouraged, too.

No wonder he couldn't concentrate on the therapist and bedsores. For entire hours of the day — even in the midst of rehabilitation — John could do nothing but remember. How the earth felt beneath his feet as he flew down the football field; how easily he'd strolled in front of his classroom day in, day out for the past twenty years. How his children had bounced on his knee as babies, and how he'd carried them on his back when they walked through the zoo.

How Abby's legs felt near his when they danced at the end of the pier. How her body felt beneath him when they —

"Mr. Reynolds, I'd like you to explain it back to me now." The slender therapist tapped his clipboard, his expression one of scant tolerance. "How often should you check your body for sores, especially after atrophy sets in? Have you heard anything I've told you? Mr. Reynolds?"

John looked at the man, but he couldn't bring himself to answer. The miracles he'd expected weren't happening, and he'd reached the next stage in what would be the rest of his life. The life without dancing or running or making love to Abby. It was a stage he hadn't anticipated, hadn't planned for. And for one reason alone it was more painful than even the first days after learning he'd been paralyzed.

Reality was setting in.

Eighteen

———◆———

Abby had never felt more stressed in all her life.

In part, she wanted a glorious home-coming. It was Christmastime, after all. They should have had the tree up and decorated, their home looking festive like it always did. She pictured a houseful of guests there to greet John as he arrived, and sweet conversation throughout the evening.

But John wanted nothing of the sort.

"Just get me home and let me sit in the living room with my family, Abby. Nothing else."

She spent every waking hour trying to be whatever John needed at the moment. When he was subdued, she was the quiet supporter. When he was angry, the patient listener. And when he showed signs of determination, of a willingness to fight the terrible curse that had come upon him, she cheered him on. If she couldn't read his mood, she maintained a false sense of euphoria — her way of convincing him that she was okay with his paralysis, that the changes in their life were not enough to take away her joy.

But it was all a lie.

She wasn't happy. Hadn't been since John's accident. But she owed it to John to appear happy and positive. He needed that from her. The trouble was, she had nowhere to let her guard down, nowhere to weep and wail against the twists life had taken.

And so she kept it bottled deep inside her heart, where the only thing it did was make her a basket case. Anxious and uptight and alone.

In the end, Abby did as John asked and kept his homecoming celebration to a minimum. Kade, who had gone back to school to finish the football season and the semester, was home for a month on Christmas break. He and Sean had picked out a tree and brought it home before John's arrival. Nicole and Matt and Jo and Denny had helped decorate it.

Dr. Furin released John at one that afternoon, and an hour later Abby and he pulled up in front of their house. She turned off the engine, and for a moment neither of them moved.

"Can you imagine, Abby?" John stared at the front door of their home. "I'll never drive again. Have you thought about that? I mean never again."

"You'll drive, John. They have hand-operated vehicles set up for people with —"

"Abby, can you just let me accept the truth for a minute?" His tone was sharp, but immediately he let his head fall back against the seat. "Ugggh. I'm sorry." He looked at her, and she could see the heavy fatigue in his eyes, his features. "I didn't mean to snap at you."

"I was trying to help. They have special cars . . . lifts . . . that kind of thing." Abby's hands trembled and she couldn't draw a full breath. How was it going to feel, pushing John into their house? Knowing he would never walk up to the door beside her again? She clenched her teeth. She'd keep her sadness at bay if it killed her. John deserved at least that.

"Do you know how much we take for granted? The little things in life? Like jumping in a car, and driving, and running up the sidewalk to your front door?"

Abby held her breath. "I know." Did he want her to cry with him, or play the role of encourager? And what about *her* feelings? The loss she was suffering? She blew out a shaky breath and filled her lungs again. "Let's go in. The kids are waiting."

John nodded and opened the door. Looking like the athlete he still was, he swung his legs out of the car. Abby tried not to notice the grotesque way they hung limp and fell onto the curb. He did his best to straighten them, but it didn't help.

He looked back at her, and she jerked into action. "I'll get the chair."

John hung his head while she hurried around, popped the trunk, and heaved his wheelchair onto the road. Abby tightened her jacket. It was cold but at least it wasn't snowing. For nearly a minute she struggled with the latch, ripping a fingernail off in the process. "Yikes." She shook her hand to stave off the pain.

"What's wrong?" John craned his head but he couldn't see her bloody nail base.

"Nothing." Abby blinked back tears. How strange it felt to be struggling this way and not have John's help. He was ten feet away. Just ten lousy feet. But he couldn't stand up and help her. "I'm . . . I'm trying to open the chair, but it's stuck."

"The latches are on both sides. Can you see them?" John was trying, doing his best to help her, but she needed more than his suggestions. She needed his strength.

"They won't budge." She pulled at it again, this time with more force. *Don't let him hear me crying, God . . .* "It doesn't work."

Abby struggled a moment more, and then in a flurry of angry frustration, she tossed the wheelchair on the grass beside the curb. "I *hate* that thing!" She fell against the side of the car and hid her face in her arms. "I hate it!"

"Abby, come here." John's voice was gentle.

She wanted to turn and run a hundred thousand miles away, off to some place where John didn't need a wheelchair to get into the house. But that wouldn't do any good.

God, I'm falling apart. Catch me, Lord . . . please, catch me.

Lean not on your own understanding . . .

It was the same Scripture that had come to her the last time she felt this way. What could it mean, though? Lean not on her own understanding? Was there a different way to understand the things that had happened in their lives? Could there be a *good* aspect to John's paralysis . . . ?

Abby didn't see it.

"Did you hear me, Abby? You're killing me." John's tone was louder now. "You're crying, and there's nothing I can do about it. Not a single thing. At least come here so I can hold you."

A quick pain sliced into her, cutting her to the quick. She hadn't thought of that before. How helpless he would feel. Always before if she was upset, he could come to her. Now he couldn't even do that. She dried her face and went to him, falling to her knees before him. His legs were in the way, so she put her hands on his thighs and pushed them apart. It wasn't the first time she'd moved them on his behalf, but she still wasn't used to the sensation. They didn't move easily, but slow and heavy, like the legs of a dead person.

When the space between his knees was big enough, she moved closer, pressing her body against his and laying her head on his shoulder. "I'm sorry for crying. This was supposed to be a happy moment."

"Aahhh, Abby." John nuzzled his face alongside hers. "There's nothing happy about it."

"Yes, there is." She spoke near his ear. "You're *alive*, John. And you're home in time for Christmas. That's plenty to be happy about."

"So those are tears of joy?" He ran his lips lightly along the side of her neck.

"I hate your chair."

"It's my only source of freedom. My only way to get around anymore, Abby."

"I know. I'm sorry."

"It's okay." He brought his lips to hers and kissed her, soft and tender. When he came up for a breath, he caught her eyes. "I hate it, too."

There was a sound behind Abby and she looked over her shoulder. It was Kade, bounding down the walkway.

"Hey, what's taking so long? We're in there waiting, and you two are out here hugging or something."

Abby studied their older son. The pain in his eyes was a mile deep, but his smile was genuine.

Abby stood and wiped her hands on her jeans. Her finger still throbbed where the nail ripped. "I can't open the chair."

"Is that all?" Kade reached for the wheelchair, checked the latches on both sides, and then with the toe of his shoe, he flipped a third near the base. With a single flick of his wrist, the chair opened, and Kade snapped it into position. He did a sweeping bow. "Your chariot, sir."

Abby stepped back, awed. "I fought with

that stupid chair forever." She shook her head. "How'd you know how to work it?"

"I practiced at the hospital." Kade shrugged one shoulder. "Too much time on my hands, I guess."

Abby watched as Kade positioned the chair in front of John, then slid his forearms beneath his father's armpits and eased him onto the padded seat. The scene made Abby's heart catch. How must John feel? John who had always been stronger than Kade . . . John the mentor and teacher and coach . . . now having to be lifted onto a wheelchair? By his son? And what about Kade? The boy was only eighteen, yet he gave the impression that helping John this way was a routine event.

When John was buckled into his chair, Kade took the handles and pushed him up the walk. "Well, Dad . . ." Kade opened the front door and wheeled John inside. "Welcome home."

And with that, a new chapter of their lives began.

The black cloud that had settled in around John was darker than ever.

He appreciated the reception and was grateful to be home and surrounded by his family. But no matter where his mind settled, it always wound up in the same sorry place: deep in self-pity and regret. A place from which he simply couldn't escape.

Sure, he went through the motions. He accepted his family's cards and well-wishes and encouraging statements about how good he looked and how wonderful it was that he'd survived.

But all the while he could only think of one thing: *Why me, Lord? Why now, when Abby and I had just worked things out? When we were just learning to dance again?* Since coming home, he'd been short with Abby, short with anyone who had an answer for his poor attitude. He didn't want a wheelchair van, or an invitation to the Special Olympics.

He wanted to walk. Just once more . . . so he could savor every step and appreciate the feel of his shoes on his feet, wonder at the balance in his legs and the graceful way it felt when he jogged around the track at Marion High.

Just one more day to say good-bye to the legs that had gotten him through every major event in his life. Not that it would help, really. One day wouldn't be enough. But if he could only move his feet and legs again now, he'd appreciate them every day for the rest of his life.

Too bad that wasn't going to happen. And neither was any other good thing until he could find in God the strength to will away the black cloud.

Two hours after getting home, the kids had returned to their activities. Abby was in the kitchen, but John still sat in the chair, facing out the front window.

God, I know You're still there, watching me, loving me. You have a plan for my life, even now . . .

"But what could it possibly be?" His ragged whisper tore through the silence around him. "What good am I?"

Another hour passed. At least three times John thought of something he wanted to get or look at or check somewhere in the house. Each time he would grab hold of the chair's armrests and make an attempt to stand.

And each time his body would jerk up against the safety belt and snap back into place. He realized what the problem was. He didn't yet think like a paralyzed person. His brain still gave him reasons to move and stand and walk, but his legs no longer heard the discussion. He wondered if it was this way for everyone who suffered from sudden paralysis. And if so, how long would it be until his mind gave up, too?

Until his brain no longer thought of his legs as anything more than dead weight?

John had always loved the view out the front window of his house. Trees and a winding drive that looked like something out of a painting. But right then he couldn't take another moment of sitting in one place. He worked the muscles in his jaw and slipped his hands around the wheels on either side of his chair.

Specially designed for paraplegics — people who still had the use of their arms — the wheelchair maneuvered more easily than most. John gave the wheels two hard shoves — and zipped backward so fast he crashed into the coffee table.

"John?" Abby's voice was filled with alarm. She appeared at the doorway, drying her hands on a towel. "Are you okay?"

He glanced at her, then let his gaze fall to his knees. "I'm fine, Abby. Every time I crash the chair into something doesn't mean there's a crisis."

The moment he said the words he was sorry. Why did he have to take out his frustration on her?

She came to him, slowly, tentatively. "I'm not worried about the table." He could smell her perfume, feel her presence beside him. Normally on a day like this he would tickle her or pin her playfully against the wall until she begged for mercy. Then, if the kids were busy, they might wind up in their bedroom for the better part of an hour.

His longing for her was still as strong, but how spontaneous could he possibly be now? Even if they were able to find a way to be physically intimate — which the therapist insisted was possible — it would require the type of planning that had never marked their lovemaking.

She rested her hand on his shoulder. "Is there anything I can do?"

"Nothing." He reached up and held her hand, savoring her skin against his, hoping she could feel how badly he wanted her. "I'm sorry, Abby. I've been a jerk lately. You don't deserve it."

"It'll take time. Dr. Furin . . . the therapists . . . everyone says so." She bent down and kissed his cheek. "Life won't always feel like this."

"I know." He caught her face between his fingers and brought his lips to hers. They kissed again, longer than they had outside a few hours earlier. "Pray that we find a way to live again, okay?"

"I am, John." Her eyes glistened, and he

knew her heart. She had probably been praying for him constantly. More than he'd prayed for himself.

He realized then where he wanted to be. "Abby, take me outside. To the pier, could you do that?"

"The pier?" She hesitated. "It's a little cold, don't you think?"

Abby was right. Temperatures were in the low thirties that day. But John didn't care. He wanted to sit out there in that familiar spot and watch the lake, look for signs that God was listening, that He hadn't walked away and left John to live out his days suffocating beneath a sad, dark cloud.

"I'll wear my jacket. Please, Abby. I need to be out there."

"Okay." She breathed out a little louder than usual. Loud enough to tell John that she didn't think it a good idea. People with paralysis rarely got enough exercise to fully expand their lungs. Diminished lung function meant a greater risk of pneumonia. Knowing Abby, she would have preferred John stay indoors all winter.

She found his jacket, the one with the Marion Eagles insignia across the back and over the front left pocket. After she helped him slide into it, she wheeled him out the patio door and into the backyard.

Abby had hired a handyman to build a wheelchair ramp up and over the sliding door tracks, and down from the deck to the yard below. Once they reached the grass, the ride was bumpy, but John didn't mind.

There was another ramp from the ground to the pier, and Abby struggled to get him up and onto the flat surface. "Good?"

"Closer to the water."

"John, think about your safety." She positioned herself in front of him where he could see her. "The pier has a slope to it. If your brake fails . . ."

If his brake failed, the wheelchair would roll forward and fall into the water, taking John with it. The lake was deep enough at the end of the pier that unless someone saw it happen, John wouldn't have a chance.

"It won't fail." He looked straight at her. "Come on, Abby. I can't watch the lake from back here."

"Fine." She released the brake with her foot and pushed him almost to the edge. He could hear her jam the lever down and give it a test push. "Is that better?"

He twisted around so he could see her.

She was angry. "Thank you."

She planted her hands on her hips. "When do you want to come in?"

If it weren't for the brake, he would've made his way inside by himself. But when the back brake was in place, John couldn't move without someone releasing it. "An hour."

Her hands fell to her sides again. "I'm sorry, John. We'll have to find our way through this. I just . . . I wouldn't know what to do if you fell in, and . . ." She hung her head for a moment before finding his eyes once more. "I can't lose you, John. I need you too much."

His neck burned from craning toward her, but he nodded. "I'm okay, Abby. I promise."

She held his gaze a few seconds longer, then turned and went back in the house.

John relaxed his neck and stared out over the lake. His other injuries were healed now, his throat and a few cuts and bruises on his face and arms. The accident had thrown him onto the truck's floorboard, breaking his neck in the sudden jolt.

Other than that, he'd fared miraculously well. But why? What could God have left for him now? The next several months would be focused on rehabilitation, which meant he was unable to teach. He could go back in the fall if he wanted, but it would be tough. The constant pity he was bound to receive would get old after a few days, let alone another ten years.

John watched a couple row out toward the middle of the lake and cast a line. All his life he'd made his mark through sports. What good was he now, like *this?* And what sense did it make that Jake Daniels would spend the rest of his life paying for it? Yes, Jake shouldn't have agreed to race. But what about his father, Tim? Wasn't he partially to blame for buying the boy a car that cried to be driven at high speeds?

John had no idea how the boy was doing. Jake and his family had sent John a card, apologizing and wishing him a quick recovery. None of them had been by to see him.

"So, what am I going to do with the rest of my life, Lord?" The words dissipated in the cool breeze that blew up from the lake.

He remembered a verse he'd loved as a boy, one that had helped him last year when it seemed he and Abby would divorce: Jeremiah 29:11. *"I know the plans I have for you . . . plans to give you hope and a future, and not to harm you."*

Okay, so if that was true, what were the

plans . . . and how was he supposed to get through the next several decades feeling anything but harmed? Most of all, where was the hope?

His thoughts were interrupted by the back door opening. The muscles in his neck still hurt from the way he'd craned around to see her earlier. He waited until she was standing in front of him.

"That was the district attorney on the phone. The hearing to determine whether Jake will be tried as an adult is tomorrow morning." Abby's voice was flat. "He said the judge might be more likely to decide in our favor if you're there in person."

John cocked his head to one side. "What's in our favor?"

"Obviously the D.A. assumes we want Jake tried as an adult." Abby sighed. "The penalties are much tougher that way."

John's head was spinning. Seeing Jake sentenced to prison as an adult would be as devastating a blow as the accident. "You sound like you agree."

She squatted down, resting her knees on the pier and sitting back on her heels. "I don't know what I think." Her eyes fell to his wheelchair. "People shouldn't race their cars on city streets."

"Putting Jake in prison will change that?"

Abby's voice was barely audible. "I don't know."

John leaned forward and took gentle hold of Abby's shoulder. "Don't you think Jake's learned his lesson?"

"I'm not sure." She looked up at him again. "I suppose."

"I'm serious, Abby. Do you think a day will ever come when Jake Daniels agrees to race like that again?"

"No." She shook her head, her eyes never leaving his. "He won't. I'm sure of it."

"So why send the kid to prison?" John was surprised at the sudden passion in his voice, his heart. "Send him to a dozen high schools where he can tell other kids not to race. Send him to college and pray that he grows up to teach or coach or pass the joy of playing football on to hundreds of kids like himself." He shook his head and glanced away before meeting Abby's eyes again. "The district attorney is doing what he thinks is best. That's his job. But I know Jake Daniels. Prison won't help him or me or anyone else. And it won't stop the next kid from saying yes to a street race."

A hint of fire sparked in Abby's eyes, something he hadn't seen since his accident. In a flash of realization, John understood. Hearing determination in his voice was a victory, a milestone. The corners of her mouth lifted just a bit. "What should I tell the D.A.?"

John clenched his fingers around the wheels of his chair. For the first time in weeks, he had a purpose.

"Tell him I'll be there."

Nineteen

———◆———

Jake Daniels was sitting between his parents and his attorney when he saw something that made his stomach turn.

The glimpse of a wheelchair.

Before he could do anything to stop the moment, before he could hide or cover his eyes or turn and run, the rest of the wheelchair appeared. In it was Coach Reynolds, being pushed by his wife.

The adults around Jake turned to see what he was looking at, and A.W. muttered an expletive under his breath. "We don't have a chance if he testifies."

Jake's parents were quick to turn back toward the front of the courtroom. But Jake couldn't stop looking, couldn't take his eyes off his coach. If it wasn't for the Marion Eagles baseball cap he wore, Jake would barely have recognized him. He'd lost weight — a lot of weight. And he looked smaller, older somehow.

For a moment, Coach didn't see him, but then he turned before Jake could look away, and their eyes met. Jake was spellbound, unable to blink or breathe or move. He'd spent hours imagining what Coach looked like in a wheelchair, how sad it would be to see such a tall, strong man condemned to spend the rest of his life sitting down.

But Jake had never expected this.

From across the courtroom, Coach Reynolds smiled at him. Not the big, full-faced smile he had in the locker room after an Eagles victory, or the silly smile he wore when he was pulling some crazy stunt for his health class. But a sad sort of smile that told Jake's stunned heart that his coach didn't hate him.

Coach nodded once at Jake, then Mrs. Reynolds wheeled him to the corner of the courtroom at the end of one of the spectator benches. She sat beside him, and the two began to whisper.

"Jake, you need to know how serious this is." A.W. seemed irritated at the exchange that had just taken place between Jake and the coach. "If Mr. Reynolds testifies, the judge will almost certainly decide to try you as an adult."

"Coach."

"What?" A.W. pushed his glasses back up the bridge of his nose.

Jake turned to look his attorney straight in the eyes. "*Coach* Reynolds. Not *Mr.* Reynolds. Okay?"

"Jake, your attorney is only trying to help." Jake's father put an arm around his shoulders and looked at A.W. "This is the first time he's seen Coach Reynolds since the accident."

The attorney waved his hand near his face as though his father's information was trivial. "The point is, Jake's in trouble. If the judge decides to try him as an adult, we'll have to ask for a significant continuance. We're looking at three to ten if he's convicted."

"You don't really think that'll happen, do you?" His mother was rubbing her hands together. A habit she'd picked up in the past six weeks. "Even if he's tried as an adult he could be acquitted, right?"

"It's very complicated." A.W. took out a pad of paper and a pen and began diagraming. "There are several ways a jury could look at it, starting with the felony assault charge and . . ."

Jake tuned out and positioned his head just far enough to the side so he could see Coach Reynolds and his wife. They were still talking, their heads bowed together. After a few seconds, the district attorney joined them. The conversation between the three didn't last long, and then the attorney took his seat on the other side of the table.

Jake was being rude; he knew it. But he couldn't force himself to look away. Seeing Coach in a wheelchair was the most horrible thing he could imagine. *Get up, Coach . . . run around the room and tell us it's all a big joke. Something you'd pull in one of your health classes. Please!*

But the man didn't move a bit.

The hearing would start any minute, and for the first time since hitting Coach's pickup truck, Jake didn't want to run away. He wanted to get up and go to Coach, tell him how much he'd missed him and how sorry he was. How sorry he would always be.

Then Jake saw something even worse. Coach's foot slipped off the chair and hung loose and limp to one side. And this was the awful part — Coach didn't even notice! It was his wife who saw it first. She stooped down and *lifted* his foot — like it was a book or a plant or something — and set it back on the chair.

Jake felt tears well up. *Coach, no!* How

was it possible? Coach couldn't even feel his own feet? Was it that bad? Jake brushed a single tear off his cheek. Since his parents' divorce, he'd spent little time praying. But he had prayed once. When he'd desperately needed help, in the moments after hitting Coach's truck. Back then Jake had screamed out for God's help.

And God had brought it.

So, why not do the same thing here and now? Jake closed his eyes.

God, it's me — Jake Daniels. I'm sure You know I've ruined everything. My whole life's shot but the sad thing is, my coach's life is shot, too. And it wasn't his fault, not at all. So You see, God, I have this favor to ask. I believe You can do anything, God. You can make blind people see and deaf people hear — at least that's what my Sunday school teacher used to say.

Tears streamed down his face, but none of the adults around him seemed to notice. *God, I remember a story about a paralyzed man. He had a mat with him, I think. And a bunch of friends. And Lord, I know You made him walk again. I'm pretty sure one minute he was lying there and the next he was walking around.*

Jake opened his eyes and snuck another quick look at Coach.

So, please, God . . . could You do the same thing for Coach Reynolds? Could You make him walk again and run again? Just do whatever You did to that other guy and let him have his legs back. Please, God.

How long had it been since he'd prayed that way? Jake wasn't sure, but it felt wonderful. And even though his parents told him Coach would always be paralyzed, Jake was sure God could change that if He wanted to.

Coach caught his eye, and Jake made a quick turn toward his parents. He dried his cheeks and stared at his mom and dad, hating the way they listened to everything A.W. said. The attorney saw Coach as the enemy . . . but his parents didn't feel that way, did they? Not that many years ago his parents had been friends with the Reynoldses.

Jake sniffed and studied his parents.

What was going on with them, anyway? Now that the trial was coming up, his father had taken a personal leave from work. He was staying at a hotel not far from where Jake and his mother lived. Jake spent the days at continuation school, wondering why he wasn't in jail where he belonged.

But what about his dad? Where was he spending the days lately? At his mother's house? If so, were they getting along or just trying to figure out what to do if Jake went to prison? They still sat with space between them, so there couldn't be anything that good happening.

The space between them was the first sign there'd been problems between them, back before their fighting overtook the house. Lately, though, they hadn't fought once. Not since this whole mess with the accident.

The judge walked in and the hearing began. The woman had already heard from Jake's parents on why he should be tried as a minor, but now she glanced around the courtroom and asked A.W. a question. "Is there any new evidence the court should consider before making a decision in this matter?"

Jake's attorney stood for a moment. "None, Your Honor."

The judge turned to the district attorney. "Counselor?"

The man stood and looked toward the back of the room. "Yes. The state would like to call Mr. John Reynolds to the stand."

Jake could hardly breathe as Mrs. Reynolds wheeled Coach to the front of the courtroom. This was the part where

Coach would say how wrong it was to street race, and how Jake must have known what he was doing.

But Jake didn't care. He deserved whatever happened next. The only thing that mattered was Coach's legs, and whether this would be the moment God would choose to heal him.

Or if that would come sometime later.

Twenty

Every eye was on John.

Abby knew they were staring at him, thinking him painfully thin with useless legs strapped to a prison of metal and wheels — but it didn't matter. She couldn't have been more proud of him. His back was still sore, and this morning the pain had been so bad he could hardly sit up. But still he'd come.

The district attorney didn't know what he was in for.

Abby parked the wheelchair near the witness stand. She took a seat in the front row, not far from John. When he had stated his name for the record and explained his role in the hearing, the judge turned the floor over to the state. "Proceed with your witness."

"Thank you, Your Honor." The district attorney was a plain-looking man whose square jaw was his most prominent feature.

He wore a short-sleeved shirt and inexpensive dress pants, but he looked kind. Abby hoped he would understand what John was about to do.

The attorney walked John through a series of quick questions, designed to put him at the scene and verify for the court that his paralysis was, in fact, the result of Jake Daniels's street racing.

"Mr. Reynolds, let's talk about the defendant for a moment." The attorney kept his distance. Probably so he wouldn't block the judge's view of John in his wheelchair. "You know Jake Daniels, don't you?"

Abby's heart raced. Here it was.

"Yes, I do." John cast a look at Jake. Abby followed his gaze, but Jake was studying his folded hands. John turned back to the district attorney. "I've known him for several years."

"You've seen him grow up; would you say that, Mr. Reynolds?"

"Yes." John rested his hands on his lap. "I've seen him grow up."

"Now, Mr. Reynolds, you're aware that this court is about to decide whether the defendant should be tried as an adult, is that correct?"

"Yes, I'm aware."

"Is it your understanding that the defendant is only months away from his eighteenth birthday, an age that would make him legally an adult?"

"It is."

"Very well then, Mr. Reynolds, is it your opinion that a young man almost eighteen years old, who agrees to participate in an illegal street race, should be tried as an adult?"

Abby caught a glimpse of Jake's parents. They were both grimacing, holding their breath while they waited for John's condemnation.

It never came.

"No, sir, I don't believe Jake Daniels should be tried as an adult." John looked at Jake while he spoke. "Jake is one of the good kids, actually. In the months before the accident, he had shown significant maturity, choosing to go his own way instead of following his peers."

John paused, and the district attorney pounced. "Now, let me see if I'm understanding this correctly, Mr. Reynolds. You saw significant maturity in the defendant in the months leading up to the accident, but you *don't* think he should be tried as an adult. Is that right?"

"Exactly." John smiled at the D.A. "See, the fact that someone like Jake could be at a party, refusing to drink and in general being a good example for the others seems proof that he is capable of standing trial as an adult."

Abby shifted her gaze to Jake's parents. Tara was quietly crying, her hand over her mouth. Tim had his arm around Jake. Their faces were shrouded in disbelief.

John continued. "But anytime a good kid like Jake agrees to something as terribly wrong as street racing, I can only surmise one thing." John hesitated. "He's still a kid. A kid who used poor judgment to make a bad choice."

He looked at Jake, and this time the boy lifted his eyes. He was crying, and in that moment, everyone in the courtroom must've seen the truth. Jake wasn't a man; he was a boy. A frightened, shame-filled, guilty boy who would have given his life to take back the consequences of his decisions that awful Friday night.

The district attorney deflated like a worn-out tire. "Is that all, Mr. Reynolds?"

"Not really." John rotated his chair so he could better see the judge. "Your Honor, I'd like to go on record saying that I don't believe jail time is best for a boy like Jake. If he was a repeat offender, that would be different. But Jake isn't a defiant kid. He's not anxious to get his license back so he can go out and race again. He doesn't need prison time; he needs to take his story back into the schools, to talk to kids and tell them the truth about street racing. I'm willing to bet everyone who hears him will feel what *he's* feeling. And maybe then we'll stop this from happening to someone else." He nodded once. "That's all, Your Honor."

John wheeled himself back to Abby. In his eyes she saw hope. A hope she'd been afraid was gone forever.

"You did good."

"Thanks."

In the background, Abby vaguely heard the D.A. call for a meeting with the judge. Before she had time to give it much thought, the hearing was over and Jake's attorney was at their side. He kept his chin low, his hands clasped behind his back, a properly meek stance in light of John's condition. But the exuberance in his face was undeniable.

It made Abby's stomach turn. John hadn't given his speech to make a defense attorney look good. He had given it to save Jake, a boy he knew and trusted and still believed in.

The attorney effused on about John's

graciousness, his act of kindness. But before John could respond, the judge called the hearing back to order.

"In light of the testimony given today by the victim in this case —" the judge glanced in Jake's direction — "I have decided to hand the defendant over to be tried as a juvenile."

Behind them, Abby heard Jake's mother contain a cry. The hum of whispering overshadowed the judge's words, and she rapped her gavel on the bench. "That will be enough of that." The room fell quiet once more, and the judge looked at the D.A. "The attorney for the state has asked for time to talk with the defendant's attorney about a plea bargain. They will set that meeting up, and we will convene again in three weeks to determine if this case will require a trial or not."

Abby flashed a look at Jake's attorney. The man was grinning, shaking Tara's hand and then Tim's, and finally Jake's. Again, the windows in Abby's soul shook with frustration, until she caught the expressions on the Danielses' faces. Jake and his family were not smiling. Their attorney might have seen today's outcome as merely a legal victory, but not the Daniels family. They were as painfully aware as she that

John was still paralyzed.

Whatever penalty the courts meted out to Jake, in many ways they were all losers.

The hearing was over, and Jake's attorney pulled Jake aside. Abby stood and wheeled John around. As she did, her gaze landed squarely on Tara and Tim Daniels. Tara was gathering her things when her eyes met Abby's. The two of them hadn't spoken since the accident. Other than their sympathy card, they'd kept their distance. Abby understood. It was as tumultuous a time for the Daniels family as it was for hers.

Abby wheeled John closer, maneuvering him between the defense table and the first row of spectator benches. Her heart beat faster than it had all day.

The moment grew more awkward until finally John broke the silence. "Tara . . . how's it going?"

"I'm —" Tara's voice cracked. She and Tim moved closer, and the four of them formed a small circle. Tara's eyes filled, and she took one more step toward John. As she did, John reached up his hand, and she took it, her fingers trembling. "I'm so sorry. We would've been by but . . . I didn't know what to say." She lifted her eyes. "I'm sorry, Abby."

The tears came in streams. Abby moved around John's chair and took Tara in her arms. "Jake didn't want this any more than we did." She kept her voice soft, her sobs muted. Their hug ended, and they stood there, each planted in the awkward soil of unfortunate circumstances.

Tim cleared his throat and met John's gaze. "It's been a long time."

"It has." John shook the man's hand. "You never said good-bye."

"The situation wasn't —" Tim glanced at Tara. "It wasn't good, John. I'm sorry."

He pressed on. "You remarried now?"

"No." Tim's cheeks grew red. "I took a leave from work. I've been staying at a hotel in town." Again he looked at Tara, and something curious washed over Abby's heart. Were Tara and Tim having feelings for each other? After years of being divorced? Tim shifted his gaze back to John. "We've been talking about a lot of things. Why I left, for instance. And why we couldn't make it work."

John glanced back at Abby, then leaned forward slightly. "Would it shock you to know that Abby and I nearly made a decision to divorce this past summer?"

Tara's eyes flew open. "Abby? You and John?"

"We'd been talking about it for three years." Abby wanted to stand on the judge's bench and shout John's praises. He was the one whose life had been forever changed because of the accident, yet here he was getting to the heart of an issue that — for him — would always be even closer to his heart than his legs: the dissolution of marriages. Especially Christian marriages.

Tim stuffed his hands in his pants pocket. "So . . . what happened? I mean . . . you're still together."

"We remembered why we got married and all the memories we'd made along the way. And most of all how dismal the future looked if we didn't have us anymore." John craned his neck again until his eyes found Abby's. Then he returned his attention to Tim. "Things are better than they've ever been."

Tara wiped at a tear and sniffed. "Tim wants us to talk about taking another try at being married." She shook her head. "But I can't do it. The divorce about killed us the first time. A second failure would do me in."

"I tell you what . . ." John reached back for Abby's hand, and she came up alongside him. Sincerity rang from his voice. "As long as you're in town, how about you and Tara come by the house a few nights a week? Just to talk things through."

Abby caught John's vision, and her heart leaped. "Maybe we can share something from our story that'll help you."

Tara looked doubtful. "I don't know."

They were quiet for a while, then Tim looked at the ground, his feet restless. When he looked up, there were tears in his eyes. "I'm sorry, John. About your legs."

John shrugged, his expression more at peace than it had been in weeks. "It wasn't your fault."

"I bought the car." Tim's face was ashen. "Tara was right. It was the wrong thing for a teenage boy. I'll . . . live with that the rest of my life."

Ten feet away, the defense attorney patted Jake on the shoulder and made a quick exit. When he was gone, Jake stared at the four of them, then approached with clearly hesitant feet. Abby studied the boy. She wasn't sure what she felt. Sometimes she hated him. Jake's decision had cost John his ability to walk, and changed their lives forever. But other times . . .

She simply didn't know.

This was one of those times.

When Jake reached them, he looked at

his parents. "Can I have a minute with Coach?"

"Of course." Tara collected her things and she and Tim moved toward the door. "We'll be out here when you're done."

Abby gave John's shoulder a light squeeze. "Want me to leave?"

"No." Jake answered before John could speak. "Please, Mrs. Reynolds . . . I want you to hear what I'm going to say."

Abby pulled a chair from the defense table and positioned it near John. When she was seated, Jake crossed his arms and inhaled. Abby tried to read the boy's eyes. Was this a thank-you speech concocted by his attorney? Or was there something real on Jake's heart? Even before he spoke, Abby knew it was the latter.

"Coach, my attorney just got done telling me I was lucky." Jake huffed and the air left his body in a single burst. "Can you believe that?"

John said nothing, just kept his gaze on Jake and waited.

"I want you and Mrs. Reynolds to know that no matter what happens with the hearing in a few weeks, I am *not* lucky." Jake's eyes welled, but he didn't cry. "I made a stupid decision, and it . . . it . . ."

He bit his lip and hung his head. For a

long time he stayed that way, and Abby understood. His emotions were too near the surface to let go now. Not when he had more to say. Jake held his breath and looked at John again. "It was my fault, Coach. I never should've raced him. Never." The boy's knees shook. "I saw your truck pull out that night, but I was going too fast. I couldn't stop."

Abby's heart fell. *God . . . couldn't You have held John back an extra minute? Enough time to spare him this?*

Lean not on your own understanding, daughter . . .

She blinked. The strange words that played across her soul felt almost like a direct response from God. And with the same Scripture that had come to mind again and again.

Is that You, God?

I have told you these things, so that in Me you may have peace. In the world you will have trouble. But take heart! I have overcome the world.

Jake was going on, explaining how quickly the accident had happened, but Abby wasn't listening. Chills had gone down her spine the moment the Scripture flashed in her heart. It was a verse she'd read that morning in her devotion time. In fact, she and John had looked at it a little while ago . . . after Nicole's wedding, when they first began reading the Bible together again.

It was the perfect verse, the one that described their situation exactly. She understood that now even more than she had back in the hospital in the days after John's accident. The Word of God, His promises, these things God had spoken to them so that they would have peace. In the world they would have trouble — most definitely. First on the football field with parents and the administration. And then with John's accident.

But in the end, though they didn't see it now, God would win. God would always win. He would win over deceitful parents and spineless administrators; He would win over John's car accident, and even his paralysis.

He would win even if John spent the rest of his life in a wheelchair.

Jake was saying something about Casey Parker leaving the scene and then coming back to call for help. "We were so scared, Coach. We thought you were gonna die." The boy squirmed, his tears finally splashing onto his tennis shoes. "I'm so sorry." Jake sank into a chair across from

John and let his head fall into hands. "I'd give anything to take back those few minutes."

Casey Parker hadn't been to see John, either. Ever since finding out that the boy's father had written the notes about John, Abby wondered if the man was maybe glad about what had happened to John. Not that he'd been injured, of course, but that he wouldn't be coaching. It was an awful thing to think, but Abby couldn't help herself. She was a coach's wife, after all. And people tended to reserve some of their greatest disdain and poorest behavior for coaches. It was a fact of American life.

If John was thinking those things, he never mentioned them.

He leaned forward now as far as he could and gripped Jake's knees. "Jake, look at me." John's voice was kind, but stern. The same tone Abby had heard him use with their own children when they were down on themselves.

Jake barely lifted his head and then let his fingers cover his face once more.

"I'm serious, Jake. Drop the hands and look at me."

Abby was quiet, watching from her place at his side. This was the John she knew and loved, the one who would see something wrong and right it with a passion that couldn't be contrived — or resisted.

This time Jake's hands fell to his lap, and he met John's gaze. Tears ran down both sides of his face. "Coach, don't make me look at you. It's too hard."

The sorrow in Jake's eyes softened Abby's heart. He really *was* just a kid, a boy drowning in a river of guilt, with no way of reaching the other side.

John leaned closer still. "Jake, I forgive you. It was an accident."

"It was *stupid!*" Jake's features twisted and he uttered a soundless cry. "You're in a chair, Coach. Because of me! I can't take that." A single sob slipped from Jake's throat. "I *want* them to put me in prison. That way I don't have to pretend my life is fine when I'm the one who wrecked yours."

"You didn't wreck my life. There's nothing I can't do if I work hard enough, and I'm going to work, Jake; you better believe it. I never let you boys settle for second, and I'm certainly not going to settle for second, now."

Abby's heart skipped a beat. This from the man who sat alone on their pier the day before, isolated and discouraged? She wanted to raise both hands and scream in victory, but she resisted.

Jake rubbed his knuckles into his forehead and shook his head. "It isn't right, Coach. What you did for me today. I don't deserve it."

"It *is* right. You do no one any good sitting in a prison cell, Jake. You made a bad decision, and your life changed in a few seconds. Mine, too. But you won't save anyone by sitting behind bars. Not the next street-race victim, not yourself. And definitely not me. You need to be out there sharing that message, telling kids to say no if someone challenges them to a race. That way you'll save lives."

"Coach —" torment wracked Jake's face again — "that's not enough punishment. How can I look in the mirror? I mean . . . it's crazy. You and your family . . . you could never really forgive me for what I did. You *shouldn't* forgive me."

"Jake . . ." John's tone was quieter than before. "I already have."

"Don't say that."

Abby closed her eyes. She could sense what was coming. *Don't make me forgive him, too, God. Not yet . . .*

John settled back in his chair some. "The minute Abby told me what happened . . . that it was you driving the other car . . . I made a decision deep inside to forgive you." John gave a single sad sort of laugh. "How could I hold it against you? It was an accident, Jake. Besides, you're like a son to me. I forgive you completely."

Abby shifted in her chair.

Speak, daughter . . . forgive as I forgave you . . .

The prompting in Abby's soul was undeniable. *Lord . . . please. Don't make me say it now. He doesn't need my forgiveness.*

"Abby does, too." John turned to her, his eyes so transparent she could see straight to his heart. Whatever other feelings John might wrestle with in the coming months and years, she doubted a lack of forgiveness would be one of them. He was being honest with Jake. He harbored no resentment or ill will toward the boy. None at all. John was still looking at her, waiting. "Tell him, Abby. You forgive him, right?"

"Of course." She had to say it for John; she could sort out her feelings later. "We all do."

Jake hung his head again. "I hate myself."

"Then *there's* the real problem. Forgiving yourself." John dug his elbows into his knees, and Abby was struck by a thought. *He can't feel it . . . like he's resting his arms on a table or a desk.*

Jake was silent.

"Then that's what I'll pray for —" John bit the corner of his lip — "that God will give you the grace to forgive yourself. The way *He* forgives you."

"God?" Jake's eyes lifted once more. "Someone like God isn't about to forgive me. Coach, it was my fault!"

"Have you told Him you're sorry?"

"Yes!" The pain intensified. "A dozen times that first night. But still . . . I need to pay my penalty. I wouldn't expect God or you or . . . or Mrs. Reynolds . . . or anyone else to forgive me until I've gone to prison for a long, long time."

"Why?"

"So I can make up for it."

"Make up for taking away my legs?" John's eyes showed the hint of a sparkle, and the corners of his mouth lifted. "You'd have to be in there an awful long time if that were true. Because I had some mighty fast legs, Daniels. Mighty fast."

Again, Abby wanted to clap or shout out loud. John was joking! Playing up on an old bit of banter he and Jake had exchanged since Jake was a middle-school boy. Back in the days when his parents would come over for the occasional Sunday dinner.

Abby could still hear them, still see them the way they'd been five years earlier. Jake's family would enter the house and John would welcome them. Jake would put himself toe-to-toe with John, his eyes wide. *You gotta race me, Coach; I'm getting faster!* And John — whom Jake had always called Coach — would give a soft laugh. *I don't know, Jake. I have some mighty fast legs.* To which Jake would raise an eyebrow and pretend to punch John's shoulder. *Come on, Coach, they're not that fast. Nothing like mine!*

Chills danced across Abby's arms as she understood. John was tossing Jake a life rope, a chance to be rescued from the waters of guilt.

Abby stood stone still, her eyes on the weeping boy. Suddenly the lines around his eyes and forehead eased.

"Come on, Coach —" his voice cracked, and a tear slid onto his cheek — "they weren't that fast. Nothing . . . nothing like mine."

"Thatta boy, Jake." John gave him a light smack on the knee. "I may be paralyzed, but I'm not dead. I don't want you hanging your head every time we see each other. Because then I lose twice."

"Twice?"

"My legs . . . and then you." John paused. "Don't do that to me, Jake. It'll be hard enough getting my routine down without wondering whether you're okay or not."

Once again Jake let the tears come. As he did, he looked twelve, and Abby felt her heart grow still softer toward him. Maybe she could forgive him, after all.

"But I'm so sorry. I gotta do something, Coach. Something to make it right."

"Listen, Jake . . . every time you walk into an auditorium packed with teenagers and tell them your story, I want you to remember something." His voice dropped a notch. "I'm with you, Daniels. Right there beside you, step by step. And that'll make everything right."

Twenty-one

Nicole was nauseous nearly every day.

Not because of morning sickness. That had passed weeks ago. Now that she was almost halfway through her pregnancy, the sick feeling came from one thing: it was almost Christmas, and her dad still couldn't feel anything in his legs or feet.

The moment she'd heard the news about his paralysis that terrible afternoon in the hospital waiting room, Nicole prayed. Since then she'd spent hours pleading with God, believing He would work a miracle in her father. She had no idea how it would come about, just that it would. It *had* to. Every time she prayed about something and had this feeling, things went the way they were supposed to.

But as the days passed, her prayers slowed and finally stopped. In the process she'd come to grips with something that turned her stomach.

Things didn't always go the way they were supposed to.

If they did, she wouldn't have gotten pregnant for another three years, her parents would never have argued, never considered divorce. More to the point, Christians wouldn't lose loved ones to illnesses and accidents. They'd never suffer from depression or pain or money troubles.

They'd certainly never be paralyzed.

No, if things always went the way they were supposed to, they'd never have anything but blue skies until the day — as a very old person — they would lie down at night and wake up in the arms of Jesus.

But that wasn't how it worked. And the truth of that left her with a sort of sick feeling about her faith, a feeling as new as marriage and loss and disappointment.

Maybe God intended to use her father's injuries as a way to change the kids at Marion High School. Nicole didn't like that option, but it was a possibility. She'd heard rumors from Kade — who still kept in touch with a few kids at Marion High. Talk around school was that since her dad's accident attitudes had improved and kids were kinder than they'd been before. There was even talk of some sort of

"Coach Reynolds town meeting," though neither Nicole nor Kade had mentioned that to their father.

He had enough on his mind, what with learning to get around in a wheelchair and coming to grips with his injury.

If that's why God had allowed her father's injury, Nicole should have felt some sort of quiet peace, a sense that the Scripture in Romans was right, that all things really did work to the good for those who loved God.

But she didn't feel that way at all.

She just felt nauseous.

Her doctor had warned her that constant anxiety wasn't good for the baby. After that she'd made a promise to Matt and herself to spend more time reading Scripture and praying, trying to ease the stress.

But every time she tried to read a favorite verse or talk to God, she found herself thinking about the accident. Why had God allowed it? Couldn't her father have left the office five minutes earlier? Seconds later? After all her parents had been through, after their hearts and souls had finally come back together? After Dad had been going to church with them again?

The questions Nicole had for God outweighed the things she wanted to pray about, so her anxiety remained. It wasn't that she was angry at God, exactly. She just wasn't sure she could trust Him. The truth about these feelings was something she didn't share with anyone. Even herself.

Because the Nicole Reynolds she'd been until her dad's accident would never have doubted God. That old Nicole had been more aware of God's whispered voice, more reliant on Bible verses and prayer, than anyone in her family.

Only lately had Nicole finally understood the reason for her deep faith. It had nothing to do with believing she was better than the others, or somehow having a greater need than the others for God's peace and presence. No, that wasn't the reason at all.

The reason was Haley Ann.

Which was something else she hadn't shared with anyone.

No one knew she remembered losing her little sister. She might have been not quite two years old, but there were scenes from that sad day that stayed with her still, written with the indelible ink of a little girl's tears. Haley Ann had been sleeping in her crib, taking a nap, Nicole understood now. Most of the details were fuzzy, but Nicole could still close her eyes and see big men rushing into Haley Ann's room, working over her, trying to get her to breathe.

Everyone assumed that because Nicole was young, she didn't grieve back then. But Haley Ann was her sister! Her only sister. Nicole remembered one conversation she'd had with her mother about losing Haley Ann.

"She's in heaven now, darling." Her mother had been crying the way she did a lot back then. "But as long as you love God, you'll always be only a whisper away from her. Understand?"

Nicole had understood better than Abby could have imagined. If loving God was the way to be closer to Haley Ann's memory, she would do so with all her heart. And she had. Every month, every year . . . until now.

Now everything had changed, and the reason was obvious. She simply wasn't sure she could trust God anymore. Not with her deepest prayers and concerns. After all, she had prayed for the safety of everyone in her family. The very morning of the accident in fact. But that night, there she was, in the hospital beside her mother, wondering what had gone wrong.

Wondering where God had been when

they'd needed Him most.

The feelings she had about the entire matter only added to her anxiety. Even worse, Matt talked constantly about God's will this and God's best that and God's miraculous hand in saving her dad's life. He would find her at the most inopportune times — when she was working on a homework assignment or folding laundry or getting ready for school.

Two nights ago they'd had their first real fight over the issue. She'd been on the Internet looking for bargains on eBay.com when he came up behind her and massaged her shoulders. His tone was even gentler than his fingertips.

"Nicole, get off the computer."

She gave him a quick glance over her shoulder. "Why?"

"Because you're running."

"From what?" Her attention was back on the computer screen and the list of items there.

Matt breathed out in a sudden burst. "From everything. From talking to me . . . from your dad's situation . . . from your pregnancy." He hesitated. "From God."

Even now Nicole wasn't sure why his comments made her so angry. Words began tumbling out of her mouth before she could stop them. "Who are you to tell me what I'm running from?" She spun the chair around and glared at him. "Just because I don't want to delve into the deeper meaning on every topic doesn't mean I'm running."

"Praying with your husband isn't exactly delving into the deeper meaning, Nicole."

"Okay, fine. You want me to pray, I'll pray. But don't ask me to put my heart into it because I can't. Right now I need a little time before I go calling on God."

Matt had looked at her, clearly dumbfounded. "You don't sound anything like the girl I married."

"Thanks a lot."

"I'm serious. You used to talk about God constantly. Now you'd rather pretend He doesn't exist."

"That isn't it." She huffed. "It's just that there isn't a lot left for me to ask Him. Let my dad's legs be okay? Too late. Let us wait and have babies in a few years. Done deal. I'm not running, Matt. I guess I just don't see the point in praying."

Matt motioned to the computer. "And playing on eBay will help you work through that?"

"It's better than wasting every moment

praying when in the end God will do whatever He wants."

Matt had stared at her for a long time after that. When he spoke, his voice was quieter than before. "As long as one of us still believes in prayer, I want you to know something."

Nicole was silent, her cheeks burning.

"I'll be praying for you, Nicole. That God will help you remember who you are."

Since then his words had played in her head, easing their way across her heart. What was wrong with her anyway? She still believed in prayer, didn't she? After a lifetime of seeing God's answers, her life's situations now couldn't be enough to actually shake her faith, could they?

She slipped into a black stretch skirt and a white silk blouse. Her belly was protruding now, but not so much that she needed maternity clothes. She was grateful. It was Christmas Eve, and they were invited, along with Jo and Denny, to her parents for dinner. Matt's parents were already downstairs with Matt, waiting for her.

Nicole grabbed a pair of black hose, and as she slipped them on, her eyes fell on a Scripture plaque near their bed. It was a verse from Hebrews, one that had always been a favorite of Matt's.

"Let us fix our eyes on Jesus, the author and perfecter of our faith . . ."

The pantyhose fell still in Nicole's hands. Maybe *that* was her problem. She hadn't had her eyes fixed on Jesus much. Not since her father's accident. They'd been fixed on his injury, her pregnancy, and the sorrow and frustrations that went along with both.

But not on Jesus.

Wasn't there another Bible verse about God being the author . . . of something? Nicole closed her eyes for a moment, and it came to her. The author of life. That was it. God was called the author of life. And if He was the author, it was His decision whether some characters would go through life unscathed or whether they'd fall victim to a car wreck.

The idea didn't ease Nicole's burden. And it certainly didn't increase her desire to pray. If God was the author, then the book was already written. They could love God, and He could love them. But prayer wasn't going to change anything. Not if the pages had already been written.

"Nicole, are you ready?" Matt's voice carried up the stairs. They'd both apologized since the fight the other day, but nothing had been the same between them. Matt thought she'd changed, and she thought he'd become insensitive. It was one more thing to add to the list.

She stuck her head out the door. "In a minute."

"Hurry." He shot a look at the clock on the wall. "We're already late."

Nicole began working on her pantyhose again. "Merry Christmas to you, too." She hissed the words quietly, so Matt wouldn't hear her. As she did, she sat on the edge of the bed and raised one foot. She was pulling the hose up past her ankles when it happened.

Deep within her she felt a fluttering.

As though someone was tickling her from the inside. Nicole's heartbeat quickened, and she stayed still. Was that what she thought it was? Nearly a minute passed and it happened again. It felt like the paws of a sleepy kitten, tapping at her from somewhere behind her lower abdomen.

When it happened a third time, Nicole knew. It wasn't a kitten.

It was her baby. The baby she had never quite accepted, never quite been happy about. But now here this little child was, moving and stretching and becoming. The beautiful sunrise of vibrant joy exploded in

Nicole's heart. God was knitting a new life within her! How could she be anything but thrilled with that truth?

She hugged herself, wondering for the first time what the baby would be like. A boy or girl? Tall like Kade or bigger-boned like Matt? With her mother's intensity or her father's determination? Tears stung at her eyes, but she refused to cry. Whatever other problems she needed to work through, Nicole was suddenly ready to love this child within her.

And maybe one of these days she'd be ready to talk to God again, too.

The door burst open and Matt stared at her. "It's been five minutes, Nic. What're you doing?"

A single laugh bubbled up from Nicole's throat. "The baby . . ."

Matt entered the room and took a few steps closer, his expression blank. "What about the baby?"

"I felt the baby move, Matt." Another breathy chuckle slipped from her mouth. "Just a few little flutterings, but I'm sure that's what it was."

"Really?" The tension around Matt's eyes eased. He moved onto the bed beside her and lay his hand on her tummy.

"You won't be able to feel it." She covered his hand with hers. "It was soft. I would've missed it if I hadn't been sitting here."

Matt's eyes met hers. "You sound happy about it."

Had her disappointment been that obvious? Nicole's heart grieved at the thought. "Of course I'm happy." She leaned over and kissed him.

For a moment he looked at her, his eyes full of questions. But just when she thought he was going to ask her about prayer and God and her attitude, he smiled. "Let's get to your parents' house and tell them."

Nicole's love for Matt swelled as it hadn't in months. He wanted so badly to fix her, to make her feel and think and act the way she used to. But here, when he could have used this moment as a way of convincing her that God was working in her life, he'd been willing to wait. "Thanks, Matt. For not pushing it."

"I love you, Nic. No matter what you feel or think or believe." He reached for her hand. "When you're ready to talk, I'm here."

Abby was struggling.

It was Christmas Eve and the kids would

be there in five minutes, but nothing felt right. She took one last look in the mirror and sucked in a steadying breath. John's good days had outnumbered the bad this past week, and Abby thought she knew why. It had everything to do with seeing Jake Daniels. John's time in court that day to talk with the boy, laugh with him, offer him hope, had done more for John than any amount of therapy so far.

If only it had helped her. She just couldn't get past her anger, couldn't seem to download it so it didn't stay bottled up inside her, eating at the lining in her stomach.

Friends from church would call, but she'd tell them all the same thing: "We're doing great . . . thanks for praying . . . John's feeling better . . . getting used to the wheelchair."

If only she had the courage to tell it like it was: "I'm furious . . . disappointed . . . heartbroken. And not sure I like the idea of spending the rest of my life watching John pine away in a wheelchair."

She was supposed to be strong, determined, positive. That had always been her role, even when she and John had been facing a divorce. Now, it felt as though every person who called — whether they were a longtime friend or a student of John's — was looking for her to encourage and uplift them.

Why did everyone in her world depend on her to have a good attitude about John's injury? John . . . the kids . . . their family and friends . . . it was as though they'd all gotten together and decided, "Hey, if Abby's okay, everything's all right. We can breathe a sigh of relief and move on with life."

Being positive, at peace, was the right thing to do. The expected thing. No one would know how to act if Abby wept every time someone asked her about John. Or if she threw her hands in the air and told the truth about how she was struggling inside.

She studied her reflection once more.

Whatever was brewing in the basement of her heart, she'd have to hide it a while longer. It was Christmas, after all. And the entire family would expect her to be full of good cheer and pleasant conversation. Of course, last year she'd silenced her feelings about the trouble in their marriage, and it had only made things worse . . .

But this was different. She had to keep quiet now or none of them would survive.

She held her breath as she made her way out of the bedroom. Holding her breath was one way to keep from crying. *Let it go, Abby . . . don't think about your own feelings. Think of something else . . .* She blinked hard. Kade. That was it: she could think about Kade. At least things were going better with him. He had been meeting with a counselor from church ever since he'd been home on Christmas break. The other night Kade told Abby and John that he hadn't looked at any pornography, Internet or otherwise, since his discussion with John that day on the lake. Kade's counselor had asked Kade to study a couple who seemed to best illustrate true intimacy.

Kade had chosen Abby and John.

She reached the bottom of the stairs and could hear a chorus of voices in the next room. She turned the corner into the living room and was immediately greeted by Jo and Denny.

"Now, Abby, don't you just look like a Christmas angel." Jo took three giant steps and circled her arms around Abby in a quick hug. "I'm always telling Denny you look like an angel. You know . . . that blonde halo and all. But now I have to say I've never been more right about it." She elbowed Denny. "Isn't that right, Denny?"

The man had his hands in his pockets

and he gave a shy nod. "She's a pretty one; that's for sure."

"Thanks, guys. You look nice, too." Abby smiled. Compliments were wonderful. Too bad they didn't make her feel better. "Dinner's ready in the kitchen. Let's go find everyone else."

The meal was cheery and upbeat. Cinnamon candles burned on either end of the table and Abby had cooked a turkey for the occasion. John sat at the head of the table — not because he'd always sat there in the past, but because it was the only spot that would accommodate his wheelchair. Abby tried not to think about it.

"You know, Dad —" Kade finished a bite of mashed potatoes — "one of the guys at school told me his football coach spent the last five years of his career in a wheelchair. A muscle disorder or something."

Abby flashed a quick look at John, but he was nodding thoughtfully, his eyes on Kade. "I know. It wouldn't be impossible."

"So, you should do it." Kade set his fork down and leaned his elbows on the table.

"If things were different, I might."

Nicole wiped her mouth. "You mean the kids?"

"Yep. That and the parents." John shook his head. "My injury hasn't changed anything at school. Parents wanted my head, remember? I was about to be fired when the accident happened."

"Aw, Dad." Kade shook his head. "They never woulda fired you. You're too good for that."

"Doesn't matter." John took a long drink of water. "If the administration doesn't support what you're doing, it's not worth the effort."

"So you're quitting?" Kade's voice fell.

A sad smile lifted the corners of John's mouth. "I'll write the resignation letter sometime next month."

"Well, all I can say is whoever's at the top o' the heap at that school needs their head examined." Jo had finished her first plateful and was helping herself to more of everything. "Lettin' you get away'd be like hooking the biggest steelhead that side of the Mississippi and cuttin' it free before a single picture was snapped." She looked around the table. "Know what I mean?"

Sean paused, his fork midbite. "What's a steelhead?"

Even Abby laughed, though Jo launched into an explanation of the kinds of lakes where steelhead might be found and what sort of bait was best for catching them.

When they were finished eating, they exchanged gifts around the tree in the living room. One gift each on Christmas Eve. That was the family rule. And no sorting beneath the tree, either. First gift with your name on it was the one you opened.

Keeping with tradition, John was last. He chose a small package that happened to be from Jo and Denny. Wads of wrapping paper dotted the floor, and each of them sat beside a newly opened gift while they watched John open his.

At first, Abby couldn't make out what it was. Then as John opened the wrapper, she could see it clearly. It was a pair of gloves. The fingerless kind worn by serious bicyclists.

Or men in wheelchairs.

John slipped them on his hands and fastened the Velcro straps around his wrists. "These are great, guys. Thanks."

But even as he was thanking Matt's parents, Abby saw tears gathering in Nicole's eyes. Jo seemed to sense that somehow her gift was causing sadness around the previously happy circle. "See —" she waved her hands in the air — "Denny and I always think of John as active. Going here and there and making the rest of us look pretty lazy, if you know what I mean." She laughed once, but it rang hollow across the room.

Denny tried to rescue her. "What Jo's trying to say is that we figured John would be getting around more in the weeks to come. Maybe taking the chair around the track at school . . . something like that."

"Right, and the gloves . . . well, it's obvious what they're for. Otherwise John's hands would get plum tore up. All callused and blistered and banged up." She looked at Abby. "And we can't have that. Not on a man as nice-looking as John Reynolds, right, Abby?"

It was happening again. Everyone was looking to her to save the moment, to speak something encouraging and upbeat that would give the rest of them permission to cheer up. But this time she wasn't sure what to say. It wasn't Jo's fault. She and Denny had meant well with the gloves. One day very soon they'd probably come in handy.

But right now — with Christmas knocking on the door — Abby didn't want a reminder of John's handicap. She wanted packages of sweaters and scarves and cologne. Favorite books and CDs and candy.

Not gloves that would make it more comfortable to get around in a wheelchair.

When she couldn't think of anything to

say, Nicole spoke up. "Jo, they're perfect." She sniffed and wiped at a tear. "I think we're all a little sad that Daddy needs them. But still . . . they were very thoughtful."

"Definitely." John held up his hands, admiring them.

"Well, I didn't mean nothin' by it." Jo's chin dropped a bit. "Just wanted to keep his hands nice."

Sean stood and moved next to John. "They're cool, Dad. Can I wear them when I ride my bike?"

The group laughed and the tension dissipated as quickly as it had built. Abby exhaled softly. She was grateful. Her bank account of ways to look at John's situation in a positive light was running frightfully low.

And come spring, when John should be out on the football field running laps with his players, she was pretty sure she wouldn't have anything positive left to say at all.

Even if everyone she knew was counting on her.

John was the only one awake. He was staring out the front window thinking of Christmases past, when he heard a sound.

"Dad?" It was Sean. The boy's quiet footsteps approached from behind.

John turned and found his son's eyes in the dark. "I thought you were sleeping." He held an arm out, and Sean came to him.

"I can't."

Only then did John realize his younger son was crying. "Hey, buddy, what's wrong? You're not supposed to cry on Christmas Eve."

"I . . . I feel like everything's a mess."

John's heart broke for the boy. How little time they'd spent together since the accident . . . yet certainly the changes in their lives were affecting him, too. Obviously more than John had realized. "You mean because of my legs?"

Sean hung his head, his lips pursed. Even in the shadowy moonlight John could see anger in the young boy's eyes. "It isn't *fair*, Dad!"

John waited. Sean had always needed more time than their other children to share his feelings. Whatever torment the boy had gone through since the accident, John was grateful he was finally sharing his heart. "I'm listening."

"I know I shouldn't be thinking about myself." He shrugged and wiped at his eyes. "You're the one hurt. But still . . ."

"Still what?"

Sean lifted his eyes and met John's straight on. "What about *my* dreams, Dad? Have you thought about that?"

John wasn't sure what his son meant. "Your dreams?"

"Yeah." The boy crossed his arms, and it looked like he was barely containing the struggle within. "You coached Kade until he was a senior, but what about me? I'll be at Marion High in two years, remember? How can I play football for someone else?"

Realization washed over John's soul. Of course . . . why hadn't he thought about this before? In his busyness with rehabilitation and coming to grips with his altered life, John hadn't thought once about how his injury might affect Sean. They'd always talked about how John would coach Sean, too, the same way he'd coached Kade. But John hadn't known until now how much the boy had counted on the arrangement. Sean was only in sixth grade. To John, his younger son's football days seemed light-years away.

But to an eleven-year-old boy . . . they were right around the corner.

"Sean —" John tightened his hand around Sean's waist and hugged him closer

— "I'm so sorry, buddy."

Looking more like a child than he had in years, Sean hung his head and wept. They were tears John understood, tears of sorrow and frustration and guilt at what he obviously thought were selfish feelings. This time when he looked up, his eyes pleaded with John. "Didn't you hear Kade tonight? You can coach in a wheelchair, Dad. There's no rule against it or anything."

John gave the boy a sad smile. The situation was so much more complicated than that. But right now his son didn't need to hear a list of specifics and details. He needed a reason to believe things were going to be okay, that life would somehow, someway be good again even if he had to let go of this boyhood dream of his. *Give me something to say, God . . . something that'll restore the peace in his heart . . .*

Then it hit him. He cleared his throat. "I'll always be your coach, Sean. Whether I'm out there on the field or not."

Something changed in his son's expression. The anger and sadness wasn't gone exactly, but his gaze held the beginning of hope. "Really?"

"Of course. We'll work out together . . . learn plays together." John felt his enthusiasm building. It was true. He might hang up his Marion High whistle, but he'd never stop coaching his boys. Especially Sean, who had so many years of football ahead. "I'll teach you everything I taught Kade."

Sean stood a little straighter. The worry lines across his forehead relaxed some. "Even in a wheelchair?"

"Even in a wheelchair."

For a moment neither of them said anything, then Sean put his hand on John's shoulder and sucked in a quick breath. "Can I tell you something, Dad?"

John reached up and tousled the boy's sandy blond hair. "Anything."

"I'm so glad you didn't die."

Tears stung at John's eyes. Again he was struck by how little he and Sean had talked lately. They needed this . . . this and many more times like it. He grinned. "Me, too, buddy."

Sean leaned down and hugged him, and they held each other for a long while. Finally Sean stood up and yawned. "Well . . . I guess I'll go back to bed."

"Yeah . . . don't wanna catch Santa Claus sneaking around the living room."

The boy's giggle was like an infusion in John's soul. *Thank You, God . . . thank You for this time with my son.*

"G'night, Dad. I love you."

"Love you, too. See you in the morning."

Sean left, and for a long while John sat there, pondering their conversation. Sean would be a joy to coach, as quick and easy to teach as Kade had been. And John would most certainly make good on his promise, working with the boy whenever they had a chance. Not just because Sean had always wanted to learn from him, but because he finally understood.

Even though he was about to resign from coaching the Eagles, as long as he had Sean, he would still be a coach.

And that, all by itself, was the greatest Christmas present anyone could have given him.

Twenty-two

———◆———

John had been dreading the moment all winter.

By the first week of March, when grass began poking through the melting snow, he knew it was time. He hadn't heard from Herman Lutz or any of the other school administrators, but there was no point waiting another day. This was the beginning of the academic hiring period, and the school officials deserved to know. They weren't going to fire him — he'd guessed that much after a few conversations with other teachers. Not this year, anyway.

"They're worried about how it would look," one of the math teachers had told him. The man had overheard Herman Lutz talking with the principal in the office one day in January. "They said the public would come unglued if the school fired you now. Just a few months after you'd been paralyzed."

So the administration was willing to wait a year, but they still wanted him gone. Still didn't trust his character enough to believe he never would have allowed his players to drink or race cars if he'd known it was happening. And they still were willing to bow to the complaints of a few parents, rather than support him and the work he'd done at Marion High.

Yes, it was time to resign.

John asked Abby to help him dress warmly that day, two pairs of sweats and an extra sweatshirt. Then he bundled into his warmest jacket and grabbed his laptop computer.

"I've got a letter to write." He winked at Abby.

She waited a moment before answering him. "Okay. I'll be here if you need me."

He smiled, but it didn't fool her. By the time he moved out the door and into the backyard, they both had tears in their eyes. John stopped and surveyed the path ahead of him. Before the first snow, they'd hired a contractor to pour a cement pathway to the pier. Now it was cleared and salted, surrounded by remnants of ice on either side.

John filled his lungs with the sweet air of early spring. His therapy still hadn't yielded the results he prayed for, but he'd learned to be more independent. He could get to the pier by himself now. The doctor had prescribed a new chair for him, one with a firm brake in hand's reach. And his upper body was stronger than before, strong enough to propel himself up hills and ramp-ways.

Carrying his laptop on his knees, he made his way almost to the end of the pier where he set the brake firmly in place. As he opened the computer, he caught sight of his legs. They'd wasted away, just like the therapist had said. Before the accident they'd been twice the size of Kade's. Now they were smaller, thinner, and John knew it wouldn't be long until they were little more than skin and bones.

He flipped the computer screen up, hit the start button, and stared at the keyboard. When the program was ready, he opened a new document and waited, his fingers poised over the keys. What was he supposed to say? How could he put into words that he was ready to give up his lifelong passion?

He began to type.

To whom it may concern: This is to inform you that I am hereby resigning as varsity football coach at Marion High. As you know, I've been the Eagles coach since the school opened in 1985. In that time, I . . .

His fingers stopped.

In that time . . .

So much had happened since he'd taken the job at Marion. And even before that. When had he fallen in love with the game anyway? His eyes drifted up from the screen and gazed out across the lake. Wasn't it when he was just a baby? There were pictures of him holding a football before he could crawl.

Images flooded his mind, memories he hadn't walked through in more than a decade.

His dad's life had revolved around the game, much like Abby's father's always had. The two men had played at University of Michigan, where they'd become best friends.

John's father had gone into banking after college, but not Abby's. He'd coached the game, too.

"It's in my blood." He always grinned when he said that. "I wouldn't know what to do with myself if I wasn't around football."

That's how it had been for John. It didn't matter that his father rarely talked about his prowess on the field. When John was old enough to wear a uniform, he begged his parents to sign him up. From the moment he took his first down as a player, John knew he'd play the game as long as he lived.

An image came to him then . . . him and his family visiting Abby and her parents at their lakeside home in Lake Geneva, Wisconsin. He'd met Abby before, but that year he was seventeen and a senior in high school. She was a freshman, just fourteen.

But she was a football coach's daughter, and it showed in everything she did. She could throw and catch a ball better than most boys her age, and the two of them spent hours barefoot on the beach tossing the pigskin back and forth.

"You're not so bad for a girl," John had teased her.

She had held her head a bit higher. Older boys hadn't intimidated her, not when her father coached sixty of them every year at the high school. John knew the team often hung out at Coach Chapman's house, playing on the lake or eating barbecued chicken with her family.

Abby's response that afternoon was something that rang clear in his memory. She had stared at John, her eyes dancing. "And you're not so bad for a *boy*."

John had laughed hard, hard enough that eventually he took off after her, tickling her and letting her believe she could outrun him. The truth was he could run like the wind back then. Like his father, John had become a great quarterback and was being pursued by a dozen major universities — including their fathers' alma mater, Michigan.

One night that summer, the two families brought blankets down to the sandy shoreline and Abby's father built a bonfire. They sang songs about God. Not the usual silly campfire songs about chickens or trains comin' round the mountain, but sweet songs about peace and joy and love and a God who cared deeply for all of them. When the songs ended and the adults were lost in their own conversation, John moved next to Abby and poked her with his elbow.

"You got a boyfriend, little Miss Abby Chapman?" He grinned at her, imagining her in five years or ten. When she'd grown up some.

Again she kept her cool. "I don't need a boyfriend." She bumped his bare foot with her own.

He nudged her back. "That so?" A grin spread across his face.

"Yes." Her head raised another notch and she leveled her gaze straight at him. "Boys can be very immature." She studied him for a moment. "Let me guess . . . you've got a different girlfriend every week, right? That's how it is with Dad's quarterbacks."

John laughed out loud before he looked at her again and answered her question. "I guess I'm different."

Abby's eyes grew wide in mock amazement. "What? John Reynolds has no girlfriend?"

He reached for the football — one was seldom more than an arm's length away that entire summer — and tossed it lightly in the air a few times. "*This* is my girlfriend."

Abby nodded, eyes twinkling. "She'll make a great prom date, I'm sure."

He pushed her foot again and lowered his eyes with a wink. "Shhh. You'll offend her."

John blinked, and the memory disappeared.

After that summer, John was certain he would marry Abby Chapman one day. It wasn't something he made a conscious decision about, like deciding what college to attend or what discipline to major in.

Rather it was something that grew from his heart, a truth that simply was.

But since that had been a long way off, John had poured his heart and soul into his first love — football. Especially the following year when he accepted a scholarship to the University of Michigan.

John lifted his chin a bit and scanned the tops of the trees. How far could he throw the ball back then? Sixty yards? Seventy? He closed his eyes and remembered the feel of the earth beneath his feet, the explosive push with every step, as he flew out of the pocket, looking for a receiver downfield.

His parents never missed a game, but one contest would always stand out in his mind. It was at the end of his junior season, a game against Michigan's chief rival, Ohio State. Michigan won by three touchdowns that afternoon, and after the game John and his father had walked through one of the neighborhoods and found an old bench at Almondinger Park.

"It feels so good seeing you out there, son. Watching you lead that team the way I did all those years ago."

John's father was rarely in a pensive mood, but that afternoon was different. John kept quiet and let his father talk.

"Sometimes watching you is like watching myself, every step, every throw . . . as though I'm down there doing it all over again, living it all over again."

"There's nothing like it."

"No." His father had teared up then, something John had seen only a handful of times in his life. "Definitely not. Out there on the field . . . it's you and your team and the ball, living out a drama, a battle, so rich and powerful that only another player could understand."

"Yes, sir."

"And time's a thief, son. You only get so many downs, so many whistles. So many games. Before you know it, you'll be grown up and watching your own son play. Then you'll know what I mean."

Of course in the end, his father had been right. John's years of Michigan football flew by, and late in his last game as a senior, he snapped the ligaments in his knee. Though he'd had pro scouts calling earlier that year, they disappeared after his injury and no one had to tell him to look at the clock. The truth was as real as his impending graduation.

His football playing days were over.

John kept the tape of his last game handy in the file cabinet of his mind. He remembered suiting up in the locker room, bantering back and forth with his teammates and swapping barbs as though they had forever.

Four quarters later, John was huddled on the bench, his knee swathed in three rolls of Ace bandaging, when the final whistle blew. Even now he remembered how strange it felt. How right up until that whistle, he and his teammates had just one thought in mind: beat Illinois.

They'd needed a victory in order to get a bowl bid that year. But after John's injury, Illinois ran a punt back for a touchdown and Michigan never regained the lead. Only then, in the sad silence that followed, did the reality sink in.

It was over. The game, the season . . . and John Reynolds's career.

John had glanced up at the stands, at the people filing out, and wondered what they were thinking. Better luck next year, maybe? Or what's wrong with the Wolverines? Whatever their thoughts, only one man knew how John was feeling that afternoon . . . how it felt to play a game for sixteen straight seasons and then have it be over in as much time as it took a referee to blow a whistle. Only one man knew how John's heart had ached that day, the man who hugged him an hour later after he'd turned in his uniform and showered and changed. A man who said nothing while he quietly grieved the fact that it was all finally and suddenly over.

His father.

John swallowed and remembered how proud his dad had been when he called him that afternoon in 1985 and told him the news.

"They hired me, Dad! I'm the head coach at Marion High."

"Marion, huh?"

"Yep. It's a brand-new school, and I've got a truckload of ideas. I'm going to build a program here, Dad. Something new and different and better than anything in the state."

"New programs are hard, son. Have you talked to Abby's father?"

"Not yet. And you're right." John had been barely able to contain his enthusiasm. "I know it'll be hard. But I can't let that bother me. We have good kids in this town, good teachers. A good administration. We'll start at the bottom, and in a few years we'll be league contenders. After that, who knows?"

"Is Abby excited?"

"She's happier than I am. She said she'll

write press releases about the team for the paper and start a booster club. And when Kade's old enough, I'll take him with me to practice."

His father had chuckled. "Kade's only two, son."

"But he's already walking. I'll let him come to practice with Abby even this year."

"Okay, but don't forget what I told you."

"About what?"

"About how it feels to watch your son play. I hope I'm there to see it happen." His dad laughed again. "Your day's coming."

And so it had . . . but not in time for his father to see it. Four years after John took the job at Marion, his father died of a heart attack. Only Abby knew the extent of John's loss — how he'd lost not just a father, but a mentor and coach. And most of all, a friend.

Coaching football was the cure for John's grief. It turned out to be almost as great a thrill as playing the game. But there was one very wonderful difference. A player's days were numbered. A few years in high school, a few years in college for the talented ones.

Not so for a coach.

Every year a group of teary-eyed seniors would play their last football game for Marion High. Then, come fall, John and his staff would be back, welcoming in a new crop of freshmen and making plans for another season. John planned to coach until he retired. At least.

That was true even through the hard years at Marion, the years when parents grumbled that he wasn't winning games fast enough and that maybe a different man should have been hired for the job. But those seasons led to John's first state title in 1989.

By then everyone in Marion loved John. And in 1997, Kade joined the team. Only then did John get a true sense of what his father had been talking about that day at Almondinger Park.

Watching Kade play football left John just one regret — that his father hadn't lived to see it. Kade was everything his father and grandfather had been, and then some. He was taller, quicker, and lightning fast on his release of the ball. John couldn't count the times he'd stopped in his tracks as he watched Kade line up, watched him bark out an audible and then speed to the back of the pocket, his arm ready to fire the ball at a receiver.

His father had been right.

Watching Kade, he could almost feel the pads sliding against his shoulders, smell the rich grass beneath his feet. It was a heady experience, one that was second only to being out there and playing the game himself.

The current problems at Marion hadn't started until that past summer, a few months after Kade's graduation.

John shifted his gaze back to the water.

What would his father have thought about the attitudes among his players and parents this year? Would it have jaded him? Made the game seem less somehow? And then there was the thing John liked to think about least of all.

How would his father have handled John's resignation?

The man would have been crushed to see John in a wheelchair, to know that John would never walk or run again. And certainly he would have been saddened to know that parents were trying to get John fired. But how would he have felt knowing John was going to step down as varsity coach? Walk away without looking back?

John drew a deep breath and let his eyes fall to the computer keyboard once more. His father would have understood. Because he would have known John would have given up coaching only for one reason: if the game had changed.

And it had.

Yes, his father would've supported him completely. In fact, somewhere in heaven, his dad would most certainly know how hard the letter of resignation was to write. And as John returned his fingers to the keyboard, as he found the strength to do what he never thought he'd do, he felt convinced of one thing.

His father must be aware of all that had happened and even now, in the most difficult moment of John's football career, his dad was sitting on the fifty-yard line of heaven, cheering for him the way he'd done as far back as John could remember.

Twenty-three

John was just finishing up the letter when Abby joined him on the pier.

Her eyes were bloodshot and pensive, like she'd been crying. She sauntered out toward him and pulled a bench up next to his wheelchair. "Finished?"

"Yep." He typed his name. "Just now."

She stared out at the lake. "It's the end of a chapter."

"It is." He reached for her hand and laced his fingers between hers. "You okay?"

Her teeth stayed clenched, but a tired sigh eased through her lips anyway. She turned to him, and he saw something that hadn't been there for months: sheer, undeniable anger. Her mouth opened, and for a while, nothing came out. Then she narrowed her eyes. "No, I'm not okay."

For a long time he'd suspected things weren't as well with Abby as she tried to make it seem. He asked her about her feelings now and then, but always she said the same thing. She was fine . . . she was grateful . . . she was happier than ever. So glad that he'd lived . . . so glad their marriage was back to what it had been when they were younger.

All of it sounded good, just not exactly real. Not that John didn't believe her. Somewhere in her soul, Abby meant every positive thing she said. But she had always been intense, and it had seemed strange to John that in this — their greatest physical challenge as a couple — she would be passive and accepting. He waited for her to continue.

"John, I've done everything I can to make this easy for you and the kids and . . . well, easy for everyone we know." She shrugged and leaned forward, digging her elbows into her thighs. "But I'm not sure I can do it anymore."

Panic flashed across the horizon of John's heart. She couldn't do it anymore? Where was this going? "Okay. You wanna explain?"

Abby clenched her fists and gritted her teeth as she continued. "I'm so mad, John! I'm so mad I can't even stand it." She opened her hands and made circles with them. "It's like a tornado building up inside of me. Every day I'm madder than the day before."

John chose his words carefully. "Who are you mad at?"

"I don't know!" Abby's tone was loud, seething. "I'm mad at you for staying at school that night when you should've been home." She stood and paced to the end of the pier and back, her arms crossed tight in front of her. "I'm mad at Jake for hitting you, and at the doctors for not being able to make you better. I'm mad that no one thinks I might be mad about this whole thing." She let her hands fall to her sides. "And I'm mad at God for letting it happen."

John bit his lip. "You're mad at me?"

Something in his question caught her off guard, and though she tried to contain it, a single ripple of laughter spilled through her teeth. Immediately, she regained her composure. "John, don't."

"Don't what?"

"You're supposed to ask me about the last part . . . about being mad at God."

"I don't know." John lifted one shoulder and leaned back in his chair. "I can understand about being mad at God. I mean, I get mad at God sometimes." He angled his head, his eyes narrow. "But me? Come on, Abby, what'd *I* do?"

She exhaled hard. "You should've come home with me, that's what." She gave him a light push on his shoulder. "Then none of this would've happened."

"Oh . . . well . . . I guess that makes sense."

"Never mind, you big jerk. This is supposed to be my time to get angry." Abby made a sound that was more laugh than cry, and she pushed him again. This time he caught her hand and pulled her onto his legs. She slid the laptop computer out from beneath her and set it on the pier. At the same time he released the brake on his wheelchair.

"John!" She let loose a scream. "What're you doing? We'll both fall in the lake."

He gripped the wheels and whirled the chair around just before they went over the edge of the pier. "What's this? No trust from my fair maiden?"

She grabbed a handful of his shirt and he grinned. "John, stop! You've lost your mind."

Instead, he wheeled the two of them to the far end of the pier, turned once more and let gravity pull the chair back down the wooden slats toward the water. Abby screamed again and tried to break free, but John held her firmly in place, one hand around her waist, one hand on the wheel of his chair. "Take it back."

They were halfway down the pier and moving fast. "What?" Abby's voice was a shrill mix of terror and exhilaration.

"Tell me you're not mad at me."

"Fine!" The water was closing in on them. "I'm not mad at you."

In a single, fluid motion, as gracefully as he'd once thrown a football, John grabbed both wheels and slowed the chair into a controlled spin. When they'd come full circle, he set the hand brake and wrapped both hands around Abby. Her eyes were wide, her body heaving to catch her breath.

"That was the craziest thing you've ever done, John Reynolds." She pushed his shoulder once more, this time harder than before. "What if you hadn't stopped in time?"

"It was under control, Abby." His tone was soft, the teasing gone. "Just like your emotions these past few months."

She froze and he could see the tears form across the surface of her eyes. "It was that obvious?"

"Of course."

A tired sigh worked its way up from somewhere deep within her. "I was afraid to tell you how I felt."

"Why? You've never been afraid before.

Even when we weren't getting along."

"Because —" she let her head fall against his chest — "I was afraid you'd never recover if you knew how upset I was."

"No." He waited, choosing his words with careful precision. "I'll never recover if you can't be yourself, Abby. We can't pretend everything's okay, don't you see? There'll be days when you can't take another minute of helping me get dressed . . . days when you want to scream you're so angry. But there'll be days when I feel the same way. No matter how upbeat we pretend to be. The only way we'll survive this is if we're honest. Do you understand?"

"John . . ." The tears spilled onto her cheeks. "I'm so mad this happened to you. It's not fair. It's just not fair."

"I know, honey." He cradled her close, stroking her back. "I know."

She brought her face up against his and dried her tears on his cheeks. "I want to dance again. Don't you ever feel that way?"

"All the time." He released the hand brake again and wheeled her once more to the far end of the pier.

"John . . . what're you doing?" Her body grew taut in his arms. "Not another trip down! We'll fall in for sure this time."

"No, Abby —" they reached the top of

the pier and he turned so the wheelchair was facing the water — "just lean back against me and relax."

She hesitated and for a minute he thought she might jump off. "You're serious?"

"Yes." He patted his chest. "Come on, lean back."

"What're we doing?"

"It's sort of a tango dance step. Something I've been practicing." He eased Abby back against him so they were both facing forward. "Okay . . . now you've gotta let everything go . . . your anger, your frustration . . . all of it. The dance doesn't work otherwise."

She giggled and the sound did wonders for his soul. "Okay. I'm ready."

John released the hand brake and the chair began rolling down the pier toward the water. Abby's laughter grew louder and she pressed her back against him. "It's kinda fun when you're not scared."

"The tango always is."

"Perky Paula would be proud."

The chair picked up speed, and their laughter built until, a few yards from the water, John slowed the chair and turned it for one final spin. After that he wove the chair back and forth, his voice a gentle whisper in Abby's ear. "Do you hear it?"

"Mmmmm." Her soft moan sounded

deep against his chest. "I think so."

"The dance steps might change, Abby —" he kissed her earlobe — "but the music's still playing."

They stayed that way, swaying to the distant breeze and the rustling of still bare branches, until finally Abby shifted herself onto one of his knees and kissed him, long and slow. "You know what?"

"What?"

"I'm not angry anymore. At least for now."

"See . . . the tango, Abby." He brushed his nose against hers. "Works every time."

"No —" their lips met again and again — "your love works every time."

John was about to kiss her once more when it happened. It was so brief, so fleeting, John knew it might be nothing. But then . . . he paused, going stone still. What else could cause it to happen?

Abby drew back a few inches. "What is it, John? You're scaring me."

He gulped and concentrated on the place where he'd felt it. Then, as though God wanted him to know it wasn't a fluke or some figment of his imagination, he felt it again. Sort of a twinge or a burning sensation in his big toe. A place where he hadn't felt anything since the accident.

"Abby, you're not going to believe this."
He looked straight at her, seeing past the
surface to the heart of this woman he
loved.

"What? Tell me." Abby leaned back further, looking down the length of him. "Is
something wrong?"

"No." He pointed to his feet, his heart
thudding hard against the wall of his chest.
"Just now, just a few seconds ago . . .
something happened. Something I can't
explain."

"What was it?" She climbed off him and
stood, studying his legs.

Suddenly he realized that what he was
about to say would sound ludicrous.
Maybe it was only phantom pain, something he'd read about where months or
even years after paralysis a person might
have the memory of sensation.

He couldn't say something that would
build false hope only to destroy it when
they found it wasn't so. He'd tell her soon,
but not yet. Abby was staring at him,
waiting. *Think, John . . . come on . . . make
something up.*

"Well . . ." He smiled big at her. "I think
we invented a new dance step."

The wind left Abby's lungs in a rush.
"John, I thought you were hurt . . . like

maybe you couldn't breathe or something."

He chuckled, hiding the excitement welling in his soul. "Nope. Don't you know, Abby? Dancing is good for the lungs." He patted his chest. "After a routine like the one we just did, I'll be breathing good for days."

"You're such a teaser." Abby reached for his hand, and together they made their way up the pier and toward the house. "You shouldn't do that. I really thought something was wrong."

They were halfway up the yard when it happened again. This time John had no doubt about what he was feeling. This was no phantom pain, no memory of previous sensation. He felt a burning twinge in his toe. And this time something else happened. Something he could barely keep to himself.

His toe moved!

John had no idea what that meant or why it was happening. But he had the strangest sense that something — or Someone — was working on his spine. It didn't feel like the hands of a doctor or a therapist.

It felt like the very fingers of God.

Twenty-four

—◦◦◦—

Chuck Parker had just walked in the door when the call came in.

He was an insurance broker, and this past winter had been busy — busier than any in his life. Not only was business booming, but with Casey's driver's license suspended for a year, Chuck or his wife had to drive the boy everywhere he went.

The worst part about being so busy was that Chuck hadn't had time to stage the meeting. Ever since finding out about Coach's paralysis, Chuck had wanted a group discussion at school about the way they'd handled Coach Reynolds this past season. He'd made a handful of phone calls, but no meeting had materialized. The trouble was time. With so much on his plate, the idea had simply gotten away from him.

But no worries. As long as he and the other parents had backed off from pressuring Herman Lutz, Coach Reynolds's job was safe. Maybe they didn't actually need a meeting. When Coach returned next fall, certainly he'd see that everyone had changed after what had happened. The players, the students. Even the parents.

The phone rang three times before Chuck grabbed it. "Hello?"

"Mr. Parker? This is Sue Diver down at Marion High."

Sue Diver . . . Chuck wracked his brain. Oh, right. Sue. The secretary at school. Carried a whole-life policy he'd written up for her back in '98. He glanced at his watch. He had three evening appointments starting in thirty minutes. "Hey, Sue . . . what's up?"

"A letter came into the office today." Her voice was low, troubled.

"Okay . . ."

"I don't know if I'm supposed to be telling you this."

"I'm sure it's fine, Sue. Otherwise you wouldn't have felt the need to call."

His words seemed to work. He could hear her take a quick breath. "It's a resignation letter from Coach Reynolds. He's resigning effective immediately. Says that the game has passed him by . . . and that

378

the parents no longer respect him."

What? Chuck felt as though the floor beneath him had given way. Why hadn't he scheduled the meeting sooner? Now it was too late. If Herman Lutz read the letter, he'd have Coach Reynolds's job posted on the state listing in twenty-four hours. Probably believing it was what everyone wanted.

Only that wasn't true at all. Not anymore.

He closed his eyes and pinched the bridge of his nose between his thumb and forefinger. "I'm gonna need some phone numbers, Sue. Can you get me the names and numbers of all the guys on the team?"

"I think so."

"Good." He looked at his stack of appointment files. "I'll make the calls tonight. What's the next available time on the school calendar?"

The sound of rustling paper filled the background. "Today's Monday, let's see . . ." More muffled paper sounds. "How about Thursday night?"

Chuck looked at his calendar. He had four appointments scheduled for that night. "Perfect. Let's set it for seven o'clock. In the auditorium."

"Okay. I'll run it by the administration, but it shouldn't be a problem. Parents are allowed to use the building for school-related meetings."

Sue sounded worried, like she was trying to convince herself. But it didn't matter. After months of procrastinating, Chuck had the meeting scheduled. Now all he needed were the phone numbers. "You have those numbers nearby?"

"Uh . . . can I fax you the list?"

"Absolutely." Chuck rattled off his fax number. "I'll be waiting. And, Sue, thanks for the tip. We'll have to get together one of these days and see if we can't upgrade your policy."

"Sure, Mr. Parker. Listen, I have to go."

The moment Chuck hung up, his fax line began to ring. Chuck made three quick calls to cancel his appointments. Then, when he had the phone list in hand, he took a deep breath and began to call.

John refused to get Abby's hopes up.

But that night, before they went to bed, he casually mentioned that he needed to see the doctor. Soon, if possible.

"Why?" Abby had helped him into bed, and now she was getting ready.

"I'm just concerned about my legs."

John forced himself to look relaxed. "They're too thin."

"Honey . . ." Abby stopped and gave him a sad look. "The doctor said that would happen. It's normal."

John searched for a way to convince her. "Not this thin . . . and not this fast." He pressed the blankets down against his legs. As he did, his right toe moved just a bit. "I'm wasting away, Abby. The doctor needs to hear about it."

"Really?" A puzzled look came over her face. "Well, if you think so. I'll call Dr. Furin in the morning."

The next day after breakfast John was drinking coffee in the kitchen when Abby found him. "He can see you at eleven today."

"Good." He blew at the steam rising from his cup. "I'm sure there's something he can do."

"Mind if I drop you off?" Abby was a blur of motion, straightening the kitchen and sorting through a stack of papers on the counter. "We need a few things at the store."

"Sure. Fine . . . I'll be in the waiting room whenever you get back." John couldn't believe his good fortune. The last thing he wanted to do was talk about his toes moving in front of Abby. As hard as the past few months had been on her, there was no point getting her hopes up now.

Two hours later, John was in the examination room when Dr. Furin walked in. "John . . . I understand you're worried about the wasting process in your legs."

John gave a short laugh. "Actually, that's not it at all. I just . . ." He reined in his enthusiasm so he could think more clearly. "I couldn't tell Abby the real reason I wanted to see you. I didn't want to get her hopes up."

"Okay." Dr. Furin set his clipboard down near the sink. "What's the real reason?"

"Doc —" John's smile worked its way up his cheeks — "I'm feeling something in my right toe." John held up one hand. "Not constantly and not a lot. But several times yesterday and again today. Sort of like a burning feeling, a flash of pain, maybe. And a few times I've felt the toe move."

Dr. Furin's mouth hung open. "You're serious?"

"Completely. You're the only one I've told."

The doctor stood and paced to the window and back, taking slow, deliberate steps. "When we checked your X rays the first time, it looked almost as though you were one of the lucky ones. Your break was in an area where people sometimes regain feeling. But usually that happens within a few days, after the swelling goes down."

He paced a bit more, stroking his chin and staring vacantly at the floor. "Your feeling didn't come back, so we took more pictures, did more tests. And after that it looked like I was wrong. Like the break was just a hair into the area where paralysis is permanent."

John studied the doctor, trying to understand. "So, why am I feeling something in my right toe?"

"In all my years working with people who've injured their spinal cords, I've never treated a patient whose break fell so close to the dividing line. A fraction higher, you walk again. A fraction lower, you're in a chair for the rest of your life. But maybe . . ."

John waited until he couldn't stand it another minute. "What?"

"Recent research has shown that in a few rare cases, a break is so close to the separating line that surgery can be done to wire the spinal cord back together. Sometimes, after surgery, feeling can be restored. Even when it appeared that a person was paralyzed for life."

The news was more than John had hoped for. His hands shook as he stared at Dr. Furin. "And you think maybe I might be one of those people?"

"We'll have to do tests, but if I remember right, the first symptom is feeling in one or more toes. And I'm already certain your break happened in the area where research is being done."

John wanted to shout, to raise a fist in the air and holler at the good news. Instead he stayed quiet and turned his thoughts heavenward. *God . . . thank You. Thank You for this second chance.* He couldn't wait to begin the tests. Whatever needed to be done, he wanted to do it. Because if a surgery might restore feeling to his legs, he was ready to go under the knife that afternoon.

"Can you stay awhile?"

John laughed. "Operate on me now, Doc! I'm ready."

"You need to know something." Dr. Furin frowned. "Even if you're a candidate for the surgery, there's no guarantee it'll work. The research is too new. So far it looks like only about half the people who undergo surgery ever regain feeling in their extremities."

"Look, Doctor, those odds are a whole lot better than what I had before I came in here. When can we start testing?"

"I'd like to take more pictures and run a few more specific tests — tests that must be done in the hospital. Normally it takes weeks to schedule these types of pictures, but I had a cancellation today." He hesitated. "I do think you need to tell your wife what's going on. The tests will take most of the afternoon, and she'll need to drive you to the hospital so you can take them."

John nodded. How would she react? Would she be afraid of being disappointed? Anxious? Excited? Either way, the doctor was right. It was time for her to know.

Dr. Furin took a set of X rays, and thirty minutes later, John was in the examination room when Abby walked in. "Sorry." She leaned over and kissed his cheek. "It took longer than I thought."

"Abby . . . sit down." He motioned to a folding chair against one wall. "We need to talk."

Her face went slack, and he knew it was from fear. But she did as he asked, and when their knees were nearly touching, she swallowed hard. "What's wrong? Don't tell me there's something else."

He couldn't keep her waiting another minute. "Abby, yesterday . . . when I told you something strange was happening . . ."

She thought back and then remembered. "When you invented that new dance step?"

"Right." He reached out and she took his hand in hers. "Well, that wasn't exactly what was going on."

Her chin fell a little, but she said nothing.

"The truth is, I was getting pains in my right toe." His voice grew soft. "I was feeling it, Abby. I really was. Then when we walked into the house, my toe moved." He glanced around the room, looking for a way to describe how it had felt. "I thought maybe I was imagining it . . . like maybe it hadn't really happened. But then I felt it again before we went to sleep and again this morning."

"That's why you wanted to come today?"

John nodded. "I had to tell Dr. Furin. Because everyone had told me I'd never have feeling like that again. Phantom pain, maybe. But not real feeling. And there was no doubt this was real pain . . . real movement."

"So —" Abby ran her tongue over her bottom lip — "what'd Dr. Furin say?"

John did his best to explain the situation, how once in a rare while a certain type of broken neck could be operated on and feeling, possibly restored. "It's still a long shot, Abby. He wants to do more tests this afternoon. If I'm a candidate for surgery, he'll know after that."

Abby's mouth hung open, her eyes wide as she took in the news. She leaned forward, grabbing his chair with both hands. "You're *serious?*"

"Completely." John loved the hope in Abby's eyes. *Please, Lord . . . get us through this. Give us a miracle.* There was no audible answer, not even a still, silent whisper in his soul, but John was suddenly overwhelmed with an indescribable peace.

"Okay, then. Let's get you over to the hospital."

The tests took five hours and were as exhausting as they were long. Abby contacted Nicole midway through the day and asked her to pick up Sean when school was out.

"What's going on?"

"I'll tell you later." Abby hurried through the conversation, anxious to rejoin John. "I promise."

Dr. Furin arrived near the end of the day and began reading the results with a team of spinal cord specialists. Finally, at six o'clock that evening John's doctor met them in the hospital lobby.

John prided himself on being able to read a person's expression, but Dr. Furin could've made his living playing poker. It was impossible to tell the results from the look on his face. He motioned for them to follow him to a quieter corner where they wouldn't be distracted.

Abby held tight to John's hand, so tight he could feel the pulse in her fingertips. "What'd you find out?"

Dr. Furin allowed just the hint of a smile. "John's a candidate for surgery. His injury is almost textbook perfect, the kind they've done research on."

For a moment, John let his head fall. He'd been granted a second chance! An opportunity, no matter how slim, to have his legs again. It was more than he could imagine, more than he could bear.

When he looked up, he saw that Abby had covered her mouth with her free hand. Small soblike sounds were coming from her throat, but her eyes were dry. She was probably in shock, like him. Who'd have ever thought it possible? After so many months of being paralyzed?

John had never heard of such a thing. "When can we do the surgery?"

"No time soon." Dr. Furin folded his hands and leaned forward. "I'll want the nation's top experts to perform the operation. I'll assist, but since it's their research, they should do the surgery."

"They'll come here?" John still couldn't believe he was having this conversation. "I thought with specialists you have to go wherever they're based."

"They do most of their work in Arizona, but they're willing to travel for an extraordinary case. I'd say yours fits that description."

"So when, Doctor?" Abby's palms were damp. "How soon?"

"It's March now. I'd say four weeks. Sometime in mid-April. It'd probably take that long to pull the team together."

"Is there anything we can do between now and then?" John eased his arm around Abby's shoulders and hugged her close. The feeling of hope was so strong it was almost a physical assault. If the doctor hadn't been there, John would've pulled Abby onto his lap and held her until they were ready to talk about the possibilities.

"Yes." Abby's teeth chattered. "Anything we can do so the surgery will be more successful. A special diet or exercises? Anything?"

"Yes." Dr. Furin looked from Abby to John, and back again. "In a situation like this, there's one thing I'd recommend." He paused and his eyes shifted to John's once more. "Go home and pray. Have your kids and your friends and your family pray. Get the whole town praying. Pray for us . . . pray for yourself . . . pray for a miracle. After that we'll put you under the knife and do our best. It's the only chance you have."

Dr. Furin explained a bit more about the operation, and then he left. The moment he was gone, John turned to Abby and held out his arms. She climbed on his lap like a child who'd been lost for a week. Then, unconcerned with whoever else might be in the waiting room or passing by in the hallways, John and Abby brought their heads together and prayed. Not just because it was doctor's orders, but because a miracle was standing on the front porch of their lives. And John intended to beg God night and day to open the door and let it in.

Jake Daniels had a funny feeling about his mom and dad.

His hearing was in one week, the one where he and his attorney would agree to plead guilty to a list of charges, things A.W. and the district attorney had agreed on. His dad had extended his leave of absence from work and was still staying at the hotel in town. But Jake wondered if sometimes he might be really sleeping on the sofa downstairs.

There were nights when his dad was there, talking to his mother, long after Jake turned in. And in the mornings, his father would be in the kitchen making coffee. The whole situation felt strange. After all, his folks were divorced. But sometimes — when Jake wandered downstairs before breakfast and found his dad in the kitchen — it was sort of nice to pretend that his family had never really split up. Or that they'd somehow gotten back together.

It was possible, wasn't it? After all, they were out together tonight.

Jake flopped down on his bed just as the phone rang. He caught a glimpse of the alarm clock on his dresser. Nearly nine o'clock. Only a few people could be calling this late. His attorney, or his mother.

In fact, Jake was almost positive it was his mom. Lots of times when his mother was out late with his dad, she'd call and give him some kind of explanation. Dinner was served late . . . or they'd gotten into a long conversation.

Jake didn't care.

As long as they were together, there was a chance they'd work things out. He stretched across his bed and grabbed the receiver.

"Hello?"

"Jake . . . Casey Parker."

Casey Parker? "Hey." Jake sat straight up and dropped his face in his hands. He hadn't talked to Casey since the accident. "What's up?"

"I shoulda called you sooner." There was a hitch in Casey's voice, like he was trying not to cry. "Listen, Jake. I'm sorry. About asking you to race and all. Really, man. I'm . . . I don't know what to say."

Jake searched his mind, trying to imagine why Casey would call now. "We need to move on, I guess."

"You're out at that continuation school, right?"

"Right. It's okay. I've got straight As."

"You gonna get to come back to Marion in the fall?"

It was the question his mother asked him at least once a week. The counselor had said it was okay, as long as he wasn't in a juvenile detention center. By then Jake would be finished with his mandatory house arrest — a time when he wasn't allowed to go anywhere but to continuation school and home again. If he wasn't locked up, he'd be involved in community service, telling teens at other schools why they needed to avoid street racing.

Everyone seemed to think he'd be better off at Marion in the fall, spending his senior year at his own school, being a living reminder to his peers that racing could have tragic consequences. But Jake wasn't sure. It was one thing to talk with Coach Reynolds in a courtroom. It would be another entirely to watch him wheeling his way around Marion High.

"I'm not sure."

"Yeah, well. I don't blame you. It's tough being at school." Casey hesitated. "Coach is still at home. Everyone says he'll be back in the fall."

"Yep." Jake felt sick to his stomach. Where was the conversation going? "Hey, thanks for calling. I gotta get some rest before —"

"Wait." Casey's voice was urgent. "That's not why I called."

"Okay."

"We're having a meeting for Coach Reynolds."

"A meeting?" Jake's heart skipped a beat. "What kind of meeting?"

"I guess Coach sent in a resignation letter, saying he was done with football because he didn't have —" Casey's voice cracked some and it was a while before he could speak again. "He didn't have the support he needed."

Jake's heart broke at the news. Not only did Coach have to deal with his injury, but he had to live with the fact that right before he'd gotten hurt, the parents had ganged up against him. "What's the meeting for?"

"A lot's changed since Coach got hurt, Jake. We've had a chance to . . . I don't know, maybe look at ourselves a little closer. I think we realized — even the parents — that it wasn't Coach after all. It was us. You know what I mean?"

"I do. So it's a good meeting?"

"Absolutely. Anyone who wants Coach to stay with the Eagles next year is supposed to come and talk. The guys'll start spreading the word tomorrow at school. I think a lot of kids are gonna go. A lot of parents, too."

Jake was certain he could get permission from the judge to attend. He had just one question. "Has anyone invited Coach Reynolds?"

"Well . . ." Casey paused. "We were kind of hoping you could do that."

After all that had happened, Jake felt nothing but honor at the chance to call Coach Reynolds and invite him to the meeting. "I'll do it as soon as I hang up."

"Okay. The meeting's Thursday night at seven."

"See ya there."

Jake hung up and imagined Coach Reynolds surrounded by a huge room full of people who loved him. The thought gave Jake more peace than anything had in months. He smiled to himself, thinking of what he'd like to say if he could get up the courage. Then he did something he never expected to do again as long as he lived.

He dialed Coach Reynolds's phone number and waited.

Twenty-five

The Marion High auditorium was filled with police officers.

Chuck Parker took the microphone and started to talk, but the officers threw things at him and shouted for John. Slowly, uncertainty in his eyes, John wheeled himself up onto the stage, but the entire auditorium booed him. The moment he reached for the microphone, a dozen officers rushed the stage and handcuffed him. One of them looked at the crowd and said, "Coach Reynolds knew his players were drinking . . . he knew they were street racing. Now it's time for him to pay."

They pushed John off the stage, and not once did he speak up for himself.

"John . . . tell them what really happened!" Abby stood and yelled at him from the back of the room. "Tell them you didn't know about those things."

But John only turned around and waved

at her. "It's my fault, Abby . . . it's my fault . . ."

She tried to run after him, but an officer grabbed her arm and began telling her something about having a right to remain silent.

"Don't *touch* me! My husband did nothing wrong . . . nothing! This whole meeting is a setup and —"

Something caught her attention. A buzzing or a hum of some kind. It grew louder and louder . . .

Abby sat straight up in bed, gasping for breath. She glanced at John. He hadn't been taken away by police. He was asleep beside her. The sound came again and suddenly she realized what it was.

John was snoring.

She fell back against the pillow. The week's emotional chain of events was almost more than Abby could bear.

First, the doctor's determination that they could operate on John's back, and the knowledge that maybe — just maybe — he might regain use of his legs. Then the call from Jake Daniels. The team, the parents . . . nearly the entire school planned to turn out for a meeting on John's behalf.

But what exactly did they want to say? Abby felt her heart rate return to normal.

Obviously she was worried about it. Whatever it was, the idea of meeting with the very people who had tried to ruin John did not sit well with her.

The day passed in a blur of housework and other errands until finally it was six o'clock and the meeting was in just one hour. John was shaving upstairs, and Abby stared at the telephone. There was time for a quick call to Nicole. The poor girl had wanted desperately to go to the meeting, but she'd already made plans to have Matt's parents over for dinner. Besides, she was seven months pregnant and more tired than usual.

Neither Nicole nor the other kids knew about John's impending surgery. Abby and John wanted to tell them on the weekend, when everyone was at the house. Then as soon as the details were out, they could place a speakerphone call to Kade and share the news together.

Nicole answered on the first ring. "Hello?"

"Hi, honey. It's Mom."

"Oh, hi. Aren't you supposed to be at the meeting?"

"It's not till seven." Abby poured a bit of lotion on the palm of her hand and worked it into her fingers. "How are you, dear? It

398

worries me that you're so tired. Usually the seventh and eighth month aren't like that."

"I don't know, Mom." Nicole lowered her voice. "I don't want Matt to worry, but this afternoon while I was making spaghetti sauce, I had some of those false contractions. Only this time they were pretty strong."

"Is the baby moving around okay?"

"Not so much this evening. But earlier it felt like she was doing backflips."

"She?" There was teasing in Abby's voice. Matt and Nicole had decided not to find out whether they were having a boy or girl. They wanted to be surprised. "Are you trying to tell me something?"

"It's just a guess. I have a hunch it's a girl. Matt thinks it's a boy. So I guess one of us'll be —" Nicole groaned.

"Nic, what is it?"

"Ugggh." Nicole grabbed a few quick breaths. "Just another false contraction. See what I mean? They're getting harder all the time."

Abby worked to keep the concern from her voice. "Honey, you need to write down the time and keep track of them. If they get stronger or start coming more regularly, have Matt take you in. Please, sweetie. That's nothing to mess with."

Nicole promised she'd keep track of the pains, and then she asked Abby to pass a message on to John. "Tell Daddy Matt's been praying for him. That whatever's said at this meeting will be an encouragement."

"*Matt's* been praying? What about y—"

"Don't start, Mom." A sigh sounded across the phone lines. "You know how I feel about it."

Abby did know, and she still couldn't believe it was happening. Life was tragic enough when having her husband lose his ability to walk. But watching Nicole lose her ability to pray? They chatted a bit more and Abby was careful not to be critical of Nicole. She needed Abby's love, not her condemnation. The phone call ended, and Abby closed her eyes.

God . . . work on her heart. Please . . .

Have peace, daughter . . . no one can snatch her out of My hand . . .

The words were like a balm to her soul, filling in the worn-out places of her assurance with a peace that was beyond description. *No one can snatch them out of My hand.* It was a Scripture from Abby's college days. She had memorized it after having a discussion with a youth pastor about salvation.

Nicole wasn't rejecting her faith. She

was merely struggling. She thought about her daughter's contractions. Certainly God would meet her where she was, one way or another, and see her through this season of doubt. And someday very soon, Abby believed with all her heart that Nicole would pray again.

Maybe even yet that night.

The meeting was already underway when John and Abby snuck in through a back door in the auditorium. The lights were low, and John had been certain the action would come to a complete halt the minute they arrived.

Instead, Abby opened the door and slipped in first, while John wheeled in behind her without a sound. Abby found a chair against the back wall and John positioned himself beside her. They stayed there in the shadows near the back while Herman Lutz took the podium.

"You're gathered here tonight for a parent-staged meeting. As you know, our district makes school buildings available for such discussion times." He held up a piece of paper and read its contents in a slow, unpracticed manner. "As athletic director at Marion High, I wanted to make sure you're all clear on the boundaries.

Please keep your comments as positive as possible, and let's avoid any name-calling. In addition, you should know that the opinions expressed here tonight are not those of the administration or staff."

The man seemed bored and condescending. The same way he acted around the coaches and students at Marion. John tried not to let his attitude bother him.

Lutz shaded his eyes and gazed at the front row of seats. "Mr. Chuck Parker, you called this meeting, so please get the discussion started."

So it was true. Chuck Parker had called the meeting. The very man who had argued with John before the season about whether his son should play quarterback, and — according to Jake, anyway — the one who had spearheaded the attack against his character. John leaned back in his wheelchair. As he did, he felt Abby's hand alongside his. He held it, glad for her presence, and even more glad that they hadn't been spotted.

Now that his eyes had adjusted to the light, he could see the auditorium more clearly. It was packed. Hundreds of people had turned out. What in the world could all those people have to say?

Chuck Parker made his way to the microphone and, for a long while, said nothing at all. He cleared his throat and glanced at his shoes. When he looked up, his cheeks were deep red. "I called this meeting for one reason. To apologize publicly to Coach John Reynolds."

Abby squeezed his hand, her voice barely audible. "It's about time."

John strained to hear. He didn't want to miss a word.

"Many of you remember how I acted last season. To satisfy my own agenda, I tried to convince you Coach Reynolds was not the man our Eagles needed on the football field." He glanced down once more. "But I've done a lot of thinking since then."

Chuck looked up and paced a few steps in either direction. "What happened with our boys this past season was *my* fault." He pointed at the audience. "And the fault of any of you parents who tried to turn your kid against Coach Reynolds." He hesitated. "What hope did my boy have as an Eagle when all he heard from me were cuts against his coach? The more I attacked the man, the more Casey lost respect for him. Once players lose respect for the coach, it doesn't matter what the man might do or what kind of talent the team might have. Everyone loses. It's that simple." He paused. "But it took a tragedy for me to sort it out and see it for myself."

John wondered if he were dreaming. Never in his wildest imagination had he thought Chuck Parker would face the Marion faithful and admit he'd undermined John's coaching authority. He shot a quick look at Abby. There were tears on her cheeks, but she was quiet, soaking in the things being said.

"I tried to get Coach Reynolds fired. But I was wrong." Parker shrugged and seemed at a loss for words. "Coach sent in his resignation letter this week. I guess if there's another reason I called this meeting, it's to convince Coach we want him back at Marion High. The program won't be the same without him."

Chuck opened the meeting up to whoever wanted to speak. Several parents went first, and John's astonishment only grew. These were people he'd always assumed had supported him. Yet one at a time they apologized for siding with a handful of parents who'd had an agenda against him.

One parent said, "What we did to Coach Reynolds last year made us losers, and it made our sons losers. I'm ashamed of myself, and I'm glad for the chance to tell the rest of you how I feel."

John shifted in his chair. No wonder he'd felt such pressure. Even parents who smiled at his face had talked behind his back. He and Abby exchanged a look. It was easy to see she was thinking the same thing.

Next at the podium was a wave of parents who had publicly opposed John. They, too, expressed sorrow at what they'd done.

"Not just because he's hurt now," one father said. "The reason we're here today isn't because we pity Coach Reynolds. It's because we're ashamed of ourselves and the way we treated him."

Thirty minutes into the meeting, the first of several players stood to speak. He was a lineman, a soft-spoken athlete named Buck, whose intensity came out only on the field.

Until now.

"Coach Reynolds was not a regular coach, not the kind of man you take for granted." Buck looked uncomfortable at the small podium, but he continued, passion ringing in his voice. "Coach had us to his home for movies and dinners. One time he told us if we ever needed a place to go so we wouldn't drink at a party, we could come to his house." Buck's voice lifted louder. "He loved us that much. See, that's the thing I want you parents to know. You took a stand against a man who cared about us more than any coach I've ever heard of. We were the luckiest athletes in the state of Illinois. Because Coach loved us." He hung his head for a moment. "All I'm saying is, now it's time to get the message back to Coach . . . that we love him, too."

A lump formed in John's throat and refused to budge. He blinked back tears and listened as, one after another, his players took the podium and echoed Buck's thoughts. So they did care, after all. It was worth more than John could have imagined. He brought Abby's hand to his lips and gave it a tender kiss.

She smiled at him and mouthed, "They love you, John."

Finally there was a lull in the action and a ripple of whispers fanned across the spectator section. All eyes were on someone, but John couldn't make out who it was. Finally the boy came into view.

Jake Daniels.

John hadn't seen him since that day in court, and he looked different now. Older, more grown up. He was no longer the carefree star athlete he'd been back in November.

Abby leaned closer. "What's the commotion about?"

"Jake hasn't been back at Marion High since the accident."

"Oh." Her eyes grew wide. "I didn't know."

"This must be hard for him."

Jake was neither shy nor awkward. Instead he handled the microphone like a professional, making eye contact with different sections of the audience.

"I'm here to tell you the truth regarding some rumors that went around about Coach Reynolds last year." He paused, his eyes intense. "First of all, yes, some of us guys on the team drank during summer camp last August. I was one of them. And a few guys raced."

John exchanged a look with Abby. So, Jake had been one of the drinkers. John was fairly sure the boy hadn't raced, though. At least not back then. It wasn't until his father bought him the Integra that he'd been tempted to do that. And even then he'd done it just one tragic time. Still, he didn't claim innocence, nor did he point out which players had violated rules.

Jake slipped one hand in his pocket. "I look at our team last year, and I know what one of you said earlier was true. We were losers. Not just on the field, but off the field. Most of us were rule-breakers. Drinking, racing, getting into pornography."

Abby flashed John a look of alarm. She kept to a whisper. "In high school?"

"I guess."

"Was Kade involved last year, too?"

"No." John was careful to keep his voice low. His conversation with Kade that day on the fishing boat was still fresh. "Not until he got to college."

"It's that rampant?"

John nodded. "And getting worse." He had a thought then . . . Why not ask Kade to talk to the team about how pornography progresses and becomes addicting, about breaking free from it and getting help? It could have a real imp—

Then he remembered. He wouldn't be coaching next year. The new coach might not be interested in having the boys stay clear of pornographic material. And it would be up to him to plan speakers for the team.

Jake was still talking. "If that wasn't bad enough, we walked around campus thinking we ruled the school, treating other people like dirt. Making Marion High a miserable place for anyone who didn't play ball." Jake stopped and squared up to the edge of the stage, his eyes searching the audience. "We thought we were better than everyone. Even Coach Reynolds."

Jake paused. Even from the back of the room John could tell he was trying not to cry. Finally he cleared his throat and found voice enough to speak. "Coach wanted us to be upstanding, moral young men. Men of character. Anyone who's played for him has heard him say that a hundred times. He led by example."

The image of Charlene came to mind, and an arrow of guilt sliced through John's gut. He hadn't always been moral. But because of his faith, because of God's strength and not his own, he'd walked away from that situation, and steered clear of others that would have led him down the wrong path. Only by God's grace did Jake and the others see in him the type of character they now wanted to imitate.

"We had the best coach in the state. Like Buck said, a coach who loved us. And we let him get away." Jake sniffed and again seemed to be trying to get hold of his emotions. "I'm still believing that somehow God will heal Coach Reynolds, but maybe not. What I did by racing that day might have ruined Coach's legs forever." A single sob caught in Jake's throat, and he placed his fist over his mouth until he had control again. "But I think what our team did by going against him last season is worse, because we ruined his desire to coach." Jake shook his head, his voice strained. "I can only pray that someday Coach will come back and some lucky group of guys will be smart enough to know how good they've got it. Smart enough to listen to him, act like him, and play for him with all their hearts. The way I wish we would have."

John blinked back a layer of tears and looked at Abby.

"He's grown up." She had tears in her eyes.

"Yes." John turned and watched Jake leave the stage. "He has."

For several seconds there was a lull, and finally Chuck Parker took the podium. "I had hoped Coach Reynolds might be here tonight, but I think it's understandable why he isn't. Not just because of his injury, but because of the way we treated him last season. Why would he come?"

Abby nudged him. "Say something."

"Not yet." John felt awkward shouting out while Chuck was at the microphone. "Wait till he's finished."

Chuck shaded his eyes again and

scanned the front of the auditorium. "So if no one else wants to say anything, I've brought a petition asking Coach Reynolds to reconsider and come back as coach for the Eagles. If each of you could sign it before you —"

"Wait!" A tall figure entered the auditorium from one of the side doors and strode toward the front of the room.

Chuck looked surprised and more than a little nervous. The student ambled onto the stage and approached the podium, and then John understood.

The boy was Nathan Pike.

John stared. It *was* Nathan, but he wasn't dressed in black and his arms and neck were free from spiked collars and leather bands. He looked like any other kid at Marion High, and there was something else. His expression was softer. So soft John almost didn't recognize him.

Nathan looked at Parker and extended his hand. "Sorry, I'm late. I have something to say. Would it be all right?"

Relief flooded Chuck's face. John was pretty sure most everyone at school had heard the rumors about Nathan. How could they not, after the football game where the boy was arrested? School officials later caught a boy from the opposing team for making the threat, but the incident hadn't helped Nathan's image, and John had heard that some still feared he might do something crazy.

But Chuck didn't hesitate. He handed over the microphone and stepped back, giving Nathan the floor. "First of all —" Nathan looked toward the back of the auditorium — "Coach Reynolds *is* here. He and his wife are in the back. I saw them when I came in."

A jumble of voices started talking at once as people craned their necks and pointed toward where John and Abby sat.

"So much for anonymity." Abby sank lower in her seat.

"Coach?" Nathan peered into the darkness. "Could you come down here?"

John's stomach fluttered and his hands felt damp.

"I'll be praying," Abby whispered.

"Thanks." John wheeled himself along the back wall and up the aisle toward the front of the room. He could feel every eye on him as he crossed the front and made his way up a ramp onto the stage.

At first the parents and players could only stare. The last time they'd seen him, he'd stood six-foot-four, bigger and stronger than life, a walking illustration of the physical power necessary for the game of football.

Now he was reduced to a wheelchair, forty pounds lighter, his legs strangely thin.

After several seconds, Jake Daniels stood and began clapping. Not polite applause, but loud, single claps that ignited the room. Before Nathan could say another word, Casey Parker stood, then Buck. Finally the entire audience rose to its feet and clapped for John in a way they'd never done before.

It was an applause that in sixty seconds made John forget an entire season of criticism and complaints. An applause that told him, yes, his players and their parents had done him wrong, but they knew they'd made a mistake and they were sorry. Not sorry for him — though certainly they were that, too. But sorry they hadn't supported him and given him a chance that past season.

When they'd taken their seats and the room was quiet again, Nathan spoke. "I think we've learned something about forgiveness tonight. Kids like me have to forgive kids like you." He looked at the place where the players sat. "And kids like you have to forgive kids like me. Those are lessons Coach taught me, things I'll remember forever." He paused. "But mostly, Coach Reynolds has to forgive us all."

John was too stunned to do anything but listen.

"Right now —" Nathan moved closer and took hold of John's wheelchair — "I'd like everyone to come up and gather round Coach while we pray for two miracles."

What was this? Nathan wanted people to pray? The entire scene was so strange it was unbelievable. Yet, it was actually happening. John stilled his mind enough to listen.

"The first miracle we need here is obvious — that Coach will walk again. The second one is just as hard to imagine. That Coach'll change his mind about resigning from the Eagles. Because we need him. We all need him."

One at a time they came — players and parents and students, many who hadn't spoken, but wanted to show their support all the same. The cluster of people on the stage grew until everyone was circled around John. Everyone except Herman Lutz and a janitor in the back of the room.

John saw Abby work her way up the aisle to the middle of the stage. She placed her hands on John's shoulders, and as the voices around him began lifting prayers to heaven, John felt movement in his feet. This time from both his big toes.

Then and there, in the quietest corner of his heart, he could almost hear God whisper to him.

Lean not on your own understanding . . .

As John closed his eyes and joined his silent voice with those of the others, as he realized the good God was indeed working out of the disaster of his past year, he knew something for certain.

He would never lean that way again.

Twenty-six

At eleven o'clock that night, Nicole remembered how to pray.

By then she'd been charting contractions for most of the night, and though they hadn't been regular, they were definitely getting stronger.

She'd played them down to Matt and his parents, not wanting to bother anyone if they were only false contractions. She'd done the same at nine o'clock when her mother called to update her on the meeting at school.

"How're the pains, Nic?" There was worry in her voice.

"Fine. Nothing out of the ordinary."

Now two hours had passed, and she was in so much pain she'd moved to the downstairs sofa, both to keep from waking Matt and to chart the contractions. But something else bothered her — almost more than the pain. Something her mother had asked earlier that night on the phone.

Was the baby still moving?

At first, Nicole had said yes. There had still been movement, even if it was less than before. But since then she'd paid more careful attention. And now, an hour after Matt's parents had gone for the night, she was starting to panic. She hadn't felt the baby move since after dinner. Not once.

And that's what had led Nicole — for the first time since her father's accident — to pray again.

At eleven o'clock, as a pain worse than any of the others seized her and knocked her off the sofa onto her knees, she prayed as instinctively as she breathed.

God, what's happening to me? Help me, Lord . . . It's too early for the baby to come!

Silence.

When the pain ended, Nicole began to cry. There was no way to describe how she felt — both horrible and wonderful at the same time. Horrible because of the contractions, but wonderfully at peace because for the first time in far too long she'd spoken to God.

What had she been thinking these past months? Why had she convinced herself that prayer was useless? Look how faithfully God had answered her prayers about her parents. And about a thousand other things every day of her life.

Then it hit her. The reason why she'd stopped praying.

She had only seen God as faithful when her prayers were answered the way *she* wanted them answered. What did the Bible say about making requests to God? That He heard them, and that He would be faithful to answer.

Not necessarily faithful to grant the request, but faithful to move in the situation as He saw best.

She remembered something else. All prayers were not answered immediately. Otherwise there would be no need to pray without ceasing, as Scripture said to do.

Nicole climbed back onto the sofa, her abdomen still tight from the last contraction. Why hadn't she remembered those things sooner? And how could she have gone all these months without talking to God?

What a fool she'd been . . .

Tears nipped at the corners of her eyes and sorrow overwhelmed her. Had she really thought she could get through life without a relationship with her Creator? A relationship so vital she'd built her life around it? The answer resounded in her soul. No, she could never have walked away from God forever. She was merely mad at Him for allowing her father to be paralyzed.

But God never promised life would be problem-free. Nicole had always known that, had heard it all her life, but she'd never had to face it before. Never had to wrestle with the dichotomy of an all-loving, compassionate God who didn't stop terrible things from happening.

And yet . . . as she lay there, she thought back over all the years, all her life, all the ways God had touched and blessed and moved. He'd proven Himself over and over. And His Word proved even more. It told her the truth: God promised peace amid pain, and He promised life everlasting. Wasn't that more than anyone could hope for? Especially since this life was so fleeting, so unpredictable.

Another cramp gripped her stomach and this time she cried out. "Matt! Help me."

Even while the contraction was gaining strength, she glanced at the piece of paper on the arm of the sofa. The last pain had been at 10:58. She checked her watch, pursing her lips and pushing air out the way they'd taught her at the childbirth classes.

It was 11:04. Only six minutes had passed, and just seven minutes between that one and the one before it. They were getting stronger and closer together. *God . . . what should I do?*

In response she had an overwhelming sense to call Matt again. And as the pain eased she did so, this time louder than before. "Matt . . . I need you!"

She heard his feet hit the floor above her. The stairs shook as he took them two at a time. He was breathless when he turned the corner and saw her, huddled in a corner on the sofa, tears on her cheeks.

"Honey, what's wrong?"

"The baby's coming, Matt." She sobbed, still exhausted from the last contraction. "I'm having pains every six or seven minutes, and they keep getting worse."

Matt's face went pale, and he took a step back toward the stairs. "I'll get dressed and we'll go to the hospital. Wait there, okay?"

Though it only took Matt a few minutes, and despite the fact that he sped all the way to the hospital, it was nearly midnight when they admitted her. By then they'd given her a shot of something to stop the contractions, but all it had done was make her jittery and weepy.

"I need to call my parents." She reached

for Matt's hand. "What if the baby comes tonight?"

"I'll call them as soon as they get you into a room."

A doctor wheeled her out of the emergency room and into an elevator, up two floors to a delivery area. "We're doing everything we can to stop your labor, Nicole, but your cervix is dilated to five centimeters and the contractions are still coming."

Five centimeters? Everything Nicole had read about having a baby agreed on one thing: rarely did labor stop once a woman was dilated that far. The doctor wheeled her into a room with bright lights and a shiny steel table. "We're still trying to stop the contractions, but you need to know the truth. You could deliver within the hour."

Nicole opened her mouth to speak, but another pain came. She rode it out, while Matt asked the questions. "My wife's only seven months pregnant, Doctor. What's that mean for the baby?"

The doctor frowned. "We'll have to wait and see. Babies born that prematurely can survive. The problem is the lungs on a child that little don't work on their own. Survival is a case-by-case situation."

A case-by-case situation? The words

pelted Nicole's heart like so many rocks. This was *her* child they were talking about! The baby whose reality she had refused to embrace until that Christmas Eve in her bedroom when she'd first felt the child moving inside her. Since then she'd formed a bond with this little one, a bond deeper and stronger than anything she could have imagined possible.

"Nicole —" the doctor was trying to get her attention, and she blinked, meeting his gaze — "when's the last time you felt the baby move?"

"It's . . . it's been a while. Usually she's more active."

"Hmmm." The doctor moved a stethoscope over Nicole's belly. It took a minute before he spoke again. "The baby's showing signs of distress. It looks like we may have to let the birth happen if we're going to have a chance at saving the child."

The doctor hooked her up to another monitor. "I'll be back in a few minutes. Stay as still as possible."

He was gone and Nicole grabbed Matt's hand again. Her heart raced within her. *Please God . . . save my baby. Please.* "Matt . . . call my parents. We need everyone praying."

Matt moved toward the phone on the

table near her bed. But then he stopped. "Did you say . . . ?"

"Of course." She locked eyes with him, knowing he could see her fear. "I was just mad before. I started praying a few hours ago and I haven't stopped since." A sob caught in her throat. "Now, please . . . call my parents."

Matt nodded and grabbed the phone. As he dialed, she could see another emotion join fear and worry and helplessness, those already working his features.

Relief.

Abby awoke to the shrill jangle of the phone ringing.

She jolted upright and caught her breath. Who would be calling at this hour? She reached for the phone. "Hello?"

"Mom, it's Matt." He paused long enough for her to recognize panic in his voice. A rush of adrenaline surged through her veins. Was something wrong with Nicole? She sat up straighter as Matt hurried on. "We're at the hospital and . . . the doctors can't stop Nicole's contractions. It looks like the baby's going to be born anytime. She wanted you to pray."

Abby's heart slammed against the wall of her chest. Nicole was only seven months along. That meant the baby couldn't weigh more than a few pounds at best. Suddenly she remembered Haley Ann. Would Nicole have to lose a child, also? *God, no . . . don't let it happen.*

"Mom, are you there?" Matt's voice was so tense, Abby barely recognized it.

"We're on our way."

When she hung up, she woke John. Twenty minutes later, they pulled into the hospital parking lot and made their way up to labor and delivery. Matt met them in the hallway. He was dressed in a hospital gown and paper face mask.

"They've tried everything, but they can't stop her labor." His eyes were red. "They say the baby's in distress."

Abby took another two steps toward the room where Matt had just exited. "Where is she?"

"The delivery room. The doctor said it could be any minute."

John wheeled himself closer. "Can we see her?"

"Not yet. I'm allowed back in, but the doctor wants you to wait across the hall. It's a private room. I'll come get you as soon as I know anything."

Matt hugged them both. "Nicole wanted you to pray for the baby, but pray for her, too. She's bleeding internally. Her blood pressure is way too low."

Abby had to force herself not to run down the hall and find Nicole. It was one thing that the baby was in danger . . . but Nicole? Abby hadn't even considered that possibility. Certainly God wouldn't allow something to happen to Nicole. Not now, when so much had happened. They'd already lost one daughter.

God wouldn't take a second one, would He?

Matt took off down the hall, and John reached for her fingers. "Come on." He led her to an armchair in the private waiting room and positioned himself as close to her as possible. With careful hands, he framed her face and forced her to look at him. "I know what you're thinking, Abby. But you need to stop. We have to believe God's here with us, that He'll help Nicole and the baby get through this."

Abby was too afraid to do anything but nod. "Pray, John. Please."

He bowed his head close to hers and placed Nicole and the baby in God's hands. "We trust You, God. No matter how the situation looks, no matter what else has happened before, we trust You. And we believe You'll work a miracle for our daughter and her baby."

As John prayed, Abby realized how strongly she still believed. Despite everything that had happened, God's fingerprints were everywhere. John had survived the accident, hadn't he? The two of them loved each other again, didn't they? And she'd finally been able to be honest with her feelings.

A wave of panic overshadowed her peace, but only for a moment. There was no time to fear. Not with Nicole and the baby fighting for their lives down the hallway. Even now, in the midst of a crisis, God was at work somehow.

Abby had to believe that.

Otherwise, she wasn't sure she'd make it through the night. Without her faith, another loss now would certainly send her over the edge.

A full hour passed before Matt appeared in the waiting room. He looked ten years older, but Abby felt a surge of elation. He was smiling!

"Nicole's okay. The bleeding was because of a tear in the placenta, something that can be fatal." He sucked in a slow breath, his eyes red and bleary. "I waited with her until her blood pressure came back up. She's tired, but the doctors say she's not in danger."

Abby exhaled hard. "Thank God . . . I knew He'd save her."

"What about the baby?" John put his hand on Abby's knee, his features taut.

Matt's smile faded. "It's a girl. But it doesn't look good. She's barely two pounds and she's having trouble breathing. They put her in intensive care."

So Nicole had been right. A baby girl . . . but now it looked as though none of them would even get to meet her. Poor little thing, alone in an incubator, struggling for every breath. Abby's arms ached for the chance to hold her. "Can we see either of them?"

"Nicole's back in her room. She might be asleep, but I know she'd want you to come in." Matt's gaze dropped to the floor for a moment. "I'm not sure about our little girl." His eyes met theirs again. "She's so small. I've never seen a baby that little."

They followed Matt to Nicole's room, and as they went, John tapped Abby's leg. She turned to him and he pointed to his feet. "Let's tell her."

Of course! The news about John's surgery, the chance he might walk again! It was bound to encourage her. "You tell her."

They entered the room, and Nicole opened her eyes. "Hi." Her voice was groggy. "How's the baby?"

"They're working on her, honey." Matt was at her side instantly, soothing his hand over her forehead.

Nicole looked past him to Abby and John. "She's absolutely wonderful. The littlest bit of dark hair and perfect tiny features. Have you seen her?"

"Not yet." Abby bit her lip. "She's very small, Nic."

"I know, but she's going to be okay. I feel it in my bones."

John glanced at Abby, and she nodded. A distraction would be good. Especially the type of distraction John wanted to share. He moved his wheelchair to the foot of her bed and took hold of her toes. "There's something I need to tell you, Nic."

"Okay." She blinked, her lids heavy, a smile lifting the corners of her mouth. "Sounds serious."

"It is." He looked at Abby once more. "This week I saw the doctor. He ran some tests and decided they could operate on my neck. The surgery's set to take place in about a month."

Nicole's eyes grew wide, and Matt

turned an open mouth toward John. Nicole sat up straighter in bed, wincing at her soreness. "What for?"

"Well . . . I've been having feeling in my toes. Once in a while they even move a little." John's eyes twinkled. Abby doubted she'd ever been happier for him. "I guess in rare cases this kind of operation can repair the break."

"But what about your legs?" Matt's tone was gentle, awed.

John's chin quivered, and he struggled to find the words. Abby cleared her throat and finished for him. "He could regain full function."

Nicole hooted out loud. "Dad! That's amazing!"

"It's just a chance, but we're praying." John sat back in his chair and chuckled. "A while ago your mom thought God was up to something big in our lives. It looks like she was right."

"She is. I know it. Your legs and our little girl's survival." Nicole folded her arms. "You have to see her, Mom. She's so beautiful."

Sorrow circled Abby's heart, but she forced herself to smile. "I'm sure she is, honey."

"You guys are grandparents!" Nicole's

voice was tired again, but her enthusiasm hadn't waned. "Can you believe it?"

Abby hadn't given the idea a single thought. The only thing that mattered was the safety of Nicole and the baby. Now that the little girl was born, she hadn't yet acknowledged the truth: she and John were grandparents. It was unbelievable, and for the briefest moment she wondered how this scene would've played out if they'd gone ahead with their divorce plans. Most likely he wouldn't have been here for this event. It would have been too awkward, too difficult.

How good God had been to them! She slipped her arm around John's shoulders and studied Nicole, the peace in her eyes. "Have you named her?"

Nicole and Matt had gone through dozens of names, never really settling on one for either a boy or a girl. But now they gave each other a subtle grin, and Nicole looked at Abby. "Yes. Haley Jo. After my sister . . . and Matt's mother."

"Oh, Nic." Abby could do nothing to stop the tears. "That's beautiful."

There was silence between them then, silence and the soft sound of tears. Abby guessed they all were thinking the same thing. The first Haley hadn't survived, and now this Haley might not either.

Before anyone could speak, the doctor came in. "Nicole, your baby's in serious distress. I know you're tired, but I'd like to get you in a wheelchair and take you down to the neonatal intensive care unit. I think it might help if she felt your touch, heard your voice."

In a blur, Nicole was lifted from the bed into a chair, and she and Matt left the room with the doctor in tow. Only Abby and John were left in the room. "What if she dies before we get a chance to see her?" Abby fell into John's lap and circled his neck with her arms.

"Then she and Haley Ann will have a party in heaven." John kissed her forehead. "And one day when it's our turn, they'll be there to greet us."

At three o'clock that morning, Matt found them again in the waiting room. This time his voice was thick with tears. "The doctor says you can go in." Matt folded his arms. "She might not make it. Nicole wanted you to see her before . . ."

He didn't finish his thought. John wheeled himself toward Matt, and Abby kept in step behind him. "We'll follow you."

Matt showed them into a sterilization

area, where they were both given hospital gowns and directed to wash their hands. Afterward, a nurse met them at the entrance to the special unit. "It'll have to be quick. We're working very hard to save her."

The nurse led the way, followed by John and Abby, and finally Matt. Abby couldn't speak as they stopped at an incubator. The nurse laid her hand on top of the clear cover. "This is Haley."

Matt stayed a few feet back so Abby and John could get a clear look. Nicole had been right. The child was gorgeous, a miniature of Nicole at that age and even . . . yes . . . a strong resemblance to — "Do you see it, John?"

His eyes glistened with tears as he nodded, never taking his gaze off the tiny infant. "She looks like Haley Ann."

"Really?" Matt poked his head between them, staring at the tiny child. "Nicole and I couldn't figure out who she looked like."

Abby studied the baby again. Her tiny fingers were no thicker than spaghetti noodles, and her entire body would've fit comfortably in one of John's hands. There were hairlike wires attached to her at several places, and she was nearly covered with monitoring patches and bands. Her skin that did show was pale and translucent. Clearly not the normal skin of a newborn.

Abby placed her palm against the warm glass. "Come on, little Haley, keep breathing. We're pulling for you, baby."

John squeezed her knee, but said nothing. Her quiet words had spoken for both of them. Suddenly Abby realized that Matt's parents weren't there. She looked over her shoulder at him. "Have you called your mom and dad?"

"Their phone's off the hook or something. Every time I call it's busy."

"We'll go by and tell them on the way home." John wheeled himself back a bit. "You and Nicole need your time. But we'll be praying for Haley. And we're only a phone call away if anything changes."

John was right, but Abby wanted nothing more than to sit beside the baby's incubator, willing her to breathe. The entire scene reminded her of that final morning with Haley Ann, when Abby had laid her down for a nap and found her two hours later, dead in her crib.

If only she'd stayed with her, watched her breathe . . . jolted her into catching her breath the moment her body stopped drawing air. Then Haley Ann would've lived. And maybe the same was true for this Haley, also. This precious grand-daughter.

John was waiting for her, but Abby studied little Haley one more time. *I'm giving her to You, God . . . watch over her. Keep her breathing, please.*

An image filled Abby's mind, that of a smiling, youthful Jesus cradling Haley Jo in His arms and holding her close to His chest. Convinced of that, Abby was finally able to pull herself away. The message she'd gotten from the image was clear as air. There was nothing Abby could do for Haley that Jesus wasn't already doing.

Her life, her future . . . her next breath . . . were all in His hands.

Twenty-seven

When the doorbell rang just before noon, Abby was certain it would be Jo and Denny. Nicole had called that morning to say that Haley had survived the night. After Abby and John had alerted Matt's parents, they went straight to the hospital. Now, Abby figured, they were coming by to share their fears. Certainly to join Abby and John in their concern for the tiny baby.

But when Abby opened the door, it wasn't Matt's parents.

It was Jake Daniels's.

Tara and Tim stood on the front mat, looking at each other like awkward teenagers, and then at Abby. Tara spoke first. "Can we come in?"

"Sure." Abby stepped back, surprised. Since that day at court, neither of them had made contact with Abby or John. "I was expecting someone else."

The Danielses moved into the entryway,

but Tim stopped. "If you're having company, we can come back."

Abby waved her hand. "No, nothing like that." She hesitated. "Nicole had her baby early this morning. I sort of expected her husband's parents to stop by."

"Is the baby okay?" Concern flashed in Tim's eyes.

"No. Not really." Abby's voice was suddenly thick. "She's two months early. We're praying for her."

John must have heard their voices. He came wheeling down the hallway and waved. "Come on in."

They moved into the living room. John positioned himself close to Abby's chair. "Still on leave from work, Tim?"

"Yes." He exchanged a look with Tara. "Jake's hearing is Thursday."

"He might get a year at a juvenile detention center." Tara slid a little closer to Tim. "But that'd be the worst of it."

Abby squirmed in her chair. Was this why they'd come? To talk about Jake's sentence?

"We didn't come to talk about that." Tim folded his hands and planted his forearms on his knees. "Remember in court that day . . . you told us the two of you almost divorced last year?"

John nodded.

Tara raised an eyebrow. "We've wanted to come ever since, but . . . I couldn't." She crossed her legs and leaned closer to Tim. "Now the hearing's next week, and after that Tim needs to get back to work. That means our time together is almost over, and we still haven't talked about what we're feeling. Or whether we should get back together."

Abby understood. "You're afraid."

"Tim and I fought so much before he left. Then, when he was gone, all I could think about was what we'd thrown away. The love and laughter and memories. All of it was gone."

"I felt that way, too, but Tara doesn't believe me." Tim tossed his hands in the air. "There's no question we want to be together, but we can't get beyond the past."

Tim and Tara's words could have been their own a year ago, when Abby's father died. Without a doubt Abby and John knew that day that they still cared for each other, still wanted each other, but the mountain of hurt was simply too high to scale.

"After Tim moved away, he began dating." The pain showed in Tara's eyes. "Here I was grieving all we'd lost, and he's out in New Jersey getting a new haircut, a new job, and a new girlfriend. Sometimes every few weeks. How could I compete with that?"

Tim turned his hands palm up. "Those girls meant nothing. I was running from the pain. Everything I did was my way of running. Even buying Jake the Integra."

There was silence between them for a moment, and Abby drew a quiet breath. "May I say something?"

"Please." Tim was quick to answer. "That's why we came."

Abby looked at John, silently asking him if it was okay to share the details of their situation. The peace in his eyes told her that he would have it no other way. She smiled and then shifted her gaze to Tara.

"When John and I were having trouble, he spent time with one of the teachers at school. She doesn't work there anymore, and her name isn't important. The thing is, it made me mad. Jealous, really. She was younger than I was, more professional. I figured I couldn't compete with her, didn't *want* to compete with her. I still felt angry and jealous even after John began doing everything he could to make things right between us."

Tara nodded. "Exactly."

"The thing I had to learn was this: Sometimes love makes a mistake. Even a series of mistakes. When I married John, I promised to love him in good times and bad. No matter what happened." Abby kept her voice tender, but let her passion show, too. A passion she hoped Tara would hear. "John wanted to make things right between us, but I wasn't willing to forgive him. And you know what? At that point he wasn't the one breaking our wedding vows — I was. I refused to trust him, even after he'd told me time and again that he hadn't had an affair. I wanted to punish him for even finding another woman attractive, for befriending her and being tempted by her. And because of that I could justify treating him —" she searched for the right word — "cruelly. Because my feelings had been hurt and I thought he deserved it."

A quiet settled over them again. John looked at Tim. "Of course, I didn't understand any of that. I just figured she wasn't capable of forgiving me."

There were tears in Tara's eyes and she dabbed at them discretely. "How . . . how did you get past it?"

"Memories." John sat back, his eyes only semifocused. "Our divorce plans ran right along the same time frame as Nicole's engagement. It was wedding dresses this, and churches that, and what about our vows, Daddy . . ." He shook his head. "What else could we do but remember how it had been for us twenty years earlier."

"How we fell in love as kids and how magical it was when we first got married." Abby smiled. "Even then it wasn't easy."

"The memories came at us separately." John gave a sad chuckle. "Neither of us knew how to approach the other about them, and because of that, we were ready to go ahead with our plans."

"What stopped you?" Another tear spilled onto Tara's cheek.

"God." John and Abby said the answer at the same time and then looked at each other and grinned. John shot a pointed look at Tim. "God might as well have sent us a telegram." John deepened his voice. " 'John and Abby Reynolds . . . do NOT get divorced. I made you for each other . . . forgive and forget . . . and move on in the joyful life I have for you.' "

Abby met Tara's eyes. "Do you ever feel that way, Tara? Like God wants you to let go of the hurt and anger and simply love each other?"

"All the time."

"Then why haven't you done it?"

"Because. I'm afraid it'll happen again."
She looked at Tim. "You're the only man
I've ever loved, but when you left me, I
hated you. And . . . and I swore you'd
never break my heart like you did before.
Even if you begged me to come back."

"The problem —" John's voice was
gentle once more — "is one that's gotten
mankind into trouble since the beginning."

"*Which* problem?" Tim wrung his hands.

"Pride." John smiled. "It's why Adam
and Eve took the apple — because they
thought they were smarter than God. They
wanted to be like God. And it's why good
couples — loving couples like the two of
you or Abby and me — start going in different directions and wind up believing divorce is the only solution." He took Abby's
hand. "When really, the only solution is to
grab tight to each other, forgive, and go
on."

For a while none of them said anything.
Then John made one final point. "Remember, the devil has always been behind
the sin of pride. He wants us to think we
can't forgive, can't live humbly with each
other. But the devil has an agenda. He
wants us to be miserable."

Tim stared at John. "And you think

that's all divorce is? Two people listening to the devil's lies?"

"Most of the time, yes. When we say those wedding vows, the last thing on our mind is divorce. Isn't that right?"

Tara and Tim nodded.

"For me, I was up there knowing Abby was the only woman I'd ever loved, the only one I wanted to spend the rest of my life with."

"That's exactly how I felt." Tim set his hand on Tara's knee, and she let it stay there.

"So only a lie could change that, right? Otherwise the love I shared with Abby should've gotten better with each year." There was regret in John's voice. The regret Abby knew they both carried. A regret that realized the value of all those years they lost back when they were living separate lives under one roof.

"Instead —" Abby finished John's thought — "we began thinking badly of each other. Pretty soon we were listening to the lie, believing we deserved something better than a life together."

"When we really needed to stop running, forgive each other, and remember all the reasons we got married in the first place."

Tara sniffed, her eyes dry now. "It's all about forgiveness."

"Yes." Abby's heart went out to the woman. "It is." She felt a pang of regret. How awful it had been living on the other side of forgiveness. Holding on to bitterness and working to hate the man she'd pledged her life to.

John leaned back, more relaxed now. "The Bible tells a story about a man who was forgiven a great debt by the king. The moment he was free, he ran through the streets looking for his fellow servant. When he found him, he grabbed the man by the cloak. 'You owe me, buddy,' the guy said. 'Pay up or I'll throw you into debtor's prison!'

"When the king found out what happened, he called for the man. 'The debt I forgave you was far greater than the debt your fellow servant owed. Now, since you couldn't find it in your heart to forgive the smaller amount, neither will I forgive you the large amount.' And with that he threw the man into prison."

Abby loved the way John could come up with an illustration from Scripture like that. He had always been a storyteller. It was what made him a good teacher, a strong communicator. But now that he was back at church with Abby every week, he constantly came up with stories like the one he'd just told.

Abby searched Tim's and Tara's faces and saw that they understood.

"God's forgiven us —" Tara sniffed — "much more than we could ever need to forgive someone else."

"Exactly." John's tone rang with compassion.

Tara moved to the edge of her seat. "Pray for me, will you? That I'll find a way to forgive."

Without hesitating, John did just that. When they were done, he looked at Abby. "Honey, take off my shoes, will you?"

She wasn't sure what he was up to, but she liked his grin. With a light heart, she stooped down in front of him and slipped his shoes off. Then she returned to her chair and waited.

Tim and Tara looked at his feet, their faces a twist of curiosity.

"Watch." John pointed to his toes. "There's something I want you to pass on to that son of yours."

Whatever he was about to do, even Abby had no idea. It was one thing that John's toes had occasionally moved in some involuntary manner. But this . . . what was he up to?

Then, with all of their eyes glued to his two big toes, Abby saw it. The toes moved! Both of them. Just a little wiggle, but there was no denying the fact. Abby let out a cry and threw her arms around John's neck. "It's happening, John. I can't believe it."

Across the room, Tim and Tara looked stunned, like they'd just seen John levitate. Tim was the first to recover. "What . . . how did . . . John, does your doctor know about that?"

"Yes." John pulled Abby over onto his lap. "It's a form of spinal shock. Really rare. They're operating on me next month. There's a chance I'll get full use of my legs back."

"Oh my goodness." Tara's hands flew to her mouth. "Jake told me he asked God for a miracle. That you'd . . . you'd walk again someday."

Tim looked at her. "He didn't tell me."

"It's true." Her eyes were still wide, still focused on John's two big toes. "He thought God had told him that's exactly what would happen. Coach Reynolds would get better. But as the months went by, nothing happened. Jake . . . he stopped talking about it."

"Well, tell him to keep praying." John grinned, his arm tight around Abby's waist. "Miracles happen to those who believe."

Long after Tim and Tara had gone, after John had gone into their new first-floor bedroom for a nap, Abby sat at the dining room table and stared out at the lake. John was right. Miracles did happen to those who believed. After all, Nicole had prayed for Abby and John. And Jake had prayed about John's damaged legs. And now the boy had a sense everything was going to work out for John.

She sat there a long time, praying for baby Haley, talking to God and marveling at His plan for their lives. The more she thought about the discussion with Tim and Tara, the more convinced she became that whatever was happening with John's legs, it was only part of the miracle Jake was about to receive.

The other part, Abby was almost certain, would happen any day now, when a certain couple just might walk through the door and announce that by God's grace and forgiveness, Jake's father was never moving back to New Jersey.

By Sunday afternoon, the baby had survived three days, which was more than the doctors had thought possible. She still struggled for every breath, but Nicole had recovered quickly and spent nearly every waking moment anchored beside the baby's incubator. She was allowed to reach inside and run her finger along Haley's small leg or arm. The opening was just large enough so Nicole could see her baby respond to not only her touch, but her voice.

There was a tap on her shoulder, and Nicole turned around. It was Jo, her eyes red and swollen. "Hi."

"Jo, hi . . . sit down."

Jo nodded and slid a chair over next to Nicole's. "How is she?"

"Holding on." Nicole studied the woman. Jo defined intensity. Whatever her mood, she played it to the furthest degree. But here, now, she was quiet, pensive. Defeated, even. "You okay?"

"Sure." Jo's eyes grew watery. "Where's Matt?"

"At home getting some sleep. He's barely closed his eyes since the baby was born."

For a while they sat that way, watching little Haley, willing her small chest to continue it's up-and-down struggle. After five minutes had passed, Jo drew a sharp breath. "Nicole, I have something to tell you."

She turned her head enough to glance at Jo. "I'm listening."

"Oh, brother." Jo rolled her eyes and dabbed at her nose. "Never in a million years did I think I'd ever tell anyone about this. Least of all you or Matt."

Nicole studied the woman. Whatever it was, the burden of it weighed on her like a diesel truck. "You can tell me, Jo."

She cast Nicole a wary eye. "Don't hate me, okay?"

"Okay."

"See . . ." She huffed hard, searching for the words. "It happened a long time back, back when me and Denny were first married." Jo wiped her hands on her pant legs and stared at baby Haley. "We were young and stupid, and just a few weeks after the weddin' we found out I was pregnant."

Pregnant? Nicole tried not to act surprised. Jo was right. Neither she nor Matt had ever heard this story. She waited for Jo to continue.

"We were scared, I mean really scared." Jo shook her head. "Like a coupla fish at the end of a line. No matter which way we turned, didn't seem to be no way out. You know?"

"I do." Nicole hoped her face reflected the empathy she was feeling. It was exactly how she'd felt when she found out she was pregnant. The way she probably still would feel if God hadn't changed her attitude.

"Back then . . . well, me and Denny didn't have God. No one around us did, either. So . . ." Her voice cracked, and she hung her head. "I'm sorry. I don't know if I can finish."

A dawning of understanding shone across the landscape of Nicole's heart. Had the woman done something to end her pregnancy? Nicole reached out and took Jo's weathered hand in her own. "Nothing you could tell me would make me love you less, Jo. You don't have to share this . . . but I want you to know that."

Jo struggled to regain control. When she could speak again, she cast a quick look at Nicole. "I got an abortion, Nicole." She nodded, giving a single loud sniff. "Denny drove me to the clinic and waited in the lobby. And back in one of them dingy rooms, this handsome man came to me and told me it was all going to be okay. All I had to do was lay real still and tell him if I felt any pain. The pregnancy would be gone in no time."

Tears spilled onto Nicole's cheeks, and her heart broke for Jo. She wasn't sure what she should say, so she kept quiet.

"Isn't that something? The pregnancy would be gone . . . as if there wasn't any baby involved." Jo wiped her eyes. "But it was more than a pregnancy. I was five months along by the time I went in and one of the nurses told me." The words caught in Jo's throat for a moment. "It was a girl, Nicole. A little girl like your Haley. Only instead of helping her live, I helped her die."

Jo dropped her head in her hands and stifled a sob.

"Oh, Jo . . ." Nicole rubbed small gentle circles on her back and searched for something to say. But she could think of nothing.

Finally, Jo found her voice again. "A year later I got pregnant with Matt. We were going to have another abortion, but something stopped me. I can't remember what it was, but somehow I knew it wasn't right. It didn't matter if we were young and poor. It wasn't the baby's fault, and I wasn't going to go back to that awful place again."

Nicole's heart skipped a beat. If Jo had aborted Matt . . . She couldn't think about it. There was enough pain, knowing about Jo's first abortion. "Matt doesn't know?"

"How could I tell him? How do you look

your son in the face and let him know you killed his sister?"

"Come on, Jo . . . don't." Nicole put her arm around Jo's neck and brought her own younger face against Jo's older one. "You didn't know what you were doing."

"But I know now." Jo's tears came harder, and Nicole saw a few nurses glancing over at them. Jo seemed to notice, too, and she lowered her voice. "Ever since Matt was born, I've regretted what I did. I'd a done anything to get that little sweetheart back, to have it to do over again."

Nicole released the hold she had on Jo and settled back in her chair. "God forgives you, Jo. You know that, right?"

Jo nodded and sniffed again. "After I gave my life to Jesus last year, I had a chat with Denny. I told him what we'd done was wrong and he agreed. We went to church that night all by ourselves and had a little service for the baby. We got down on our knees and told God how sorry we were." She lifted her chin a bit. "I never seen a grown man cry like that, Nicole. And I knew then that I wasn't the only one who missed that baby girl."

Nicole was struck by the image Jo painted. Both parents taking responsibility for what they'd done and asking God's forgiveness. "What a wonderful thing, remembering her together that way."

"Well, it wasn't wonderful. It was painful. Hurt more than anything in my life, if you wanna know the truth. After we told God we was sorry, we asked Him to take care of our baby up there in heaven. You know, give her little hugs and kisses and pick wildflowers with her on a summer day. Teach her how to fish and laugh and love. Watch over her until one day we could be up there to do it ourselves."

Jo was quiet again, studying baby Haley. "We sort of pictured our little girl like an orphan. A heavenly orphan." Jo gave Nicole a sideways look. "And that night we promised God if He'd take care of our little orphan girl in heaven, we'd take care of His orphans down here on earth."

Suddenly it was all coming together. "Your trip to Mexico?"

"Yes." There was a quivering in Jo's lip. "That's why we're going."

"Wow . . ." Nicole inhaled sharply. "That's beautiful, Jo."

"Yeah, well, the rest of what I have to say isn't so pretty."

Nicole's heart rate quickened, but she stayed silent.

"Ever since I heard about little Haley,

me and Denny have prayed till I thought our teeth would fall out." Jo placed her hand alongside the incubator. "But every time I pray, God gives me a picture that scares me."

Nicole wasn't sure she wanted to know, but she couldn't help herself. "What's the picture?"

"It's a picture of three little girls, running through the fields of heaven, arm in arm." Jo paused and Nicole wanted to cover her ears. "One of them is your sister, Haley Ann; the other is our little girl; and the third one . . . the third one is your little Haley Jo."

It took a moment before Nicole could breathe again. When she could, she forced a quiet chuckle. "Now, Jo . . . is that what's bothering you?"

"Of course." She cast a surprised look at Nicole. "I want little Haley to live more than anything in the world. More than I've wanted something for a very long time. But if God knows my heart, why do I keep getting that picture?"

Nicole sounded stronger than she felt. "Maybe because I got pregnant early, too. Maybe because you know that if Haley . . . if she doesn't make it, she'll be happy in heaven with her two aunts." Nicole tossed her hands a few inches in the air. "I don't know, but it doesn't mean God's going to take Haley home. You can't think that, Jo."

Something in Nicole's words or maybe the tone of her voice, caused Jo to relax. The fear and torment left her face, and in its place there was only a distant sorrow. "You're right. God's going to save little Haley. I have to believe that."

After a while Jo left, and Nicole stayed there by herself for nearly an hour, watching Haley, silently urging her to keep breathing, keep living. And praying that when Haley was old enough to run through fields of flowers, they would be the ones in their very own backyard.

And not the ones in heaven.

Twenty-eight

It was the day of his hearing, and Jake felt he'd aged ten years in the past four months.

Not a bad kind of aging, but a good kind. The kind that made him feel more sure about his faith and his future and his plans to help other teenagers avoid the mistakes he'd made.

If he didn't get sent to a juvenile detention center, Jake planned to return to Marion High in the fall. Everyone he talked to agreed it was the best choice, the way he could most impact his peers about the dangers of street racing. Besides, that way he could be around Coach Reynolds again. And after four months away, Jake had no intention of finishing his high-school education any place except the campus where Coach could teach him. If not on the football field, then certainly in the classroom. If the court let him, that was.

He'd decided something else, too. He

wanted another shot at football. Not so he could show up the underclassmen or put himself on a pedestal among his peers, but so he could play the game the way Coach had taught him to play. With heart and class and honor.

Of course, A.W. had been straight with him. He might not get the chance. The judge could easily sentence him to a year in juvenile hall, and if that happened, he'd spend his senior year in confinement.

Jake had prayed about the outcome of today's hearing, and if that's where God wanted him, that's where he'd go. There was no question, he deserved whatever punishment he was given.

The courtroom was filling up, and Jake glanced at his parents. They were talking near the back door, looking friendlier than they'd looked at any time since the accident. He had asked his mother on occasion if anything was happening between them, but she was always evasive.

"We have a lot to talk about, Jake. Your father's only helping me through this."

Jake would raise an eyebrow, but leave it alone. Still, they spent enough time together now that he'd added it to his list of God topics — things he talked about with the Lord.

The judge entered the room and immediately his parents left their conversation and took their places on either side of him. A.W. straightened a stack of papers and whispered, "Here goes."

When the judge was seated, she called the court to order. Jake's case was first on her docket. "I understand the defendant in *State v. Daniels* would like to enter a plea; is that right?"

A.W. was on his feet. "Yes, Your Honor. We've reached an agreement with the state on the correct charges."

"Very well. Will the defendant please rise?"

Jake stood up, awed at the strange calm that had come over him. *Your call, God . . . whatever You want . . .*

The judge glanced at a sheet of paper on the bench. "Mr. Daniels, you are being charged with the gross negligent use of a vehicle, reckless driving, and illegal street racing — all misdemeanors." She looked at him. "How do you plead?"

"Guilty, Your Honor. On all charges." The words felt wonderful. He *was* guilty. There was no sense playing games about it. Whatever the judge did next was fine with him.

"Mr. Daniels, you're aware that each of

these charges carry with them a maximum of six months in a juvenile detention facility?"

"Yes, Your Honor."

"And that the combination of charges means you could serve up to eighteen months in such a facility?"

"Yes, Your Honor."

The judge sorted through a file of papers. "I see that your attorney has provided me with letters on your behalf. I'll recess this court for twenty minutes while I read through the file." She looked at A.W. "At that point I'll return and hand your client his sentence; is that understood?"

"Yes, Your Honor." He barely paused. "I'd like you to also consider the fact that my client has already signed up for community service events. He plans to speak to students at four high schools a year for the next five years as a way of helping kids avoid the mistakes he made."

The judge was quiet for a moment. "Very well. I'll consider that along with the letters."

Court was adjourned, and Jake's parents hugged him from either side.

"You aren't nervous, are you, son?" His father searched his face, clearly surprised.

"No. Me and God already talked it out. Whatever happens, that's what He wants. I'm not afraid."

A.W. gave a nervous laugh. "Well, I am. If that makes you feel any better." He nodded toward the judge's chamber door. "She's a tough one, that judge. No matter what the letters say, she could make an example out of you."

Jake saw his mother wince at the thought, and he patted her back. "Mom, you gotta trust God on this one. If He wants me at a detention center, that's where I'll go. And everything will work out fine."

"I know. I just . . . I'd like to see you back at Marion. Your ideas . . . about football and helping your friends . . . they seem so good."

"How many letters were you able to get?" Jake's father directed his attention to A.W.

"Five. That's more than enough." The attorney gazed up, trying to remember. "One each from you and Tara, one from Jake's parole officer, one from the person at community service he's been working with. And the best one of all — from John Reynolds."

Coach Reynolds? Jake's stomach flip-flopped inside him. "You asked Coach Reynolds for a letter?"

"Yeah, why?"

"I can't believe you did that . . . he's gone through enough without having to write a letter for me. I mean, whoever told you to do something like that, when . . ."

A.W. held up a hand, and Jake stopped his sentence short. Though he was quiet, he was fuming. He hadn't been this angry in a while. The nerve of asking Coach for a letter that would help him get a lighter sentence.

"I didn't ask Mr. Reynolds for a letter." A.W. tilted his head, a look of vindication on his face. "Mr. Reynolds offered."

Jake's stomach stopped flipping and sank to his knees. What? Coach Reynolds — in the midst of dealing with his sick granddaughter and an upcoming surgery — had taken time to write a letter on his behalf?

Jake looked at his parents and saw they were feeling the same thing. They had all known Coach Reynolds was a great man. But this great? This concerned about a kid who had put him in a wheelchair? For the first time that day, Jake felt a lump in his throat.

The judge appeared and once more called the court to order.

"In the matter of *State v. Daniels*, I have reached a decision, one that even I am not certain is fair."

She's sending me to juvie . . . Jake blinked and tried not to feel afraid. *Help me here, God . . . help me.*

The judge continued. "Will the defendant please rise?"

Jake stood, his knees knocking ever so slightly.

"As I mentioned, it is within my right to sentence you, Mr. Daniels, to eighteen months in a juvenile detention center." She paused and glanced at the district attorney. "But in this case, I have been inundated with requests to act otherwise."

Jake saw his parents link hands.

"The letter that most affected me was the one written by the victim — Mr. John Reynolds." She held up a piece of paper. "Mr. Reynolds writes, 'I beg you to let Jake work off his sentence while attending Marion High in the fall. For you see, that is when I will return to school, and if the accident had never happened, it would have been Jake's senior year. Being on campus without Jake will be a daily reminder of what happened that awful November night. Locking Jake up won't make him a better driver or a wiser young man, nor will it lessen the impact of my injuries. But seeing Jake on campus at Marion High would be almost as good as walking again.' " She paused and looked at Jake before finishing. " 'Please, Your Honor, I ask you to help my recovery by punishing Jake some other way. He's changed since the accident, and Marion High needs more kids like him on campus.' "

Throughout the courtroom the only sound was the faint sniff of his mother's tears and the thud of his own heartbeat. Had Coach really said that? Seeing him on campus would be as good as walking again?

The judge set the letter down and glanced around the room. "For that reason, and because the defendant is pulling straight As at the continuation school, I am hereby waiving all juvenile detention center time. Instead, I will agree to the community service plan, where the defendant will speak to high-school groups four times a year for the next five years."

Jake was so happy he could've floated out of the courtroom. Not because he'd dodged a bullet, but because he was going back to Marion High, back to the same campus as Coach Reynolds! And because he'd have one more chance to play football the way he should have played it all along. *God . . . I'll make it up to You . . . I promise . . .*

Beside him, his parents looked suddenly a decade younger, and Jake realized something. They'd been more worried about his being sentenced to a detention center than they'd let on.

The judge rapped her gavel on the bench. "Order." When it was quiet, she continued. "In addition, the defendant's driver's license shall remain revoked, and he shall not be permitted to apply for a new license until his twenty-first birthday. Between now and then, he will attend a ten-week driver's safety course, this year and every year until he is twenty-one." She looked at Jake. "Most often when I hand down a sentence, I have a sense as to whether justice was served." She angled her head. "This time I'm not sure."

"Yes, Your Honor."

"You're getting off very easy, son. I don't want to see your face in this court or any other ever again. Is that understood?"

Jake nodded. "You don't have to worry, Your Honor. I won't be back."

Just like that, the hearing was over and Jake was being congratulated by A.W. and his parents, and a few Marion High football players who had stayed in the back of the courtroom.

"Jake, man, this is good. We need you back next year at QB." It was Al Hoosey, a wide receiver. He slapped Jake on the shoulder. "Way to go."

Jake met the eyes of the boy. "It'll be different next year, Hoosey. Much different."

The boy blinked. "That's a good thing, right?"

This time Jake couldn't contain his smile. "A *very* good thing."

Other people milled around him, and he felt someone tug his elbow. He turned and found himself looking into the face of the district attorney. "Listen, about the judge's comment . . . that she wasn't sure if justice had been served?"

"Yes, sir?" Jake pivoted so the man had his full attention.

"I have a sense about those things, too. And this time I'm sure. Justice *was* served." The attorney's face was serious, somber. "Now go out there and make sure those friends of yours stay away from street races, okay? That'll make my job a lot easier. Deal?"

Jake swallowed hard. "Deal."

The crowd thinned out and his own attorney gathered his things and left. Finally it was just Jake and his parents.

"Amazing, huh, son?" His mom and dad were still holding hands. They seemed in no hurry to leave.

"God must have big things for me next year at Marion." Jake shot a look at the clock on the courthouse wall. "Let's get home. I have a thank-you call to make."

His mother smiled and brushed her fingertips across his forehead, straightening his bangs the way she'd done back when he was a little boy. "Coach?"

"Yep. Can't wait to tell him."

"Son . . ." His father sat up a bit straighter, and Jake had the sense he was about to say something important. "Before we go, your mom and I have something we want to tell you."

Abby never expected it to take place in a restaurant parking lot.

She had known there would be a time when her family would come together to pray for John. But with Haley still fighting for her life, the days got away from them. Finally, it was Sunday, the day before John's surgery.

Kade was home for an extended spring break, and John and Abby took the family

465

to brunch after church. Before the group broke up, Abby looked around the circle. "We wanted everyone to pray together . . . before John goes in tomorrow."

"Great idea." Jo held her hands out to either side, closed her eyes, and hung her head. "Who's gonna start?"

A few of them shared quiet smiles. Then they did the same, joining hands and bowing their heads there in the parking lot. Kade was the first to pray, and Jo and Denny added their sentiments before Nicole and Matt and Sean took turns.

Abby struggled to speak. All she could manage was a quick thanks to God for giving them even a glimmer of hope.

Then it was John's turn.

He opened his mouth to pray, but nothing came out. Then, after several seconds, he began to sing.

"Great is Thy faithfulness . . . oh God, my Father. There is no shadow of turning with Thee . . ."

The hymn had been John's father's favorite, long before John was even born. One at a time the others added their voices, unconcerned with the looks they got from passersby. When they reached the chorus, they sang about the greatness of God's faithfulness and the truth from

Lamentations that His mercies were new every morning.

No matter what.

Abby found her voice and sang clear, her heart caught up in every word. She'd never forget this. When the song ended, John looked at the faces around him. "Thank you. God is faithful; I believe that. No matter what happens."

Several of them blinked back tears as the group exchanged hugs and talked about their plans for the next day. Jo and Denny would meet the others at the hospital sometime after the surgery. Sean and Kade would be there all day, as would Nicole and Matt — who would primarily be with Haley, but would check in often to see how John was doing.

"Haley's on the third floor and you'll be on the fifth, Daddy." Nicole hugged him tight. "Isn't that something?"

Abby watched John. The strain of what the next day's events held was finally starting to get to him. He kissed Nicole on the cheek. "You just take care of my little granddaughter for me, okay?"

"Okay." She wiped a tear. "We'll be praying."

Sean rode home with Kade, so once John was strapped in and Abby took the driver's seat, they were by themselves. "Notice how no one said anything about you walking again?"

It was a beautiful April day, the kind that shouted of the coming summer. John stared out the window. "I think they're afraid to hope for it."

They were quiet the rest of the way home, but once they got out of the car, Abby had no doubts where they'd wind up. Without saying a word, she followed John into the backyard, down the cement path, and up onto the pier. They moved toward the water. Abby sat in the chair, with John beside her.

"What're you thinking, Miss Abby?" He turned so his eyes met hers.

"Miss Abby . . . you haven't called me that since we were kids."

"Really?"

"Really."

John chuckled. "Well, not because I haven't thought it. You'll always be my little Miss Abby." He waited a moment, allowing the breeze from the lake to wash over them before he tried again. "You didn't answer me."

"Hmmm." The sun was directly overhead, and it caused an explosion of light on the lake. She stared out at the water. "I guess not."

"So . . . you aren't thinking anything special, or you don't want to tell me."

"Neither." A lazy grin spread across her face.

He pursed his lips, trying to figure her out. "I'm not sure I get it."

"I *am* thinking something special —" she lowered her chin, enjoying the easy banter between them — "and I *do* want to tell you."

"Okay." He crossed his arms. "So tell me."

"I was waiting for the right time. Because what I have to say is important. I want you to hear it straight to your soul, John Reynolds."

He maneuvered his chair so he could see her better. Their knees were touching, though Abby knew John couldn't feel the sensation. Not yet, anyway. "I'm listening, Abby. Heart, soul, and mind."

"Good." Abby drew a deep breath and her eyes settled on his. "I've given your surgery a lot of thought, John. I've dreamed about what it would be like to have you healed." She paused.

"I do the same thing." His eyes narrowed. "I think of all the ways I'd use my legs if I had even one more hour, one more day."

"What would you do?" Her words were

slow, easy. A hawk circled overhead.

"I'd run a mile in the morning, play football with Sean and Kade, and make love to you all afternoon, Miss Abby."

"Nice." She smiled, feeling the hint of warmth in her cheeks. "My thoughts are pretty much the same."

"That's what you wanted to tell me?" He leaned over and gripped her legs, rubbing his thumbs gently along the inside of her knees.

"No." She looked deeper, to the center of his soul. "I wanted to tell you that it doesn't matter."

John waited for her to finish, his head angled.

"It doesn't matter if you get your legs back, John. There was a time when I would've told you anything other than a complete recovery would be tragic, hard on our lives and hard on our relationship." She shook her head. "But not anymore. Over the past five months I've learned how to love you just like this. I love helping you in and out of bed; I love being there to pull your pants up for you. I even love the way you wheel me down the pier at twenty-miles-per-hour in some newfangled version of the tango."

She studied him, her eyes unblinking.

"What I'm trying to say is, I want your legs back as badly as you do, but if you come out of the surgery tomorrow the same as you are today, that's okay, too. I couldn't love you more than I do right now."

For a long while, John said nothing. Just stared at Abby while the two of them soaked in everything about the moment. "What if we hadn't talked that night after Nicole's wedding?"

"I can't imagine." Abby's voice was tight, her throat thick with emotion.

"I love you so much, Abby. Thank God we were smart enough to hear His voice, smart enough to find each other again." His eyes reflected the lake. Abby felt herself drowning in them, unaware of the world around her. "You're everything to me, Abby. Everything."

"I believe with all my heart that God will be there tomorrow, in the operating room, guiding the surgeon's knife and bringing healing to your back. But remember something, will you, John?"

"Anything."

"I'll be there, too." She pressed her fingers over his heart. "Right here . . . the whole time."

"You know what we need to do first?" John's expression lightened and his eyes shone the way their sons' eyes shone when they were up to no good.

"First? Before the surgery, you mean?"

"Yep."

"Okay . . . I give up. What do we need to do first?"

He patted his lap.

"Oh, no. Not the tango."

"Yes, Abby . . . come on. We're just getting good at it."

Laughter formed in her heart and found its way out of her mouth. She stood and dropped herself unceremoniously onto his lap. "I won't be able to do this after tomorrow, you know."

He turned the wheelchair and began heading toward the far end of the pier. "Why not?"

"Because after tomorrow you'll *feel* me, silly. I'll be too heavy for you."

"You? Too heavy?" He reached the top and spun the chair around, using the hand brake to stop it. "Never, Abby. We'll save the chair and do this once a week for old time's sake."

"Oh, quit." She pushed at his shoulder. As she did, John's elbow released the hand brake, and the chair began rolling down the pier.

"Here we go." He guided the chair with

one hand and grabbed hers with the other, holding it straight out in front of them, tango-style.

She pressed her cheek against his as they passed the midway point, plummeting faster and faster toward the water. Her voice was loud, breathless. "Have I mentioned that this dance terrifies me?"

"Ah, Abby . . . so little faith . . . we'll have to do it again until you're not afraid anymore."

Just before they reached the end, John spun the chair in a graceful circle. But this time the wheels skidded and the chair flipped over, spilling John onto his back near the end of the pier, and Abby on top of him.

Abby muffled a scream that was more laughter than fear. She lifted her face and held it inches from his. "Nice move, Reynolds."

"I practiced that for weeks. I thought you'd love it." He ran his hands along her back, pressing her against him. They kissed then, their lips meeting each other first briefly, then in a way that spoke the things too deep for words.

Abby started laughing.

"Hey, wait a minute." John grabbed a quick breath. "You're not supposed to laugh. This is part of the dance."

"I can't help it." Abby rested her forehead on his shoulder until she could breathe again. She raised up a bit and looked at him. "Remember that day in the hallway? How you fell backward trying to lead me into the kitchen?"

John chuckled, still stroking her back. "One of my finest moments."

"You said you'd never be mature, remember?"

The laughter came more loudly for John. "Even Paula's dance classes couldn't help me."

"Apparently not."

They laughed and kissed, and laughed some more, until the sounds of their happiness drifted across the lake and mingled with the afternoon winds. Only then, when they were tired from laughing, did Abby pick herself up and right the wheelchair. She helped John back into it and pushed him slowly up the pier.

As long as she lived, she'd never forget this afternoon. The depth of love and laughter, peace and acceptance. She had told John the truth. She could never love him more in all her life, and that would be true tomorrow, too.

No matter what else the day might bring.

Twenty-nine

———◦◦◦———

Jake woke up the next morning at seven o'clock and looked at his calendar.

This was the day. He could feel it as surely as he could feel his own heartbeat. He'd been praying, not just for Coach Reynolds, but for the man's little granddaughter as well. And God had practically told him that sometime that morning there would be drastic miracles for both of them.

His job was to keep praying.

So before he climbed out of bed, before he got dressed or ate breakfast or did anything else, he rolled onto his stomach, buried his face in his pillow, and prayed. Not the way he used to pray back when he was a kid, before the accident.

But like a man.

As though his very life depended on it.

There was a flurry of activity around Haley's incubator.

Nicole had slept down the hall in the same room where she and sometimes Matt had stayed since Haley was born. The little girl had survived four weeks, longer than the doctors had dared hope. But still her lung activity was weak. If the situation didn't improve, she was a prime candidate for pneumonia, which in her frail state would almost certainly prove fatal.

As always, Nicole had asked the nurses to get her if anything about Haley's condition changed. But no one had come for her, and now her heart raced as she saw half a dozen nurses gathered around her baby. She moved quickly down the aisle, past several incubators until she was as close as she could get to Haley's.

"Excuse me . . ." Nicole peered around the nurses. "What's going on? That's my baby in there."

A nurse Nicole recognized spun around and hugged her. "It's a miracle!" She pulled Nicole back a few feet away from the commotion. "This morning your baby's numbers looked worse than before. We were going to wake you up and have you come see her, but then at a little past seven o'clock, everything changed."

Nicole's mind raced almost as fast as her heart. "Changed? What do you mean?"

"Her lungs. It's like they opened up for the first time and actually sucked in a complete breath. Right away her blood oxygen level soared into the healthy range."

"So . . . so she's doing better?" Nicole strained to see Haley, glad that the other nurses were going about their business again.

"Not just doing better." The nurse positively beamed. "She's turned a corner. The doctor was just in and he upgraded her condition from critical to serious. If things stay this good, she can go home as soon as she's gained enough weight. No one can believe it. That's why the other nurses are here. Things like this don't just happen. Not to sick babies like yours."

There was finally an open spot alongside the incubator, and Nicole pressed in as close as she could. "Can I touch her?"

The nurse grinned. "Definitely."

Nicole worked her hand through the sterile opening and soothed a finger over Haley's legs and arms. "Honey, it's me. Mommy." Tears spilled onto her cheeks, and Nicole uttered a single laugh. "God saved you, Haley. He's going to let you live."

She remembered the image Jo had seen so often. Three little girls running and skipping through the fields of heaven. Nicole shuddered. How close they'd come to having that be true.

Haley stretched her legs, her hands flailing at the touch of Nicole's skin. Nicole glanced back at the nurse. "She wants me to hold her."

"She does?" The nurse raised an eyebrow. "We'll weigh her later today, and if her breathing is still this good, you should be able to hold her this afternoon."

Nicole wanted to shout out loud. Haley was going to live! Her mind raced, thinking of what to do next. She needed to tell Matt and his parents, needed to tell her parents —

Her parents!

It was just after eight o'clock, and her father would be wheeled into surgery any minute. He couldn't go without hearing the news. Nicole whispered near the hole in the incubator. "Haley, baby, get some sleep. I'll be back." Then she turned to the nurse. "Watch her for me. I have to tell the others."

Nicole hadn't run this fast since before the baby was born. She bounded down the hall and into the elevator, and darted back out the moment it reached the fifth floor. Quick as her feet would carry her, she made her way to the nurses' station. "I'm looking for my dad, John Reynolds."

The nurse pointed. "He's on his way to surgery."

"Thanks." Nicole took off down the hall. *Oh, not yet . . . please, God, let me catch him in time.*

She rounded a corner near the elevator and ran smack into Kade, who tripped, toppling both of them onto the floor, their legs and arms tangled. From her position on the hospital floor, she shouted at her father. "Don't go anywhere, Dad. I have to tell you something."

Her mother helped her to her feet, while Kade flopped onto his backside and struggled to get up. "Nice tackle." He straightened his baseball cap. "You missed your calling, Nicole. You shoulda been a lineman, not a teacher."

"Sorry." Nicole brushed the dust off Kade's jeans and then her own. "I had to reach Dad before he went into surgery."

Her father was lying on the stretcher, just outside the elevator doors. He was quietly laughing, his eyebrows raised. "Whatever it is, it must be good."

Nicole nodded to Sean and moved closer to her father. A technician stood at the foot of the stretcher, watching her like she was a crazy woman. She waved at him. "Hello . . . sorry about the excitement."

The elevator door opened, and Nicole shook her head at the man. "Not yet. Give me a minute, okay?"

"Nicole, whatever is going on?" Her mother came up beside her, searching her face.

"Just a minute. Dad —" she turned her attention back to her father — "Haley's turned a corner. She's breathing like a regular baby and . . ." Nicole could barely catch her breath, first from the hospital sprint, but also from the sheer exhilaration of the miracle that had occurred. She exhaled, struggling to compose herself. "The doctor said she's turned a corner. She's out of danger, Dad. Isn't that *amazing?*"

Now it was Kade's turn to tackle her. He lifted her in a bear hug while Sean and her mother circled their arms around her. Her father reached for her hand and squeezed it. "Are you serious, sweetheart?"

Nicole worked herself free from the group hug. "Yes, Daddy." She bent over him, searching his eyes. "And God's not finished yet. I couldn't let you go into surgery without knowing what God was doing. What He's still going to do for you before the day is up."

"So, honey, what happened? She just breathed on her own for no reason?"

The elevator doors opened again, and Nicole flashed the technician a smile. "One more minute? Please?"

He shrugged. "They can't start without your father."

Nicole looked at her mother. "No one knows what happened. Sometime around seven o'clock she sucked in a full breath of air. The monitors all went off, telling the staff that she was finally breathing on her own. She's been breathing great ever since."

"Yes!" Sean raised his fist in the air. "My little niece is gonna live!"

Nicole's voice grew softer. "So, Dad . . . now it's your turn, okay?"

Her father smiled, his eyes dry. "You tell that little girl of yours that one day soon, her grandpa's going to take her for a walk."

"Okay." Nicole stepped back and nodded to the technician just as the elevator doors opened one more time. "Go get 'em."

She linked arms with Sean and Kade and Mom. The last thing any of them saw as John was wheeled into the elevator was a smile that stretched across his face. That and his raised fist as he flashed them the thumbs-up sign.

Seeing it made Nicole's eyes fill with tears. It was the sign her father had always flashed from the football field, but not before every game.

Just those he was sure they were going to win.

Abby had never paced in all her life, but she was pacing now. Not the slow, musing type of pace reserved for pensive moments. Rather a quick one. Fast steps across the waiting room to the wall of windows, and then faster steps back again.

Nicole and Matt were downstairs with Haley, the boys had gone to the cafeteria for something to eat, and Jo and Denny weren't there yet. So, Abby was alone. The operation had been underway for nearly an hour, and Abby had more energy than she knew what to do with.

Yes, she would love John the same if the surgery didn't restore feeling to his legs. But what if it did? What if he could actually walk and run and drive a car again? How amazing would that be? Not only would they have found a deeper love because of the accident, but they would have a second chance to enjoy it.

The possibilities made Abby's heart race, and the only way she knew to work through it was to pace. Hard and fast, in a way that gave her nervous energy an escape.

Dr. Furin had told them the operation could take four hours. They had to identify each strand of John's damaged spinal cord and painstakingly repair it. If they were right, if he was to have any chance of walking again, they would find a few strands still intact. That would explain the feeling and movement in his toes.

But that was only half the battle.

The other half was making sure the repair went perfectly well. Strand by strand, hour after painstaking hour.

Abby paced faster.

She was still pacing when Jo and Denny came down the hall and stopped at the entrance to the waiting room. "My land, Abby, what in tarnation are you doing?" Jo came up beside her and took hold of her arm. "Trying to wear a hole in the floor?"

For the first time in half an hour, Abby stopped. "I don't know what else to do."

"Well, that's easy as fly bait." Jo led Abby to the nearest sofa, with Denny still watching from the doorway. "You sit yourself right down here and pray." She motioned for Denny to join them.

As he did, he pulled a newspaper section

from behind his back and handed it to Abby.

Jo beamed at her. "Then, when you're finished praying, you can read this. After that I don't think you'll feel much like pacing."

Abby took the newspaper and nodded, closing her eyes while Denny prayed for the surgeons' hands to be guided by God's mighty grip. When they were finished, Abby held the paper up and stared at it. For a moment, she wasn't sure what she was seeing. The entire page was filled with column after column of names. Then her eyes shot to the top of the page. What she saw made her gasp out loud.

It was a full-page ad, and the headline read, "We're praying for you, Coach!"

Beneath that was a smaller section that said, "We, the students and teachers at Marion High, wish to publicly thank Coach John Reynolds for everything he's done to make us winners. Today, as he goes into surgery, we will be praying for his complete recovery. And that next year he might still be head coach of the mighty Eagles."

The sentiment was followed by a list of names too great to read through in one sitting. Hundreds of names, names of teachers and students and players — many Abby didn't even recognize.

"See." Jo gave a firm nod. "I knew that'd stop your pacing."

The newspaper shook in Abby's hand. "John won't believe it."

Jo was right about her nervous energy. After seeing the full-page ad from the community at Marion High, Abby felt strangely peaceful. She passed the next three hours either praying or playing cards with Jo and Denny.

When they weren't in the cafeteria eating, Kade and Sean kept busy with Sean's NFL Game Boy. Occasionally Nicole and Matt found their way up to the waiting room anxious for a report.

But there was none.

Abby tried not to see that as a bad sign. Dr. Furin had said he'd do his best to give the family updates throughout the surgery. Almost four hours had passed, and still they'd heard nothing.

"Shouldn't we know by now?" Denny peered over the cards in his hand and sent Abby a quick look.

"I thought so." She drew a steady breath. *Come on, heart. Stay steady.* "I guess we'll just have to wait."

"A good fisherman knows all about

waiting." Jo played a card. She looked completely unfazed, as though they were passing the afternoon in a sunny parlor and not the waiting room of a hospital. "Only instead of casting a line, today we're casting our cares." She grinned at Abby. "Beats pacing, don't it?"

Another thirty minutes passed, and Abby didn't care if Jo was right. She had cast her cares on God a hundred times in the past hour, and the anxiety was back. "Okay, guys —" she looked at Jo and Denny and motioned for the boys to join them — "it's time to pray again."

But before they could utter a single word, Dr. Furin appeared. Abby squinted to make out his expression. She had seen the hint of a grin play on the man's face before, but she'd never seen his face fully taken up with a smile.

Until now.

Abby was on her feet immediately. "How is he?" The others stayed perfectly still, staring at the doctor, waiting for the news.

"He came through the surgery beautifully." Dr. Furin took a seat across from them. "His break was just as we hoped it might be. We had barely enough cord to work with."

Abby was frantic for the news. Her entire

body trembled. "Can you tell yet? Whether it worked?"

The doctor's smile got even bigger. "He's already coming out of anesthesia and we've gotten reaction from all of his major reflexes." He held his hands out to his sides. "The operation was a complete success. He'll need therapy, of course, to regain the strength in his legs. But I expect him to make a full recovery."

Jo stood up and stared down at the doctor, her hands on her hips. "I'm a lot simpler than most folk, Doctor. I don't want this full recovery or therapy business. The question is: Will the man walk again?"

"Yes." Dr. Furin laughed out loud. "He'll beat you in a footrace before summer."

"Yahoo!" Jo raised her fist straight into the air. "Thank You, Jesus!"

Kade and Sean slid onto the sofa on either side of Abby and hugged her. They were both crying. "I didn't think —" Kade was too choked up to say more.

"What he means is —" Sean wiped his tears — "neither of us thought it would really happen. We thought . . . we thought you grownups were crazy to think an operation could help Dad walk again."

"I feel so bad." Kade sniffed, his face still buried in Abby's shoulder.

Dr. Furin nodded at her and quietly stood to leave. They could talk about the details later. For now she had two boys to comfort.

Jo took Denny by the hand and whispered to Abby, "I'll go tell Nicole."

Abby nodded and waited until they were gone. Then she soothed her hands over the backs of her boys. "It's okay . . . you don't have to feel bad. Daddy's going to be fine." They might be teenagers, but inside they were still children, still desperately in need of consoling. Especially with all that had happened in their lives this past year.

Kade coughed and lifted his face enough so Abby could see his swollen eyes. "I didn't believe, Mom. I've been a Christian all these years, and . . . and Matt's parents had more faith." He twisted his face in anger. "What does that say about me?"

"Me, too." Sean sniffed. "I knew everyone was praying for a miracle. I mean, I prayed for Dad to be okay. But I never really thought he'd walk again."

"You're not the only ones, boys. There were times when I felt the same way. I had to believe the operation wouldn't work and imagine my life that way. Even today I had trouble believing it would actually happen."

"Really?" Kade sat up a bit straighter. He dragged the back of his hand beneath his eyes. "I thought that kind of thing didn't happen to people your age."

Abby chuckled, giving Kade a soft punch in the gut. "People my age?" She raised her eyebrows. "I think it happens more to people my age." She thought of Haley Ann and her laughter dimmed a bit. "Because we've had a chance to see the truth that sometimes God doesn't give us the answer we want."

"So, Dad's really going to walk again?" The reality of what had happened was sinking in, and Sean couldn't contain himself. He bounced up and down on the seat. "Maybe he and I can go jogging this summer. Like, every day for a mile or two."

Kade laughed. "Give him time, buddy. First he has to get his legs strong enough to move them."

They were discussing the process of muscle atrophy, when Nicole and Matt came tearing around the corner. "Is it true?" Nicole grabbed Abby's hands. Her eyes were wide and filled with tears.

"My parents told me the operation was a success. They're taking a turn with Haley, but we had to come up and ask for ourselves. Is that really what the doctor said?" Matt blurted out.

Abby grinned and the feeling seemed to come from the depths of her soul. "To quote the man, he said your father will beat people at footraces before summer hits."

"*Yes!*" Nicole flew into Matt's arms, and then moved around the room, hugging Abby and her brothers. "I knew it was going to be a day of miracles. I just *knew* it."

As her children began talking all at once, laughing and smiling, filled with a hope they hadn't had before, Abby felt the nervous energy come over her again. Not because she was worried or anxious, but because there was something she had to do. Something no amount of pacing would satisfy.

"I'll be right back." Abby stood and headed down the hallway.

"Wait." Nicole called after her. "Where're you going?"

Abby only grinned, this time bigger than before.

"That's not fair. I want to see him, too."

"Me first. If he's awake, I'll come get the rest of you." Abby sent them a look that said they better not follow her. Then she practically ran toward John's room to do the one thing she'd wanted to do since his operation began.

Walk up to him, kiss him on the lips, and challenge him to a June footrace.

She slowed her pace as she neared his room. She didn't want to wake him if he was asleep. He was probably exhausted, and definitely still sedated. There were no sounds coming from his bed as she leaned her head inside the room, and then crept up alongside him.

"John, you did it, baby!" Her voice was a tender whisper, the kind she hoped he could hear in his dreams.

For a while he stayed still, but then he let out a weak moan. His neck was stabilized, so he couldn't turn his head. But his eyes began to move beneath the lids. After a few seconds he blinked, and Abby saw panic fill his expression.

"Honey, it's okay. The surgery's over."

He shifted his eyes toward her voice. The moment he saw her, the panic faded. "Hi."

She ran her fingers over his arm and bent down, kissing him on his forehead. "Hi."

"How long've I been here?" He winced, straining against the neck brace.

"Not long. An hour maybe."

The fog of medication seemed to clear, and his look became more intense. "Tell me, Abby . . . did it work?"

"Oh, honey, yes!" A single laugh escaped Abby's mouth, and she smothered it with her hand. She couldn't stop the tears that gathered in her eyes. "It worked perfectly. Dr. Furin says your leg reflexes are all normal."

"So . . ." He swallowed hard, and she could hear how dry his mouth was. "So . . . I'll be able to walk again?"

Abby nodded. "Try, John. Try to move your legs."

His head was strapped to the bed, but he stared down the length of his body. Abby watched as both his legs trembled beneath the sheets. If it had been any other time, if he hadn't just come out of surgery, Abby would have thought the movement an involuntary shivering.

But not this time.

John met her eyes again. "Did you see that?"

"Yes!" She brought her face close to his, not sure if she wanted to laugh or cry. "Did you feel it?"

"I did."

Abby stood again and this time she saw

something she hadn't seen since John had been injured. He was crying. Not the way their sons had cried earlier, but in a quiet way that didn't seem like crying at all. Rather, it looked as though John had sprung a leak on either side of his face.

She kissed one of his cheeks, tasting the salt of his tears. "It's a miracle, John."

He sniffed and laughed at the same time. "How long before I can walk?"

"The doctor said you'd be winning footraces by summer." She kissed him again. "But I told the guy he was crazy. I'm a faster runner. I'd beat you. No contest."

"Oh, yeah?" John's voice was tired again, and a sleepy smile drifted across his face. "Is that a challenge?"

"Absolutely." She giggled, anxious for the days and weeks to pass. Desperate to see him fully recovered.

"Okay, you're on." His lids grew heavy and finally closed altogether. "June it is."

Abby stepped back and leaned against the wall. "Goodnight, John."

He was already asleep, the smile still on his face. She knew the others were waiting for a chance to see him, but she couldn't tear herself away, couldn't stop staring at him, reminding herself that it had really happened. The surgery had fixed John's legs!

She closed her eyes and lifted her face toward heaven.

God . . . thank You doesn't come close to telling You how I feel. First Haley . . . now John. You are so good, God. No matter what happens, there You are. Giving us peace . . . teaching us how to love . . . restoring us to a life bursting with hope. Thank You, God.

She remembered some of the verses that had pulled her through the dark days of John's paralysis: *"In this world you will have trouble. But take heart! I have overcome the world"* . . . *"Lean not on your own understanding, in all your ways acknowledge Him, and He will make your paths straight . . ."*

Abby marveled at the promises. God had definitely delivered — and long before John's successful surgery.

A dozen moments flashed in her mind. The day when John would take his first steps, the morning when he could finally come home, the time when he would first push little Haley in her stroller . . . the moment when he would run again.

And on some far-off June afternoon, the time when they would line up along one end of their backyard and race to the other. Of all the athletic feats John had accomplished, that single run would be the greatest of his life.

Thirty

As movement went, it wasn't much.

They had to gather close around John's bed, their faces inches from his covered legs, just to see it. But Abby couldn't have been happier if John had jumped on top of the bed and danced a jig on the hospital sheets.

"See —" John pointed to his legs — "watch, I'll do it again."

Kade and Sean and Nicole and Matt closed in and stared at John's legs. His left knee rose half an inch, then his right, followed by the faintest rustling of all ten toes beneath the blankets. "It's amazing, Dad." Nicole took his hand. "You and Haley . . . on the same day. Only God could've worked that out."

It was Wednesday night, three days after the surgery, and Dr. Furin's reports had been nothing but glowing. John had surface and muscular sensation in nearly all sections of his lower extremities. The skin on the back of his calves was still somewhat numb, but the doctor wasn't worried. Rarely, in the few incidents where spinal cord injuries had been reversed, did complete sensation return just days after surgery.

"You're an exceptional case," Dr. Furin told him earlier that day. "You must have taken my advice."

John winked at the doctor. "Absolutely." He pointed to the full-page ad hanging on his hospital wall. "Most of Marion was praying for me."

Abby stepped back and let the kids ooh and aah over John's ability to move his legs. Everything about the past few days had been unforgettable. Seeing John that first day, watching their kids' faces when they were able to see for themselves that, yes, John had feeling in his legs once again.

And especially handing him the newspaper ad.

She'd given it to him the morning after the surgery, and at first he'd had as much trouble as Abby trying to make sense of it. Then he read the headline and the copy beneath it and stared at her, unable to speak.

"They love you, John." She shrugged,

her voice tight. "I guess they always did."

"So they were . . ." He looked at the list of hundreds of names. "They were all praying for me?"

Abby nodded. "Apparently Kade told some of the guys on the team that Dr. Furin wanted everyone praying." She smiled. "A few of them took the order literally and began getting signatures. Anyone who would promise to pray, anyone who wanted to thank you for what you've done for that school, got their name on the list."

John had stared at it for a long time, scanning the names. "It's unbelievable."

"Not just that, but you had our prayers and those of Jo and Denny."

A chuckle worked its way through John's stiff neck and slid through his teeth. "Jo's someone I'd always want praying for me."

"She doesn't so much ask God, as she demands. Almost like she already knows it's going to work out, so let's get it worked out already."

"Exactly."

In the days since his surgery, they had shared many precious hours. So far only family had been in to see him. Family and Jake Daniels. Nothing could've kept the boy away. Abby guessed he'd be back again later that night. But now John was ready for other visitors as well.

John was feeling so good that Abby had given the green light to several people who wanted to come by. Already three players and their parents had stopped in, and now the kids were here. John never got tired of moving his legs on command — even a little. The atmosphere was as festive as Christmas Day.

"Hey, Dad. How come you can't lift your knees up or get out of bed yet?" Sean ran a finger over John's knee, staring at it. "I thought your legs were better."

"Dork." Kade elbowed his younger brother. "His leg muscles are gone. I told you, remember? He doesn't have any strength. He'll have to work to get them moving again."

John grinned at the exchange. "Yep, your dad's about as weak as little Haley."

Abby looked at Nicole. "How's she doing, sweetheart?"

"Wonderful. I get to hold her whenever I want." Nicole looked better than she had since she'd had the baby. Happy, content, and well-rested. "She weighs three pounds and she's gaining a few ounces every day. Her breathing is normal and she has no cerebral palsy from the early delivery."

Nicole clasped Matt's hand. "She could come home in just three weeks if everything goes well."

The hospital door opened and Jo and Denny walked in. Jo was carrying a big wrapped box with a giant fish balloon floating from it. The fish read, "What a Catch!" Jo smiled big as she handed it to John.

He stared at it and bit his lip. "Thanks, Jo . . . Denny. You didn't have to do this."

"Ain't that the best balloon you ever saw?" Jo looked straight up at the green-and-gold mylar fish dancing above John's bed. "Denny told me it wasn't appropriate for a get-well gift, but I think it works." She looked at John, her face earnest. "See, once you're up and runnin' around again, you'll wanna get out in that boat of yours and do some fishin'. At least that's what I'd wanna do. And the minute you're back behind the rod, I know it in my bones you'll catch the fish of your life. So, see, the balloon works. 'What a Catch!' "

Abby and the others struggled to keep from laughing.

Denny rolled his eyes and shook his head in Jo's direction. "The woman's delusional."

Jo spun around and gave Denny a light

kick in the shins. "I am *not*." She turned back to John. "It works another way, too. When you're up and feeling better, those strappin' sons o' yours will have you on the football field in no time. Now I know your legs might take a bit gettin' used to, but not that arm you got." Jo brought her hand up and back behind her head, like she was about to throw a ball. "There you'll be, winding back, throwing for all you're worth . . . and one of these here boys will catch the ball. And you'll say —"

"What a catch!" John winked at Denny. "Makes perfect sense to me."

John was able to sit up now, and he positioned himself a little higher on the bed. He still wore the neck brace, and would for several weeks. But it didn't keep him from enjoying the celebration. He slid the paper off the gift box, opened it, and pulled out a pair of well-worn Nikes.

They were dirty, with barely any sole left, and two large holes near the tips.

"Okay." Jo motioned to the old shoes. "Let me explain."

A few giggles rose from Sean and Kade, but Jo waved her finger at them. "Hey, there . . . don't laugh. There's a story behind them shoes."

"Here we go." Denny shook his head. "I

told her to give you flowers or candy like a normal person, but . . . well, you know."

"Stop." Jo snapped her fingers. She looked at Abby, then back to John. Abby could only guess what sort of story she was about to tell. "I hear tell you and Abby's gonna have a footrace sometime this June." She flashed a quick glance at Abby. "Ain't that so?"

Abby lowered her chin, doing her best to keep a serious face. "It is."

"Okay, then." She looked at John again. "I got the idea the other day when I was lookin' at your feet. I said to myself, 'Jo . . . why those feet look almost the same size as my Denny's feet.' " She cupped her hands around her mouth and whispered the next part. "Denny has big feet for a small man."

"Thank you, honey."

"You're welcome." Jo smiled and resumed the story. "So I started thinkin' about the time when Denny had the darndest run o' great fishin' days. I mean one day he'd catch three prize babies and the next he'd catch four. Went like that for weeks on end. And these —" she snatched the old shoes from John's hands and held them up for everyone to admire — "these were the shoes Denny wore back then." Her head jerked in a quick nod. "Saved 'em all these years in case we ever needed a pair of lucky shoes."

"So . . ." John reached for the shoes again and grinned at them. "You want me to wear these when I race Abby. Is that it?"

"'O' course." She shook her head and shot a look at Abby and Nicole. "Men aren't the quickest study, are they?"

Abby opened her mouth to answer, but Jo beat her to it. "Okay, everyone, listen up. Denny and I got an announcement."

Abby and Nicole exchanged a quick giggle, before covering their mouths and giving Jo their attention again.

"Jo . . . we already told 'em." Denny's cheeks were pink, and he wore an apologetic look on his face. "Her memory's a little dim these days."

Her hands flew to her hips. "It is not. Besides, I never told 'em the facts." She turned to the others once more. "Me and Denny bought our tickets to Mexico." Jo winked at Nicole, and a knowing look filled Nicole's face. Whatever Jo was about to say, she'd obviously already shared it with Nicole. Abby made a mental note to ask Nicole about it later.

Jo whipped two small folders from her purse and held them up. "These are stamped and dated. Good for two one-way flights to Mexico the third of June."

"One-way?" Matt took a step closer and scrutinized the tickets. "You're coming back aren't you."

"Yes. Six months . . . a year maybe." Jo slipped the tickets back in her purse. "Don't worry, I can't miss little Haley growin' up."

"We'll come back to the States every few months for a visit." Denny slipped his arm around Jo. "But we have to go." He and Jo swapped a tender look. "It's something we promised God."

"By the way —" Jo tapped Kade on the shoulder — "Denny says you've been talkin' to the pastor at church."

Kade looked startled. "Uh . . . yes." The look he shot at John and Abby was uncertain. "We've gotten together a few times."

"Well, that's not the point." Jo waved her hand in the air. "The point is, maybe you're thinkin' about being a pastor. Are ya?"

"No . . ." Kade's eyes grew wide. "Not really."

"A missionary, then?"

"Not so far."

"Well, that don't matter." Jo flicked her fingers over her head as though she were shooing away a fly. "Point is, we could use a strappin' young lad like you down in Mexico for a few weeks in July." She glanced at Denny. "Ain't that so, honey?"

Denny nodded, clearly embarrassed by Jo's approach. "That's what the pastor said. They want a team of volunteers to put a new roof on the orphanage."

Abby studied Kade and watched his confusion turn to curiosity. "Really?"

"Yes." Jo slapped Kade on the back. "And it's just a few weeks. Your football team won't miss you for a few weeks in July."

Kade asked several questions about the trip. When it was exactly . . . and whether some of his football buddies could come.

Abby watched in silent awe. A year ago Kade was heart-deep in the stench of pornography . . . and now he was considering a stay in Mexico to build a roof for orphan children. He'd been meeting with their pastor whenever he was home, and the change that had come about was amazing. Kade was tender and kind, more aware of spiritual issues. Walking daily outside God's plan for his life had caused calluses on his soul, but they were gone now, all of them. God, Himself, had removed them.

Nicole and Sean joined the conversation, asking more about the orphanage and the types of children who lived there. John reached over and linked fingers with Abby. "Maybe we should go, too."

Abby raised an eyebrow. "A footrace is one thing, John Reynolds. Building roofs in Mexico is another." She looked at Jo. "Ask us next year."

"Actually . . . it might be good therapy if —"

The door opened and Tim and Tara Daniels walked in. Jake was with them, a grin plastered across his face. He looked at John and the two swapped a knowing look. Abby knew immediately. The two of them were up to something.

"This a good time, Coach?" Jake moved in front of his parents and anchored himself near the foot of John's bed.

John did a quick survey of the room. "I believe it is."

"Hi, everyone." Jake waved at the others.

Abby could sense a slight hesitation on Nicole's part, but otherwise the group smiled and bid the boy hello.

"We won't be long. Just wanted to be here for a couple announcements." Jake nodded to his parents. "My folks can go first."

Tim took a step forward and looked from Abby to John. "Tara and I . . ." He reached back for her hand. "We wanted to thank you for praying for us. We've . . . we've talked it over and decided we never should've gotten divorced."

A quick giggle came from Tara's throat. "We wanted you to be the first to know."

"Other than me, of course." Jake stood between his parents and flung his arms over their shoulders.

"Of course." Tara smiled at Jake and then turned back to the rest of them. "Tim and I are getting married the first Saturday in June." She looked at Abby, tears welling in her eyes. "We want you and John to stand up for us. Be our best man and maid of honor."

"Right." Tim nodded. "Because it wouldn't have happened without you two."

"Isn't that awesome!" Jake gave a high-five to Kade and Sean, John and Matt. "My parents are getting married!"

"Oh, you guys." Abby moved around John's bed and hugged them, first Tim, then Tara, and finally Jake. "That's wonderful. Of course we'll be there."

Who would've ever thought a year ago — back when she and John were determined to divorce — that God would not only save their marriage and make their love stronger than ever, but that He'd use them to reach two people like Tim and Tara.

John's eyes danced and he pointed to the fish balloon. "In honor of your engagement, Tim, I think you deserve my balloon." He grinned at Tara. "I mean, what a catch!"

Everyone laughed and then Jake waved his hands. "Okay . . . quiet . . . it's Coach's turn."

A strange feeling bounced around in Abby's gut. Coach's turn? What was this about? And why hadn't John told her he had something to say?

"Dad?" Kade gave John a curious look. "You have an announcement?"

John shrugged as best he could with the brace in the way. His lopsided grin told Abby all she needed to know. Whatever he was about to say, he and Jake had this part planned out. "Yeah, I guess so."

"Go on, Coach. Tell 'em."

"Okay." John straightened himself once more. "Jake and I did a little talking the other day, and he told me next year'll be his best ever. I mean . . ." John angled his head, a grin playing on the corners of his mouth. "He'll be a senior and all."

"And for the first time I'll be really listening to Coach . . . you know, doing whatever he asks me to do . . ."

Abby held her breath. Could he be about to say — ?

"So I decided to revoke my resignation." John lifted his hands and let them fall to his lap. "I'm going to coach next year, after all!"

The room erupted in a chorus of congratulations and hugs, high-fives and laughter. Jo slapped her leg. "That settles it. The Marion High athletic director — what's his name?"

"Herman Lutz." John grinned.

"Right, that's it. Lutz. Well, *he* gets the fish balloon. I'll take it into his office myself and hand it to him. 'What a catch, buddy!' I'll tell him, 'It's your lucky day because you just got John Reynolds back as coach!' "

Again everyone lit into conversation, guessing at the team's record next year and making predictions about how well Jake would do. Abby tuned most of it out and leaned against the hospital wall. Her eyes found John, and she saw that he wasn't listening either.

Instead they held a private conversation with their eyes. A dialogue where Abby told John how proud she was that he'd stood his ground and won, that he'd been willing to take a second look at the coaching job at Marion and realize it was where he belonged. And John silently thanked her for standing by him. Not just through the difficult days last season, or the horror of his accident, but during his wheelchair days and the anticipation over his surgery. And even now, when he was choosing to take time away from her once more to do the thing he loved.

"I can't wait." She mouthed the words, enjoying this private moment while the rest of the room celebrated loudly around them.

"Me, either." He held his hand toward her and she came, linking her fingers with his and feeling his love with every fiber of her being. "You know what, Abby?"

"What?" They were still whispering.

"It's going to be the best season ever."

Abby smiled and squeezed his hand. They had come so far, through so much. Yet now she was back where she'd started so many years ago. Looking forward to September and the warm glow of stadium lights on the face of the man she loved more than any in the world. Being caught up in a series of Friday night games, the way she'd been since she was a small girl.

The summer lay ahead of them, and

with it no doubt dozens of small miracles. Haley would come home, and John would be up and walking again. But right then and there, Abby was consumed with one tantalizing thought.

John Reynolds was going to coach again.

Abby could hardly wait for the new season of their life together to begin. John was right . . . it was going to be the best ever.

Author's Note

———⟳———

Paralysis is a devastating condition. In our country today, the foremost cause of sudden paralysis in people is a gunshot wound to the neck or back. Car accidents follow as the second most common cause. The technology and treatment described in *A Time to Embrace* are futuristic and not yet in use. However, according to the American Association of Neurological Surgeons and the Congress of Neurological Surgeons, even at this very moment, the field of spinal surgery is enjoying an "explosion of new surgical techniques" designed to reduce or reverse spinal cord injuries.

In many cases these new surgical techniques are still in need of financial support and testing before they can be implemented. Some are years or decades away from working the way they worked on John Reynolds. I chose to allow Coach Reynolds to be an early benefactor of such new surgical techniques to demonstrate what I pray and hope will one day be a reality for anyone who has fallen victim to this devastating type of injury.

A Word to Readers

Dear Reader Friends,

Thank you for traveling the pages of Abby and John's story . . . through their seasons of grief and gladness, joy and pain. This is my second book with these characters, and as such I have come to care for them a great deal. And to learn from the lessons they have taught me.

The most important may very well be this: life is made up of seasons.

You don't have to be married to a coach to recognize the fact. Some months we're busy and distracted, others we can barely concentrate for the consuming thoughts of love that fill our hearts. Love for our spouse, our families, our Lord. There are seasons of joy and seasons of pain, seasons of grief and those of growth. Of heartache and hope.

If you ventured with John and Abby through the first part of their story — *A Time to Dance* — then you know the celebration they experienced at the end of that book. After very nearly giving in to their own separate desires, after making plans to divorce, they allowed God to rescue them.

I've talked with dozens of couples who have been through what John and Abby experienced in the first book. Couples who loved each other and intended to stay together a lifetime, only to find their marriage, their love, their oneness derailed somewhere along the road to forever.

God tells us in Scripture that He will never let us be tempted beyond what we can bear, but that when we're tempted, He will provide a way of escape.

That is always true, even when our marriages begin to crumble.

Of course, too often one or both spouses is not willing to look for that escape route, not willing to hear the voice of God above the voice of their own desires. But when both people will follow God's way of escape and put away their differences, the result is something more beautiful than you could dare to dream.

If you've read my other novels, you know that we have six children, the youngest of whom had heart troubles as an infant. Little Austin was born with a defective aorta, the main artery out of the heart.

In what was a very delicate surgery, doctors removed the bad sections of Austin's aorta and replaced it with a piece of artery from his left arm. The whole thing seemed unbelievable to me and my husband.

"What if the patch job doesn't take?" I asked the doctor after the operation.

"Oh, it'll take. In fact the area where there was trauma and healing will actually be stronger than the unaffected sections."

I thought about that for a long time and marveled at the truth there. Where there was trauma and healing, that section would be stronger than any other.

And so it is in our marriages.

Trauma will come to most relationships. Disagreements, differences, arguments. Even sometimes betrayal. God knew we'd stumble along the way, so He gave us His Word wrought with advice on how to handle it. How to make points of trauma, places of healing.

And come out stronger in the end because of it.

Forgive as the Lord forgave you.

Love is patient.

Love is kind. . . . It is not easily angered.

Be completely humble and gentle.

Love covers over a multitude of sins.

Bear with each other. Encourage one another.

Yes, God knows what it is to be wronged. Remember the first Good Friday? There He was with His closest friends, each of them making grand promises of loyalty and commitment, when suddenly a troop of soldiers appeared.

What did Jesus' most faithful followers do? They ran.

And that's the same thing we're tempted to do when our marriages don't go the way we expected, but we'd do well to follow Christ's example. Not only did He forgive His friends, He embraced them. When He appeared to them in the upper room after that glorious Resurrection Sunday, He comforted them with no thought of the wrongs they'd committed against Him.

When I finished *A Time to Dance*, many of you wrote to me wondering what happened to Abby and John . . . how they were able to work their reconciliation into an everyday life without falling prey to the problems that plagued them at first.

It was then that I realized the lesson of trauma and healing. The couples I know who have found glorious restoration in their marriages, almost always do so in a way that makes their relationship better, stronger, more loving than ever before.

The reason? A troubled marriage is a tested one. And when we look to God together as a way of passing the test, we will always be closer in the long run.

Please don't read into this a callousness toward those of you who've suffered through a divorce. It is the rare exception when two people determined to walk away from each other stop and look to God instead. Many of you would love to have a spouse willing to listen to God, willing to look for the escape route that would lead you away from divorce.

But far too often that spouse still leaves, completely hardened to God's voice.

For you, I pray God's tender mercy and healing upon your life. That you would look to Him, the Author of life, for whatever your next step should be, and that you would believe He is the God of second chances. That He has good plans for you even now.

For those of you considering a divorce, mired in the throes of bitterness and betrayal, my prayer is that you stop attacking each other. Stop thinking it's your husband's fault or wishing you had a different wife. Realize, instead, that the enemy of our souls is the one who destroys what God has created. And the oneness of marriage is definitely a God-given gift.

Get counseling . . . pray together . . . pray for each other . . . look for ways to honor your spouse. And most of all search for the route of escape. Quite often that escape route is as simple as making an apology. Then allow God to heal your broken love. Let Him give you a time to laugh and love and live in peace.

A time to embrace.

And see if the bond you share isn't much stronger as a result.

On a personal note, we have had our adopted Haitian sons home for more than a year now and life couldn't be sweeter. Our biological children have embraced their new brothers in a way that can only be considered miraculous. Our entire family owes a debt of thanks to so many of you who have prayed for us along the journey.

We have had some hard times as well. After fourteen years of coaching basketball, my husband will be taking a few years off. Without getting into great detail, I can say this: some of the issues John Reynolds experienced the season before his injury were very, very close to home. We are, of course, glad to have Don home with us. The kids love it when he holds "minicamp" in the backyard.

But still, there is loss.

If your son or daughter participates in organized sports, I have this challenge for you: thank the coach. If he or she is someone who cares for your child, someone who doesn't use foul language or abuse your kids for the sake of a victory, take time to be grateful. After every game, every practice, make it a habit to find those coaches who volunteer their time or who get paid only pennies for doing the job, and thank them. Coaches — *good* coaches — are hard to find. And when parents fail to see that, everyone loses.

As always, I pray this finds you and yours well, and feasting on our Lord's rich promises. We look forward with you to whatever adventures the Lord has around the corner. Keep praying that I write the books God places on my heart in a way that will leave a life-changing mark on yours.

In His love, and until next time . . .
Karen Kingsbury

P.S. As always, you can E-mail me at rtnbykk@aol.com, or contact me at my Web site: www.KarenKingsbury.com

Acknowledgments

As always, whenever I put together a novel there are hosts of people working behind the scenes to make it possible. On that note, thanks must first go to my husband and kids, for understanding my need to hide away when deadline calls. There were reasons why this book was harder to finish than most. I couldn't have done it if you hadn't pulled together and allowed me the time to write. I love you all!

Also, thanks to my family support team, especially my mom and dad, and the rest of you who take time to read my books and offer valuable insight. A special thanks to my niece, Shannon, for always being the first with feedback. One day I expect to be reading your books, honey.

Prayer support is crucial when writing a novel — especially one with God-given truths woven throughout. I would be unable to write the stories God has given me if not for the prayers of my husband and kids, my family, and friends. I'm blessed to have not just those people praying, but also Sylvia and Walt Wallgren, Ann Hudson, and so many of you faithful reader friends who constantly lift me up in prayer. Thank you for your faithfulness. I pray you enjoy the fruits of partnering with me in this writing ministry.

Also, a special thanks to my assistant, Amber Santiago, for being everywhere I can't be as I set about the business of writing. Please know that your time with Austin and the hours you put in making my house livable are an amazing blessing to me. Thank you for your servant heart, Amber. I appreciate you more than you know.

In the writing of this book, I found myself desperately in need of quiet time. When that happened, I called up new friends of mine, Louise and Warren, and snuck off to their bed-and-breakfast for a few days of solid writing. Thank you for providing me with a quiet, phone-free environment in which to work. I am certain I'll spend many more hours at your hideaway.

Thanks also goes to those people who read galley proofs for me: Melinda

Chapman, Joan Westphal, Kathy Santschi, and the Wallgrens. Your expert eyes have helped me turn out a novel I can smile about. Thank you!

On a business note, I'd like to thank Ami McConnell, Debbie Wickwire, and the good folks at W Publishing Group for their commitment to excellence in women's fiction.

I had the privilege of working with my favorite editor, Karen Ball, in the course of this book. It was a difficult season for Karen, as she lost her dear mother, Paula Sapp, days before editing my manuscript. Karen, I ache with you at your loss and believe along with you that your mother is finally free. That even now she watches over you, praying for you, longing for the reunion that will take place one far-off day. Thank you for being willing to work with me even amid a season of heartache.

It is my belief that God teams writers up with agents for a good reason. As such, I am eternally grateful that the Lord brought Greg Johnson into my life. Greg is an author's dream-come-true agent, looking out for every aspect of my writing career. If you're reading this book, you can thank God for Greg's role in my life. I couldn't do this without him.

Also a special thanks to Kirk DouPonce of Uttley-DouPonce Designworks. Kirk and his amazing team of artists are quite simply the best cover designers in the business. If I had my way, every book I ever write would have their artwork gracing the front. Thank you for pulling off another amazing cover! You're the very best.

Study Guide

1. Was the love between Abby and John stronger or weaker in light of the fact that they had so recently changed their minds about getting divorced? Explain.
2. Describe a time when you had a falling-out with someone you love. Was the love between you stronger or weaker afterward? Why?
3. Trust takes time to build again, especially in a relationship that has fallen victim to betrayal. How did this truth present itself in Abby and John's relationship?
4. Has trust ever been an issue between you and someone you love? Describe that situation.
5. How were you able to finally trust that person again?
6. The Reynoldses' son was involved in Internet pornography. What are your

thoughts on whether this form of sexual sin is addictive? What examples from the book do you think would help in breaking that addiction for you or someone you love?

7. What role did Abby play in the family drama after John's injury? Why was this damaging to her?

8. Describe a time when you felt you had to fix everyone's problems. How did this make you feel? How were you able to move past that season?

9. John's emotions varied quite a bit in the days after his injury. What event finally changed his attitude for the better? Why?

10. Nicole experienced a blow to her faith after her father was paralyzed. Why do you think this was? What finally helped her come back to a place of believing?

11. Have you ever suffered through a time that tore at your faith? What made believing in God so difficult during that time? How did you work through that time?

12. Jake's reaction to his role in Coach Reynolds's injury was one of horrendous guilt. What were Jake's feelings regarding his possible punishment?

How did he grow during this season of sorrow and guilt?

13. Describe a time when you did something for which you couldn't forgive yourself. What brought about those feelings? How were you able to get past them and finally heal?

14. What were some of the ways the love between Abby and John grew during his wheelchair days? Describe your favorite moment between these two. Why was it special?

15. Love is not always easy. Describe a time when you were able to share love with someone through a difficult time. How did it strengthen your relationship? What did you learn in the process?